The Moonstone Hero

Moonstone Landing Series
Book 5

by

Meara Platt

ARE YOU SIGNED UP FOR DRAGONBLADE'S BLOG?

You'll get the latest news and information on exclusive giveaways, exclusive excerpts, coming releases, sales, free books, cover reveals and more.

Check out our complete list of authors, too!

No spam, no junk. That's a promise!

Sign Up Here

www.dragonbladepublishing.com

Dearest Reader;

Thank you for your support of a small press. At Dragonblade Publishing, we strive to bring you the highest quality Historical Romance from some of the best authors in the business. Without your support, there is no 'us', so we sincerely hope you adore these stories and find some new favorite authors along the way.

Happy Reading!

CEO, Dragonblade Publishing

Dark Gardens Series
Garden of Shadows
Garden of Light
Garden of Dragons
Garden of Destiny
Garden of Angels

The Farthingale Series
If You Wished For Me (Novella)

The Lyon's Den Series
Kiss of the Lyon
The Lyon's Surprise
Lyon in the Rough

Pirates of Britannia Series
Pearls of Fire

De Wolfe Pack: The Series
Nobody's Angel
Kiss an Angel
Bhrodi's Angel

Also from Meara Platt
Aislin
All I Want for Christmas

Chapter One

Moonstone Landing
Cornwall, England
July 1829

"**G**ET OUT!"

With no further warning, a tin cup flew past Lady Ella Stockwell's head as she stepped into the private hospital quarters reserved for wounded sons of England's privileged elite on what should have been a quiet Monday afternoon. The cup hit the door with a solid *thwack*, spilling cider mostly on it and the floor. A few drops splattered onto the apron Ella had thought to wear over her gown. "Try that again, Caden Seaton, and I shall ram that cup down your throat."

She took a moment to pick it up, and then wet a cloth to quickly wipe down the door and sop up the small puddle on the floor. Fortunately, clean cloths, a basin, and a ewer of fresh water were kept in every room. She had only to grab whatever she needed from those items neatly placed on a table beneath one of the large windows. Also on the table was a vase filled with lavender, its refreshingly subtle scent filling the air.

Ella could have left the task of cleaning the spill to one of the hospital workers, but they were already stretched thin caring for the batch of newly arrived wounded soldiers carried off the Royal

Navy frigate that had docked in the harbor this morning.

"You really are too much," she muttered, frowning at the difficult man who merely glared back at her with wild obsidian eyes. Most of these sons and grandsons of peers were not only privileged, but arrogant, and none more so than Caden Seaton, grandson and heir to the powerful Duke of Seaton.

"Do I know you?"

"Yes, you clot." She did not know the specifics of how he had arrived in his bruised and battered condition in Moonstone Landing's Fort Arundel Army Hospital earlier this week, but the anger with which he had hurled that cup spoke of significant damage to his soul as well as his body. Yet, by the newspaper accounts lauding his military campaigns, he had come home a hero, ready to be showered with more medals and honors than most generals received over decades of service.

But this man did not look like a hero, not even while his dark hair, masculine face, and broad shoulders were illuminated in the afternoon's golden sunlight that surrounded them.

In truth, he looked like he wanted to crawl into a dark cave and die.

"Your voice is familiar, but that changes nothing. Get out!" He ignored her by turning his back as she approached his bed. It was the only one currently occupied in the spacious and sunlit room overlooking Moonstone Landing's harbor and the glistening sea beyond.

"You were an arrogant lout when I first met you, and you haven't changed one bit. Recognize me yet? I don't suppose you would. It would require your thinking of someone other than yourself for once."

She saw him stiffen, and then he emitted a soft chuckle. "I might have known it was you."

However, he refused to turn toward her. "Get out, Ella," he said more gently, still refusing to properly acknowledge her. "I don't want you to see me like this. Please...just go."

How could she remain irritated with him now?

His voice resonated not only with anger but shame, pain, and utter misery.

What had happened to him?

She drew up a chair beside his bed. "I am not going to leave, so you may as well turn around and face me. I've brought a book of poetry to read to you. However, I think we can skip it for today. If I dared open it, you would probably grab it from my hands and hurl it at the door as you did the cup. Or perhaps you would toss the book out the window, and me along with it."

He said nothing, just continued to stare at the wall.

She sighed and settled into the chair. "Major Fionn Brennan is in charge of the army fort and the hospital attached to it. Have you met him yet? I'm sure he must have come by to greet you. He makes a point to spend a moment with every soldier brought here, even the arrogant, privileged ones like yourself who are given private rooms instead of placed in the common wards. His wife, Lady Chloe, is my Aunt Phoebe's sister."

"Fascinating. Just what I needed to hear today—irrelevant details of your family tree. As if I were not bored enough. If you wanted to put me in a coma, you could not have chosen a better topic."

Ah, Caden always knew how to level the sarcasm with biting condescension.

Too bad his insufferable attitude hadn't changed.

"Aunt Phoebe's other sister is Duchess Henley, wife of the Duke of Malvern. She is known as Duchess Hen. Her husband, Cain, is a big bear of a man and probably the largest landowner in the area. He will maul you if you dare speak to him as insolently as you spoke to me just now."

"Positively delightful," he grumbled. "Any other scintillating facts you wish to share before I fall irrevocably into that coma?"

"I've had two offers of marriage."

That got his attention.

He slowly turned to face her, and then winced as he struggled to sit up. He wore a white linen nightshirt that was a tight fit on him. Ella could make out the flex and tension of his muscular arms and broad chest as he moved into a sitting position with obvious difficulty. "Two offers? Is that all? I would have expected more suitors flinging themselves at your feet, desperate to marry Lady Ella Stockwell, the *ton*'s most brilliant diamond."

She wanted to help him settle more comfortably, but refrained. He was feeling helpless enough already, and her fussing would only anger him. Besides, he really was a cynical clot, and she would just as soon punch him as tend to him. She was only in here because none of the other ladies who volunteered to read or chat with the wounded soldiers would go near him. "Let me amend that," she said. "I actually received eight proposals in all, but only two were worthy of serious consideration."

"And are you hoping for a third from me?" His gaze was now fully trained on her, those dark eyes searching her face. His nicely shaped mouth twitched at the corners, as though he found the notion amusing.

"I would have to be desperate or deranged to wish that on myself," she remarked, wanting to be honest with him. Although he was one of the handsomest men of her acquaintance, every encounter with him felt as though she were walking into a tiger's cage. But, *dear heaven*, he was gorgeous. "Fortunately, I am neither of those. Should I refer to you as Lord Mersey or Colonel Seaton, or perhaps you prefer Colonel Lord Mersey?"

His grandfather had given him the courtesy title of Marquess of Mersey several years ago, but now that he was a distinguished military figure, she did not know if he preferred to go by his military rank.

He grunted. "Caden will do. How have you been, Ella?"

"The more important question is: how have *you* been?"

He glanced away. "Is this why they shoved you in here? To get answers out of me?"

"No one shoved me in here. I only came to sit with you because none of the other ladies will have anything to do with you. Someone had to pop their head in to make certain you are still breathing. I had no idea it was a charged question. You needn't answer it. I can see you are in agony, both physically and in spirit. Is this why they brought you here? Have you managed to frustrate, insult, and offend every hospital commander between here and Dover?"

He surprised her by grinning. "Yes, something like that."

It was an appealingly lopsided grin tinged with a dash of wickedness, because this was Caden, sinfully handsome and extremely dangerous to a girl's heart.

Hers was always guarded around him.

Nevertheless, it gave a little flutter when he smiled, for she did not think he had been remotely mirthful in a very long time. She was tempted to reach out and brush down the boyish cowlick that stuck up amid his slightly unkempt hair, but dared not be so familiar.

Instead, she clasped her hands and rested them on her lap.

Oh, yes. Much safer never to get too close to Caden Seaton. One risked getting eaten alive by this dark-haired, dark-eyed beast of a man, for he was that dangerous tiger pent up in his cage. She had not seen him in over a year, and he had grown handsomer than ever, that big, muscled body of his having filled out nicely, even though he appeared to have lost a bit of weight. This was no doubt due to his injuries. However, there was no denying his appeal. Despite his languid attitude and air of disaffection, she knew one did not remain as fit as he was by living a soft life.

He was never a lazy man and did not shirk hard work.

It was not as though she knew him well. They had only met last year in London during her debut Season, sharing a few conversations at various affairs, until he claimed her for the supper dance during Lady Marston's ball. That supper dance was a waltz, and then he had escorted her into supper, where they truly had the chance to talk. A few days later, his regiment had shipped off for parts unknown.

Well, unknown to her.

He was back now after having marched into the jaws of

death, judging by how battered he appeared. She resolved to read up on the newspaper accounts, for this past year had taken him to a very dark place in his soul, never mind the miles from England. If she was going to help him recover, then it was important for her to find out what had happened to him during his time away.

"They consider me a disciplinary problem and are not certain what do with me," he muttered, "especially now that some idiotic committee of generals has decided to make me out to be a hero. In their infinite wisdom, they have lined up innumerable awards ceremonies across England to tout my valor—which, by the way, is nonexistent."

"I find that hard to believe. You were insufferable, but never a coward."

"Don't make excuses for me, Ella," he said harshly, the angles of his face hardening as his temper flared. There had always been a hardness to him, as though his handsome face and the heart he always kept securely hidden were carved out of granite. But that ruggedness suited him. Firm, masculine jaw, high cheekbones. An almost aquiline nose that might have once been broken and created that attractive imperfection. Broad, sensual mouth.

"I am not making excuses for you, Caden. If you wish, I will embellish the list of things I dislike about you. It is quite extensive. I'm sure I will come up with more as I get to know you better."

"I have no doubt. But do not bother to get to know me better. You will not like what you find."

"I expect you are right," she admitted. "Good grief, you turn every conversation into a battle. You are far too complicated for me. But do not pretend you have no honor. I will believe many things about you, but not this. You are right that I do not know you well, but a coward does not climb onto a rain-slicked rooftop to save a shivering kitten, or put himself between two drunken boors to keep them from hurting each other at Lady Marston's ball last year. So, you do not need to tell me what happened to you in the year since I've seen you, because—"

"I am not going to talk about it."

"As I said," she continued with gentle insistence, "I am not going to ask you about any of it, but do not ask me to swallow that fable you are putting about. Lack of valor was never one of your flaws. Shall we move on now?"

He nodded. "You can move on right out of my room."

"Ah, you are delightful as ever. No, I have a full hour with you. We can talk about me, if you like. Or this lovely village of Moonstone Landing. Or anything else you wish to discuss."

He folded his arms across his chest and stared at her as though he could see straight through her garments and into her heart. She did not understand why his gaze bothered her so much, for he was not leering or ogling her, as other men sometimes did. Perhaps it was the piercing darkness of his eyes that unsettled her, for they were not completely black but a deep mahogany brown, only ringed by an outer circle of black. "Who has offered for you?"

"The Earl of Maxton and the Earl of Whitfield." She stared back at him, awaiting his insulting comments.

He merely gave a dismissive snort. "Which one will you choose?"

"How is that any of your business?"

He grinned. "It isn't, I suppose. Those were the two drunkards I had to break apart last Season. They were fighting over you?"

She nibbled her lip as she nodded. "I certainly gave them no encouragement."

"I did not mean to suggest you did. Of all the young ladies making their debuts last Season, you were the last I would ever accuse of manipulating suitors. You were refreshingly honest; I will give you that."

She put a hand to her ear in jest. "Wait, was that a compliment I heard escape your lips? A *compliment*, Caden?"

He managed a chuckle, then winced and put a hand to his side to quell the stitch of pain. "It is nothing more than a statement of fact. But it is one of the reasons I noticed you and asked to claim the supper dance. One leaves these affairs exhausted trying to figure out who is lying to you and who is not. For me, I just assume all the young ladies are lying to me. They want the title, not the man."

"Yes, it is one of the aspects I hate most about the Marriage Mart. There is little romantic about making a match there. Mostly, it is a horse auction."

He glanced down at himself. "So, what do you think? Am I still a fine stallion?"

She cast him a mirthful smile. "You may appear splendid at first glance, but you are not nearly so fine as you think."

"I'm not?" His grin was unguarded, and its gentleness caused her heart to flutter again.

"Decidedly not. You are surly and unmanageable. Prone to colic, I expect. You certainly give others colic whenever they are around you," she muttered, the comment getting another grin out of him. "You are also arrogant, acerbic, and, as I have already mentioned, generally insufferable."

He chuckled. "Ah, thank you, Ella. See, this is why I held out hope for you. It was rather refreshing to hear you insult me to my face when we danced the waltz last year."

"Can you blame me? All you did the entire time we twirled around the floor was insinuate I only wanted you for your wealth and title. Rest assured, I had no interest in digging into your pockets for gold back then. Nor do I care to do so now."

"I know. You were the only one who ever gave me the set-down I deserved. Obviously, I was goading you."

"And I rose to the bait."

"It wasn't bait. It was a test, and you were the only one who passed it. All those other *ton* diamonds just smiled and fawned over me, pretending to find me charming—which I am not, as you well know—but they were never going to tell me the truth because I am heir to the elderly Duke of Seaton. They thought because he is getting on in years that I would be duke soon. They could not be more wrong. My grandfather is a tough old bird and has more strength in him than many men in their prime."

"Do not be too hard on the ladies, Caden. Many of them are forced to find a rich husband in order to save their family from financial ruin. I am fortunate with mine. My father is cautious and wise. He loves me and Imogen, and will never leave us in dire straits. Nor would my Uncle Cormac—he's the Marquess of Burness. He has settled here in Moonstone Landing, and my sister and I have been visiting him every summer since we were little girls."

Caden shook his head and laughed. "Do not give me that family tree again. But I know of Burness. Every soldier does. His bravery is legendary."

"He acquired Westgate Hall and resides there now with Phoebe and their twin boys. He and the Duke of Malvern have settled here permanently, only returning to London when Parliament is in session. Oh, they still have their other estates to manage, but their lives are here. Major Brennan, too. He is actually Viscount Brennan, but hates for us to refer to him as that. The Duke of Claymore has also settled here, but Brenna, his wife, was born and raised in Moonstone Landing, so it is little surprise they decided to remain. Claymore's mother and orphaned nephew live with them."

"Ella, stop tossing names at me. I know of them all. However, I do not want to see any of them… Maybe Burness, though. He's the only one who might understand."

"I could arrange it. As I said, he is my uncle and dotes on me and Imogen. Our best memories are of summers here with him. He's a wonderful man and would be—"

"I know of his reputation. Good, honest, a bit of an arse."

"Just like you," she teased.

He laughed. "Yes, but do not invite him yet. I am not ready."

She nodded. "All right."

He closed his eyes a moment, as though absorbing the weight of the world he had placed upon his shoulders. She wondered whether he had drifted off to sleep, for his every movement seemed painful and drained him. He must have expended quite a bit of anger just throwing that cup at her.

As his breathing evened, she quietly rose to walk to the window and look at the view of the glistening sea visible from his room. The curtains were drawn aside to allow in the sunlight, and all the windows were open to allow in the cooling breeze.

The room itself was sunny and cheerful, but she did not know if Caden was in any condition to appreciate the serenity that surrounded him.

Perhaps it gave him pain.

Everything seemed to give him pain.

As she watched him from the short distance, he opened his eyes again to stare at her, those dark orbs penetrating her heart. "You did not answer me regarding your two suitors."

"Oh, are we back to them again?"

"Yes, them again. Which one did you accept, Ella?"

Chapter Two

C ADEN DID NOT know why he had asked the question, or why he cared for Ella's answer. Perhaps because he did not think much of either Whitfield or Maxton. They would make decent husbands, he supposed. But not to someone like Ella, this golden-haired angel who stood beside the window, illuminated in the sun's shimmering light.

She wore a muslin gown and crisp white apron.

That prim look suited her…and drove him wild.

He wanted to peel those very proper garments off her body and trail his hands slowly over her every sinful curve. Apparently, being a physical mess had not dampened his lustful urges. He ached to roll Ella under him, press his weight lightly atop her body as he kissed her, tasted her, explored every inch of this young woman he had not been able to get out of his thoughts the entire year he had been away.

Did she wear a corset beneath her gown?

He did not think so, for the natural shape of her was perfection. Softly rounded shoulders, slim hips and waist. Full, perky breasts.

His mouth went dry. "Well, Ella? Whom did you choose?"

Even her eyes were unbearably beautiful. There was a fae quality to them that had stolen his breath the first time their gazes met. They appeared even lovelier now, a pale green that sparkled like the magical fairy pools found only in the Highlands.

"Will you make a jest of it if I tell you?" she asked.

He shrugged. "Depends on what you tell me."

"Must you always be so difficult? I will not have you laughing at me."

Why would he ever laugh at her? She had intelligence, wit, and charm, in addition to being a delicate beauty. She also had a quiet, thoughtful nature that he liked very much. She was not one to dazzle when first walking into a room, although she would never go unnoticed by those with a more discerning eye.

"I give you my word of honor that I will not make fun of you." He had thought to dismiss her as another empty-headed hopeful when they were first introduced last Season, but something about her kept drawing him back to her. Perhaps it was the look on her face whenever he approached, that *Oh, Lord, not him again* look she did not bother to hide from him.

He was the first to admit he goaded her, teased and tested her.

But she always held her own against him.

She wasn't afraid of him, either.

In truth, she handled him more politely than he deserved, because there was also a sweetness about her that he found fascinating. No one in his family had ever been sweet or kind. Perhaps he came closest, and he was an utter arse.

Her sweetness did not make her weak, but somehow strengthened her. He had been in the middle of trying to figure out why this quiet beauty had such a pull on him and what he was going to do about it when his regiment received their orders and immediately shipped out.

"Ella? Which one of them did you accept?"

She patted her golden curls that shone like silk in the bright sunlight, a giveaway that she was uncomfortable about responding. Her big eyes stared back at him. That combination of magical eyes and full, pouty lips got to him, turning up the furnace on his battered body. "I did not accept either of them."

"Truly?" Her response surprised him. "Why reject them? After me, they were considered worthy catches."

"Ah, and you think you were the Season's prize?" She shook her head and laughed. "Considering how self-absorbed you are, I don't know that you would ever understand my reasons, or ever care."

But he did care, more than he would ever let on or desire to think about.

"Tell me anyway, Ella," he said with a wry smile, liking that she had a quick wit and gave back as good as she got. "I could do with a laugh."

She frowned at him. "You promised you would not make a jest of my Season."

He held up his hands in mock surrender. "Lord, you can be a prickly pain sometimes. I am not laughing at you, just at those two clots who fought over you. Your worth far exceeds theirs."

"Well, I don't know about that." She stopped frowning at him, picked up the book of poetry she had intended to read to him, and then sank down into her chair beside his bed and set the book casually on her lap. "I felt much the same as you felt when dealing with the debutantes who sought to catch your eye. They did not really care to know you. It was the same for me. Both earls knew the exact details of my dowry and my family connections, but they never once asked me what I cared about or the sort of woman I hoped to become. They just assumed I would leap at the chance to be their countess."

"Well, you were raised for the role and would be perfect for it."

"I don't think so. I am too outspoken. Those men are looking for biddable wives."

He closed his eyes a moment, for his head was pounding. The small strip of bandage around his head suddenly felt tight and itchy. "I'm glad you rejected them. You can do better than Maxton or Whitfield. Ella, would you mind drawing the curtain? The clouds seem to be disappearing, and the sunlight is too bright. It is shining in my eyes and giving me a headache."

She gave a soft gasp and rose immediately to attend to it. "I won't draw them closed all the way. A refreshing breeze is blowing off the water, and I don't wish to shut it out. Nor should you be left in complete darkness. Your soul is too dark as it is."

He gave a bitter laugh. "So I have been told."

She stood outlined in the lone ray of sunshine now spilling into the room, her graceful form turned away from him as she smoothed out the curtains, then drew them open just a little more before nodding in satisfaction. "It is a good thing you have come to Moonstone Landing."

"Why? Because the chirpy Lady Ella Stockwell is here?"

She walked back to his side, frowning at him again. "You really are exhausting, you know. Were you raised on curdled milk? I mentioned the village because it is someplace quite special."

"What makes it so special?"

Her eyes turned bright and sparkling. "You will understand what I mean once you are recovered enough to walk around. The air here is fresh, and our sunshine warms your bones. The sunset on the water is breathtaking, as is the sunrise, although I am rarely awake at that hour to enjoy it. We have woods and meadows full of flowers. A good harbor and plenty of fishing boats. Beaches and splendid cliff walks. We even have a pirate cave or two. And we can claim the best tea shop in all of England."

"Your eyes sparkle when you speak of this village. You really love it here, don't you?"

She nodded. "I would stay forever if I could. London is fine to visit, but I much prefer the quieter society offered here. My parents would be very disappointed if I told them, but I expect they know how I feel. I am fairly obvious about it. Do you enjoy sweets?"

He shrugged. "Depends on the sweet."

He would not mind tasting Ella.

His thoughts momentarily drifted to all the parts of her that would be honey on his tongue. But that was just him being crude. She meant much more to him than that. He had decided to court her, and would have done so had he not suddenly been called to duty a thousand miles away.

"What is your favorite cake, Caden? Or do you prefer pies? Or tarts?"

He had sampled a tart or two, but those were elegant courtesans trained in the art of pleasure. Not what Ella meant by *tarts*. "Lemon cake is a favorite."

She laughed. "Why am I not surprised?"

"I am not always sour," he said, casting her an unexpectedly warm smile to prove it.

"Perhaps you will surprise me one day and actually be merry. I will not hold my breath on it happening anytime soon. What else do you like? I'll bring you a treat from Mrs. Halsey's tea shop tomorrow. You will not be disappointed. Oh, are you permitted?"

He nodded. "My innards are working fine. I am only suffering from a cracked skull and a few broken bones."

"And you were shot in the leg." She plunked herself back down in her chair. "Caden, I am so very sorry. The doctor only mentioned the leg to me. He wants you to walk a little and thought I should encourage you."

"Not yet. Perhaps when my arm heals a little more. Right now, I am off balance and will fall if I dare stand up."

"Your arm? Was it broken?"

"Just the wrist." He drew back the sleeve of his nightshirt just enough to show her the binding. The bruise ran down his palm as well, but only the wrist hurt. His ribs hurt as well. Two of them were broken, but the others were merely bruised. He mentioned those, but only to stop her when she bent over him to examine him closer.

He did not want her touching his body.

Everything hurt, but this was not the main reason for keeping her away. He did not need to embarrass himself by responding with arousal to her touch.

"Is there anything else you would like me to bring you?" she asked, frowning again, but this time out of concern.

"No, Ella. I am well attended here."

"Does it get lonely for you in this private room?"

"No, I prefer to be in my own thoughts. Not that I have any privacy, even though I am presently the only one in this room. People are constantly walking in to ask me how I am doing. They do not leave me alone. Will I get lonely if I am ever left in peace? No, it would be a relief for me. I am not fit company for anyone just now."

She shook her head. "It is not always healthy to be alone when thoughts are as troubled as yours. In truth, it is probably the last thing you need. I will come by tomorrow afternoon. Would you like a book to read? Or newspapers? We even receive the gossip rags here. You can catch up on all the juicy scandals."

He laughed, then winced as he felt a tug at his ribs. "I'll be all right. Thank you for coming by."

Lord, he hadn't meant for that to slip out.

If anything, he needed to push Ella away.

She leaned forward, her eyes bright and smile lovely as she said, "What was that? A polite *thank you*? Be still, my heart. You must be heavily drugged."

He grinned. "No worries. It won't happen again. A complete accident."

"I will see you tomorrow," she said, her smile gentle and radiant.

He grunted in response.

In fact, he probably was drugged.

Until a few days ago, he had been drifting in and out of consciousness. But his head had been much clearer these past few days. He had no idea what he might have said to Ella had she seen him last week.

Something stupid might have slipped out.

Yes, something very stupid… Something like an admission

she was the woman of his dreams. She would never believe it. After all, he could hardly believe it himself. Perhaps she had been that for him last year. But he was no longer the same man, the arrogant duke's heir who thought he knew everything and could conquer worlds.

Lord, he wanted to forget all of this past year.

The blow he'd received to his head had cracked his skull open, but not stolen his memories. Those remained vivid and horrible.

Nighttime was worst, for those memories crept in, surrounded him amid the silent darkness, and threatened to suffocate him as they tore at his soul. But he never quite suffocated, just lay there helplessly as the agonized cries of his men rang in his ears, of the men he had been forced to watch die and could not save.

He wiped a tear that rolled down his cheek.

More humiliating than having Ella see him aroused was Ella seeing him cry. Lord, why did he have to end up here, of all places?

And why did she have to be here, putting herself in charge of him when she had a line of suitors awaiting her in London?

Well, she *was* here, and he did not want to chase her away quite yet.

She was a soft breath of relief amid his unrelenting agony.

All of England thought him a hero.

What had he done of merit but survive?

He pondered the question for hours, ate his supper, and then fell into a fitful sleep, relieved only by the heavy dose of laudanum the doctor had given him shortly before bedtime.

It was approaching noon by the time he awoke on Tuesday morning. A young lad was in his room, drawing open the curtains and checking on the water in his ewer. "Good morning, my lord. Dr. Hewitt thought you might wake late today. Are you hungry?"

"What did you bring me?"

The boy pointed to a tray of eggs, sausages, fresh bread, and a cup of coffee set on the table beneath his window.

Caden nodded. "Bring it closer."

"Aye, m'lord." The boy carried the tray over, his smile broad and attitude cheerful.

Was there something in the water that made everyone happy here?

"What's your name, lad?"

"Elmer Angel, my lord. My father is Constable Malcolm Angel. He keeps order in the village, although Major Brennan and his soldiers also step in whenever necessary to keep the peace."

"I got the impression this was a quiet village." Caden sat up, ignoring the stab of pain to his ribs, and another stab as he inhaled the enticing aroma.

"Oh, it is fairly quiet. On occasion, we have rowdy sailors off the Royal Navy vessels, or rowdy lords on holiday here who think they are above the law. My father can handle them, but it is often easier to bring in Major Brennan at those times to put in a word. He's a viscount, and the rowdy lords especially seem to respond better to one of their own. Some of them only think of us as dirt beneath their boots."

"Yes, I know. I went to school with many of those pompous elites." This was one failing he'd never had, although he certainly had been raised to think of himself as above everyone else. Heir to a duke. He'd even received a cuff to the head a time or two from his grandfather, who did not want him showing any deference toward their servants. His grandfather did not even like Caden speaking to their estate stewards or solicitors as though these men were their equals.

The old goat had seen to it that everyone feared them and toadied to them, but no one actually *liked* them. This seemed to suit the old man just fine, but Caden did not like it one bit. How did one earn the loyalty of workers who always felt the boot on their neck?

Well, it wasn't his problem yet.

Caden devoured his breakfast as he listened to the boy go on about the village and his life here, which seemed idyllic. "I went to school, too, my lord. We have a good one here in Moonstone Landing. But I'll not be sent off to university. I'm not smart enough. That is, not in any book-learning way like my cousin Brenna. She taught at an exclusive girls' school in Oxford, and the whole town knew she was the brilliant one in the family. But she's married to the Duke of Claymore now."

That remark caught Caden's attention, for Ella had briefly mentioned this as well. "Is she?"

The boy nodded as he watered the lavender flowers in the vase on the far table near the window. "And my cousin Cara married the Duke of Strathmore."

Was this boy having him on?

"Your cousins both married dukes?"

The boy laughed. "Yes, but my cousin Felicity only married an earl."

"Elmer, are you by any chance jesting with me?"

"No, my lord. You can ask anyone. They'll tell you. That is why we have been getting ladies arriving here by the dozens lately. They think to catch themselves a title. But they never will. It is the heart of a person that matters. Goodness and kindness, not greed or tricks. One needs to feel cared about for who they are and not what riches they might bring, don't you think?"

Caden laughed. "Elmer, you are a very wise young man. Yes, it is exactly so."

"Lady Ella and Lady Imogen are nice like that. You will never hear a cross word or condescending remark from their lips. They are true ladies. Quality, and it shows." Elmer glanced at the now-empty tray of food he had brought up. "Ah, you liked it. Well, everyone likes Mrs. Halsey's cooking. She can bake, too. Her tea shop is the best around."

"So I've heard." Caden leaned back as he continued to watch the boy bustle about the room.

"I'll help you wash up, if you're now done eating."

"Just bring the ewer and basin close to me. I'll take care of the chore myself."

"All right, if you're sure. I've brought you a clean nightshirt and a fresh cake of lavender soap, too. You'll probably need help getting the old shirt off and the new shirt on over your head. I've noticed you wince every time you raise your arm even a little. It is because of your broken ribs, I'll wager."

"I can manage. They are almost healed." Of course, this assumed he had not done more damage to them by hurling the cup at Ella when she had walked through his door yesterday. He never would have done so had he realized it was Ella—not that this was any excuse for his behavior. "I'm sure you have more work to do around the hospital."

The boy nodded as he helped Caden take off his sweat-stained nightshirt. "I'll drop it off at the hospital laundry. Yes, we're short-handed, what with new wounded soldiers arriving all week. But you are the only nobleman we have received so far."

"The others were smart and bought out their commissions."

"No, m'lord. You are the smart one. It is men like you this country needs, not those soft cowards."

Caden liked young Elmer. The boy spoke with refreshing frankness.

"The soldiers at the fort help out in the hospital as much as they can, but most aren't really all that helpful." He tossed Caden a grin. "They want to be off fighting, not cleaning out bedpans. I'll stop in to check on you once I am through delivering everyone their meals. But ring the bell by your bedside if you need me sooner. Can't have you sitting here naked as a jaybird. You'll shock our lady volunteers."

Caden wrapped the bedsheet around his waist. "I'll make certain to stay modestly covered."

The boy took off with the empty tray and dirty nightshirt.

Caden washed himself as best he could. Perhaps he ought to have allowed the boy to help, because he yelped in pain every time he raised his arm. The ribs poked into him, and those acute stabs shot straight into his head. Also, he was bandaged and needed to use extra care around those sites. Head, leg, ribs, wrist.

He removed the bandage around his head in order to wash his hair. The doctor had told him the blow to his skull was healing nicely and that the binding would be removed today. Still, he used care.

Washing his legs and chest was not too difficult. Nor did he have much trouble washing his left arm. But with a broken left wrist, he found it difficult to keep hold of the soap or wet cloth in order to wash his right arm.

Scrubbing his back proved impossible. That would have to wait until tomorrow, with Elmer's assistance.

He was struggling into his fresh nightshirt and cursing, as he had difficulty lifting his arms high enough to get his head through the opening, when he heard a light trill of laughter.

Ella.

Blessed saints.

Was the sheet covering his privates?

"Let me help you," she said, and marched to his bedside.

"Get out!" he roared as she ignored him and took the night-shirt from him. Her soft hand burned into his skin as she placed it over his heart to calm him. Of course, it had quite the opposite effect and—Lord help him—ignited a fire below.

"For pity's sake! Must you shout in my ear?" She took his injured arm and held it very gently. "Stop struggling."

"Ow!" He grabbed his pillow and shoved it onto his lap for good measure. Was the girl out of her senses? To barge into his hospital room unannounced? And him not dressed. "What a bloody nuisance you are. Get out!"

"You are going to bring everyone running in here if you do not stop howling. Then Fionn will hear about your being undressed in my presence and come here to punch you. Not to mention, Uncle Cormac will gut you and have your entrails thrown to the dogs. I did not realize you were sitting here naked underneath the sheet. Did you just bathe?" She inhaled by his neck. "Ooh, nice. Much better than yesterday."

"Ella!"

"It isn't as though I saw anything unmentionable."

"All of it is unmentionable," he said with a growl, for his arms, chest, and shoulders were exposed. So were his legs below the knee. Not that he was in any way prudish, but this was Ella. He wanted to see *her* naked, not the other way around.

"I'm glad you were attempting to bathe yourself, although you've obviously had a hard time of it. And an even harder time getting your nightshirt back on. You really ought to learn to accept help when it is offered to you. Your chest is bandaged. Because of your broken ribs, I suppose. Oh, dear. You are bruised all over your chest."

"I am acutely aware."

"It must hurt every time you breathe. But it does not seem to prevent you from shouting in my ear. Here," she said after getting the shirt over his head, "put your arm through the sleeve. If you resist, it will only hurt more, and you still won't be able to get the shirt on by yourself."

He sighed and stopped struggling.

"That's better, you stubborn clot," she said with a soft laugh, and helped him on with his other sleeve. She then tugged the shirt down as far as she dared before turning away and walking across the room to stare out the window. "Caden, can you draw your nightshirt down further? Let me know once you have it properly fixed about yourself."

He growled again.

"Stop complaining. The worst is over. You smell very nice, by the way."

"So you've mentioned. I feel like I've rolled in a field of lavender," he grumbled.

"It is better than the alternatives."

"Such as blood and vomit?"

"Must you be so annoyingly *you*?"

"Yes, I must," he said with a chuckle. "Leave if you find me too insufferable."

She sighed and shook her head. "I love how you make a person feel welcome."

After a few grunts and groans, he managed to make himself moderately presentable. "All right. Done. I am safely dressed, and the covers are securely tucked around me. You need not suffer the sight of my pale arse."

"Ever the gentleman," she muttered, turning to him with a smile. "Are you sure you are comfortable? Do you need another pillow at your back?"

"No, I'm fine. I only need you to go away." He brushed fingers through his wet hair so the water droplets did not drip onto his face.

"I have signed up for a full hour every day this week. I meant it when I said none of the other ladies want to be anywhere near you. It isn't the shouting they mind so much as the brutal sarcasm. You know how to reduce these poor volunteers to tears."

"You seem impervious."

"Because I'd met you before and had a glimpse of your good qualities. Yes, you do have some, although you were very much an oaf last year, too."

"Ah, Ella. Be kind to me or I shall cry."

"Ha! You? I would be shocked to learn you had ever shed a tear. There is a very hard edge to you, Caden."

Because this was the mask he always wore, the icy lack of concern he made a point of showing to others.

But he certainly had shed tears.

So many bloody tears.

In truth, he did not know how to make them stop. They remained well hidden, for he only shed them in the wee hours of the night when all was dark and silent. But there seemed to be an endless supply of them, and the agony he felt was ripping his heart to shreds.

Now, the brainless dolts in the House of Lords, along with some witless generals who had never been close to a battlefront, had tossed medals galore at him and wanted to trot him around the country like a prize show horse.

A hero.

He would laugh hard if his ribs weren't still sore.

"You've brought a basket with you," he said, glancing at the object she had set down by the door before rushing to his side. "What's in it?"

"Books. A few newspapers. And a few scandal sheets. I thought it would be fun to read the gossip to you. The other material is for you to peruse in your own good time. But let me know if you would rather I read to you. Do your eyes strain easily?"

"Yes, sometimes. They tend to blur on and off throughout the day."

She frowned. "What does the doctor say about it?"

"That the headaches will diminish and I will recover my sight fully, but it could take months for those bouts of blurriness to subside. The bones, too. They are healing. I was faring quite poorly on the voyage home. There were moments I wasn't certain I would make it. But I am fairly certain to recover now. I just need time."

She regarded him thoughtfully. "You are in a good place here. Don't let them transfer you out. You need to be in Moonstone Landing."

"Why? Because you are here?"

"No, it has nothing to do with me. It is just this place. It is good for the soul, and yours is in desperate need of restoration."

He shrugged. "I will consider it. What is that scent *you* are wearing? It is making me hungry."

"A blend of cinnamon and apples. It is one of the Farthingale soaps." She approached his bedside, leaned close, and turned her head aside so he could breathe her in. "I have an entire collection of scented soaps. Aunt Phoebe enjoys them, too. I bring a boxful for her from London every summer."

Unaware of the turmoil caused by the light scent of her skin and the fact his lips had softly brushed her neck, she turned away and scooted to the door to fetch her basket. Blessed saints, it was a good thing his covers were securely around him. Was it just Ella or merely abstinence that had him in this roiled state?

"I also brought you some of Mrs. Halsey's lemon cake," she continued, unaware of the effect she was having on him. "It is still warm from the oven. I would offer you a drink, but first you must promise not to hurl it at me."

He arched an eyebrow and grinned. "No more tossing drinks, I promise."

She nodded. "Give me a moment and I'll fetch you some cider. Or would you prefer tea?"

"Cider will do. Bring a glass for yourself. Join me."

"I ate just before coming over here. I'll share some with you tomorrow. Do you like apple pie?"

"Yes, but I prefer ginger cakes. Does Mrs. Halsey make them?"

"Of course. It is another village favorite. I'll bring you ginger cake and apple tarts tomorrow. She also has strawberry, peach, quince, or apricot tarts. Raisin scones. Crumpets. Almond biscuits. Sally Lunns and maids of honor. Damson jams."

"Stop. Now I am starving again, which is ridiculous, because I just finished a large breakfast."

She cast him a soft smile, the sort that made him want to reach out and draw her into his arms. It was something to consider once he stopped howling in pain every time he moved a part of his body. Lord, she had a lovely smile. "I'm glad you are regaining your appetite," she said, giving her hair a light pat, since getting close to him obviously made her fidget. "You could do with putting a little meat back on your bones. Well…I had better get the cider for you. Don't run off. I'll be right back."

"I doubt I'll get far while dressed as I am." His nightshirt was light and thin, perfect for the summer weather, but probably too sheer to walk around in the sunlight without giving her a view of his arse or privates. No, he would need a proper robe if he ever got out of bed. "Ella…"

She turned back to him as she was about to walk out the door. "Yes?"

"You said you rejected Maxton and Whitfield…"

"Yes, and I don't regret it. Why do you ask?"

Because she overwhelmed him.

Because those feelings she had stirred in him all those months ago in those glittering London ballrooms were not mere happenstance.

There was no glitter here. Only Ella in her natural beauty.

In London, they called her a diamond.

Here in Moonstone Landing…she was a shimmering light of heaven.

How could every eligible bachelor in England not be after her? Or were they? Just because she had rejected Maxton and Whitfield did not mean she was on the shelf.

"No reason. Just curious. Is anyone else courting you at the moment?"

Chapter Three

"SEVERAL GENTLEMEN ARE courting me," Ella said. Why was she asking? Idle curiosity? Or did he actually care? She hurried out of his room before he could toss more questions at her, and made her way to the hospital kitchen to fetch a small jug of cider and a mug.

She ran into Dr. Hewitt on her way back upstairs. He was the local Moonstone Landing doctor, but often volunteered his time at the army hospital whenever there was an overflow of wounded coming in, as it seemed there had been lately. "Lady Ella, how is the patient behaving?"

"Better than yesterday. He is now offering to drink his cider instead of hurling it at me," she said with a gentle laugh.

The doctor joined her in a chuckle. "Well, that is a welcome improvement."

"We shall see how it goes. He was a surly man before his injuries, and I doubt that will change. But at least he is not raging. I volunteered to read to him for the rest of this week. Perhaps by next week he will behave himself for someone else."

"Maybe. I expect his grandfather will order him moved to London as soon as Dr. Spencer gives him clearance to travel." Ella knew Dr. Spencer was the one in charge of the medical staff at this army hospital and responsible for signing off on all discharges.

"Oh, no," she said, her eyes rounding in alarm. "You must speak to him. He mustn't allow Lord Mersey to leave yet. His heart is not well. I don't mean physically. I'm not sure what is going on with him, but there is agony in his eyes, and I don't think it has to do with broken bones."

"Ella, this is important… Has he said anything to you about his time in West Africa?"

She shook her head. "No, and I am afraid to press him on the matter. I'm sure he's given a full report to his superiors."

Dr. Hewitt cleared his throat. "What I heard from Dr. Spencer is that Lord Mersey told them all to go to hell."

She sighed. "Sounds just like him. Well, I had better get back. I will let you know if he tells me anything significant. However, I will not betray his trust. If he asks me not to repeat what he tells me, then I won't."

"Nor would I want you to. The generals can do a little work on their own and get their information from other sources."

She hurried upstairs, waving to Fort Arundel's commanding officer as she rushed by. "No time to chat, Fionn! See you tonight."

She was slightly out of breath when she walked back into Caden's room. Between one thing and another, it had taken her longer than expected to return. The curtains had been drawn, leaving him in the dark. "Has someone been in here?"

He nodded. "Some woman who introduced herself as Lady Dowling. She said she was here to take over for you, but I knew you had not asked her. First of all, she would have returned with the cider. Second of all, you would have come up here to tell me yourself instead of simply running off. There's something about her I did not like, so I told her I was tired and just wanted to sleep. Open the curtains and allow in the light, Ella. I'd like you to read to me."

"I am not too fond of her myself," she admitted, crossing the room and drawing aside the curtains to allow in the sunshine and a pleasant breeze off the sea. "She amuses herself by causing mischief between sweethearts."

He grinned. "Are we sweethearts, Ella?"

She rolled her eyes. "Oh, do be serious. No, we are not. But Lady Dowling must have heard we knew each other, and thought there might be something between us. This is what she does, insinuates herself between a courting couple. Sometimes husbands and wives. I really don't understand her. She can be nice when she wants to be, but I would never confide in her or trust her with anything important for fear she would find a way to use it for her own purposes at a later time. I suppose she heard you were heir to a duke and wanted to get a good look at you."

She returned to his side, poured some of the cider from the jug into his cup, and then set the jug on the small table beside his bed.

He took a few sips, then stared into the swirling amber liquid. "Who are the gentlemen currently courting you, Ella? Anyone I know?"

"I expect you know them all. I'll be returning to London at the end of the summer, and I am fairly certain they will come around to see me once I am back home. I am not serious about any of them yet."

"Are you saying this in the hope I will court you?"

She looked up in surprise, her gaze caught in the grip of his dark eyes. "No. I've told you, it is exhausting to be around you. You are constantly pressing and pushing, never content to simply enjoy an affair or dance a dance. You are unable to play cards and think only of the game. Your mind goes to a thousand places, and none of them content you. I feel like a limp rag after spending time with you."

"I'm sorry I make you feel that way," he said with unexpected sincerity.

She cut him a slice of lemon cake and exchanged the mug in his hand for the plate before continuing. "Sometimes you go easy with me, such as now. You are quite pleasant in those moments. I like that Caden very much. But usually you are irritating and give me a headache. How do you like the cake?"

He took a healthy bite and swallowed before replying, "Delicious. I'll have some more."

She smiled as she cut him another slice, watching as he devoured the first with a hearty enthusiasm that meant he was regaining his strength.

"Ella, are you sure you will not join me?"

"Tomorrow, I promise. I'll bring up lemonade, too. Do you like lemonade, or do you prefer cider? I would offer ale, but I am not certain it is permitted for you. You are wobbly enough on your feet without imbibing spirits."

"Ale is hardly that, but I shall survive without it. The cider or lemonade will do just fine. Whichever you prefer." He polished off two more slices of lemon cake in short order and took another sip of his drink. "Read me some of the gossip rags. Let's see if they reveal who else is courting the Season's most dazzling diamond, Lady Ella Stockwell."

"It is no secret. Viscount Tremell, for one."

"Oh, not that fool," he said with an aching groan. "He's an utter arse. Ella, you can do much better than him."

"Did I ask for your opinion?" Was he going to disparage all her suitors? Well, she was curious to learn what he thought of them. Men knew each other's strengths and weaknesses better than she ever would. The entire point of courtship was to show one's best side and hide one's faults. But Caden had gone to school with these men, or knew of them from their clubs or mutual friends. They drank together, rode together, and sometimes hunted together.

Ladies only got to see the polite side of these gentlemen, the façade they wished to show while on their best behavior at the various balls, assemblies, and musicales hosted throughout the Season.

He polished off his cider and poured himself another. "No, you did not ask for my opinion. But I shall give it anyway. Who else?"

"The Marquess of Brodick."

Caden merely grunted.

She arched an eyebrow. "Nothing to say about him?"

"No. He's a decent fellow."

"Thank you. That is good to know. How about Lord Harvey and Lord Eckleston?"

He grunted again.

"What? No disparaging comments?" She laughed. "They did seem to be decent fellows. I shall discourage Viscount Tremell's pursuit of me. Thank you for the warning. He did strike me as oily. But I will agree to see the others. Well, my return to London is several months away, and much can change in that time."

She picked up the gossip rag that had just arrived this morning. "Oh…"

Caden leaned forward. "What is it, Ella?"

"We can strike Brodick from the list." She knew she ought to feel some disappointment, but she mostly felt mild curiosity about the young lady he had chosen. "He is now betrothed to a duke's daughter."

Caden regarded her with unexpected kindness. "I'm sorry, Ella. Who's the girl?"

"Lady Jane Grimsby, eldest daughter of the Duke of Hawes."

He shook his head. "A money match, for certain. That girl's name suits her. She is a grim one. Poor Brodick. I had no idea he needed to marry a fortune."

"I suppose that is all he wanted of me, as well. But I was slow to come around, so he moved on." She was not disappointed in losing the man, but did not know why the notion still overset her. In truth, she was never going to fall in love with Lord Brodick. But she had been fooled by his affection for her. She thought he sincerely liked her, and confided as much to Caden.

"He probably did care for you, Ella. Very much. I'm sure he hoped you and he would be a match. But desperate times call for desperate measures, and he did not have time to wait around to win your hand. Nor were there any guarantees he would come out the victor, since you had three other suitors already in the game."

"Love shouldn't be a game."

"No, it should not be. But the Marriage Mart is not about love. It is about securing futures and gaining fortunes."

She nodded. "I know, but I still don't care for it."

"Nor do I." He took the gossip sheet from her hands. "Let's see what other dirt is revealed. Ah, Lady Melinda Wycliff is betrothed to Lord Jeremy Flint. Poor Flint."

"Who is she? I thought I knew most of the young ladies making their debuts."

"I'm surprised you haven't met her or at least heard of her. She is the young lady my grandfather hoped to match with me."

"Oh, I'm sorry. Seems we've each lost a potential mate." She did not know why the thought of Caden betrothed was wreaking havoc on her heart. It should have come as no surprise that his grandfather had arranged a wife for him. The agreement might have been reached between the families years ago, when Caden and Lady Melinda were just children.

"Don't be. This is the best news I could receive. Although I do feel sorry for poor Flint. He'll be stuck with her now."

"Is she that odious? You don't have much regard for women, do you? First you disparage Jane Grimbsy, and now Lady Melinda."

"I like women well enough, just not those two. Do not weep for them, Ella. They are not particularly nice. Nor is Flint any prize himself. I'm sure he's arranged to take Melinda's money, set her up in a fine house in London, and then take himself off to Pembrokeshire with his mistress and two children."

Ella gasped. "What a wretched thing to do! Lord Flint has children? With his mistress?"

"Yes, although they'll never inherit his title. He'll do right by them. As for Melinda, do not cry for her. She will enjoy herself quite nicely."

"As his abandoned spouse? Living without her husband?"

Caden shook his head. "Ella, stop being so innocent. Yes, without her husband. She does not want him around to interfere with her and her fast friends. Why do you think I am cheering? My grandfather and I heartily disagree on matters of matrimony. He refused to see beyond her wealth and royal connections. I saw her as a spoiled, ill-tempered shrew who was going to cuckold me at every turn."

"So, you want a wife in more than name only," she remarked, somewhat surprised that he cared at all about matters of the heart.

He grunted again. "Why shouldn't I be selective? She will be the mother of my children. I would like to know they are mine and not some other man's offspring. I would also like to see them grow up with intelligence, common sense, and an understanding that wealth is not the end-all and be-all. How much wealth does a man need to accumulate in his lifetime? At what point does the damage caused to others by his greed become intolerable?"

"I think you would like my father and Uncle Cormac very much. They think very much as you do. Not every venture is worth the investment, even if it is a sure thing. But they are also firm believers in a love match, having made such matches for themselves. They are so happy. Even as the world presses down upon their shoulders, the burden is easier to bear because it is shared with the wives they love."

"Well, it makes sense for you to make such a match, because you take things very much to heart. You need someone who will love you and make you happy. Marrying merely for wealth or a title is out of the question for you."

"And yet that perfect person is not so easy to find," she admitted. "Who do you think would suit me best, Lord Harvey or Lord Eckleston?"

"Neither."

"Neither?"

Caden shook his head. "There's no sparkle in your eyes when you mention them. Ella, you are not the sort who can give herself to a man you do not love. And before you huff in indignation and suggest you could grow to love one of them, forget it."

"Why must I forget it? Does love not grow stronger over time? And what makes you the expert? You don't like anyone."

He laughed. "I assure you, I do like some people. But you are right that I find most exceedingly tiresome and unworthy of my esteem or trust. However, I know what I want in a woman."

Ella rolled her eyes. "And have you met this paragon of perfection yet?"

Yes. You.

He shrugged. "It does not matter if I have or not. I am in no position to do anything about it right now, am I? I cannot even use a bedpan without someone holding me up so I do not fall flat on my face."

She set her hand ever so lightly on his forearm, careful not to put any weight on it. "We will get you better here. I am certain of it, Caden."

He sighed. "Read on, my ministering angel. Let's get to the scandals. I need to be amused."

She read him an item about Lord P and Lady G caught in a hayloft. "Who do you think they are?"

"That would be Sir John Peveril and Lady Sarah Graystone. A sad affair, that. Her father is a viscount and did not consider Peveril, a mere knight, worthy of his daughter. He refused Peveril's offer of marriage and had her betrothed to the Earl of Graystone. A mismatch if ever there was one. It is a dangerous triangle, and one of them is going to get shot someday, because Graystone is not one to share his wife with others."

"Oh, that is terrible for all of them. How unhappy they must all be."

"You are being too soft-hearted again, Ella. Graystone knew of her affections for Peveril but went ahead and offered for her anyway. What did he think was going to happen?"

"He might have hoped she would fall in love with him instead, given the chance."

Caden snorted. "Perhaps, but that was a foolish notion on his part. Lady Graystone has never had a sensible thought in her entire life. She responds to everything with theatrical affect, as though she is the tragic heroine and everyone ought to feel sorry for her."

"But we should not?" Ella asked, caught up in the gossip.

"No, we should not. The lady is tiresome, and one can never do enough for her. She needs to be constantly worshiped. That is not in Graystone's nature. However, Peveril is also prone to the dramatic. He and Lady Graystone view themselves as tragic lovers, like Romeo and Juliet."

Ella edged closer to his bedside. "Hence your theatrical reference."

He nodded. "I am fairly confident their grand *amour* would quickly die out if they actually had to live together. The lady is a peahen, and Peveril would soon tire of her constant demands and insecurities."

"Why should she take all the blame? Perhaps she would tire of him, since he sounds like a bit of a numbskull to me."

"He is," Caden said with a light nod. "And to take Lady Graystone to a hayloft? Gad, that must have been uncomfortable for them. Those bits of straw and rough-hewn wood poking into their backsides as they rolled around. Hard to rouse passion under those conditions. She must have complained all the while."

"And then to get caught on top of it all." Ella shook her head as she studied him. "You sound as though you've tried it."

He cast her an appealingly wicked grin that she should not have found appealing at all, but there was something irresistibly attractive about Caden that could not be denied. "Only once, and not with her, that's for certain," he said. "I was very young and stupid at the time. Let's move on to the next scandal. Doing the naughty deed in a hayloft is not an appropriate conversation to be having with anyone as innocent as you."

"All right." She studied the gossip sheet and found the next item. "Lord M and Lady F have run off to Italy together, abandoning their spouses. However, it is also reported that neither abandoned spouse is bereft over this turn of events. It appears Lady M and Lord F have retired to Lord F's country estate and are enjoying the rustic life together."

"Switching spouses? Well, I suppose it is an agreeable outcome for them. Their children will be confused as all hell."

"Do you know who they are?"

"Yes, Lady M is Lady Markwood and Lord F is Lord Farraday."

"For a man who disdains all manner of social games, you certainly know who all the players are."

He shrugged. "Some of these men turn to me for advice, and the—"

Ella laughed. "Surely you jest. Why would they trust you on matters of love? Your answers would only be cynical and probably wrong."

He leaned back against his pillows and regarded her with amusement glittering in his eyes. "You have such a low opinion of me. Do you think I give no thought to life or love, or what I would hope for in my future? Even cold-hearted clots like me think of these things. Let's move on. What else has happened in London in our absence?"

Ella read him an item about the elopement of a young couple. "They dashed off to Gretna Green, with her father close on their heels."

"Did the father catch up to them before the border?"

Ella perused the rest of the story. "No. The couple are now wed." She paused to stare at him. "Are you going to give me your thoughts on the matter? I know you have opinions about everything."

"Actually, I have no opinion on this. They've made their choice and are now stuck with it. I expect their happiness will depend on how willing her father is to now accept him. They will have a very hard life if he chooses to cut them off. It may also be that the bridegroom is a hard worker and can make something of himself even if the father does not help them out. The marriage might succeed. But if I were a betting man, I would bet against them. The stardust in a bride's eyes will quickly fade when the realities of a hard life are upon her."

Ella then read two more stories about a wife abandoning a husband for his horse trainer, and a husband bringing a mistress to live under the same roof as him and his wife. "Oh, Caden. That is awful. How cruel of the man to show such little respect for his wife."

He nodded. "It is an exceedingly low thing to do."

"Would you ever do such a thing?"

He appeared surprised by the question. "Me? How can you even ask? No, I would not. Nor would Harvey or Eckleston. They are decent men."

She set the gossip rag aside. "I often enjoy reading these juicy tidbits, but they strike me as terribly sad today. Wives and husbands trapped in unhappy marriages with no way out unless they do something scandalous and foolish."

"That's what happens when one marries for alliance reasons. Some endure quite nicely. Some even grow to care for each other. Some find a discreet compromise. And some simply explode in a public and often humiliating fashion."

"I suppose." She set aside the gossip sheet and picked up one of the newspapers, but then immediately set it aside. The leading story was about battles in Africa's Gold Coast region between the British and the Ashanti tribesmen. She knew this was where Caden had served this past year, and so she quickly tucked the paper back in her basket, concerned he might know some of the soldiers listed as deceased.

Their hour had passed quite nicely, and she found his opinions surprisingly thoughtful and interesting. He was a practical man and looked at everything with reason and logic, even matters of the heart. But she sensed these stories about the Ashanti wars would set him off. This was something more suitable for her Uncle Cormac to discuss with him.

Caden was now yawning. He was tiring.

He had eaten four slices of lemon cake and imbibed three glasses of cider, all the while talking to her. She had not checked on the time, but it was well past their hour. This was a good moment to take her leave. "I shall see you tomorrow, Caden. I'll leave these books for you, should you feel the urge to read. One is a mystery story, another is a book of poems by Shelley, and the last is an account by the renowned explorer, Lord Roger Hillingsworth, on his travels around the world."

"Thank you, Ella. But I doubt I will be able to read these yet. I'll only get through a page or two before my eyes strain."

"Oh, yes. You've mentioned. I'll leave them here for you anyway. Choose one you might like, and I'll start reading it to you tomorrow." She rose and placed the books on the small table beside the jug of cider. However, she left the newspapers tucked in the basket and meant to take them away.

"What are you hiding from me, Ella?"

She blushed. "Nothing. It is just more news about disasters and other sad events."

"Leave the papers. I am not a child who needs to be sheltered. What did you see in them that makes you determined to keep them from me?"

"More sad things." She clasped her hands together and began to wring them. "Please, Caden. Let me take the newspapers home."

"They contain accounts of the Ashanti battles, don't they? That war has been going on for years. We kill their soldiers. They kill ours. And what is it for? So some rich merchants and their investors can get even richer on the gold and cocoa to be found in the region? We wouldn't be there if there was nothing of interest to be grabbed. Leave the papers here. I could do with a good laugh."

"No, I am going to take them back with me. We'll talk about it tomorrow."

He attempted to reach for her, but fell back against his pillows in pain. "Don't treat me like a child, Ella."

"I assure you, I am not. But you almost died over there, or may have lost good friends. I don't want you reading about others who—"

"Others? There are no others. All my friends are dead," he said with unrestrained bitterness. "There's no one left in my regiment but me. The idiot governor appointed by the Crown came into the region knowing nothing about the local customs and traditions. He insulted everyone, including the British troops assigned to the area. After riling the tribesmen, he..." Caden turned toward the wall and groaned with such a raw ache, it made her shiver. "Go away, Ella. I'll see you tomorrow."

She took several deep breaths, struggling to remain calm when she had obviously brought up the worst possible topic for him. "I'm so sorry, Caden. Truly, I am."

"I know you are. It's all right. I'll see you tomorrow, my innocent dove."

Dove?

Well, her heart was quite fragile at the moment, as easily torn apart as the wings of a gentle dove. She wanted to bend over and kiss his forehead, but dared not. She would melt and do something improper if he closed his arms around her. "Yes, until tomorrow."

Her eyes began to fill with tears, for the thought of his losing every friend assigned with him simply tore her to pieces. She did not even know them, but he had served with them and gone into battle with them. No wonder his soul was in anguish.

She sniffled as she picked up her basket.

"Blast it, Ella. Are you crying?" He did not appear to be angry with her. In truth, his voice was achingly gentle. "You didn't cause anything bad to happen. It is a craven world we live in. Sometimes we manage to avoid looming disasters, and sometimes we find ourselves caught up in the middle of them with no hope of escape."

"I'm so sorry I ruined this day for you. We were having a nice time, weren't we? Then I went ahead and drew out that newspaper."

"It was a good day," he insisted, shifting his position so that he now sat upright. "Ella, you are still looking at me with big, sad eyes."

"I cannot help it. I meant to cheer you, and instead I've made things worse."

"You are not to blame. Despite appearances, you have made things better." Ignoring the pain he felt with every movement, he reached out and caressed her cheek.

It was such a kind and thoughtful gesture, it left her undone. "How is it that you are making the effort to cheer me up when I am the one who should be doing this for you?" she asked in a ragged whisper.

"You have cheered me, Ella." He took her hand and drew her closer so that her hip leaned against his bed. "Close your eyes."

Instead, they widened. "Caden, I forbid you to kiss me."

He drew her closer still. "What makes you think I intend to kiss you?"

Had she misread that look in his eyes? "Oh, because we are suddenly very close to each other. I can feel the heat of your body and breathe in the lavender scent of your skin. But...I'm sorry. I thought... Aren't you?"

"Going to kiss you?" His dark eyes turned smoldering. "Do you want me to?"

Her face turned hot as the blush crawled up her neck and spread onto her cheeks, which now burned with embarrassment.

"Ah, you do like me after all. Close your eyes and trust me, Ella."

"Oh, dear heaven." Well, she owed him that much for opening up his painful wounds, did she not?

She held her breath and shut her eyes.

He placed his hand to the back of her head, his roughened fingers exciting her as he drew her ever so slowly closer. She felt their breaths mingling, then felt the whisper-soft touch of his lips to hers, those full, manly lips that now sank down on her slightly parted ones with possessive heat and surprising tenderness. There was something exquisite about his kiss, conquering but also quite protective, as though he was claiming her for his own, but also promising to watch over her, guard her and keep her safe.

Well, there was nothing halfway about Caden. If he wanted something, he went for it in a completely commanding and breathtaking way.

Did he want her?

He drew her up against his hard body.

Was she hurting him? She was almost atop him and pressed immodestly against his chest.

He did not seem to mind or care.

Well, why would he? He seemed to be enjoying her surrender.

She felt strength in those magnificently muscled arms of his that now surrounded her.

She inhaled the heat of his skin, the maleness of it and the light lavender scent of his soap that he complained made him smell like a girl.

It didn't.

Caden was all hard, stubborn male.

She felt the tip of his tongue slide along the seam of her lips before he suddenly drew away and nudged her off his bed. "Bollocks. Bad timing."

She wasn't certain what was happening until Elmer came bounding in. "Oh, Lady Ella. I did not realize you were still here." Fortunately, the boy was oblivious to the reason her face was in flames. She dared not touch a finger to her lips that were still tingling from Caden's kiss.

Instead, she turned away and pretended to fumble through her basket in the hope Elmer would not notice her appallingly heated response to the cad now grinning at her from his bed.

She tossed Caden a disapproving frown.

He stared back at her, his smile smug and conquering.

Lord, he was such an oaf. Did he have to be so obvious when gloating?

But he certainly knew how to kiss a woman. The impact of his kiss was still rippling through her body.

She cleared her throat. "I was just leaving, Elmer. Um, you caught me checking that his pillows were properly set at his back."

Caden's smile turned surprisingly gentle. "Ella, I enjoyed my time with you. Don't forget the ginger cake tomorrow."

She was still feeling those ripples as she nodded numbly. "What?"

His smile broadened. "The ginger cake, Ella."

"Oh, yes." She stumbled over her chair, quickly recovered her balance and righted herself, then hurried out.

What had she done?

"Dear heaven." Every lesson ingrained in her as she prepared for her debut was this exact warning about never kissing a beau. Caden was not even a beau. Worse, he was a surly rake who knew how to make her melt.

Would he kiss her again?

She dared not allow it.

But what a splendid first kiss he had given her.

Did he suspect she had never been kissed before?

Her thoughts were in a whirl as she hurried out of the hospital building and scampered over to Mr. Bedwell's mercantile, where the Moonstone Cottage caretaker, Mr. Hawke, was waiting in his wagon to drive her back to her Uncle Cormac's home. Westgate Hall was on his way, and he often picked her up from there and dropped her off in Moonstone Landing, then returned her to Westgate Hall on the return trip.

"Lady Ella, is something wrong?" Mr. Hawke asked. "You seem flustered."

"No, all is fine. Just trying to keep a list in my head of all the things I must do tomorrow. Lost in my own thoughts." And those thoughts were all about Caden and the kiss they had shared today that still had her tingling and reeling.

Would he attempt to kiss her again tomorrow?

Dear heaven.

How would she respond if he did?

Chapter Four

CADEN SPENT THE following morning exercising his limbs. Having to raise his arms, put weight on his injured leg—even turn his head right and left—was exhausting and painful. But he needed to get out of his sickbed and start walking around. With crutches, of course. He was not yet able to walk on his own.

But he needed to do something, *anything*, to stop thinking of Ella and how much he wanted to kiss her again.

What a fool he was to think one taste of her would ever be enough to satisfy him.

He ought to have been prepared for the impact to his heart. After all, he had spent an entire year in a hot, dusty garrison thinking about her to the point of obsession, worried he might lose her on the Marriage Mart. In truth, this had been his greatest fear, returning to England only to find she was married.

He had yet to calm down from the joy he felt in finding her unattached.

If he could have leaped out of bed and danced a jig, he would have done so. He was a cynical arse and had little faith in any higher being, but he once again gave silent thanks for Ella coming back into his life.

He had done the same at least a dozen times last night, thinking of her every time he awoke in a cold sweat and with tears in his eyes for his fallen men. Thoughts of her helped pull him out of despair, for he had returned to England truly on the brink of madness. Seeing Ella again had sent his heart soaring.

His heart was still soaring, even though every bone in his body ached from this morning's exertion.

He had overdone it and now smelled like a wet sock.

But that did not bear mentioning.

He glanced toward the door, eager to see her again, and even more eager to feel the sensation of her lips on his. How was he going to impress her when he could not even stand on his own?

It did not matter.

She was not going to go near him as he was now, an odorous mess. She, on the other hand, was always as sweet and fragrant as a meadow flower. Yesterday, her lips had tasted of wild honey.

How would they taste today? Perhaps of the ginger cake she had promised to bring him.

Now having a purpose to his recovery, he took up his crutches again and forced himself to walk around the room once more.

Every organ, bone, and pore in his body protested.

"Don't overdo it, you arse," he cautioned himself, for it was quite possible he would lose his balance and crash to the floor if he did not stop right now.

Ella would get an eyeful if she walked in while he was on the ground, just lying there in a nightshirt that barely fell to his knees.

Not that he expected her yet. She had torn out of his room yesterday as though the devil were on her tail.

And what a delightful tail she had.

He leaned against his bed a moment and took a few breaths to settle himself until his dizziness passed. Besides making himself fit for Ella, he needed to do this for himself. It was not in his nature to lie abed, and now one of the clerks from the Royal Marines headquarters had sent him a list of proposed stops around the country for his "I am a *bloody* hero" tour.

He had ripped it up and sent a missive back telling them to kiss his arse.

Not the brightest thing he had ever done.

Two things were likely to happen once that message was received in London. The first: a contingent of soldiers would arrive and take him under their "protection" until he agreed to go along with this farce of a tour. The second: his grandfather would come for him, raging and blustering about dishonoring the family name by refusing to cooperate with his superiors.

Before either of those things happened, he wanted to spend as much time with Ella as possible. Lord knew why, for he was in no fit condition to court anyone, or even be in anyone's company for too long. But she was special, a thing of beauty.

His gentle dove.

His.

"Ah, Lord Mersey, you are up and about," Dr. Hewitt said, looking quite official with his spectacles perched atop his head and medical instruments dangling out of his coat pocket. "Careful not to overdo it."

Caden laughed. "That warning is probably too late. I never do anything by half measures."

"Well, you need to take it slow now. This is serious. I don't want you to rupture any organs."

"All right." But he bridled at the caution, for he was tired of lying abed and impatient to recover, especially now that he had kissed Ella.

Having kissed her, what next?

He wanted more, of course. But not even he was that much of a wretch to coax her beyond what was proper. Not that kissing her passionately was proper. Nor were his thoughts about that exquisite body of hers remotely proper.

Of course, he had to restrain himself, or else she would believe those kisses meant something more than a bit of fun.

Perhaps they did mean more.

Yes, they did.

He could not breathe for wanting her.

And now, Dr. Hewitt had him seated at the edge of his bed and was asking him to take deep breaths. "Hold to the count of three. One. Two. Three. Good, now release."

Caden let the air rush out of him with a groan. "Bollocks."

"Did that hurt? Well, those ribs are still sensitive. Do not bend over and do not lift anything heavier than a cup for the next few days. I promise you will feel much better soon."

"I'll hold you to that promise." He wanted to spend time with Ella, and not just here while lying in his hospital bed like a big, helpless lump. As for courting her, he dared not think that far ahead, not while those generals and his grandfather were furious with him and trying to break his will.

Well, they could kiss his arse. He was not going to take that "look at me, I am a *bloody* hero" tour until he was good and ready.

Lord, why did he always have to be so difficult?

Well, Ella handled him easily enough. She made it look effortless and reminded him why he had been so drawn to her last year, too. He was not ready for any commitments, but nor did he want to lose her.

Despite everything else going wrong for him, he knew she was the one right thing in his life.

But his life was such a mess.

He was an utter mess inside.

Was it fair to take all he could from this girl when he might not be able to give her anything in return? He could never treat her as just another peahen in the flock who sought to win his favor. If he was not going to bed her and not going to dally with her, was it right to steal a few more kisses?

How could he resist? She did something to his heart.

"I'll stop in to see you later this afternoon," Dr. Hewitt said after finishing his examination. He had checked Caden's fingers and toes, making certain he was able to wiggle them about and feel sensations of pain when pinched. He checked Caden's head wound and then had him fix his gaze on a pencil that he moved back and forth in front of his eyes. "Good. Good. Get some rest now."

Caden sank back onto his bed and closed his eyes.

It was not long before more thoughts of Ella crept into his head.

Beautiful, innocent Ella.

Then he thought of the duties he would eventually have to undertake.

Everyone was tugging at him, expecting him to go around the country espousing the big lie. Wars happened; battles were fought. This is not what troubled him.

This last Ashanti battle was different.

He had not been sent off to fight for a noble cause. There was no danger to Crown interests or British sovereignty. That last battle had been all about seizing the gold mines and cocoa plantations that were going to make businessmen, including his grandfather, rich at the expense of everyone else. This was about private interests, bribery, all about lining one's pockets. Nothing to do with valor.

He heard light footsteps coming up the stairs and hoped it was Ella coming for her afternoon visit. To his disappointment, Lady Dowling breezed into the room. Lord, what did she want with him?

"Good afternoon, my lord," she said with syrupy sweetness.

He grunted. "Why are you here?"

She patted her hair and then approached his bed. "To keep you company, of course."

"It isn't necessary. Lady Ella will be here soon."

Lady Dowling appeared to be in her early thirties, a stunning woman who had retained much of her youthful appeal. But Caden was not moved or impressed in the least. Greedy women circled him all the time, and he could readily tell who they were, since they all had the same calculating expression when approaching him. "Really, my lord. Think of her reputation. She cannot be in here alone with you day after day. People will talk. I ought to take over responsibility for tending you."

"No. It shall be Lady Ella and no one else. Have Elmer stand in here with us if you are so concerned about her reputation."

She pinched her lips. "The lad has other duties." Despite not having been given permission, she stepped closer to him. "Let me adjust your pillows."

"Not necessary. I am quite comfortable."

"You do not look comfortable." She leaned into him, purposely rubbing her breasts against his chest as she uselessly fluffed those pillows.

Ella chose that moment to walk in.

Caden groaned.

She could not have appeared at a worse time, although Lady Dowling must have known she was on her way up and arranged this little scene for her.

"Please come in, Lady Ella. I have been waiting for you," he said.

She paused at the threshold, no doubt debating whether to stay or go.

He'd kissed her yesterday. Did she think he was now moving on to kiss someone else?

Caden sat up with difficulty, feeling jabs of pain shoot up his sides and tear into his head, a sign he had moved too quickly. "Bollocks. Bollocks. Ow. Don't go, Ella," he said, his voice raw and his feelings bared. Surely she had to know Lady Dowling had set them both up and meant to make mischief between them.

He turned to Lady Dowling. "You are dismissed."

The command was rude, but she did not deserve his courtesy. He wanted Ella.

He sighed and fell back against his pillows once Lady Dowling flounced out. "I did not ask her up here, Ella. Nor am I interested in anything she has to offer. Lord, she's even put her scent all over me. I wondered at the reason for her strong perfume. Will you hand me a washcloth and the lavender soap? I would rather smell like a field of flowers than that woman. She's quite the sly one, isn't she?"

Ella set her basket on the small table beside his bed, grabbed the damp cloth and soap, and then took the chair by his bedside. "Let's hope she does not start any ugly rumors."

"She would not dare," he said fiercely.

Ella smiled and shook her head. "That is quite a naïve thing to say. I should think you've had experience with a woman scorned."

"Why? Because I have a rakish reputation with the ladies?"

"Yes. Women like her do not like to be ignored."

"Well, I want nothing to do with her. There are plenty just like her in London. I did not think they were here as well. I suppose they are everywhere. They come after me. I do not chase them." He rubbed the damp cloth across his chest, neck, and face as he spoke. "Ah, that's better."

Ella took the cloth and soap and set them back on the table beneath the window.

He watched her cross the room and then come back to his side, her movements graceful and efficient. "Ella, I got out of bed and walked around a little this morning."

Her face brightened. "You did? Oh, I'm so glad. How are you feeling now?"

"Very achy," he said with a chuckle. "I expect that ginger cake will go a long way toward improving my day. Open the basket. The aroma is heavenly."

"Mrs. Halsey baked this one just for you." She reached into the basket and drew it out. Next, she removed the bottle of lemonade.

"Share it with me, Ella."

She cast him a breathtaking smile. "You do not need to ask me twice."

There was something about this girl that made him feel good whenever he was in her company. They were not doing anything important, and perhaps this was why he enjoyed their time together so much. She was gentle with him, but not cloying. If he tossed a barb, she always had a ready response because she was quick-witted and easily able to keep up with him.

She cut several slices and then poured each of them a glass of lemonade. "What shall we talk about today?"

"We could talk about the kiss we shared," he said, his gaze fixed on her pretty mouth.

She shook her head, immediately tensing. "No, it was a mistake and cannot happen again."

He was not going to let her get away with that remark. "It was your first, Ella. I could tell, so do not bother to deny it. And it wasn't a mistake. We won't talk about the kiss if you don't want to, but never call it a mistake."

"You're right," she said, now appearing ashamed. "I am so sorry. It was a perfect kiss. Truly, Caden. It was all I ever hoped a first kiss would be...even if it was with you." She held up her hand when he started to protest. "I am teasing you. It was perfect *because* it was you. And don't you dare make too much of my admission."

He arched an eyebrow.

"I suppose there is something to be said for kissing big, insufferable louts. You made my first time feel magical and special. Did you do this on purpose?"

"I'm not sure how to answer that. Yes, I wanted our kiss to be everything wonderful and memorable for you. It was special because it was you that I was kissing. It was magical because of you."

She nodded. "You made me feel desired and beautiful. Truly, it was a kiss to be treasured."

He cast her a soft smile. "Ah, more admissions."

"Yes, but I would rather not say anything more about it."

"I understand. But before we move on, I just want you to know the kiss was real for me, too. I did desire you. You are beautiful. And I want more."

"Oh." She buried her face in her hands and groaned. "Must you always make things so difficult?"

"I thought I was clarifying the situation. I am not going to kiss you again without your permission. Just let me know if you are amenable, and I will oblige."

She dropped her hands and looked up at him. "No, you are complicating the situation. Here, have a slice of ginger cake."

"Tell me about Moonstone Landing, Ella. Why do you love it here so much?" He chose to change the topic before she ran out of here and never returned. He accepted the plate she was now offering him.

She pursed her lips, reminding him again how much he wished to kiss her. But she was already embarrassed and overly skittish. He would chase her away if he came on too strong. Besides, he liked talking to her. Being with her made him forget the horrors of that last battle for just a little while.

"For me," she said, "it is the *feeling* of this place more than anything else. There is a beautiful simplicity to life here. Damaged souls can heal here."

"Such as mine?"

She nodded. "You were very angry when you arrived. This is why I hope you can stay longer and complete your recovery here. It was never about the physical mending. You are strong and healthy. Those visible wounds will mend in time. Your damaged soul will take a bit longer to heal."

"It won't." He snorted. "One cannot undo events that occur in one's life."

She set down the slice of ginger cake she was about to bite into. "I am not suggesting you will forget any of it, but it is important for you to learn to cope with whatever has happened and somehow move forward."

Cope? If only he could snap his fingers and make the pain of remembering go away. "Easy for you to say. You don't know what happened."

"Caden, I am ready to listen whenever you are willing to talk about it."

"No, and don't ask me again." Just as she did not want to talk about their kiss, he did not want to discuss the Ashanti incident.

"All right. Oh, you are frowning at me now. Have another

slice of cake. Learn to appreciate these small joys, for they are as important as the evils you have encountered. Life is a matter of balance, Caden. When you have seen things as terrible as you obviously have, there must be something of extraordinary beauty to balance it out."

"And I will find it here?"

She nodded.

It could be argued she *was* that beauty.

"I hope you will."

He shrugged and cast her a wry smile. "The cake is delicious. Being with you is also nice. You are a calming influence on me. Perhaps it is enough for me to look at you and drink you into my soul."

She arched an eyebrow. "You are a veritable well of compliments today. I'm glad I can be of help."

"You are, Ella. More than you can ever imagine." There was something about the natural ease of this moment that did his soul good. The air was soft, the sun gently warming as it filtered into the room through the large windows. The ginger cake was delicious and the lemonade refreshing.

Most of all, he felt at peace with Ella.

She would never lie to him or use him.

She sighed as she set aside her plate, the ginger cake only half finished. "I often feel so useless in London, where my days are taken up doing nothing important."

"Some would say finding a proper husband is an important role for a young lady."

"I suppose. Have you ever read Shelley's poem, 'Love's Philosophy'?"

He shook his head. "No. This may shock you, but I am not a very romantic fellow. I do not have a poetic soul."

"You don't say? I never would have guessed." She emitted a trill of laughter as she reached into the basket and withdrew a book of poetry. "When you first arrived, I was going to read you 'Ozymandias,' because I thought you were so arrogant and impossibly full of yourself. I wanted to give you a light kick and remind you that no matter how exalted we believe we are, we all turn to dust in the end. Same dust, whether king or pauper. But I think now you are worthy of the other poem. It isn't long. I'll read it to you now. For me, it is a perfect description of Moonstone Landing, a place so beautiful that one simply has to find true love here."

"Ella, you can find love anywhere. You just have to keep your eyes open to see it when it comes upon you."

She shook her head. "No, I know it must be here."

"All right, be stubborn about it." But he found himself smiling anyway because she was so inexperienced and yet so certain of how love should be for her. "Go on, read it to me."

She cleared her throat and began. He closed his eyes and allowed the melodic lilt of her voice to wash over him like a healing balm. Finding her here had been such a relief for him—to see her innocent face, look upon her radiance, and know he still had a chance with her.

Hope still existed amid the greed and carnage.

That carnage.

So senseless.

So brutal.

And yet he had survived when no one else had…all for an act of kindness. *What goes around comes around.* This was an adage he had heard as a boy, and never appreciated it as much as he had that day of battle.

It wasn't much of a battle, more of a bloodbath, for he had been sent off in command of a few hundred men to subdue Ashanti warriors numbering in the thousands. More than ten thousand had been waiting for him and his men. As it turned out, an unnecessary fight, one instigated by the corrupt territorial governor, Fulke.

Caden would kill that man on sight if he ever saw him on a London street.

He hoped the Ashanti had gotten their hands on that spineless weasel and dispatched him with the same brutality as they had dispatched his men. Was it wrong to wish that suffering on any man? Well, if that thought prevented him from getting into heaven, so be it. Some men deserved a hideous death.

He shook out of his thoughts as Ella touched his arm. "Caden, where did you disappear to just now? Are you all right?"

He nodded. "Sorry. Go ahead, read me your poem again."

She began with the first lines, her voice as soft as that of an angel.

The fountains mingle with the rivers
And the rivers with the ocean...

It was a poem about the beauty of the earth. If only he could feel this way, but he only saw death and destruction whenever he closed his eyes. And when he opened them, he saw the faces of those greedy lords who thought their wealth mattered more than the lives of simple, honest men who were duped and believed they were fighting for an honorable cause, protecting king and country.

See the mountains kiss high heaven
And the waves clasp one another;

Ah, there were such places of wonder. He recalled the wild, rough seas along the coast of West Africa and the majesty of the distant mountains. One found beauty in its rawest form there. But here in Cornwall, it was a gentler beauty. He'd spent the morning looking out his window as he practiced walking and moving his stiff limbs. The sea was calm and glistening. The hospital was built on a small promontory, a rocky ledge overlooking the harbor. Perhaps he would have Ella show him around Moonstone Landing once he was back on his feet.

And the sunlight clasps the earth
And the moonbeams kiss the sea:

What is all this sweet work worth
If thou kiss not me?

Yes, he needed to give Ella another kiss.

She set the book on the side table and studied him. "Well, what do you think?"

That I am probably already in love with you. "It's a nice poem."

"I thought so, too. Moonstone Landing is the purest example of nature's beauty. The way sunlight falls upon the meadows and shimmers on the sea. The way the moon glistens upon the water every night. They say there are moonstones beneath the sea that glow on the night of a full moon when in the presence of true love."

He arched an eyebrow. "You hope someday they will glow for you?"

She nodded. "Yes, because I know I will find true love here and not in London. Men are different here. They do not put on airs. They sacrifice for others because it is the right thing to do."

"Elmer told me about the sea captain who once owned Moonstone Cottage, how he lost his life while rescuing the schoolchildren of this village."

"Yes, they were all saved because of him. This included many of Elmer's cousins, so Captain Arundel will never be forgotten for saving all those precious lives."

"He told me his cousins, Brenna, Cara, and Felicity Angel, went on to marry noblemen."

Ella laughed. "They did. Two dukes and an earl. Fairly impressive, I would say. But these were all love marriages. Who knows what might have happened had they not survived the shipwreck? It seems Captain Arundel's act of bravery has changed the course of history. The sons to follow will have that cheerful Angel exuberance and common sense. Who among the fancy noblemen in London would ever have risked their lives to do such a brave thing?"

"There are some good men, Ella."

"Truly? I have not met anyone in London I could say this about... Well, maybe you. But you were not ideal."

"I wasn't?" He mockingly clutched his heart. "You wound me."

"What, me, pierce that tough hide of yours? I sincerely doubt it. You are still impossibly arrogant. Remember that night we waltzed at Lady Marston's ball? The entire time, I felt as though you did not see the true me. You thought I was just another in a long line of silly debutantes, and chose to amuse yourself by giving me the thrill of waltzing with you. You were so condescending, I almost wanted to refuse you."

"But you didn't."

She laughed. "No, you were too handsome, and I was too curious to pass up the offer. But I was quickly disappointed you were not bothering to see me for who I was."

"You are wrong, Ella. I saw you quite clearly. However, I was too cynical to trust what was before my very eyes. I would not have claimed you for the supper dance had I not believed you were someone special. In truth, I was eager to get to know you better. But that was last year. Too much has happened between then and now. What about your current beaus? Are you serious about any of them?"

She pursed her lips again, something she did whenever giving a matter serious thought. He liked that slight pucker of her lips, so tempting to nibble. "No, but I do not want to toss them aside without giving them a chance. Perhaps my expectations are too high. I want someone who is brave but also modest about it. Someone who is confident but not boastful. Someone who will do the right thing simply because it is right and not for the expectation of reward. I know I am asking a lot of a man, and perhaps unfairly."

"I suppose that rules me out," he said, half in jest and half in hope she might consider him. It was a dangerous conversation to have with her, since he was nowhere near ready to commit to anyone.

But once he *was* ready, he would commit to her.

There was no one else for him.

"Do you think I could ever rule you out? London's handsomest, most eligible bachelor?" Her expression turned tender as she studied him. "Not at all. You grow more likeable with the knowing. You are arrogant and ill-tempered, but you have been surprisingly nice to me since we have started these afternoon visits. You always had valor, Caden."

"Ah, yes. Saving kittens from rooftops and breaking up fights."

"Does this not prove my point? That valor is in your blood. So, I am more forgiving of your other qualities. I do not mind your arrogance, since it is also blended with confidence and a know-it-all attitude. Perhaps you are smarter than all of us and will not bend simply because everyone else has a different opinion. In truth, that streak of defiance is also something I like in you. There is nothing wrong with standing up for yourself and your beliefs. Do I even have the right to judge you? After all, what have I ever done to recommend myself to anyone?"

He took another slice of ginger cake and bit into it, laughing as he swallowed. "So, you want to hate me but you cannot?"

She released a breath and smiled. "I never wanted to hate you. But you are quite overwhelming. I know I will get hurt if I ever allow myself to get too close to you."

"No, Ella. I would never hurt you."

"Perhaps not on purpose." She turned away to put the book of poetry back in her basket, but he reached out and stilled her hand.

"Leave it with me."

"All right. Perhaps you do have a poetic soul after all."

"No, I am still pretty much an arrogant arse. But you are quite taken by these poems, so I am curious to know what you see in them."

"Is it not obvious? For me, it is all about finding true love. It is about opening one's heart and allowing the beauty around you to flow in. I hope one day those moonstones will shine for me."

"They will, Ella."

"I don't know."

"Well, I do. You will find the love you seek." The comment appeared to sadden her. "You don't believe me? Did I not admit I am an arrogant know-it-all? So, trust me. You are a catch, and any man who has been in that meat market they call the Marriage Mart will know it. This is why you have no shortage of suitors."

"But my heart does not seem to be responding to any of them."

He cast her a wicked grin. "Because you really do not want a perfect gentleman."

She took a sip of her lemonade and then set down the glass. "But I do not want a rake, either."

"What you want, my sweet Ella, is a reformed rake. Someone a little dangerous, a little exciting, but also ready to be faithful to the right woman when he meets her."

Perhaps this was him—he did not know yet. Time would tell.

However, he did know that if anyone could bring out the best in him, it was Ella.

"We are holding a recital here tomorrow. Lady Dowling—"

"Ah, the villainess who tried to steal me from you."

Ella rolled her eyes. "Lady Dowling has a beautiful singing voice and also plays the pianoforte very well. She is a favorite among the soldiers. She'll be holding a recital here tomorrow at noon. Do you think you will be able to get out of bed and join the others?"

"Will you help me?"

She nodded. "I'll find a pushchair for you, since I don't know if you can walk to the assembly room on your own even if you use your crutches. It is a long walk to the other side of the hospital."

"I don't think I can yet. Today was my first day up and about. I could only make it a few wobbling steps from my bed without tiring or stumbling. When I was shot in the leg, the ball must have also shattered bone. It is still healing. I would do better if I could properly lean on my sticks," he said, nodding toward the crutches in the corner, "but my broken wrist interferes with my ability to hold the left one."

"Plus that crack to your skull must still have you off balance."

He nodded. "I suppose, but I only feel a little dizzy when first standing. It passes after a moment, thankfully."

"Oh, dear. Caden, you are a mess inside and out. Head. Ribs. Leg. Wrist. And who knows what else? Tomorrow will be better. I'll make sure to set aside one of those pushchairs for you. Elmer can help you dress. I assume you have some clothes with you. Otherwise, I will ask Uncle Cormac to lend you some of his and bring them over in the morning."

"Not necessary. I have clothes."

"If it is a beautiful day, we can sit outdoors instead of in the crowded assembly room. We'll hear the concert just as well from the garden because the windows will all be thrown open to allow in the sea breeze. It is so much more pleasant to sit outside and listen to the music while we look out over the water. Besides, I think you need a strong dose of sunlight to help knit your bones."

"Is this what the doctor ordered?"

She shook her head. "No, just me. There's nothing more soothing than the sun on your shoulders and a beautiful seascape to excite your soul. There is something quite fascinating about the movement of the water, the waves washing in and out of the cove, and the way the sun strikes the water so that it sparkles like diamonds."

"And one must not forget your moonstones."

"They only shine when there is true love. But the sunlight on the water… You will never find anything like it in London. Nor will you ever find weather as perfect as here. London gets hot and grimy. Here, the breeze is fresh and surrounds you with cool, salty air."

"Sounds delightful. Bring more of Mrs. Halsey's cakes and we'll make a picnic of it."

Ella's eyes brightened. "Caden, that is a lovely idea."

She spoke of the sun sparkling on the sea, but Caden could swear her eyes had captured much of that sunlight, for they were shimmering as she smiled at him.

Perhaps there *was* magic in this place. There certainly was magic in this girl. Who else had fairy eyes like hers? Or lips as soft as rosebuds?

He silently berated himself.

He needed to stop thinking of Ella, not only for her sake but for his. He had sent off an angry missive to his superiors, and they were not going to let him get away with his insubordination.

At most, he had two weeks with Ella before they dragged him out of here. Two precious weeks, and he dared not waste them.

And the sunlight clasps the earth
And the moonbeams kiss the sea:
What is all this sweet work worth
If thou kiss not me?

Ah, yes. Kissing Ella. This was very much on his mind now.

What would become of them over this little time they had together? How much of herself would she give to him?

Chapter Five

"ELLA, DON'T YOU think you are spending too much time with Lord Mersey?" her sister asked as they hopped down from Mr. Hawke's wagon. It had stopped in front of Mrs. Halsey's tea shop, as usual.

"No, Imogen."

"And is it wise to be calling him Caden?"

Ella shrugged. "Why not? I would always refer to him as Lord Mersey when in the company of others."

They had volunteered to pick up freshly baked cakes and pies for today's recital. Since the two of them had been enjoying Mrs. Halsey's wares every summer for over a decade, they were well acquainted with her shop and knew just which cakes and pies were the best.

Of course, they were all delicious, so their choice was not narrowed down much, if at all.

"Fionn gave me funds to order these treats for all the hospital patients. I am purchasing them for everyone, not just Caden Seaton." Ella glanced up at the sky. It was late morning, and the day could not have turned out more beautiful. The sky was the clearest blue it had been in a while, and the breeze was invigorating as it blew off the water and cooled the air.

"Your eyes turn starry at the mere mention of his name," Imogen remarked.

Ella frowned. "They do not. It is absurd to think so. Half the time, I don't even like him."

Imogen regarded her dubiously. "Well, it is the other half that has Uncle Cormac and Aunt Phoebe concerned."

Ella entered the tea shop, greeted Mrs. Halsey, and placed her large order before responding to her sister. "If everyone is so worried about my feelings for him, then why haven't they said anything to me?"

Imogen nibbled her lip. "They will. Probably tonight."

Ella arched an eyebrow. "What do you know that I do not? Tell me, Imogen. Am I to get a lecture on the perils of consorting with men like Lord Mersey? Believe me, I am well aware. But need I point out that Uncle Cormac was far worse than Lord Mersey? And look at him now. You won't find a better husband than he is to Phoebe. Or a better father to his boys."

"But it certainly took him long enough to reform his wicked ways."

"That's just it—Caden is not like Uncle Cormac in that regard."

Imogen arched an eyebrow.

Ella ignored her. "He was never as wickedly rakish. Yes, the ladies all flock to him. But he never ran around with a fast crowd, not that I am aware. If anything, he has spent his life mostly keeping to himself. Probably closed himself off too much. And he certainly did not consort with horrible ladies of the sort Uncle Cormac used to dally with. Goodness, they were awful."

Imogen giggled. "He won't like you reminding him of it."

"Well, he'll get that reminder if he thinks to lecture me." Ella took another moment to order Caden's favorite lemon cake before turning back to her sister. "And Uncle Cormac certainly did not hesitate to kiss Aunt Phoebe after he had met her. Inappropriate kisses, and at inappropriate times, but that never stopped him. So, he had better not think to lecture me about that, either."

Imogen's eyes widened. "Has Lord Mersey tried to kiss you?"

Ella pinched her lips, silently kicking herself for mentioning kisses. "Our lips might have grazed once. More of an accident than anything intentional. It just happened. I don't think he meant it to be a kiss."

Oh, dear. Oh, dear.

She had never lied to Imogen before and felt awful about it. Sick about it, actually.

"Then what was it if it wasn't a kiss?"

"I don't know." She avoided her sister's impudent grin and took a moment to retrieve a freshly baked lemon cake from Mrs. Halsey's display. After paying for it, she walked outside to wait while Mr. Halsey packed the rest of the cakes onto Mr. Hawke's wagon.

Imogen followed her out, still pressing her for information. "Come on, Ella. We never keep secrets from each other."

"There are no secrets to tell, Imogen. Caden Seaton's problem is that he is deeply tormented, just as Uncle Cormac was when he returned from the war and lost his arm. He struggled so hard with his loss of dignity. But I think Caden is struggling with his loss of humanity."

"Oh, that is serious."

Ella studied her sister's worried expression. "I know. This is why it is so important to give him some breathing room and allow him to adjust to life in England at his own pace."

"Uncle Cormac raged at the world. He was so angry when he lost his arm," Imogen said.

"Caden is much the same. He's just as angry. Sometimes, he explodes in frustration. Mostly, he is withdrawn and quiet about it. I don't know which is worse." Ella waved Mr. Hawke on and watched as he drove his rickety wagon to the hospital to deliver their supplies. That trusty wagon had been on its last legs for years now. But somehow, it kept going.

The hospital was not a long walk for Ella and Imogen. They often fell into the routine of coming into town with Mr. Hawke. Even though he was the Moonstone Cottage caretaker, he and his wife had always looked after Henley, Phoebe, and Chloe, the Killigrew sisters who had inherited the cottage from their Aunt Henleigh. Even though the three sisters were all grown up now, married and with children of their own, the Hawkes still considered it their duty to look after them. Since Phoebe had married their Uncle Cormac, the Hawkes now took it upon themselves to look after Ella and Imogen, as well.

They did not mind at all. They had fallen into a pleasant routine. Mr. Hawke would drop them off in front of Mrs. Halsey's shop, and then leave them to tend to their chores while he picked up supplies. If Ella and Imogen had a lot to do, then Mr. Hawke would simply return at the end of the day to pick them up in front of the tea shop.

Mostly, she and Imogen volunteered at the hospital, since these soldiers seemed to do better with a woman's touch. All they did was read to the injured men, or merely sit by their bedside and talk to them. They did none of the dirtier work, such as cleaning bedpans or changing their bandages, since Fionn would not allow it.

But he did appreciate their offering conversation to many of these soldiers, who felt alone and unsure of what they would encounter upon returning to their homes.

This routine also gave Ella and Imogen a little freedom to explore on their own. Not that they were all that adventurous or ever really unsupervised, for the villagers always kept their eyes on them, and someone always knew where they were.

They never strayed far. If they were not helping out at the hospital, they were usually walking along the docks to watch the fishing vessels sail in and out. Sometimes an enormous navy frigate would sail in, the fighting ship dwarfing the other vessels in the harbor as it silently cut through the water, its white sails catching the wind.

But most days, there was little excitement, so she and Imogen would browse the fish market and stop at the local shops. They usually ended their day with tea and cakes at Mrs. Halsey's tea shop, where Mr. Hawke would pick them up.

Despite this quieter country life, they never seemed to run out of topics to discuss.

"I am going to have Caden sit outdoors with me while the recital is going on," Ella said. "We'll be in full view of everyone, so nothing untoward is going to happen. He is in desperate need of sunshine on his face and happy moments to fill his soul."

"Shall I join you?"

"I would rather you didn't. Do you mind terribly? He will never confide in me while in the presence of others." They had reached the docks, and now turned right to walk past the fishmongers and up a slight hill toward the ancient Fort Arundel and the army hospital just beyond it.

"Has Fionn asked you to pry information out of him?" Imogen asked.

"Not specifically. Caden's superior officers are trying to find out what happened to him and his men, but they are having trouble getting a report out of him. He won't talk about it to anyone. Fionn mentioned it would be helpful if I could get him to open up. But I am not going to betray a confidence."

Imogen nodded. "He needs to trust you."

"Yes, I think that is most important of all. He has to trust someone, and I hope it will be me. He remembered me from my debut Season last year. It seems he found me tolerable."

Imogen's dark curls bobbed as she shook her head and laughed. "That is quite some recommendation."

Ella laughed too. "He thought less of the other debutantes, so I suppose I ought to be flattered. But he seems to want my company, so this has to mean something. Not love or courtship or anything that significant. Perhaps a friend to trust. This is a major step in itself, that he feels comfortable around me. I am never going to betray him. If Caden doesn't want me to repeat what he tells me, then I won't."

"I think trust is just as important as love, don't you think, Ella?"

"I do. But don't get any fancy ideas about us, Imogen. He has a long way to go before he recovers. From what I gather, he is the only survivor of a battle that wiped out his entire regiment."

Imogen stopped to stare at her. "Oh, that is awful."

Ella nodded. "He is keeping the pain of it bottled up inside, and that worries me. He needs to release his anguish before he erupts like a volcano. I would hate to be standing next to him when he explodes."

"Oh, dear. Are you sure you can handle him?"

Ella emitted another laugh, this time mirthless. "No, I am not trained for this. I only hope lending a sympathetic ear is enough. I would offer a shoulder to cry on, but he is too proud ever to cry in front of me. That's why I hope Uncle Cormac comes to visit him soon. Caden hasn't wanted to see him yet, but I think the time has come. Ready or not, he has to talk to Uncle Cormac."

They marched past the ancient stone fortress that served as the garrison for the army soldiers and continued up the small hill to the hospital. It was a few years old, but still the newest building in Moonstone Landing.

In the distance, Ella noticed another Royal Navy frigate sailing into the harbor. "More wounded to unload. The hospital is already at capacity."

Imogen followed her gaze to the white-sailed speck now visible on the horizon. "Vicar Trask will take the overflow into St. Peter's Church. He's done it before. Oh, let's hurry along. I see Lady Dowling's carriage. Let's see what mischief she is up to now."

Ella stifled a pang of jealousy. She knew full well where they would find Lady Dowling, and it was not at the pianoforte rehearsing for her recital.

Imogen, whose senses were uncanny, picked up on Ella's turmoil right away. She took her hand. "Come on. The orderlies have already unloaded most of the cakes off Mr. Hawke's cart. You and I don't need to stand here watching them. We have a stray cat to declaw."

Ella wanted to laugh heartily, but shook her head instead. "Really, Imogen. It is none of my business what goes on between—"

"That is utter nonsense. First of all, she is too old for him. Does the woman have no shame? Preying on a younger man."

"He cannot be more than a couple of years younger. Hardly scandalous. Caden can defend himself, assuming he wants to."

"Ella! Of course he wants nothing to do with her. There is no question he prefers you to her. Why are you suddenly meek as a mouse? You cannot let that woman take him from you. And have you noticed how often you slipped when talking to me and referred to him as Caden instead of Lord Mersey? You had better be careful not to slip like that when speaking to others."

"I know. But you're my sister, so it is different. As for my being a mouse about his other women... Imogen, it isn't that simple."

"Yes, it is completely simple. First of all, he has no other women. He likes you. You like him. Don't you dare turn coy on me. You've told me yourself he finds Lady Dowling irritating, and he does not trust her."

"Well, sometimes things change."

Imogen rolled her eyes. "Now you are just being ridiculous. I am going to kick you in the backside if you dare spout another stupid remark like that. Come on."

Ella allowed her sister to drag her inside.

Some siblings grew up quarreling, but Ella had never had a cross word with Imogen. They were as close as two people could be. She did not even get annoyed when Imogen shoved her unannounced into Caden's private hospital room.

She stumbled in with a gasp.

Caden and Lady Dowling turned toward her.

As expected, Lady Dowling had her fawning hands all over him.

"I assure you, Lady Dowling. I can manage this myself," Caden was saying to her, but he broke off and tossed Ella a smile as she and Imogen entered his room. "You're here. Thank goodness. And is this your sister?"

Imogen stepped forward. "Yes, I'm Imogen. I've heard so much about you…since Ella cannot stop talking about you."

Ella groaned.

He chuckled. "A pleasure to meet you, Lady Imogen."

"I see you are already being attended to," Ella said, trying not to sound irked, since he had given her no cause. In truth, she had never seen a man more relieved to see her, which ought to have given her great satisfaction.

Lady Dowling still had her hands on his chest, supposedly smoothing out his nightshirt. But that shirt looked just fine to Ella, not a crease or wrinkle on it, as it was stretched tight along his broad shoulders and chest.

"Thank you, Lady Dowling. That will be quite enough," Caden said, dismissing her.

She gave a soft purr as she stroked his arm and then gave Ella a feline smirk as she glided out of Caden's room.

Ella simply stared at him, suddenly feeling inadequate and hating how this woman had managed to rattle her so easily. She knew Caden was not interested in Lady Dowling, but would the beautiful widow eventually wear him down?

"Pay no attention to my grumpy sister," Imogen said with annoying cheer. "What can we help you with before the recital begins? Lady Dowling is quite talented. She plays beautifully and has a lovely singing voice. But she's still a hateful she-cat, and—"

"Imogen!" Ella was appalled by her sister's remark.

Caden thought it humorous. "She is indeed. Quite predatory, and not one to take subtle hints. I am in need of a pushchair. Unfortunately, my leg isn't healing as rapidly as I would like. It still pains me when I put any weight on it for more than a few minutes."

"Oh, I am so sorry."

"Not your fault," he said with a shrug. "I tried to walk on it earlier today and probably aggravated it. I'll also need Elmer to help me put on some decent clothes."

"I'll go in search of him right now." Imogen bobbed a curtsy and ran off, leaving Ella alone with him.

His hawk gaze bored into her. "Ella, are you still irritated about Lady Dowling? You know she does this purely to rattle you. She means nothing to me."

She sighed and approached his bedside. "I know. I shouldn't respond to her the way I do. It is just that she is so devious and manipulative."

"Which is why I will never involve myself with her." He sat up with a struggle, careful to keep the sheet wrapped around his waist as he shifted his legs off the bed.

"What are you doing?"

"I cannot lie flat another moment. My back is sore. Does the sight of my bare legs shock you?"

She laughed lightly. "No, since you are mostly covered up. But they are quite hairy. You have big feet." She scanned upward. "And a cowlick poking out of your hair."

His smile was surprisingly warm and appealing. "I can see you are dazzled by my splendor."

"You *are* splendid, if you wish to know the truth. I like this gentler, imperfect you much better than the Greek god standing on a pedestal for all the world to admire. You are approachable and engaging like this. It is very hard to talk to you when you are standing on that Olympian pedestal."

"I was never a Greek god, and as for that pedestal… I think it has completely shattered," he said quietly. "Give me a few minutes to make myself presentable."

Elmer bounded in at that moment, his smile typically cheerful. "Lady Imogen said you needed assistance, m'lord."

"I do, Elmer. You are just in time."

Ella excused herself and closed the door on her way out to lend them privacy. She stood outside his room, preferring not to get involved with other chores. Her wait turned out to be closer to fifteen or twenty minutes. Imogen had returned with the pushchair in the meantime, so they waited together by the door and passed the time chatting.

The other patients were now being escorted to the assembly room by the hospital orderlies and soldiers from the fort who had also been invited to the recital. There was nothing for Imogen and her to do but wait for Caden to finish readying himself. "We are only going to sit outside," Ella muttered. "One would think he was dressing for a formal ball."

Imogen poked her. "He likes you and wants to look good for you."

Ella sighed. "He does not need to go to the trouble. I already think he is the handsomest man in England, and I like him more than is wise."

"I knew it!" Imogen took her hand. "Just be careful, Ella. I can see he likes you, too. But he is still quite haunted."

"I know. This is why I need to tread carefully around him. There is so much anger that still needs to flow out of him."

Imogen frowned. "What if he loses control and hits you?"

"No, he never will. He has too strong a sense of honor. But I would not be surprised if he exploded one day and began tossing furniture about like a wild ape. Nor would I want to be one of his superior officers trying to give him orders. Even with broken limbs, he can still pick them up and hurl them through the window. Good thing his room is on the ground level. They'd only fall into the bushes."

"Your wild ape is ready," Caden said with a chuckle, obviously having opened the door and overheard their conversation.

Ella blushed as she stared at him. "You heard?"

He nodded. "Your description is probably accurate, especially that part about my never hurting you. I'm glad you know it, Ella."

"I do."

He had washed his hair and shaved his overnight growth of beard. Those dark eyes of his were sharp and assessing. He had donned breeches and a fresh shirt, and wore hospital-issued slippers on his feet.

Ella had to look up at him to meet his gaze, for the top of her head barely reached his shoulders.

She had forgotten quite how splendidly big he was. Or how magnificent he looked when all cleaned up. No wonder Lady Dowling could not keep her hands off him.

"Ah, Imogen, I see you've found me a pushchair." He had used his walking sticks to cross his room and seemed to be quickly tiring from the mere effort of standing.

"Yes, do sit before you fall." Imogen steered the chair behind him, and he settled heavily into it with a grunt.

Elmer took his sticks and placed them back in their corner, then excused himself and dashed off to help the other workers settle the remaining patients.

Ella wheeled Caden outside while Imogen carried her basket that contained their picnic supplies. The hospital was built in a U-shape to give most rooms a view of the sea, and the ladies auxiliary had planted a garden in the courtyard that was at the center of the U.

Caden looked around, studying the dazzling array of plants and flowers with obvious interest. "I did not think the army cared for pretty things," he muttered.

"They don't," Ella replied. "This garden was the idea of Aunt Phoebe and her sisters. Mostly Chloe, Fionn's wife. It is designed not only for natural beauty, but for scents, as well. Inhale, Caden. What fragrances do you smell?"

He closed his eyes and inhaled as deeply as he dared. "Lavender. Roses, I think. Mint? Strawberries?"

"Yes, you have a good nose. We also have a small herb garden where we grow not only mint but sage and other herbs and spices."

Caden looked up at her. "It is a good idea. Who tends to the garden?"

"The ladies auxiliary," Imogen said. "We take turns making certain to weed and water the flowerbeds. Ella's turn is next week. Mine is the week after that. It doesn't take long, just an hour out of our day. We've also planted a few trees, mostly for shade, but they are also fruit bearing. Just watch out for falling apples," she said with a laugh as Ella wheeled him into the shade of an apple tree. "Well, I'll be off to help with the other soldiers. I'll return when the recital is over."

Ella was now left alone with Caden. "How do you feel? I hope the ride wasn't too strenuous on your ribs."

"I'll survive it." He leaned forward in his pushchair, his body almost too big for it. Indeed, he was built like a warrior and had the muscles to prove it. Sitting beside him was quite a heady experience, Ella was dismayed to discover.

Even wounded, this man was magnificent.

She sat on a stone bench beside him, both of them shaded by the large, leafy tree branches. "Take in the view, Caden. The tide is coming in. Can you hear the crash of waves as they strike the rocks below us?"

He closed his eyes and listened. "It must be quite something on stormy nights."

"We're up too high for there ever to be a risk of the hospital flooding. However, the incoming tide on one of those stormy days is something to watch. The waves are powerful and unforgiving. It is amazing how a gentle sea can turn into something so wrathful and filled with vengeance in a matter of minutes."

"That is life, Ella. Wrathful and unforgiving," he said with unreserved bitterness.

"At times," she said with a nod. "But there is also beauty. It is in little moments like these. They are important, too."

He grinned and took a slice of lemon cake off the plate she had set out. "I suppose life can also be delicious."

She sensed he was saying this merely to be agreeable, for his eyes still had that dark, haunted look to them, a sign he was not letting go of the nightmare events that held him in a silent grip. Well, she was not going to cure his anguished rage with one picnic. "Don't think too hard, Caden. Just enjoy the sun on your shoulders and the light breeze ruffling your hair. A warm lemon cake. Cool cider. Beautiful music."

He raised his glass to her. "And good company."

She liked watching him eat, for he had a healthy appetite and seemed able to scarf down those slices in the blink of an eye. As she finished her own slice of cake, the wind picked up slightly and drew a few of her curls out of place. She set aside her plate and hurriedly brushed the loose curls back.

Caden assisted her, his touch light as he tucked a curl behind her ear.

He then ran his knuckles along her cheek. "So soft. You always were a soft thing, Ella."

"Is this not a nice moment, Caden?"

"It is, my pretty dove. You needn't point it out to me."

"I'm sorry."

"Don't be. I am thinking of the poem you read to me. How can there not be love when we are surrounded by such beauty? You, first and foremost. But I also see how the sun shines like silver upon the water. Have you noticed the dolphins leaping in and out of the waves?"

She stood and scanned the water, hopping up and pointing when several suddenly leaped into the air and dove back under with a soft splash. "Yes! There they are. The birds will come out soon to forage for food. They hover over the water looking for fish swimming close to the surface."

He cast her a soft smile.

"Wait here," she said, and hurried over to the strawberry beds to pick a few for him. "Try them, Caden. What do you think? Delicious, aren't they?"

That darkness in his eyes faded a bit. "Yes. Spectacular."

"Oh, and look! We have rabbits, too." Several hopped past them.

"I can see why you love it here." Caden eased back in his pushchair and stretched his legs in front of him. His shoulders spilled over the back of the chair because he really was too big for it. But he did not seem to mind. He closed his eyes and listened as Lady Dowling now played a country reel.

The tune was playful and melodic.

Ella began to sway to the lively lilt of the song.

She did not miss much about London, but she could not deny her enjoyment of dancing. They did not hold many dances here, but there was one coming up at the Kestrel Inn soon, a little over a week from now. It was Moonstone Landing's version of an assembly ball.

But far more rustic. Few women had silks to wear or fancy jewels. Still, the ladies dressed up in their finest muslins and the men in their Sunday best. It was lots of fun.

Caden's eyes were now open and trained on her. "I remember dancing with you, Ella. That supper waltz we shared."

She tingled, remembering it very well. "You were quite magnificent," she said, her voice light and teasing.

"So were you. I think it was the last time I felt…unencumbered. Happy." His expression was now serious, those dark eyes of his burning into her soul, and his voice deep and resonant as he said, "I want to dance with you again."

Oh, dear heaven.

She wanted this too.

"Promise me a dance before I leave here, Ella."

His voice was filled with such an aching need that she knew she could never deny him. "Of course, but will you be well enough to manage it?"

"Yes—just name the time and place, and I'll be there."

Midnight.

On the beach.

Me in his arms under a full, silver moon.

Moonstones shining beneath the waves.

She could not reveal that dream to him.

Instead, she cleared her throat. "Well, there is an assembly ball to be held soon at the Kestrel Inn. I was just thinking of it, by coincidence. You'll have some work to do to get yourself in shape by then. There's still time, but you mustn't overdo it."

"I won't." But his expression was determined, and Caden never was the sort to do anything cautiously.

"I'll help you with whatever exercises the doctor prescribes."

"No, Ella. Not you."

His refusal surprised her. "Why not me? I would never criticize you or think less of you. Why am I not permitted to help you?"

A muscle twitched in his jaw.

"Caden?" She frowned lightly when he did not immediately respond. "You are not thinking of asking Lady Dowling, are you?"

He looked at her, stunned. Then he threw his head back and laughed. "I am not that much of a glutton for punishment."

"But she is beautiful."

"So are you," he said with a soft growl. "You far outshine her."

"Now I am utterly confused. If you do not find me repulsive, then why may I not help you?"

Chapter Six

"Must I give you a reason for everything I do? And don't you dare mention Lady Dowling again. Have I not made it clear enough to you that she isn't offering me a blessed thing I desire?"

What Caden wanted with an ache that grew more unbearable by the hour was Ella.

He needed to hold her in his arms. He needed to do all sorts of wickedly delicious things to her, because he was going to explode if he behaved like a gentleman around her a moment longer.

Who had rosebud lips like hers? Or eyes the luminescent green of a fairy pool? Or hair the color of spun gold?

She inhaled, drawing his gaze to her perfectly rounded breasts that were created just for his pleasure, meant to be cupped in his hands, kneaded and stroked.

Tasted.

Oh, bollocks.

His mouth had gone dry at the mere thought. Well, it was better than drooling over her like a pathetic hound.

He was done for.

All he wanted to do was carry this girl off to a secluded glen and have his way with her. Have her in every way possible, because his desire for her was insatiable. Of course, he was not going to say or do anything, since he could not even get out of this pushchair on his own yet. That was enough of a blow to his pride.

"You must have found something lacking in me, or else you would let me help you."

"There is nothing lacking in you, Ella." He was not going to allow her to watch him at his exercises, see him weak and stumbling.

No, he could not bear to have her watch him.

"Elmer is going to help me," he muttered, wanting to be clear that no other woman was replacing her. "Just Elmer and no one else. Not you. Not Lady Dowling. Not anyone else in all of Moonstone Landing. All right?"

"All right. Elmer is a sweet boy," Ella said with a nod of approval. "You mustn't bully him."

"I am *not* going to bully him."

She cast him an enchanting smile. "You bully everyone."

"I do not. Wanting things done my way is not at all the same thing." He tossed back an appealing grin.

"If you say so. But I know how eager you are to regain your strength. If Elmer suggests you stop, then listen to him."

He nodded. "Yes, I will listen. You have my word of honor."

That seemed to please her inordinately, and she smiled at him. "Thank you, Caden."

He sucked in a breath.

This girl was so beautiful, especially when she smiled.

THE RECITAL LASTED an hour, but the time passed too quickly for Caden's liking.

He had not yet tired of watching sunlight play upon Ella's face, nor had he finished staring into her fairy-pool eyes. She had been declared a diamond last year during her debut Season, but she was even more beautiful now.

He wanted to tell her so, but Ella was surprisingly modest and responded to flattery with shyness.

Anyway, he was already too obvious about his feelings for her. It was particularly dangerous, since he was not ready to make her any promises. However, there were times like these, when she had a faraway look in her eyes and resembled a delicate bird, that he wanted to toss caution to the wind and tell her how much he loved her before she flitted away and was lost to him forever.

Oh, Lord.

Love?

He dared not act on those feelings yet.

Perhaps after his "I am a *bloody* hero" tour, assuming he hadn't offended every general and government official from prime minister to rat catcher by the time the farce of a show ended.

Don't fall in love with me yet, Ella.

Falling in love with him was still too dangerous for her. What if he could not heal his soul and wound up hurting her? Yet he was encouraging her, wasn't he? Telling her that he wanted to dance with her again.

What was he thinking?

Well, he'd said it and was not going to take it back. Why should they not share a harmless dance? He would make certain she understood it meant nothing more than a simple twirl around a room.

Others were now walking out onto the courtyard.

Imogen and Elmer came over to take him back inside. "Not yet," he said, liking the breeze around him and the sight of Ella beside him.

But the pair had no sooner gone off to assist other soldiers than Caden noticed Major Brennan striding toward him. The fort's commander was a big man with a full head of dark hair and gray eyes that were as sharp as razor blades. Caden was often accused of being hard, but this man also had a look as hard as steel.

"Good afternoon, Fionn," Ella said, casting him a sincere smile.

The major did not smile back, although his tone was gentle when he replied, "Ella, I would like a moment to chat with Lord Mersey."

"Oh, all right." She rose and quietly excused herself.

Major Brennan took the spot on the bench that Ella had just vacated. Both of them watched her go back inside.

Only once she was out of sight did Caden address the man. "If you are here to lecture me about Lady Ella, you can save your breath."

The major arched an eyebrow. "I am not worried about Ella. She has a sensible head on her shoulders. Besides, you will not walk out of here alive if you hurt her."

Caden frowned. "I am not so far gone that you need to toss threats at me. Do you think I would ever purposely hurt that angel? She was the best thing in London. I haven't stopped thinking of her since I met her last year. But that is where it ends. I am in no fit condition to court anyone. And I have these damn generals ready to take me around the country and tout me as a hero. I am no one's hero."

Major Brennan returned Caden's frown with one of his own. "Are you suggesting you were a coward?"

"No. I fought alongside my men. But all I did was survive because the enemy chose not to kill me."

"Why is that, do you think?"

"The reason for my survival? Who is asking? You or those damn generals?"

He cast Caden a wry smile. "Those damn generals. They are now hounding me to convince you to go along with their plan. I don't care what they think. But I do care about Ella and how her heart could be broken."

"I know. I am doing my best to be careful around her. Just don't take her away from me yet."

Caden was surprised he had just said that. But it was true. He had no hope of healing if he was denied Ella. He did not need to kiss her, and he did not need to dance with her.

He just needed to be with her.

The request took Major Brennan by surprise. "Are you in love with her?"

Caden groaned. "I don't know. It is safer for her if I am not. My grandfather will not be pleased if I marry her. Not that I care what he thinks. He is damn well not going to choose my bride. But he can be vicious when things do not go as he planned. I will not subject her to that old demon."

"I think you have a lot to work through, Lord Mersey. About Ella and your year in West Africa. I hope you will see your way to talking to me or one of my brothers-in-law, the Marquess of Burness or the Duke of Malvern, over the next few days."

"Ella filled me in on her family tree when I first arrived here. I am well aware of her connections."

"Good, then let us know whenever you are ready to talk to us." Fionn was not much older than Caden but certainly carried himself with authority. An authority coupled with confidence and probably a hard-earned wisdom. "You claim you are not a hero, Lord Mersey."

"I'm not."

"But enemy soldiers do not simply let their captives go free after a battle such as yours. However, they will honor a warrior they believe has shown outstanding valor. This is what they must have thought of you. It is obvious to me, so do not bother to deny it. Do you know why they felt this way about you?"

Caden nodded.

"Care to share the reason?"

"No."

"Very well. However, those generals and perhaps even your grandfather will be here within the next two weeks, and they will want answers. This inevitable confrontation is going to be a bloody mess unless you give thought to what you are going to tell them. Be smart about it, Lord Mersey. You can turn this situation to your advantage. You just have to get out of your own stubborn way and work out a sensible plan."

"Duly noted," Caden said, silently hoping for the conversation to end.

But Major Brennan was not yet done with him. "I grew up on the London streets, abandoned—or so I thought—and dumped in an orphanage at birth. I had to run away when I was a mere child or else I would have died being put to work as a chimney sweep's monkey. So I made the choice to risk living on the streets. Life out there is not easy for a child."

"How did you work your way up to where you are now?" Caden asked.

"The very man who plucked me off the streets and gave me an education turned out to be the one who had been betraying me all along. But my point is, I could have wallowed in my rage and spent my life resentful. I could have given up everything good to punish the family who cheated me out of my birthright. I also could have resigned my commission and never worked another day in my life once the House of Lords recognized my claim to the title and the entailed properties that came with it. But I am no gentleman, and I knew I could contribute so much more to those who needed my help if I stayed on and saw this hospital built. I did allow myself one reward, and that was to marry the woman I had always loved. The only woman I will ever love, Lady Chloe Killigrew."

"It isn't quite the same," Caden said. "I appreciate how hard a time you had as a child."

"No, you will never understand what it was like. The nightly terrors. The starvation. The constant desperation. The friends who died and those who were caught and tossed into prison just for trying to take enough scraps of food to live. Nor will I be able to fully appreciate what you went through. All I am saying is, turn that rage toward something productive. The men who died fighting alongside you need you to make something worthwhile of their sacrifice. Decide on whatever it is you think will help most, but do it. Mouthing off might give you a momentary satisfaction, but what then? You will lose the opportunity to do something significant for those who need your leadership and voice most."

Bollocks.

Caden hated to agree with the man. Was his suggestion not better than behaving like a wild ape and tossing furniture in frustration?

"All right. Message received, Major Brennan."

Fionn rose. "My door is always open to you should you wish to talk."

"Thank you." Caden meant it sincerely.

"The Marquess of Burness will likely stop in to see you in the next day or two."

"Because of Ella?"

"Partly, but this is mostly about you."

He watched the major stride off to engage with the wounded men brought to his hospital. The man was a natural leader.

So was he, Caden realized.

Was this not a major part of his agony? His men had trusted him. They had followed him without complaint into a looming massacre. Even as they were dying all around him, not one of them ever questioned his wisdom or the cause for which they were about to lose their lives.

But he had failed them.

What could he have done differently?

Refused to follow orders? Yes, he could have done that and been court-martialed. Another officer would have taken his place. His men would still have been sent off to die. And he would have lived on in disgrace.

That was never a choice for him. He was never going to abandon his men. He'd fought fiercely by their side, fought and fully expected to die alongside them.

Perhaps Major Brennan was right. Was it not better to be

home and hailed as a hero? There was a lot of good he could do while the country worshiped and adored him. He still wanted to shoot Governor Fulke, that treasonous weasel. He *would* shoot him, too, if the man ever returned to England. Some betrayals required avenging.

But first, he had to attend to the good he could do while everyone regarded him as a hero.

Ella came back a short time later and resumed her seat on the stone bench beside him. She looked at him, staring quite openly and intently. "What, Ella?"

"Something has changed in you."

"Really? In twenty minutes?" Perhaps she was right, for Fionn's words had penetrated his thick, slightly dented skull.

She nodded. "Your eyes look lighter."

"A reflection of the sun, no doubt."

"No, Caden." She reached out and put her hand over his, but quickly drew it away before anyone noticed and gossip started. "What did Fionn say to you? He's very smart, you know."

Caden laughed. "Yes, it is obvious. He told me to stop behaving like a petulant arse and do something useful."

Ella grinned. "I'm sure he dispensed his advice with more tact than that. But I'm glad he got through to you."

"Yes, he did."

She wrapped her arms around her knees as she regarded him with her smiling countenance. "I am glad you have moved on from that sulking little boy. Is there anything I can do to help?"

Sulking boy?

Here he thought he was being deep and appealingly brooding, and she thought he was merely behaving like a spoiled child.

But she still liked him enough to kiss him. A first kiss, no less.

She must have seen some redeeming qualities in him.

Caden eased back in his chair once more and shook his head. "You are helping just by being yourself, Ella. But I may have to put a little distance between us, just for a while. Things are going to get heated between those generals and me. Not to mention my grandfather and me. I don't want you to get caught in the crossfire."

"I see."

"No, I don't think you do. I know I come across as severe and probably quite daunting. Certainly sarcastic, cold, and aloof. But I do let people in sometimes."

"Those few you trust," she said, still casually hugging her knees. This had to be a sign she felt comfortable and could be herself when with him.

"You are one of those few, Ella. But do not make too much of it. I trust you, but I also need to protect you from what is to come." He leaned forward and took her hands into his own. Her eyes widened, and she tried to slip her hands out of his, but he would not let her go. "Never mind the gossip. Everyone knows there is a spark between us. Whether I am holding your hands or not won't make any difference."

She sighed. "I suppose."

He cast her a soft smile, for she looked delicious with her brow knitted and her lips pursed as she fretted. "Ella, I wanted to kiss you and I wanted to dance with you. But I think perhaps I ought to put off those plans."

"Put them off?"

"Yes." He did not see a choice, given what he needed to accomplish.

This was his battle, and he was going to take on some powerful men. They had already proven how ruthless they could be. What would stop them from going after Ella if they knew he liked her? Would they be so low as to destroy her reputation in order to harm him? She was too sweet and gentle to survive the onslaught.

"I am sorry, too, Caden." Tears filled her eyes, but she struggled to hold them back. "As you say, it is for the best. Anyway, I have more suitors than I can handle at the moment."

He raked a hand through his hair. This was not going exactly as planned. He did not want to let her go completely, just have her remain quietly in the background for now. He did not want to lose her.

"Ella, I want you to know…there is no one else for me. It isn't about any other woman."

"But it will be. Maybe not right away, but soon enough." She swallowed hard and then released a ragged breath. "You will find someone whose father is high up in government and who will groom you to be a future prime minister of England."

"Heaven forbid." He shook his head with determination. "I could never keep my mouth shut long enough to gain supporters. I would offend everyone with my opinions within minutes of meeting them. No, I am no politician. But there are wrongs that need repairing, and for this I will need the support of Parliament and the ear of the royal family."

"Then talk to my uncle, the Marquess of Burness. Also talk to his best friend, the Duke of Malvern. I've told you they both reside here in Moonstone Landing. But they have powerful connections in London and are much admired by the public. Let them help you. You do not have to take on the world all by yourself."

"And risk bringing them down along with me if things go wrong? No, Ella. I would not do that to your family."

"Do not underestimate them. They are fighters. In truth, they are always up for a good fight."

Caden chuckled. "Well, I will seek their guidance. But nothing beyond it. Once I have set my path, it is my own to take."

"And what about me, Caden? Will I have any role in your life?"

"I don't know yet, Ella. This is as honest as I can be. But dear heaven, I cannot get you out of my soul. It is as though you have lodged yourself inside of me, and I crave you as desperately as I crave the air to breathe. However, I am a mess in body and soul, as you have pointed out more than a time or two. I do not know what additional chaos tomorrow will bring. Am I the one who will make those moonstones shine for you?"

"Do you think you might be?"

"I don't know. How can I know anything when my heart is shattered and in constant turmoil?" He sighed, shook his head, and then continued. "And yet I want to be."

Her eyes widened in surprise. "You do?"

"Yes, Ella."

She cast him an impish smile and her eyes glittered with mirth. "Oh, Caden. Dare I believe what I am hearing? I had no idea you even liked me."

He frowned. "How could you not know? I kissed you."

"So? Is this not what handsome rakes do? Kiss any girl who strikes their fancy? I was not your first."

"But I was *your* first. Being the only man to ever kiss you meant something to me." Was he more infatuated with her than she was with him? He did not like this possibility at all.

"And it meant *everything* to me," she said with sincere conviction. "Just think about letting me help you, at least with your exercises. Please, Caden. If you care for me, then don't shut me out."

Imogen and Elmer returned to their side before he could answer.

Ella took their arrival as her opportunity to leave him. He watched her walk away, her head bowed because he had given her too much to think about. No doubt, he had confused her by drawing her close, then pushing her away. Wanting her, and in the next breath warning her not to come near him.

He wasn't trying to chase her away. Hell, he did not know what he *was* trying to do.

But he could not risk having her fall in love with him, and then having his grandfather destroy her. For this reason, he was not about to make her any lifelong promises. He just wanted to insert a word of caution.

How else was he to protect her from a tough-as-nails duke and equally tough generals? Not to mention the nasty lords who were making a fortune during the Ashanti wars.

He did not care if they destroyed him. But he was not going let them harm Ella.

He caught a glimpse of her in the music room talking to several injured soldiers as Imogen and Elmer wheeled him back to his room a few minutes later.

"You like Ella, don't you?" Imogen asked as they reached his hospital room.

"Yes, I do."

"She says you are a complicated man."

He turned to glance up at Imogen, who was staring back at him with eyes that were almost the size of her face. She was younger than Ella by a couple of years and still had much of the child in her with her round face and innocent features. "I *am* complicated," he said. "But this is how life is, and one must always think things through carefully to avoid making mistakes."

"Ella is also a thinker. I think you both think too much."

He laughed. "Maybe."

"You ought to stop worrying about all the reasons things could go wrong. You will make them go wrong if you do that."

"And if I don't worry about those things?"

"I am not suggesting you ignore obvious problems. But if you shut Ella out, you will lose her. Is this really what you want to have happen?"

Chapter Seven

"LOOK AT THAT, m'lord," Elmer said with his boundless well of good cheer. "You did it!"

"Another milestone to record, Elmer," Caden replied with an exhausted laugh, tumbling onto his bed with satisfaction.

As the days wore on, Caden had found himself regaining more and more of his strength. Ten days had now passed since Lady Dowling's recital and Major Brennan's words of wisdom—words he had truly taken to heart.

He now spent his mornings exercising his leg, something that became easier as his ribs healed. He no longer felt a painful pang every time he drew a breath. The gash to his head had continued to heal, leaving behind no lingering dizziness. The spot where his head had been bashed was still tender when he touched it, so he did not touch it.

His wrist was still tender, but less so every day. His eyes still strained easily, but he was able to read more pages before the blurriness came on.

"I think you've done enough for today, m'lord. Lady Ella will be along soon, and you'll want to wash up before she does. Can't have you smelling like a cow, can we?" Elmer asked.

"Indeed, not. But I do wish you would scrounge me a bar of sandalwood soap instead of that infernal lavender. I am so sick of smelling like a damn flower."

The boy grinned at him.

Caden laughed again. "What?"

"A shipment of Farthingale soaps just came in at Mr. Bedwell's mercantile. I got you one." Elmer ran out and returned no more than a minute later with something wrapped in brown paper and tied with a green ribbon. "Here you go, my lord. Sandalwood."

Caden was now sitting up as Elmer handed him the small package and ruffled the boy's hair. "Lad, you are a genius. Did you have Mr. Bedwell put it on my account?"

"Yes."

"Good. Help me wash up and dress. I am putting on my uniform today. I think it is time I took a walk outside the hospital. Dr. Hewitt, Dr. Spencer, and Major Brennan have given their approval. I am officially released for the day."

The boy's eyes rounded in dismay. "But what about Lady Ella?"

Did the lad think Caden would ever forget about her? "I hope she will spend the day with me. I would like her to show me around Moonstone Landing."

"Oh, that is an excellent idea," Elmer said, his eyes once more bright.

Apparently, Caden was not the only one who believed he and Ella were meant to be together. The lad was fond of her, and it was quite humorous at times to watch the boy chase the other ladies away. Elmer had taken up the role of vigilant watchdog whenever Ella was not around.

Caden did not mind.

Ella had continued to visit him every afternoon, and Caden did not change that routine. He could not. She was his reward for working hard each day.

One thing that did change was his effort with the wounded soldiers who were also recovering here. Many had been shipped home from Africa, because this was the current battleground, the territory where the British government was making a determined push to bring its ideas of "civility" to the native populations. All the major European powers were doing the same throughout the region, so the battles were not always against native tribes, but often between age-old enemies.

Of course, the push to conquer was most pronounced in those areas richest in gold and other precious minerals, as well as those with fertile growing lands.

While Caden was a cynical bastard and did not believe for a moment there was a noble purpose to the Crown's desire to expand its territory, he also understood it was a necessary evil if England was to maintain its influence throughout the world.

But England also owed a duty to the soldiers who returned home injured. Caden felt he owed these men something, too. He was heir to a dukedom, privileged and elite, and ought to be a generous leader to these men. His first task was to improve morale among them. Some would be discharged from service because their wounds were too damaging to allow them to continue as soldiers. They had to be worried about what would come next.

He sat with them. Spoke to them. He listened to what they would need once leaving military service. It did not matter whether they served in the army, navy, or Royal Marines. The wounds were the same. The needs were the same.

He had just finished washing and dressing when Ella arrived, gliding into his room like a breath of fresh air.

This was what she always was, a warm and gentle breeze. Her manner was quiet and understated…but oh so delightful.

She had on a simple gown of pale blue muslin and wore her usual white apron over it, that deucedly prim thing he wanted to peel off her body along with her gown to get at her spectacular curves. Her hair was done up as it always was, swept back in a glorious, golden mass at the base of her slender neck, with a few soft waves framing her face.

"Caden, don't you look handsome?" she remarked, casting him a smile as bright as the sunshine streaming in through his windows.

He grinned back. "I wanted to leave the hospital today and walk around town with you. I needed to make myself presentable."

"Well, you will have the ladies swooning."

Elmer was still in his room, so Caden did not take Ella in his arms as he wished to do. He merely shook his head. "You are the only one whose approval matters to me."

That earned him an approving nod from the lad.

Ella blushed because his compliments still tended to rattle her. "Are you sure you are strong enough to manage a walk around Moonstone Landing on just your crutches?"

"Yes, for certain. I do not need a pushchair, so don't even think to bring one along. I am eager to see the sights you were telling me about. Dr. Hewitt and Dr. Spencer have allowed it, and Major Brennan signed off as well."

"All right. I'll have Mr. Hawke drive us back in the wagon if it proves too much for you."

Caden sighed. "Ella, I am not a delicate flower."

"Speaking of flowers…" She reached up and put her nose to his neck. "What is that scent on you? It isn't lavender."

He winked at Elmer, who giggled in return. "It is a manly sandalwood. I've had enough of smelling like a girl."

She pursed her lips, and that pretty pucker only made him yearn to kiss her. "Lavender is appropriate for everyone. It is soothing and pleasant to the senses. It is an excellent medicinal. But I suppose you are beyond needing it. The sandalwood is nice on you, too."

Caden gave her neck a quick nuzzle while Elmer was turned away a moment to collect his nightshirt and breeches for laundering. He inhaled lightly and gave her earlobe a quick suckle for no reason other than he liked to see her ruffled by his touch.

She closed her eyes and moaned softly. "Stop that."

"I cannot help it. You are sweet temptation," he whispered, loving her scent, cinnamon and apples that always made him hungry to taste her. Breathing her in was like breathing in an apple pie fresh out of the oven. How could he be faulted for wanting to lick and nibble her from head to toe?

The smolder in his eyes conveyed it. Her cheeks turned the brightest pink. The girl had fair skin, and her slightest embarrassment showed upon it.

He grinned and drew away.

Ella set aside her apron, since she would not need it to walk around town with him, and then collected his crutches. "We mustn't forget these."

He nodded. "Here, I'll carry them for now."

"Merely carry them?" She looked up at him with big, innocent eyes. "Shouldn't you be using them? Your leg will tire too quickly if you do not. Don't be so prideful. You will ruin our outing."

"All right. I'll be sensible." He did not like the idea of having to use his crutches the entire day. However, that was his pride speaking, just as Ella had accused.

They walked out of the hospital together and slowly ambled past the ancient stone fort that had been built on this spot almost eight hundred years ago. Ella gave him a brief history. "Moonstone Landing has always had a desirable harbor," she said. "It was one of the first defensive fortifications built after the Norman conquest. Possibly built atop an even earlier Roman or Saxon fort."

Both the fort and hospital overlooked the sea, and the walk from those buildings into town was quite invigorating and scenic. It was also surprisingly grueling for him. Perhaps he had attempted this walk around the village too soon, but the day was beautiful, and he'd longed to be out of his hospital bed.

They took a leisurely stroll, stopping often, but he was exhausted and in a sweat by the time they reached the harbor. Most of the fishing vessels were out to sea, but a few had returned with their fresh catch. The smell of raw fish assaulted his senses.

Fish heads, scaly skins, and blood littered the fish market

floor.

"They sell smoked haddock and pasties here. Would you like to stop a moment and have some?" Ella asked.

He shook his head, eager to get away from the pungent odors. "Perhaps on the way back."

She cast him a knowing smile. "All right. There are other shops you'll appreciate more. Rotting fish is not to everyone's taste."

But as he and Ella made their way through the market and up the high street into the center of town, a remarkable thing began to happen. Men came over, hesitant at first, and asked to shake his hand. Women came over next. Some, often the elderly ones, reached up to kiss his cheek and thank him. They congratulated him.

What had he ever done for them?

But he knew why they were gathering around him. The accounts of his return to England were still front-page news. He sold papers. He was everyone's hero. Lord knew why he had been chosen out of all the men as brave or braver than himself. However, in the weeks since his return, he had grown to understand the importance of the role he needed to assume for the sake of his fellow soldiers. He also understood what he represented to the families worrying about their sons and husbands still in the fight.

For the first time in his life, he believed he could play the role of hero. Not merely play at it, but do something useful and actually heroic.

Ella had stepped back, beautiful and smiling, to allow him to bask in the glory on his own. He drew her back to his side.

Was she not the best part of him?

Yes, she was a part of him. It was useless to deny it.

He was not the romantic sort to fawn and dote, but she had to know his feelings... Well, he had certainly muddled them, hadn't he? This was something he needed to rectify soon. Now that he was finally thinking clearly, he understood how this "hero" business would play out.

He also understood that the only thing better than a hero was a hero who was in love with a lovely English rose. Ella was certainly that—sweet and charming. She would capture the hearts of every man, woman, and child in England.

Not even his grandfather would dare interfere or risk being portrayed as the ogre by the newspapers.

In truth, why should his grandfather refuse their match? Ella was eminently suitable. Excellent bloodlines. Excellent connections. Sweet as sugar, and beautiful in a warm and approachable way.

His heart soared whenever she looked at him. She had those magical fairy eyes.

He must have shaken a hundred hands and received almost as many kisses by the time they made it the short distance to the village green. Ella drew him over to a monument standing in the green that she wanted him to see. "Please, Caden. It will only take a moment."

"All right."

His legs were tiring and his arms were sore from leaning on his crutches, but this was important to her, so he followed her to the statue and listened while she read the inscription on the plaque at its base and explained why it had been placed here. "This is the tribute to Captain Brioc Taran Arundel," Ella said, her voice quite reverential. "He saved the lives of the village children."

"I heard the story. Everyone has gone out of their way to tell me. I understand he saved several of Elmer's cousins from drowning."

She nodded. "There were ten children trapped on the sinking sloop the day that horrible squall hit and pushed their vessel against the rocks. Captain Arundel was the one who sailed out to them, braving the terrible wind and waves, and saved them all. I think you are very much like him."

Caden arched an eyebrow. "Me? I am no sailor."

"You know I am not talking about sailing boats. I am refer-ring to your valor. You have it, Caden. You were born with that sense of honor in your blood. You cannot hide it and you cannot escape it."

He snorted.

"Fine, be that way. But you do not fool me. There is a valiant man inside of you, so stop denying it. Everyone sees it, even if you refuse to acknowledge the obvious. I just want you to know how proud I am of you."

"Ella," he said with a groan, "I haven't done anything yet."

"You have already proven your merit. All you have not done yet is allow others to congratulate you for it. Today was a good start."

"It felt odd to be idolized like that."

"You give people hope. Keep doing this, Caden. Well, you really started several days ago when you walked out of your fancy hospital room and began speaking to the wounded soldiers recovering in the wards. It is one thing for Fionn to do this, to show he cares. But his war ended years ago. It was more important for you to do this. You fought beside them… Oh, not their specific regiments, and perhaps not the same enemy. But your battles are fresh, and you experienced what they experi-enced. This is why they respond to you when you show them compassion and respect."

"How could I not?"

"Do you think the powerful lords in London care about them the way you do? You must be their voice and shout loudly about their plight. You are the grandson of a duke and his heir. These soldiers all know you could have bought out your commission. You stayed and fought alongside them. Even now, you could have resumed your fancy life. But in coming to them, talking to them and listening, you showed that you care about them and are one of them. They would fight for you and die for you."

Caden shook his head. "Most of those men are never going back. The army will declare them unfit for fighting and let them go. This is the real problem. What is to become of them if they do not have families to take them in?"

"Then you must defend them."

"I know. This is something I will address on my 'I am a *bloody* hero' tour. Major Brennan convinced me this is something I must do. But I am also going to destroy the territorial governor and other greedy men like him the Crown appoints. They line their pockets, do nothing for advancing England's interests, and needlessly cause the loss of lives."

She looked up at him, obviously surprised. "Well, you are on quite the crusade."

"Yes, I never do anything by half measures." He cast her a wry smile. "Do you regret getting me started on this path? Am I too much for you to handle, Ella?"

"I don't know. Maybe."

This was not quite what he'd hoped to hear, but Ella was always going to be honest with him. She and the major had brought him around to accepting this hero nonsense. He was not merely going to ride out the glory. He was going to blast a wide hole in everyone's complacency and shake up the Houses of Parliament.

She was nibbling her lip as she continued to stare at him.

"What, Ella? You did not like me as the selfish, surly dolt. And now it appears you do not like me as the anointed defender of the people. What do you want me to be?"

"I want you to be exactly who you are, Caden. Insufferable, surly, but also valiant. I am fretting because I do not know where I fit in your plans." She shook her head and sighed. "Maybe you have not figured this out either. It is not something to be decided in a matter of minutes. Are you hungry? Let's stop at the Kestrel Inn for a bite."

"All right."

The inn, a surprisingly elegant structure just off the high street, was also a popular dining spot with the smart crowd who swelled the population of the village in the summer. Some members of Society, such as Ella's family, had settled here permanently. Apparently, the Duke of Claymore had married one of Elmer's cousins, a lass by the name of Brenna Angel, and moved his family here year round, as well.

Most of Society's elite were merely leasing pretty cottages by the sea for the summer months. Caden recognized several lords and ladies as he walked into the inn, and they recognized him.

Ella also introduced him to Thaddius Angel, the innkeeper. "Angel? That name crops up with alarming regularity around here," Caden remarked.

The amiable young man laughed. "Yes, there are plenty of Angels in Moonstone Landing."

Indeed, Caden realized this family mostly ran the village, and they were all so irritatingly cheerful. Elmer's father was constable, an uncle ran the Three Lions tavern, the young innkeeper was a cousin of Elmer's—not to mention the three female cousins who had married into the peerage. Even the bank manager was an Angel, something Caden had found out the other day when attempting to establish his credit.

Thaddius led them to the finest table in the dining room. "Order whatever you and Lady Ella like, my lord. Compliments of the house."

Caden frowned. "No, Mr. Angel. It isn't necessary. I shall pay our way."

The young man turned quite serious. "I think you have already paid more than your share. Has he not, Lady Ella?"

It did not sit well with Caden, but he understood this was how things were going to be for a while going forward. He ceased making a fuss and graciously thanked him.

Acquaintances now approached him, several lords and ladies he knew from his days as an eligible bachelor in London. He introduced them to Ella, although he expected most of them knew her or knew of her since she had made a brilliant debut.

"Yes, I remember you, Lord Waring," Ella said with an easy charm. "How did your horse do at the Newmarket races? I recall you were testing him out before attempting to race him at Ascot."

"Indeed, I am honored you remember our conversation," Lord Waring replied, obviously quite taken with Ella. "I was certain I had bored you to tears."

She graced him with one of her radiant smiles. "I was not bored at all. How did he do?"

"Alas, not well." But the fact she had remembered their conversation now had Lord Waring in raptures.

Caden stifled a grumble. Ella had gained another admirer. That she had done it so easily was rather disconcerting. Not that Ella was *flirting* with the man. She wasn't at all, just showing her natural warmth and compassion.

When Lord Waring learned she was to attend the Kestrel Inn's assembly ball in two days' time, he hurriedly claimed a dance from her.

"Yes, I shall be delighted," she replied.

Blast, did she have to smile so prettily? Caden tried not to turn into a jealous ape. He wanted Ella all to himself, and yet he was not making any motions to court her. She had to be wondering what was on his mind.

He was still trying to figure it out.

He wanted Ella in his life. But he did not want her hurt by the enemies he was bound to make.

Since his head was now pounding, he put those thoughts aside and ordered his meal. The glazed ham came on a bed of mashed potatoes and a hearty dollop of leeks, over which was poured a white sauce containing wine and chunks of apple that turned out to be quite tasty. Ella had ordered a smoked haddock, apparently a favorite of hers, since she had tried to get him to try some at the fish market.

Their meal was occasionally interrupted by well-wishers, but on the whole it was a pleasant hour. When he and Ella finished, they strolled over to the mercantile. It did not escape his notice that she was purposely slowing down for him, often finding a reason to stop and rest without making it obvious she was doing it because of him.

Mr. Bedwell tripped over himself to accommodate Caden the moment he and Ella entered his mercantile establishment. "A pleasure to see you here, my lord. Young Elmer has been giving us all updates on your health. We are glad to see you have vastly improved."

"Thank you, Mr. Bedwell." Caden purchased shaving supplies—not that he needed them at the moment, since the hospital seemed to be well equipped and even had a barber who came around to shave beards and pull the occasional tooth.

But Caden wanted to be prepared once he left the hospital and began to travel across England. He purchased a few other items that would be useful on his journey. "Have them delivered to the hospital," he said, not wanting Ella to be stuck carrying packages for him, since his hands were taken up with his crutches.

"Right away, my lord."

They next walked to Mrs. Halsey's tea shop, for Ella had warned him to leave room for tea and cakes after their meal. That was not going to be a problem for him. This first time walking around the village had proven too much of an exertion for him. It was only his stubbornness that prevented him from begging for that pushchair. He was still hungry and could have devoured another full meal without difficulty.

He also was in desperate need of a nap, and a long one at that. His legs were in light spasms and his back ached. However, he was not going to admit that to Ella.

Though she must have suspected, for she was staring at him, no doubt taking notice of his breathing and the slightest flush to his face. Beads of perspiration formed across his brow.

He hobbled into the tea shop before Ella could remark on it.

Mrs. Halsey and her daughter squealed in delight and ushered them to their finest table, which was in the corner beside the daintily curtained window. "My lord, we are honored."

"The pleasure is all mine, I assure you, Mrs. Halsey. Lady Ella said yours was the finest tea shop in England, and I must heartily agree. I have never tasted finer sweets. In truth, it is the brightest part of my day."

When he ordered a slice of apricot pie, Mrs. Halsey gave him almost the entire thing. He ordered a mint tea to go along with it.

Ella had ordered ginger cake and hot cocoa. The mention of cocoa reminded him of the plantations in the Ashanti territory, the very ones they had been ordered to seize by that idiot territorial governor. But ownership had not gone to the Crown. Instead, a consortium of investors, his grandfather included, had been given the property instead. It was that consortium who received the benefits of the subsequent government contracts for cocoa.

The Ashanti had been willing to sell their wares to the Crown on even more generous terms, but the governor had no intention of allowing them to go unpunished for their unwillingness to line his greedy pockets. So, Caden's men had to die in a made-up conflict so that his grandfather and his grasping friends could get rich on gold and cocoa.

Ella put a hand on his arm. "Caden," she said softly, "you are lost in your thoughts again."

"Sorry." How could he tell her what her simple order represented?

"Did I say something to upset you?"

"No, Ella. I think I am just tired after my first afternoon out."

She nodded. "Would you like to go out again tomorrow? Nothing as strenuous as today, I promise. You have now seen the village proper. I was hoping to take you into the countryside next. A ride along the beach and into the lovely hills. We could ride horses or take my Uncle Cormac's carriage, whichever you prefer."

"Let's take the horses. I think my ribs can stand the wear and tear. That sounds nice. Does your uncle have a mount I could borrow?"

She let out a breath. "Yes, several that will do quite nicely.

Imogen is going to join us, of course. Uncle Cormac will never allow me to ride out alone with you. He was not thrilled about my taking you out for a walk around town this afternoon, but it was just a walk, and we remained in sight of everyone."

"One could argue these villagers served as our chaperones," Caden pointed out.

"Yes, exactly. Rules are much less stringent here in Cornwall than in London. We have no *ton* Society, with their frivolous rules and restrictions. Nor are we nearly as cruel. One can be ruined and ridiculed in London just for wearing a gown that is slightly out of fashion. The gossips can be brutal."

"Then it is a good thing we are in Moonstone Landing." He cast her a rakish smile as he eased back in his chair that was too small for him. These quaint shops and their seats were designed for a woman's slender body. "I don't blame your uncle for being concerned about you. I don't trust myself with you either. I enjoyed my time with you today."

Her cheeks turned pink. This girl really did not take compliments well.

"So did I. You were very nice to everyone, even a few ladies and gentlemen who were quite persistent in gaining your notice."

"The rude louts? And the ladies who tried to slip notes into my pocket?"

Ella was surprised. "They did?"

"Yes. Look." He removed a few folded papers and tossed them onto the table. "Don't read them. They are probably lewd."

"Truly?" She dove on one and read it. "Oh my." She set it back down, her cheeks now an even brighter pink. "What are you going to do with them?"

"Burn them in the rubbish bin."

"This is going to happen everywhere you go, isn't it?"

He nodded. "It would happen even if you were with me, even if you were my wife. But what I do about these propositions is what matters, isn't it?"

"Yes." She placed her hands on the table and clasped them

together. "I suppose it makes more sense for you to be free to do whatever you need to do."

"Maybe. I don't know."

She said nothing, just appeared disappointed.

He sighed. "What I need is you, Ella. Whether you are with me or not, I would carry you in my heart. Even if I received a thousand letters propositioning me, my answer would always be the same. No. I do not want a night with some meaningless stranger. I want to build a lifetime with you."

Her eyes widened.

"I knew it after we shared the supper dance last year." Why was he telling her this? He was not ready to make a commitment to her. Yet he could not find the strength to pull away. What a confused arse he was. "I felt it acutely when you popped back into my life here in Moonstone Landing. But I am not asking you to marry me."

"Oh."

"I still have to deal with my grandfather. And I do not know if I can hold back my temper when dealing with those officious government prigs. So anything serious romantically is out of the question for now."

She looked hurt.

Of course, only he could foul up a declaration of love with such efficiency. He ought to have kept his stupid mouth shut and not said anything to her yet. Why mention marriage when he was going to shoot down the idea in his next breath? "Sorry, Ella. You know I am an arse."

She nodded. "And you keep proving it. Caden, you are as insufferable and irritating as ever. Even when you spend the day behaving as everyone's magnificent hero, you still find a way to rile me. There is one thing you and I must do before you leave here."

"I don't suppose that one thing has to do with you and me and clothes flying off."

"No, it doesn't," she said, appearing not to be offended, since she was shaking her head and chuckling. "It has to do with moonlight and a dark, clear night. We have to stand on a hillside overlooking the cove and watch for moonstones. If they shimmer, I will wait for you forever."

"And if they do not?"

"Then it will mean you do not love me."

He frowned. "Ella, I do not think that is possible. If they do not shine for us, it could mean *you* do not love me."

She shook her head. "No, Caden. I have not been able to get you out of my heart ever since we shared that supper dance. See, you were not the only one affected by it. Why do you think I have been rejecting every marriage proposal?"

"For me, Ella?" Lord, he was dense not to have realized it.

"Yes. I meant to hold out for you until all hope was lost."

Therein lay the tragedy of it.

Would it be too late for them by the time he finished doing all he needed to do? What if it took years?

How long before she gave up on him and moved on?

Chapter Eight

ELLA HAD BEEN trying very hard to shelter her heart, but it was a losing proposition. Caden had a way of melting her resistance. Yet he never quite came out and said he loved her or wanted to marry her. Quite the opposite—he went out of his way to remind her that he had no intention of marrying her now.

Or was it that he had no intention of *ever* marrying her?

He used words like *forever* and *only you*. However, there was always a condition attached to his declarations. He had to speak to his grandfather. He had to deal with his superiors and government officials. He had to complete his "hero" tour.

More telling was what he did not say. He did not come out straightforwardly and say he loved her. He did not resolve to speak to Uncle Cormac about wanting to marry her. Well, she supposed he had been clear about that. Marriage was out. Not that her uncle was the one responsible for giving consent. No, that was for her father to do. But her parents were in London and would not arrive in Moonstone Landing until it was time to bring her and Imogen home. Caden would be gone by then.

"Ella, I am going to bring my drawing pad and pencils with me for our outing," Imogen said, shaking Ella out of her thoughts as she helped her into her riding habit, a moss-green velvet that fit her to perfection and brightened the green of her eyes.

"That is a lovely idea." In turn, Ella helped Imogen into her riding outfit, which was a stunning forest-green velvet.

The two of them shared a bedchamber at Westgate Hall, her Uncle Cormac's large home at the western end of Moonstone Landing's cove. They could have taken separate rooms, for there were plenty of guest chambers available. But she and Imogen shared quarters in their London home and saw no reason to do otherwise here.

The manor house itself was perched atop a hill overlooking a private beach. These natural rock formations formed outcroppings that hid one's beach from the neighboring one. It happened that Moonstone Cottage was the property immediately to the right of Westgate Hall, so they would often skirt around the outcropping at low tide to visit Fionn and Chloe.

Moonstone Landing's beach was off in the distance and not visible from her uncle's home. However, when the sky was clear, one had only to look eastward to have a view of the village itself and its charming harbor.

"It has been a while since I sketched the countryside," Imogen muttered as Ella helped her do up her hair. "I could draw you and Caden as we picnic together."

"That is a fine idea. Just don't be obvious about it." Ella wanted a portrait of Caden that she could keep for herself to remember him. Also, Imogen had a way of capturing the honesty in a person's eyes. If Caden truly loved her, Imogen would notice and bring it out in the drawing.

But she was not going to think about this right now, for it was enough to enjoy the sunshine and vibrant blue sky.

They walked downstairs and joined her aunt and uncle by the stable. Uncle Cormac was a stern man, but he had always been exceedingly gentle with them. They ran to him and hugged him in turn. He laughed and gave them each a kiss on the forehead. "Don't you girls look lovely?"

They hugged him again.

"Don't I get a hug, too?" Phoebe remarked.

"Of course." Ella threw her arms around her aunt. Imogen

then did the same.

Aunt Phoebe was always a delight and had taught Imogen all she knew about drawing—which was quite a lot, because she was talented in her own right and could have made a name for herself even in the men's world of art.

"I have invited Lord Mersey to join us for supper tonight," Uncle Cormac said, now guiding the docile mare Ella was to ride out of the stable.

Phoebe led out an equally gentle mare meant for Imogen. This was their aunt's way of quietly helping out Uncle Cormac. He had lost his left arm shortly after the battle at Waterloo and still grew frustrated over every little thing he could not do for himself because of it. But Phoebe was always near, making no fuss as she stood by his side, her aim always to preserve his dignity.

Since he had only the one arm to lead out Ella's horse, Phoebe casually took the reins of Imogen's mount and led it out. Their groom led out the third horse, a beautiful black stallion by the name of Avenger that was readied for Caden to ride. Despite his name, the stallion actually had a good disposition, although he was still too much of a beast for Ella or Imogen to handle.

"Did he accept the supper invitation, Uncle Cormac?" Ella asked, unable to contain her curiosity.

"Yes, he did."

She let out a breath. "Good. I think this means he is ready to talk to you about what happened during his last battle."

"I hope so. Fionn says he is much improved since the day he arrived. I expect you had some influence on that."

Ella shook her head. "No, actually, I think Fionn is the one who deserves the credit. Something changed in Caden after he spoke with him on the day of Lady Dowling's piano recital. A resolve. A fresh purpose. An admirable goal to strive for, perhaps."

"Has he said anything else to you?" Phoebe asked. "I mean about his intentions toward you."

Ella pursed her lips as she gave the question thought. "Yes and no."

Uncle Cormac frowned. "What the hell does that mean?"

"Cormac! Your language," Phoebe admonished him.

His frown deepened. "You know I don't mince words. And I am sure as *hell* not going to let anyone hurt Ella."

Ella said nothing while the groom now helped her to mount the dappled mare known as Buttercup. But once she was in the saddle, and the groom had moved on to assist Imogen, she replied to her uncle. "It is a push and pull with him. I think he cares for me, but he doesn't quite know where I will fit into his life…at least not at present, while his superiors want to send him around the country on what he calls his 'I am a *bloody* hero' tour."

Her uncle laughed. "Don't swear, Ella. It isn't polite for a lady. Does he really call it that? I like his irreverent attitude."

"So do I, but it also constrains him. He knows his smart mouth is going to get him into trouble, and he doesn't want me near him when the repercussions occur."

"Well, I cannot fault him for that," her uncle admitted.

Ella patted her gentle mare. "He is always going to have a smart mouth that will get him into trouble. Will he push me away forever because of it? And why are men always so worried about the *fragile* females? First of all, we are not fragile. And it seems to me, if he truly loved me, then marriage to him would protect me better than leaving me here to be talked about as the poor, heartbroken girl he left behind."

"I agree," Phoebe said. "Cormac, he must be made to see sense. If he cares for Ella, then he ought to come right out like a man and declare himself. Is he not better off with the woman he loves standing beside him, ready to fight alongside him?"

Cormac shook his head. "Love, it isn't always that easy. I will hear him out, all right?"

Ella nodded. "Thank you, Uncle Cormac."

Imogen drew up beside her on her sweet gray mare, Honeysuckle. The groom now secured a pouch with her art supplies to the saddle.

Mr. Hawke came by in his rickety wagon, and they tied Caden's stallion to its rear gate. Ella was not surprised to see Mr. Hawke, for he often escorted her and Imogen around town and had been ferrying her to the hospital. As it turned out, Uncle Cormac had arranged for the kindly caretaker to keep them company throughout the day.

He also carried picnic supplies in his wagon—no doubt something Aunt Phoebe had requested from Mrs. Hawke, who was an excellent cook and often prepared picnic meals for them for countryside outings.

Ella ought to have realized Imogen would never be allowed to serve as chaperone on her own. She was too young and too romantically inclined, as girls budding into womanhood tended to be. Ella always thought of herself as the practical one, while Imogen was more of a dreamer.

Phoebe or her sisters, Chloe and Henley, should have taken on the role of chaperone, but they had their ladies auxiliary duties as well as their children to tend and their homes to manage. It was rare they could get away for an entire afternoon.

As for the men, Cain, the Duke of Malvern, was in Exeter on business. Fionn had his duties running the hospital and commanding Fort Arundel. Cormac was looking after Cain's operating farms and mills while Cain was away, in addition to attending to his own Burness properties.

So, it fell to Mr. Hawke, who doted on them as though he were their own grandfather.

Ella noticed Caden impatiently standing by the hospital's entrance with his arms crossed over his chest when they arrived. His eyes lit up when he saw the mount Cormac had selected for him. "His name is Avenger," Ella said.

"He's a beauty. The name suits him." He tossed his crutches into the back of the wagon, then limped over to Avenger and patted his neck. He spoke to the horse in a deep, crooning singsong, and had full command of the stallion by the time he mounted him.

Ella was impressed. She and Imogen knew very little about handling horses. They mostly rode in carriages when going around London and had never been accomplished riders. But Caden seemed to settle into his saddle as though he had been born to it.

Once they were on the outskirts of town, Caden asked about their ultimate destination. Ella pointed to a meadow in the distance that stretched down toward a cliff overlooking a beach. Fionn had taken them and Chloe there one summer to explore a pirate cave. They had since returned several times because the scenery was beautiful, and she and Imogen found the idea of pirates once smuggling in the area quite exciting.

Caden arched an eyebrow. "A pirate cave? With real pirates?"

Imogen laughed. "They haven't been active in the area for decades. The cave is just a curiosity now, something of interest for visitors to explore. But it is also a lovely spot for a picnic."

"Would you mind if I rode off on my own for a little while? I'll meet you at the meadow. But I feel Avenger is restless, and so am I. We could both do with a good run."

Ella did not mind.

"I'll meet you at the meadow," he said with the joy of a little boy granted permission to run amok.

Ella wanted to warn him not to jump any stone fences, but it was one of the first things he and Avenger did, soaring over the high stones as though they were mere stepping stools. She had no idea how Caden's ribs would absorb the landing, but she supposed any discomfort would be obvious enough once he dismounted.

She liked this adventurous, slightly reckless side of Caden, but it made her wonder if she would ever be able to keep up with him. She was much more cautious than he was. He was racing off with abandon, and she was already worrying he might have aggravated his ribs.

She was not going to say anything to him about it.

Perhaps they had healed and he felt no discomfort. After all, he was not fool enough to overdo it and puncture a lung, was he?

If he felt joy and freedom, she was not going to deny him the pleasure.

But it made her think of them as a couple. Perhaps he needed a woman who could ride like the wind as he did, and whose horse could leap over those fences with the same ease Avenger had done.

Imogen reached over and tapped her arm lightly. "Ella, is something wrong?"

She turned to her sister. "No, why do you ask?"

"You are frowning."

"Oh, it's just that the sun is a little bright."

Imogen did not believe her, but let the matter drop as they rode on to the picnic site. Ella tried not to be so obvious in her fretting, but she was concerned. What if she was not enough for Caden?

He was everyone's hero. Brave, adventurous, exuding confidence and leadership.

Who was she? What was she able to offer him as a wife that a thousand other women could not?

Since she and Imogen were never going to be able to keep up with him, they rode along at their own pace and watched in awe as he tore back and forth across the countryside. Avenger seemed to fly over those flower-dotted fields, his hooves softly pounding the earth as they ate up the ground.

As for Caden, after all those months of being trapped in bed, Ella understood how desperately he needed to feel the wind on his face and the raw power of that beast beneath his thighs.

She had worried that his leg might not hold up or that he would aggravate his bruised ribs, but he did not seem to be bothered by any of it. Perhaps riding was easier than walking, since he did not have to put weight on his leg, although he did have to guide his horse using some of his powerful muscles.

Well, Caden was a big man and had no shortage of magnificent muscles.

There were nights Ella had quietly lain awake in her bed thinking of his body and how splendid it would feel pressed atop hers. Even now, the very idea brought a blush to her cheeks. She pretended to fuss with her stirrups and forced herself to think of something other than Caden.

By the time she and Imogen reached the meadow overlooking the beach and pirate cave, Caden was already there, standing by the stream that ran alongside the gentle slope of grass. He was tending to a lathered Avenger, making certain the beast lapped up enough cool water to slake his thirst.

Mr. Hawke drew his wagon into the shade, climbed down, and also saw that his trusted mare had a drink from the stream and sufficient gorse to munch on. Ella and Imogen alighted on their own, since they were quite capable of that, and then handed over their horses to Mr. Hawke's care.

Ella and Imogen were about to lift the picnic basket out of the wagon when Caden strode over. "Let me get that for you?"

"No!" Ella cried out. "The doctor said you should not be lifting anything heavy!"

"That was at least ten days ago. Anyway, too late. Besides, it isn't heavy at all." He plucked it out as though it weighed no more than a feather.

Imogen poked her in the ribs and then grinned. "You must admit, he has gorgeous muscles. Stop gawking at him before he notices."

"Imogen, be quiet," Ella said in a frantic whisper.

She grabbed a blanket from the wagon and spread it out beneath a shady spot. Then Caden placed the picnic basket on it. Ella opened up the basket and peered inside to see what the caretaker's wife had given them. It was filled to the brim with cold meats, cheeses, fruit, and bread. Also packed inside were bottles of lemonade and ale, as well as cutlery and linens. "Mr. Hawke, will you join us?"

"No, m'lady. My wife packed a little basket for me." He excused himself to settle under a shady elm to eat and then take a nap.

While Ella carefully laid everything out, Caden escorted Imogen back to Honeysuckle and untied the pouch that held her art supplies. "What are you going to draw, Imogen?"

"The meadow. The water. Perhaps Mr. Hawke sleeping," she said with a grin. "You. Ella. The horses."

He laughed. "Well, that will keep you busy for the afternoon. Are you going to explore the pirate cave with us?"

She shook her head. "I've seen it many times. I would rather stay here and draw our surroundings."

He arched an eyebrow. "So, it is just to be me and Ella?"

"Yes," Imogen said, "but you must give me your word of honor that you will behave when you are in the cave with her."

"Of course—you have my word."

Imogen nodded. "Thank you, Caden. I knew I could trust you."

He cast her a wry smile and then turned his gaze to Ella.

Dear heaven.

She felt his dark eyes burn into her soul.

"Looks like it's to be just you and me," he said, his grin a little wicked.

"Do you mind, Caden?"

"Not at all."

Since the tide was out, Ella suggested they explore the cave before they settled down to eat. "We won't be able to explore once the tide comes in."

"Then there's no time to lose. Let's go." He held out his hand, and she entwined her fingers in his without a second thought. It was the most natural thing in the world for her, but in the next moment she realized what she had done and tried to pull out of his grasp.

Caden realized it, too. His grin was rather smug. "Stop tugging. I am not letting go of you."

Ella sighed in exasperation. "Fine, but it is not proper."

"Nor is this," he said, raising her hand to his lips and giving it a light kiss. "Stop looking around in alarm. No one can see."

Imogen had settled on the blanket with her sketchpad and pencils laid out before her, and was not looking at her and Caden. Mr. Hawke was already snoring under the shade of a stately elm.

The wind rustled through a nearby copse, whooshing softly through the silvery leaves. In the distance, Ella could hear the ebb and flow of the waves as the tide rushed out.

Caden kept hold of her hand while they made their way down the cliff steps to the pirate cave. "Are you sure you do not need your crutches?" she asked, because parts of the path were steep.

"I'm certain of it, Ella." He kept hold of her hand as they made their way down. On occasion, he wrapped an arm around her waist to hold her steady.

She thought it was rather ironic that he was helping her, since he was the one going about on an injured leg and whose balance should have been off. He had stubbornly refused to bring his crutches along to the cave, but he seemed to be managing fine without them.

When they reached the beach, she looked him over to make certain he was all right.

He grinned back. "Feels nice, doesn't it? Just you and me, enjoying the day."

She nodded.

"We feel right together, Ella. Don't we?"

She said nothing, merely turned away to adjust her riding habit so the hem of the flowing gown would not get wet.

Perhaps she ought to have agreed with Caden and told him they did feel right. But their situation was still too much up in the air for her to be convinced of it. She had already given too many pieces of herself to him.

Even if she gave all of herself to him, would it ever be enough?

"Blast," he said softly. "Ella, why are you fretting?"

"I don't mean to."

He led her along the sand, and their boots sank into the soft ground as they walked to the mouth of the cave. When they reached it, he paused to grab a lantern. The villagers kept supplies in a storage box beside the cave that contained ropes, lanterns, and chalk to mark their way. These items were a convenience for all who wished to explore.

After lighting the lantern, Caden tucked some chalk into his pocket and then turned to study her. "Won't you tell me what is wrong?"

"Nothing is wrong. It is just me thinking too hard. Imogen says I do it all the time, and I need to stop."

He cast her a soft smile. "I like this about you. You make me have to work harder to earn your approval. It keeps me from getting too full of myself when everyone else around me spouts flattering lies and panders to me. But what has you worried, Ella?"

He closed up the storage box and then took her hand in his again to lead her into the cave.

"Oh, Caden. I don't know if I should say anything to you. It is presumptuous of me, since you haven't mentioned anything about courting me. And here I am leaping ahead and…"

"Thinking of marriage?" He paused at the entrance to the cave and studied her. "You can tell me anything, Ella. You know I care for you and would never dismiss your worries."

She turned away to watch the waves gently sweeping onto the rocks below them. They would wash in with more power as the tide rolled back in. "You have so many fine qualities."

He laughed. "And this is a problem? I assure you, I am not all that fine a man."

She looked up at him and gave him a gentle smile. "You are the finest I know. You are that hero the generals have been touting. You are, Caden. Even though you deny it. In fact, you are so heroic, it has me wondering whether I will ever be able to keep up with you, whether I will ever be enough for you. I don't want to be that mouse of a wife who holds you back."

"You? A mouse?" He shook his head and laughed. "That you have a quiet nature does not make you weak or dull. You certainly know how to stand up to me."

"Because for all your barking and growling, you do not really give me a hard time. Often, you are surprisingly gentle with me. But my point is, who am I to presume you would ever want me as your wife? You've been clear about not wanting to marry me."

"My concern is only for now. Do not make more of it than it is." He groaned. "That sounded awful. I do not mean it that way."

"You are right. See, I am just being silly about everything."

She tried to walk ahead of him into the cave, wanting to hide her embarrassment. She had been too honest with him and probably made him uncomfortable. Why could she not have kept her mouth shut and simply enjoyed the day?

Caden would not let go of her hand. "Careful, Ella. It gets dark quickly in these caves. Stay close to me. We mustn't go too far in, because I only have this lantern and a bit of chalk to mark our path. The chalk can easily wash off. I don't want us getting lost. As for your not being enough for me, that is utter nonsense. I've never met anyone who would suit me so perfectly as you."

She laughed.

"No, really. Everyone who meets you is immediately charmed and adores you. There is no artifice about you, no guile or manipulation. You put everyone at ease. You go out of your way to be kind and welcoming, and are completely sincere in all you do. Even when you berate me, you are still achingly gentle. You cannot bear to hurt me."

"Why would I ever want to hurt you?"

He leaned down and kissed her lightly on the forehead. "You wouldn't. This is what makes you so special. There is not a cruel bone in your body. Believe me, you are the perfect balance for an arrogant arse like me. As for marriage—"

She groaned. "Oh, I had no right to bring it up."

"You had every right. In fact, it has been on my mind ever since we shared that supper dance last year. Ella, I never forgot you," he said with a raw ache that wrapped around her heart and squeezed it tight. His depth of feeling was evident in the strong angles of his face and in his dark eyes that looked fiery in the golden lantern light bouncing along the cave walls.

She wanted to hug him, but dared not move or breathe, dared not do anything to break the spell of this moment.

"You were always in my dreams and in my thoughts. But marriage is a lifetime commitment, especially the way you and I view it. I know you will keep to your wedding vows. Honor thy husband. Be faithful. You are too sweet and honest to do otherwise. I would do the same, promise to love and cherish you. I don't want a business alliance. I want a woman I respect to share my bed, to curl up against my body on cold nights and seek my warmth."

Ella listened as he bared his soul.

"I want a woman who will listen to my concerns and give her honest opinion."

"Well, I would certainly never lie to you."

"I know," he said with conviction. "You would always be my safe harbor, a safe place to let down my guard. I want a woman who will bear my children and raise them with love. Who else but you would fit that role? Do you know what I thought when I first laid eyes on you?"

She shook her head. "I have no idea."

"That you were the most beautiful girl I had ever seen. In fact, too beautiful to be real. I could not stop staring at you."

This admission genuinely surprised her. "You were very discreet about it. I did not think you noticed me at all."

"I could not take my eyes off you. I looked for you at every affair. Even though you never wore much jewelry, you sparkled so brightly. People were right to call you a diamond. You were one. You still are."

"Caden, I had no idea you felt this way. Why did you not tell me?"

"I wanted to, sometimes. Especially after seeing you here. I thought I was dreaming when you walked into my hospital room. *Ella.* My beautiful Ella. I was sure I was delirious and had taken too much laudanum. I believed I had made you up in my dreams."

"I was quite real."

He nodded. "There is so much I have been wanting to say to you."

"But something always holds you back."

"My anger, Ella. There is still so much of it in me. I will likely do something stupid to make enemies of powerful people, because I am still a brash arse who does not know how to curb his tongue. I know I have to restrain my temper, but it is easier said than done."

"Just keep your attention fixed on the important goals. Think of all you can do to help those injured soldiers and their families."

"It is always on my mind. But you know me better by now, don't you?"

She smiled at him. "Yes, I do. You can be a monumental clot."

He laughed. "Precisely."

He led her deeper into the cave, along a passageway that opened into a large cavern. "This must be where the pirates kept their smuggled goods," he said.

"Yes, they piled their crates onto long wooden tables to store them above the water line. This cave does not usually fill to the brim at high tide. It only partially fills, except when the moon is full and the tides are particularly strong. Or during a violent storm."

"So we won't drown if we are caught inside?"

Ella shook her head. "No, but we will get uncomfortably soaked. The water comes in fast and hard, and we might get knocked down by a particularly strong wave."

Caden had marked the passageway they had come through

with chalk, just to be sure they did not accidentally take another passage that would lead them to a dead end. Those dead ends could fill with water, so they always had to be alert as to their surroundings and the movements of the tides.

Ella liked that Caden was methodical and cautious about this.

When a little bit of water flowed into the cavernous opening, Caden took her hand again. "Looks like the tide is coming in. Come along, Ella. As you warned, it comes in fast."

"Yes, it does. Let's hurry. What a shame. I thought we had a little more time, but we must have caught the tide just as it was turning."

They spoke no more and hurried out as more water began to trickle in.

Bright sunlight momentarily blinded Ella when she walked out of the cave. By the time she regained her vision, Caden had doused the lantern and placed it and the chalk back in the storage box for the next adventurers to use.

However, they did not immediately return to Imogen.

They climbed onto a nearby outcrop of rocks instead, climbing just high enough to keep from getting wet as they watched the waves begin to flood the cave. The motion of the water fascinated Ella, the sinuous way it flowed in and out of the weathered hollows. It lulled her.

She could see it was having the same effect on Caden.

But she still felt the immense power of each wave as it broke at the mouth of the cave, its white spume dancing in the air.

No one was in danger of drowning on a day like this, but anyone used to living by the sea learned to respect it. One rogue wave could soak them and wash them out to sea.

"Shall we return to Imogen?" she asked, giving his hand a light tug, as he seemed lost in thought.

"In a moment, love," he muttered.

Ella's heart lurched.

Did he mean anything by using the endearment?

He turned to her, his gaze fiery as he regarded her. "I promised your sister I would do nothing untoward while we were in the cave. However, I did not promise to behave once we were out of the cave."

Her eyes widened and her heart beat a little faster. "What are you thinking to do?"

"What I am thinking to do and what I *will* do are quite different things. I want to do more than kiss you, Ella. But that is all I will do…for now."

He did not wait for her to accept or refuse him, although she supposed her hesitation in objecting was an indication of her desire to kiss him. A firm denial would have stopped him. But she ached for his touch, for the press of his lips against hers.

He drew her into his big, muscled arms.

Dear heaven.

She felt the strong, steady beat of his heart as she nestled against his chest.

His breath caught as she gazed up at him. "Sweet mercy, you are soft as a kitten."

He stared at her another long moment, then his mouth sank down on hers and he kissed her with scorching abandon. His lips felt rough as they ground on hers, but she liked the sensation of that urgent pressure and the heat radiating off his body. She ran her hands along his powerfully contoured arms and shoulders, desperate to touch him, to feel the heat of his hard, muscled limbs.

He made her tingle.

He made her melt.

Why did he have to be so perfect?

Why did he have to taste so perfect, too? Coffee…eggs…sausages. A hint of mint that he must have used to brush his teeth. The soap against the sinews of his neck.

She breathed him in, inhaling the fragrant sandalwood and the maleness of him. Heat, sweat, and leather.

She shook with desire.

"You are magic, Ella," he whispered, and lifted her up against him so that her bosom was pressed to his chest, and their hips and thighs molded to each other. "You and your fairy-pool eyes." His tongue slipped into her mouth, gently swirling around hers like the ebb tide swirled around the rocks and shifting sands. "You are mine."

She hoped so.

She wanted so much to be the one for him.

A wave crashed just below them, and Caden immediately drew her upward to keep her gown from getting wet. He had quick, protective instincts. "Blast, the tide is coming in fast."

She nodded. "We had better return to Imogen."

"All right." He gave a ragged laugh and took her hand. "Careful, those rocks can be slippery now that they are wet."

She was always careful, except perhaps with her heart. Why could she not control that wayward organ?

Imogen was sketching away, but set her pad and pencils aside when they approached. "How was the cave?"

"Interesting," Caden said. "But be careful whenever you come here. I think it has been used recently."

Imogen's eyes rounded in surprise. "It has?"

This surprised Ella, too. She had not noticed anything out of place in the cave. "What makes you think so?"

He shrugged. "It seems as though someone has been dragging boxes across that cavern recently."

Ella shook her head. "It cannot be. How can you tell? The tide would have washed away all signs."

"You mentioned the cave did not flood completely even at high tide. I noticed markings at the mouth of one of the rear passageways. Maybe next time I'll explore some of those other passages. We weren't really equipped to do it today."

Ella's heart began to beat faster.

She and Imogen sometimes came here on their own, and she read while Imogen drew the scenery. Mr. Hawke would drop them off and then return a few hours later to pick them up. No one thought anything of it. This village was safe. Everyone knew each other.

Perhaps not so safe anymore.

She turned to her sister. "Imogen, if what Caden says is true, then we had better not stay here by ourselves anymore."

Caden looked from one sister to the other in surprise. "You come here on your own?"

"Mr. Hawke drops us off and then picks us up later," Imogen said.

Ella nodded. "We never go down into the caves—we would never be so foolish."

"We are always careful," Imogen assured him. "I sit up here and draw the sunlight on the water. The birds circling over the cresting waves. Sometimes, I draw the stream that runs along the meadow or the way the sun catches the nearby trees and turns their leaves silvery. Ella reads her romantic poetry. But we'll make certain to keep an escort with us from now on."

Caden let out a breath. "Good."

With that resolved, Ella and Imogen set out their food.

The fare was delicious, as it always was, for Mrs. Hawke was an excellent cook. The meats were cold, but still tasty. They dined on ham and chicken, cheddar and Stilton cheeses, apples, and freshly baked bread. Caden enjoyed a mug of ale while they had their lemonade.

Once they had eaten their fill, Imogen picked up her pad and pencil, and resumed capturing on paper whatever caught her fancy. Ella and Caden stowed the remains of their picnic in the basket. She then took out her book of poetry and read aloud while Imogen sketched and Caden leaned back casually and listened to her.

"Ah, you are reciting 'Love's Philosophy' again. You love that poem, don't you, Ella?"

She smiled at him. "Yes. Is it not perfect for today?

"Yes," he said, and recited a few lines.

And the sunlight clasps the earth

And the moonbeams kiss the sea

He cast her a smile that melted her heart.

Ella set aside her book and watched the tide rolling in. The waves were now crashing against the rocks with greater force. Birds began to gather and circle what must have been a school of fish beneath the glistening swells.

The wind was picking up, as it often did in the afternoon.

Mr. Hawke awoke from his nap and ambled over to them. "Time I delivered you home, lasses."

"Oh, yes." Ella scrambled to her feet. "We ought to get back now."

Caden helped Mr. Hawke load their supplies onto the wagon. Then he went to fetch the horses that had been nibbling on the plentiful gorse beside the stream. He helped Ella to mount and then assisted Imogen. Next, he secured the pouch containing Imogen's drawing pad and pencils to the saddle.

However, Imogen had removed one of the sketches and now held it out to him. "Here, Caden. This is for you."

As he studied it, his eyes widened and his expression turned softer than Ella had ever seen before. "Imogen...I don't know what to say."

Now, Ella was curious to see what her sister had drawn. "Let me have a look, Caden."

He hesitated a moment, then nodded and came to her side to hand it to her. "What do you think?"

He rested his hand along her mare's withers as he watched her peruse Imogen's drawing. The man certainly was comfortable around horses, and they responded affectionately to him. Her mare was nuzzling his shoulder.

He casually patted the horse's neck. "Well, Ella? What do you think?"

She studied the sketch of them seated on the blanket just as they had been a short while ago. Caden was drawn with his arms back and resting on his elbows while his large frame was casually stretched out on the blanket, one leg slightly bent and the other, the injured one, lying straight. The wicker basket was behind him. Ella was seated in front of him, her legs tucked under her bottom and the book of poetry on her lap as she looked out over the water and lost herself in dreams.

Caden was depicted staring at her.

Her heart fluttered, for Imogen had captured him perfectly, his every nuance and the feelings he often sought to hide. But he could not hide them from Imogen. She captured his hunger when he looked at Ella. His eyes also reflected the memories that haunted him. There was a familiar brashness in the curve of his mouth. Valor in his posture. Frustration and anger in the curl of his hands.

It was all there, especially his affection for her.

Dear heaven.

Was it possible Caden loved her so deeply?

"It is perfect, Caden."

He nodded. "It is certainly revealing, isn't it?"

"Yes, beautifully so."

Was it possible? Her dream come true. Would those moon-stones shine for them?

Chapter Nine

CADEN WAS TIRED by the time they returned to Westgate Hall. He knew he had overdone it, but tearing across the fields and country lanes had felt so good, even though his ribs were now sore because, perhaps idiotically, he had pushed Avenger to jump fences when he should have been taking it easy. They had remained sore as he and Ella explored the pirate cave, but he'd continued to ignore the discomfort because he wanted the time alone with her and to kiss her afterward.

That kiss was not well done of him, for Imogen had trusted him.

He had kept to his word by not kissing Ella in the cave, but had completely betrayed the spirit of that promise when hungrily tasting Ella's soft lips as soon as they were back on the beach.

Now, he was to have an early supper with Ella, Imogen, and their aunt and uncle, after which Caden meant to speak privately with the Marquess of Burness.

"We do not stand on formality here, Lord Mersey," the marquess said, striding out of his elegant manor house to greet them upon their return. "Did you enjoy the outing?"

Caden dismounted. "Yes, my lord. It was a perfect day."

"Good. Good. Call me Cormac. May I call you Caden?"

"Yes, of course."

"And you may call me Phoebe," his wife said, scurrying out of the house to stand beside her husband, subtly protective of the man and his lack of an arm.

Would Ella be as protective of him?

Caden knew his wounds were going to heal in time. It was his arrogance and impatience that needed tempering. He could see Ella standing beside him, giving his arm a discreet pinch whenever his unheroic nature came out and he behaved like an arse.

The very idea had him grinning as he strode to Ella's side to assist her out of the saddle. One of the Burness grooms came running out to help Imogen down from her docile mare. Mr. Hawke had followed them in his wagon, but now handed over Caden's crutches and bade them all a good evening as he returned to Moonstone Cottage. The cottage was the neighboring property to Westgate Hall and would not take him long to reach.

Moonstone Cottage had also been the home of the village's local sea captain hero, Brioc Taran Arundel. He had built it and resided there until his death. Ella had told him all about this valiant man and the history of the house after his death. About a year after he had passed, Phoebe's aunt acquired it from his estate, ghost and all.

He studied Ella and her family from beneath hooded lids. They were so connected to Moonstone Landing with all its history and lore.

Caden had never felt connected to his family or their properties. His parents had died when he was but a child, and he was then put in his grandfather's care. The two of them together were like setting off Greek fire, the sort that burned hot and fast and never died out. They were always arguing about one thing or another.

Perhaps they were too much alike, both of them stubborn, arrogant, and impatient. Neither would bend to the other—although Caden probably should have been the one to bend, since his grandfather held the ducal title.

Caden knew he would one day become the Duke of Seaton, yet he felt no tug at his soul for the magnificent estate that had served as the family seat for centuries. Nor did he feel any particular affinity for their other holdings. For quite some time now he'd understood it wasn't just the land that mattered. People worked the land. They worked the mills. Sailed the Seaton ships. Maintained his grandfather's stately homes. Maids, butlers, housekeepers, valets, cooks, gardeners, grooms, estate managers, caretakers.

It was time to get to know them all, put names to their faces and show them that he cared for their well-being. This would probably rankle his grandfather, who had absolutely no sentiment in him. The old goat cared only for increasing his wealth and power.

He wasn't all bad, however. The properties were managed efficiently and all seemed profitable. Those who worked their lands were content and their living secure.

But what did Caden *really* know about the workings of the Seaton assets? The estate managers only showed him what his grandfather wanted him to see. He should have probed deeper, demanded more information. But he'd let the matter slide because his military duties often took him away from home, especially this last tour of duty that landed him in West Africa.

Well, things were going to change once he was through with his unavoidable "hero" tour.

He and the marquess chatted amiably as he was shown around Westgate Hall. The man was obviously proud of the large, airy rooms, and the spectacular view his home afforded of the sea. Phoebe introduced him to their energetic twin boys, then remained behind in the nursery quarters to tend to the little heathens, as Cormac jokingly called them.

Ella and Imogen had retired to their bedchamber to change out of their riding habits and dress properly for supper.

Caden and Cormac continued alone on their tour, somehow forming a silent bond due to their injuries. Caden's leg had tired out, so he had reverted to relying on his crutches.

"We have our own beach," Cormac said. "All the homes in

the area do. It is just the way the outcroppings formed. The rocks jut out just enough to give each of us privacy. When the tide is out, one can easily walk around them to the neighboring beach."

"Does it not get a bit wearying to be so close to family?"

"I was afraid it might, but it hasn't at all. Phoebe's sister, Chloe, and her husband, Major Brennan, reside at Moonstone Cottage, but he is busy every day with the fort and hospital. Chloe often stops by to visit Phoebe, but she never imposes. Much of the time the two of them are off at St. Austell Grange working with their eldest sister, Henley, on their ladies auxiliary affairs."

"Sounds very domestic."

Cormac groaned. "Yes, sometimes it is a bit too much for me. But I still wouldn't trade any of it to be back in London. Nor would I ever go back to my old ways. I wasn't just a rake. I was arrogant, insufferable, and a monumental arse, on top of it."

Caden grinned. "So I've heard."

"Gad, do my nieces talk about me? I was always on my best behavior around those sweet girls. And I have reformed since meeting Phoebe. I cannot imagine my life without her. It must be obvious ours is a love match. But it is more than that. From the moment I met her, even as she was railing at me and calling me a depraved, debauched scoundrel—which I was—there was something endearing about her. She completely ignored that I had lost my arm. She refused to see me as someone less, and yanked me out of the mud hole I was wallowing in. I credit her with restoring my dignity."

"Your nieces adore her, it is obvious."

"Phoebe is very good with all of us. Perhaps a little too good when it comes to my nieces, because they want to be here instead of London. My brother is not too happy about that, especially with Ella on the Marriage Mart and already refusing offers. But that discussion is one you and I will have another day soon."

Caden nodded. "I understand your concern and want you to know that I care for Ella very much. But I have much to get through before I dare consider marriage."

"I know very little about the Ashanti battle that decimated your regiment. This is what you and I will talk about after supper. In the meanwhile, what do you think of Westgate Hall?"

Cormac seemed exceedingly proud of it and the happy life he had made here with his wife and children, so Caden had no wish to give him less than a grand compliment. "It is quite beautiful. I can see why Ella and Imogen love it here so much."

"If you look over in the distance," Cormac said, quite pleased by the response, "you can just make out the village of Moonstone Landing and its harbor."

"Yes, I see." Caden leaned over the balustrade as they stood on the terrace, easily making out the faint outline of the hospital and fort, and the boats moored in the harbor. In truth, the views from the house were spectacular, especially on a clear day like today.

Supper was a relaxed affair, the five of them seated around a small table in the family's private dining room. The formal dining room, which could hold up to thirty or forty guests comfortably, was reserved for grander affairs. Caden preferred this informal intimacy, especially since it kept him closer to Ella, who was seated directly opposite him. This afforded him an unobstructed view of her beautiful face and those lovely lips he had not kissed nearly often enough.

The food provided for their supper was as good as any he had ever tasted, easily rivaling the repasts served at parties hosted by London's elite. Not that the courses brought out were extravagant. Quite the opposite—the fare was simple, consisting of a traditional seafood stew offered for lighter palates and a rack of lamb for those who desired a heartier main course.

The conversation flowed smoothly, and so did the wine.

Ella and Imogen did most of the talking, relating the events of the day to their aunt and uncle, who listened attentively.

After supper, Caden and the marquess retired to the marquess's study. "Care for a brandy, Caden?"

"No," he said with a laughing groan, settling in one of the large leather chairs beside the unlit hearth. "I shall fall asleep if I drink any more."

Cormac chuckled as he set aside the bottle and did not bother to pour a drink for himself. "I do not need it, either. Better to keep my wits while I listen to your story, especially since my wife is going to pry me for information as soon as you are gone. However, I give you my word of honor—whatever you wish to remain in confidence shall remain so. Not even my wife, whom I cherish more than my own life, will get it out of me. Now, care to talk about what you went through in that last battle?"

"No, it is the last thing I ever want to talk about or think about. The anguish of it haunts my dreams nightly. However, I am going to have to tell someone soon, because a bloodbath like this cannot be allowed to occur ever again. I need to confide in someone, and I believe there is no one better than you."

"I am honored," Cormac said sincerely, taking the chair beside Caden's.

"And I am grateful you are willing to listen. My grandfather will never understand the horror of what happened or care that this massacre could have been avoided. In fact, I am certain this will be another source of disagreement between us. I am not sure any of the generals will understand, either. How many of them have had real battle experience? How many of them fought against Napoleon and his armies? I mean really engaged the enemy forces in pitched assaults, hand-to-hand battles?"

Cormac nodded. "Many of them were already older when the Peninsular War began. Those generals are dead or quite infirm by now."

"Indeed, the experienced ones are mostly gone. Many of those in charge at present are just playing at being commanders. They have never set foot on a real battlefield or put their studies of the great ancient battles or tactics used by legendary conquerors to actual use. Nor do they understand the terrain or the local customs and conflicts in the countries where we have expanded our influence. Who are our friends? Who are our enemies? Why are we there in the first place?"

"It is all very different now," Cormac agreed. "Back at the height of Napoleon's power, many noblemen joined the fray. We fought in Spain. We fought in France and throughout Europe. Our enemies were familiar. We were soldiers fighting for a cause we believed in, fighting to protect our country from invasion. Our generals were not merely chess players moving men around the board as though they were mere pawns to be sacrificed. But now, everything is different."

"This is why our system must change. It is important that our very best soldiers can climb through the ranks and succeed on merit rather than on family titles or connections. Promotions ought to be based on battle experience, on military cleverness, and a nimbleness in managing our newest challenges."

"The old-timers won't like change."

Caden nodded. "But it is coming whether they like it or not. We need good men like you and the Duke of Malvern to take an active role in our military readiness. I don't mean returning to a frontline battlefield, but your understanding of strategy is invaluable at the top political and military levels. No one can object to this, for you are among the best examples of merit, despite holding family titles. My goal is not to unseat the old guard, for I would never win that argument. I just want to see new blood injected into those top ranks. Men who can adapt to our changing role in the world. As you said, with Napoleon vanquished, we are no longer fighting to save England from invasion. In many instances, we are now viewed as the invader."

Cormac listened as Caden spoke, his expression unreadable. Perhaps he now saw him as an upstart who had to be stopped, but Caden did not think so. The man was too smart and had seen enough battles to know something had to be done.

"We are sent to these faraway lands for profit and conquest," Caden continued. "There is often no formal declaration of war because they were never going to sail to England and attack us in the first place. They are not Vikings or Norman conquerors. In truth, in many of these places, the people have never even heard of England."

"But we send our soldiers anyway in order to claim dominion over their lands," Cormac remarked.

"Perhaps it is just in the nature of man never to be complacent. We have looted and pillaged each other for centuries. But the men put in charge now are different." Caden raked a hand through his hair, now agitated at the thought of men like Fulke in positions of power. "Perhaps I am wrong and they are no different than they have always been. Brutal. Intolerant. Greedy. More interested in lining their pockets than looking out for Crown interests."

Cormac shifted in his chair and leaned forward to regard Caden solemnly. "Tell me what happened to you, son. I can see you are in turmoil over it."

"It isn't about what happened to me." Caden took a deep breath and tried to keep his hands from shaking, as they often did whenever he relived that incident. "It is about all the men who rode into that Ashanti village with me and never returned. Not one of them survived."

His anguish was still raw and the memories still too vivid.

Cormac said nothing, but Caden knew he understood the devastation of those heavy losses. Before him was a man who had endured brutal winters, harsh rains, disease, lack of decent food. He had seen blood spilled. He had killed and seen men killed all around him. He had lost his arm defending his country.

Even so, Caden did not know if Cormac had ever been through a massacre. "We did not need to ride into Ashanti territory at all. The Ashanti were not denying mineral contracts to the Crown, nor were they refusing to export their cocoa. Quite the opposite—they were eager to do business with the British."

"What happened to change that?"

"That deceitful arse, Governor Fulke. He was there to line his pockets and enrich himself and his friends. He was the Crown representative, but he did not give a damn about any interests other than his own. He insulted the chieftains. Made unreasonable demands. Stirred up trouble in the hope of fabricating a reason to seize the Ashanti mines and farms. He wanted to hand them over to the men who had bribed him…my grandfather included."

"Senseless," Cormac muttered.

"Venal, cruel. He had to know this hatred he was stirring up would end with men being killed. Indeed, he knew it and sent us off anyway. To this day, I rack my brain wondering what I could have done differently. We were riding into a massacre. Fulke knew it, and had given us false information about the strength of the Ashanti forces awaiting us. I should have known better than to trust him."

"He was supposed to be on your side," Cormac said.

"Fulke was ever only on the side of Fulke. He simply did not care about anyone else. In hindsight, it is easy to see what he hoped for…a bloodbath. This way, he could further his own selfish aims by showing the Ashanti to be murderous savages. Not that I am absolving them either. They did not just kill my men, they…"

Caden broke off, appalled to realize his tears were flowing.

He buried his face in his hands and tried to compose himself. He was not embarrassed about his tears, for he trusted Cormac to understand exactly what he was feeling and respect it. Still, it wounded his pride to be sitting here and crying like an infant.

Cormac watched him quietly, not a hint of mockery on his face.

As the tears continued to fall, Caden saw the compassion in Cormac's eyes and the patience in his expression. The dam that had been holding back his anguish now burst, and all his pain came flooding out. "They mutilated the bodies of my men, obviously intending to show their disrespect of Fulke. But these were *my* men. They were good and honorable. I tried to stop the Ashanti. Finally, their chieftain put a halt to the carnage. But it was too late. There were no survivors…just me."

"Why did they not kill you, Caden? There had to be a reason they spared your life."

He nodded, using the sleeve of his uniform jacket to dry the last of his tears. "It was because of an incident several weeks earlier. Fulke, that bastard, had taken on mercenary soldiers as his private guards because he knew those of us in the Royal Marines hated him and would not do his dirty dealings. Some of those mercenaries were in the village one day, bored and drunk. They attacked a group of women and children, dragged them behind their saloon, and meant to have their way with them…even the little girls. Sick bastards. I saw what was happening and immediately put a stop to it."

"You alone?"

Caden nodded. "Yes. I used a simple military tactic."

"What was that?"

"I put a pistol to their leader's head and threatened to blow his brains out if he did not call off his men at once. Drunk as those mercenaries were, they were not going to mess with me, commander of the local British forces."

"Impressive."

Caden snorted. "No, just lucky. Any one of them could have blown my brains out and Fulke would have covered it up for them. But they were too drunk to think of it. Since their leader wanted to keep his brains intact, he ordered his men to put down their weapons. They backed off, and I escorted the women back to their homes. I apologized for the actions of Fulke's mercenaries. As it turned out, one of those women was the chieftain's wife. Two of the children, both of them little girls, were his as well."

"And this is what saved you?"

Caden nodded. "I did not realize it at first. I could not understand why they killed men all around me, but left me alive. They cracked my skull open. They shot me in the leg. They broke my ribs and wrist. I did not think I was that hard to kill. They could have put a spear through my heart, for by that time I was the only man left standing."

Cormac continued to listen attentively.

"I thought perhaps they wanted me to report back to that rat, Governor Fulke, how fierce the Ashanti fighters were and how we would all die if we ever went against them again. But it wasn't that at all. It was only because I had saved the lives of his wife and children."

"Your humanity saved your life," Cormac murmured.

"But it only saved *my* life. Not that of my men. And that spawn of Satan, Fulke, is still there to sow discord and enrich himself. Do you think my grandfather or those generals are going to let me talk about that? How fast do you think they will turn on me and shut me down? Their hero," Caden said bitterly. "What a jest. I am nothing more than their puppet."

"You are no man's puppet," Cormac said with surprising fervor. "This is what has them so scared. They know they cannot control you. The Duke of Malvern will be back home soon. This incident and the issues raised are something he and I can bring forward in the House of Lords. We'll go to London, seek an audience with His Majesty."

"No. Getting Ella's family involved is exactly what I do not want have happen."

"We are grown men and can make our own choices, Caden. Do you think to take them all on by yourself? Why? There are others who believe as you do and are willing to help you bring this change about. I am not only referring to me and Cain." Cormac grinned. "As for our changing times, Ella told me about your helper, Elmer Angel. So you know his cousins have married high-ranking peers. Lord help us, but this country could soon be governed by Angel offspring. Although that is probably not a bad thing. They are so damn cheerful."

Caden managed a smile. "Elmer certainly is. He greets each day with such enthusiasm."

"My point is, his cousin Cara is married to the Duke of Strathmore, and Brenna is married to the Duke of Claymore. This is just the sort of battle these dukes will gladly take on. I know this because it is something we have already discussed over after-dinner port. By the end of today, I can guarantee you will have three dukes, a marquess, an earl, and a viscount rallying to your cause."

Caden eyed him dubiously.

"There are more who will join us. Not only will we have Fulke removed, but we will force a review of our foreign policies regarding such appointments. I am not talking about our withdrawing from the world around us, of course. We cannot forsake our leadership role. But we can take a moral stand on how we deal with our territorial goals. It is something argued often enough in the House of Lords. We abolished slavery in England, but have done nothing so far about it in our colonial territories. Why is that? Do we not have an obligation to apply our morality equally?"

Caden had not realized the extent of the discontent. He had merely assumed all peers, especially those all-powerful dukes, felt as his grandfather did. But he was clearly wrong about this.

Cormac now had several ideas whirling in his head. "Caden, write out a list of the military needs that require addressing. Include your concerns about men like Fulke, how they are assigned to their posts, their lack of training, and their betrayal of the Crown interests. You will gain royal support if you do not blame the Crown for the venal actions of these government appointees. Make the king out to be as much a victim as your men were."

Caden frowned. "I am no political animal."

"Yes, you are. The choice has already been made for you. I can assure you, this massacre has reached the king's ears. The generals are scrambling to figure out how to protect their own hides. This is why they are so desperate to get information out of you. They may have blundered in declaring you a hero— although it seems to me you deserve this honor, and it was too obvious even for those fools to deny. They have given you that mantle and are now stuck with their declaration. Take full advantage. You have them by their nut casings. Take charge of the situation and have them do your bidding."

In truth, Caden was ready for this.

The ache he felt for the loss of his men would never go away, but he could turn the tragic incident into a lesson for the future and save the lives of others. Fionn had told him this earlier, and now he was hearing it again.

Not that Caden believed for a moment he could change the world entirely. If anything, the good he did would only be short-lived, for men had been finding reasons to fight each other and betray each other for thousands of years, and this was never going to change.

But even small victories had far-reaching effect sometimes.

"I'll give thought to all you've said," Caden assured Cormac. "Will you be at the assembly ball tomorrow?"

"Yes—not that it is my choice. But Ella and Imogen enjoy dancing, and Phoebe insists we attend as their chaperones."

"Good. I will be there, too. Do you mind if we speak more about this tomorrow night?"

"You really plan to attend?" Cormac frowned. "Are you in any shape to dance? I noticed your limping, and you winced every time you sat down or rose."

"That is because I am an idiot and overdid it today. Avenger is an excellent jumper, and we took several high fences on our ride to the pirate cave."

"And you just getting over broken ribs?" Cormac shook his head and laughed heartily. "Lord, I knew I liked you. That is exactly the stupid sort of thing I would do. Fine, I'll see you there. Anything else you wish to discuss before I have my carriage brought around to return you to the hospital?"

"Such as Ella, you mean?" Caden wasn't ready to talk about her yet.

"You mentioned her. I did not. However, now that you have brought her up, care to tell me what your intentions are toward her?"

"No, I have no wish to discuss her. And before you punch me, just know that my feelings for her are honorable. She is a treasure—how can anyone not see this? But I am not going to offer for her now. I've given it a lot of thought, gone back and forth about it. In truth, agonized about it. But my grandfather is a formidable man and has powerful friends, some of them quite nasty. I must take him and his friends on alone, especially as matters get ugly, as I am sure they will. Ella understands this."

"You are doing it again, putting the entire weight of a problem on your shoulders. Do not mistake her quiet nature for lack of strength."

Caden rose. "Duly noted, but I am not going to see her reputation torn to shreds by my ruthless grandfather and his confederates who see her as the way to weaken me. I may decide to accept your help. I certainly will seek more of your guidance. But I will never put Ella at risk. *Never.* So, if you wish for an explanation of our situation, then here it is. I have no present plans to court her. I have no present plans to offer for her hand in marriage. It is the only way I know how to protect her...even if it breaks her heart and mine."

Cormac rose as well. "All right, Caden. Fair enough. I'll have my driver take you home."

"I appreciate your listening to me spill my guts, but I would ask that you keep what I have said among the men only. I expect the women will learn of it eventually, but I cannot talk about this with Ella, and she will press me about it when she hears."

"I will keep your confidence, but why hide it? The newspapers are going to report every word you utter. The truth is going to come out soon enough anyway."

He nodded. "Yes, certainly once I am on my caged monkey tour."

Cormac sighed. "Caden, you are a hero. People need to see you and be inspired by you. Keep that in mind. Act as though you believe in this hero tour. Your attitude is going to guide theirs."

Caden shrugged. "Everyone makes too much of my importance. But my concern is for Ella. She will never move on if she hears about the massacre now. She will pledge her heart to me, and I do not have the desire or the strength to refuse her. However, it is the worst thing I can do."

Cormac shook his head. "I think it is already too late for that. She is going to pledge her heart to you no matter what you do or say."

"But I will not be here to pledge mine back."

"And you think that makes a difference?"

"I don't know. I hope so. I don't know how else to protect her."

Chapter Ten

CADEN WAS IN pain the following day.

He had overdone it badly yesterday, and now every bone in his body ached. Ribs. Leg. Wrist. Even his head throbbed at the spot where his skull had been struck during that terrible battle. Not even Elmer's boundless cheer could get him moving.

"No exercises today, Elmer," he said with a groan, and tucked the covers around his body.

The lad set down the breakfast tray he had carried in. "Are you feeling ill, my lord? Should I summon the doctor?"

"No, I'm just spent from yesterday's outing."

Elmer began to move about the room, drawing aside the curtains and opening the window to allow in the warm sea air. "Does this mean you will not attend tonight's assembly ball at the Kestrel Inn?"

"I still plan to go to that. What did you bring me for breakfast?"

"The usual, eggs and sausages." He brought the tray closer and helped Caden to sit up. "You still have your appetite. That's a good sign."

Caden hoped so.

He wanted to see Ella tonight. It had been a little over a year since they had shared that supper dance. He wanted to waltz with her again, hold her in his arms before he left Moonstone Landing for good.

Yes, he needed to dance with her and kiss her.

Well, he had gotten his kiss yesterday. The dance was not so important, he supposed. They could sit together and talk.

He shoveled the eggs into his mouth, for he was surprisingly hungry.

"My lord, what's this?" Elmer unfurled the sketch Imogen had given him. "Oh my. Did Lady Imogen draw this? It is brilliant."

Blast.

Caden hadn't meant for anyone to see it. The boy was like a little squirrel, always scampering about, digging into his belongings and setting things in order. "Yes, she's very talented."

Elmer nodded. "She certainly captured the essence of you and Lady Ella. I knew you liked her."

"I like lots of ladies."

"No, you don't. You haven't looked at anyone other than her. And now you want to go to the dance at the Kestrel Inn because she will be there. You're going to need your sticks if you feel as bad as you look right now."

"Elmer, go away."

"I'll have the doctor look in on you. You might need a bit of laudanum to ease the ache in your bones. Just a little won't hurt you. I'll come back later to help you wash and shave. I came in earlier to take your uniform and have it refreshed."

Caden grunted a thank you, for he did want to look his best tonight.

He finished his breakfast, endured Dr. Hewitt's examination and lecture, and took a little laudanum that knocked him out for several hours. He awoke again around noon and felt well enough to get out of bed. He took up his crutches and made his way over to the window. The sky had been overcast earlier in the day, but appeared clear enough now.

If there was to be any rain, he hoped it would pass quickly, because having everyone arrive soaking wet to the dance at the Kestrel Inn would put a damper on any romantic musings. Not that he had anything in mind beyond a dance—assuming he was able—or a walk in the inn's lovely garden.

As he peered down into the hospital's courtyard, he was surprised to see Ella working on the flowerbeds. This was not her week to tend them, but she did seem to enjoy working in the garden, so he assumed she had taken over Imogen's rotation for the day. Would she come up to see him afterward? He yearned for more time with her but did not want her to see him as he looked now, unwashed and with a day's growth of beard darkening his jaw.

He rubbed a hand over the itchy stubble.

She must have sensed him looking down on her, for she turned suddenly and put her hand over her eyes to shade them as she stared at his window. Then she smiled and waved to him. He acknowledged her, then retreated back to bed.

He smothered his disappointment when Elmer returned a short while later and mentioned Ella had returned to Westgate Hall.

After making himself presentable with Elmer's assistance—perhaps he ought to offer the boy a job as his personal valet and take him along on his tour of England—Caden went to the regular wards and spent time talking to the injured men, some of whom were newly arrived and scared about their fate.

He listened patiently, for had he not unburdened himself last night? Cried tears in front of Ella's uncle. He supposed everyone needed a trustworthy friend in whom to confide their thoughts and fears. Having gone through his own experience, he hoped to help others and be that trusted confidant for them.

The hospital usually quieted by evening, but there was a bit of a stir tonight, since many of the patients were curious to see Caden and the several other officers declared fit enough to attend the dance all dressed up in their military finery. Fionn's wife, Lady Chloe, had come by in their carriage to take Fionn, Caden, and these other officers to the inn.

Caden climbed into the carriage with only the slightest difficulty. But to his dismay, he required assistance stepping down from the carriage. The timing could not have been worse, for Ella had just arrived with Imogen and her aunt and uncle. They were all standing at the entrance to the inn watching him struggle as he attempted to climb down.

Blast.

Some hero he was.

But Ella's smile was genuine as she came over to greet him once both his feet were securely planted on the ground. "I'm so glad you made it, Caden," she said quietly. "I was concerned you might not attend. Elmer told me you had a difficult morning, although it is not surprising after everything we did yesterday."

"I was not that bad," he said, his pride taking charge rather than his common sense. "I saw you tending the flowerbeds earlier."

She nodded. "I was tempted to stop in to see you afterward, but Mr. Hawke came by with his wagon earlier than usual and needed to get back to Moonstone Cottage. I did not wish to delay him."

"Well, you are here now. You look beautiful, Ella." She wore a pearl silk gown and had a strand of tiny pearls beaded through her upswept hair. Her necklace was a simple teardrop pearl that drew his eyes to her slender throat and seemed to point downward like an arrow to her cleavage. It took a monumental effort to draw his gaze away. "Truly beautiful."

This was Ella, understated and elegant.

She blushed at his compliment. "Need I say how magnificent you look? I am sure you will have all the ladies in a swoon."

"Assuming I don't trip over them," he joked, glancing at the crutches that supported him.

He should not have done, but he asked Ella to remain by his side as he moved through the room and greeted her family and many of the local villagers who had approached him on his sojourn into town the other day.

Cormac drew him aside a moment. "Once the dancing gets

underway in earnest, come into the card room. Fionn, Cain, and I want to talk to you."

"The Duke of Malvern is back?"

"Yes, a day early. I told him a little about our discussion. He is eager to hear more. Claymore is going to join us as well. He is also interested."

"All right."

Ella regarded him curiously once her uncle strode off. "I don't know what you said to him, but I haven't seen him this enthused about a cause in quite a while. He is happily settled here, but I think he misses the excitement of London sometimes. Especially those shouting matches in Parliament."

"There will be plenty of those once I am through with my England tour."

"You'll be leaving soon," she said, her voice hardly audible now that the first dance was starting and the musicians struck the lively opening chords.

"Yes, Ella." He was afraid to say anything more to her, for he was already too much involved and needed to break away, at least for these next few months.

He watched the guests in attendance, and noticed Cormac and Phoebe dancing. It amazed him how smoothly Phoebe managed to fill in with a dip or a twirl to make up for the lack of her husband's arm. Fionn was dancing with his wife, his slight limp not noticeable as they moved along the line with the other couples.

Ella pointed out Cain, the Duke of Malvern, and his wife Henley. He was a big bear of a man, and his wife was slender and delicate. The same could be said of Daire, the Duke of Claymore, and his wife Brenna. She was Elmer's cousin. He noticed the Angel resemblance in the brightness of her eyes and curve of her smile.

How would he fit into Moonstone Landing?

Assuming he returned, which he would if Ella was still here. However, she was likely to be back in London by the time his tour was finished. Wherever she was, he wanted to come back for her and seriously court her.

She was right for him. He felt it in his heart.

A gentleman he did not recognize came up to Ella and asked her to dance.

"Oh…" She glanced at Caden.

"I'll be fine on my own," he assured her, although inside he was suddenly that wild ape wanting to toss furniture and punch this stranger.

"Lord Mersey," Ella said, before clearing her throat to regain his attention, which had immediately moved on to what else he might do to this stranger for attempting to take Ella from him, "may I present Lord Fielding, a good friend of the Duke of Malvern."

Caden regarded him closer. "Fielding? Of course! How have you been?"

Lord Fielding was of a similar age to Cormac and his brothers-in-law, which meant he was perhaps ten years older than Caden, and had never been married. Was he interested in Ella? Well, who wasn't? But Fielding was too old for her, at least to Caden's way of thinking.

"The more important question is how have *you* been, Mersey? It is good to see you back home and safe. I hear it is quite volatile where you were serving. Malvern and I are eager to hear more."

Caden did not wish to get into a discussion with him now, but expected Fielding would be joining the men later. He was a sensible man and very much aware of all that went on in London. It would not hurt to have his opinion.

But it did not mean Caden approved of his interest in Ella or believed him in any way suitable for her.

"Well, may I steal the lovely Lady Ella from you for a little while?" Fielding asked, rousing that ape in him again.

Ella tipped her chin up and emitted a soft huff. "Who I dance with is completely up to me. Yes, you may dance with me. Lord

Mersey does not need me to act as nursemaid to him." With that, she placed her arm on Fielding's and turned away from Caden.

He frowned.

Was this what she thought he was asking of her? To stay by him because he needed someone to nurse him? It should have been obvious to her that he enjoyed her company. He particularly liked that they did not have to talk to feel comfortable around each other.

"Ella…"

He must have appeared pathetic, for she sighed and cast him a soft smile. "Do not mind my sharp tongue. I will find you when this dance is over."

Fielding glanced from one to the other and frowned.

Good.

He should have known better than to set his cap for Ella.

The moment she walked away, women began to approach Caden. To his irritation, Lady Dowling was among them. Fortunately, he was able to blame his crutches for his inability to dance with any of them. If he danced with anyone, it was going to be Ella.

Since little remained secret in this village, the ladies knew of his exact injuries, and found it thrilling to be in his presence. He quickly realized the powerful allure of a soldier wounded in battle, especially one who was young and held a title, albeit the courtesy title of Marquess of Mersey. Perhaps this desire to fuss over him was in the nurturing nature of women, although he would not call Lady Dowling particularly nurturing. The woman obviously wanted to displace Ella and be the center of his attention.

That was never going to happen.

He repeated the same stories of his battle wounds, although he did not discuss the battle itself. He spoke of being placed on a Royal Navy frigate that was serving as a hospital ship, and how he almost did not make it home. He embellished the storms at sea. He exaggerated his fever, although he had been in a bad way for most of that trip and could have died.

Lord Fielding escorted Ella back to his side when the dance ended.

Caden noticed her hesitation and immediately drew her into the discussion before she could flit away like the silver dove she was to look for a safe place to land. "Lady Ella has been telling me of the work done for the hospital by the ladies auxiliary," he said. "I understand you all take turns volunteering to read to the injured or help them write letters to their loved ones. You also maintain the hospital gardens. I noticed you, Lady Ella, working there this morning."

"We all do the same," Lady Dowling remarked, "and not just over the summer. Lady Ella will be leaving us soon to return to London and the Marriage Mart. You'll be quite forgotten among her suitors."

Ella arched an eyebrow. "No one forgets Lord Mersey after meeting him. I look forward to sharing a dance with him once he is back in London and able to move around without his crutches. Although he knows I will always welcome his company, with or without those crutches. It is the heart of a man that matters, is it not? And no one has a finer heart than his lordship."

She then went on to tell the ladies how he had rescued a kitten from a roof last year.

Dear heaven.

The ladies were melting.

Caden had spent most of his life as a rude, disdainful arse. He did on occasion aid the weak and helpless, though mostly he did not get himself involved in other people's woes. But Ella was purposely talking him up, and there was something to be said for his laying on the charm. People responded well to him. Of course, the responses would have been different if he looked like an ugly toad and held no title. He knew the ladies considered him good looking.

They listened attentively and were sympathetic to the plight of the returning soldiers. Were they really listening or merely going off on romantic fantasies about him? It did not matter, for some of what he had been saying must have remained in their heads.

Men soon surrounded him, too. He drew them in with talk of the Royal Marines and the role of this special force around the world. However, he was also honest about the monotony and hardship, because it was not a romantic life. If the younger men were to enlist, they had to do it with their eyes open to what they would be facing. In truth, life in the Royal Navy was more lucrative. The navy men, from captain to lowliest cabin boy, shared in the spoils of any enemy ships seized.

He managed a private moment with Ella just before Cormac approached to draw him away. "You were inspiring, Caden," she said with quiet admiration. "You had such an effect on everyone."

He shook his head. "I am one of the densest men ever to exist. I truly had no idea of the strength of my influence over these strangers."

"You are what I would refer to as the full package. Handsome, titled, brave, and wounded in battle. You are also eloquent and genuinely passionate about your cause. The only way you can ruin it for yourself is to appear insincere."

"That will never happen."

"I know. Whatever happened during your last battle eats at your soul."

"As it will continue to do until England gets rid of men like Fulke. We need to overhaul the powers and standards of conduct for these governors. More important, we can never allow anyone outside of our military ranks to control the scouting reports and other reconnaissance information, or make decisions on what, whom, and when we are to attack."

Ella listened to him, gazing at him with that fairy starlight in her eyes. "Uncle Cormac is waving you over. Speak to him and the other lords as you just did with me, and you shall have your way in Parliament."

He grinned. "It is quite a strange feeling for me to engage

with people instead of pushing them away."

"Everyone will love you, Caden. I haven't a doubt."

"And you, Ella?"

"I think you will forget me very quickly."

"You are wrong about that. You know it isn't true."

She cast him a mirthless smile. "Time will tell, won't it?"

He was frustrated, wanting to say more to her. But the others were waiting, and he did not wish to irritate them before he had ever said a word to them. "Save a dance for me. The supper dance."

She laughed, this time with genuine cheer. "There is no supper dance at these local assemblies. We are not formal here. This is no London ball."

"Well, save *something* for me."

"All right." She went off to find Imogen and Aunt Phoebe.

Caden watched her make her way through the crowd, her every movement graceful as she flitted from friend to friend to greet them. The pearl silk of her gown was iridescent under the glow of candlelight and swirled sensually around her body. Yes, this was what she was…a beautiful bird, a silver dove.

His dove.

Chapter Eleven

Ella had given up hope she would see Caden before the assembly ball ended. The men in her family and several others were still engaged in deep and lively conversation with him, and she dared not interrupt.

As the night wore on and the crowd began to thin, Ella walked out into the inn's garden on her own. She stayed in full view of the assembly room, and her aunt and Imogen knew exactly where she was. But she needed to get out of that hot room filled with the pungent aromas of spilled drinks, overheated bodies, and stale perfume.

She wanted to breathe in Caden's sandalwood scent.

This would not happen tonight.

Did it really matter? He was back on his crutches and would be too off-balance to properly dance with her. She doubted he placed as much importance on sharing a dance with her, although it must have meant a little to him, since he was the one who suggested it.

But his discussion with the men was obviously of far more importance.

She put her hopes on seeing him tomorrow at the hospital during her usual afternoon visit. "But everything is changing," she whispered.

She had seen him engaging with strangers and how easily he

had them eating out of his hand. He was now a man with a purpose. This was healthier for him because it eased his torment, and Caden was indeed a tormented man.

Assuming the mantle of everyone's hero was the perfect role for him and the way to heal his heart. But it also meant she would be pushed aside for several months, perhaps longer.

This hurt. She could not deny it.

She took a deep breath to calm herself.

The air was cool and increasingly damp this evening, heavy with the scent of the sea. She noticed dew gathering on the flowers as a light mist crept in, a sign they would have rain tomorrow. Torchlights flickered around her, bathing the garden in golden light.

Ella was lost in her thoughts, staring up at the moon now barely visible through the gathering haze of clouds, and did not hear Caden when he came up to her. "There you are," he said, his voice deep and resonant, and his eyes as dark and bewitching as the night.

She smiled up at him, trying to appear casual even as her heart was fluttering. "How did your discussion go?"

"Surprisingly well." He propped his crutches against a nearby tree and then settled his large frame on the stone bench beside her. Their shoulders grazed for a moment, the innocent gesture immediately turning her insides soft. "Even Lord Fielding joined us. He and Claymore were quite enthusiastic. Clearly, I have been a political dunce all these years. But no more. I see the effect I have on the villagers, and the commitment stirred in these powerful men."

Ella nodded. "I knew you would have support even in the House of Lords."

"What makes me different, Ella? Others have been shouting about these reforms for years with nothing done."

"Because they are not you. Only you have the ability to stir passions. You are the hero everyone has been waiting for, hoping for."

He cast her a rakish grin. "Are you going to tell me again I am the full package?"

She nodded. "As often as you need to hear it, although your head is already quite swelled. Perhaps I ought to remind you, but only sparingly."

He cast her an affectionate smile. "I am going to miss you, Ella."

"No, you will be taken up by your speeches and your admirers and not think of me at all. I will be left behind. Please do not pretend it isn't so."

"I will deny it," he said with a frown. "You know my only hesitation in properly courting you is out of concern for you."

"No, Caden. If you were truly in love with me, there would be no question of where I stand with you. I would be by your side, and this is where you would always want me to be. But you have made up reasons why we should not be together and convinced yourself they are valid."

"You saw Imogen's portrait of us. How can you doubt my feelings for you?"

"I doubt because *you* still doubt. Perhaps you do love me, but you are not yet ready to admit it to yourself or to me." She knew she was making him angry, but this was the reality of their situation, and she was not going to allow him to get away with those convenient excuses to absolve himself of his inability to commit his heart to her.

He emitted a low growl. "Walk to the harbor with me. It is not far. What is the lore? Those moonstones shine where there is true love?"

"They shine on a full moon. It is not that yet. Even if it were, there is fog on the water tonight. We would never see the moonstones. Do not make this more difficult, Caden. You have your purpose. You want to be free to do whatever you must. I am not going to hold you back. You know where to find me whenever you are ready."

He regarded her as though she had put a knife through his

heart. "I will come for you, Ella."

She emitted a ragged breath. "Don't say that. I am trying to protect my heart, and you keep trying to break down those barriers I have put up. You want to pull me back to you. At the same time, you are pushing me away. Don't confuse me, Caden."

"Those moonstones will shine for us, Ella."

"Not now they won't." She left his side and hurried back indoors before she weakened and pledged to wait for him forever.

"Ella!"

The heartbreak of it was that she *would* wait forever. She loved him, and there could be no other man for her.

But she had her pride and would not force herself on him only to have him feel trapped and chained. In this moment, she was sorry she had ever met him. She was sorry they had shared a supper dance last year and sorry they had shared a kiss.

Two kisses.

She glanced back at him.

Lady Dowling was already by his side and obviously looking to comfort him. Not that Ella was jealous of the woman. But there would be a thousand Lady Dowlings eager to share a night with him. Was he going to be a monk and refuse them all? He was handsome and unattached. He could do whatever he pleased.

Ella walked over to the long tables that held the punch bowls. She poured herself a cup of ratafia punch. It tasted vile, but it suited her temperament at the moment.

How did one recover from a broken heart?

"Lady Ella, you seem overset," Lord Fielding said, regarding her with apparently sincere concern.

"No, I am fine."

"They are about to play a last waltz. Will you dance with me? We can talk while I twirl you around the floor with magnificent expertise."

She laughed lightly. "All right."

Lord Fielding was a gentleman and much admired by her family. He had never married, and she never understood why. He was handsome, honorable, wealthy, titled, and did not appear to have any of the sort of vices that ruined a marriage.

"May I ask you a question that is terribly impolite and intrusive of your privacy?"

He nodded as he led her to the circle of dancers and put his arm around her to begin the waltz. "When you put it that way, how can I say no? Go ahead, ask it."

"Why have you never married?"

"That, my sweet and lovely Ella, would take an hour to answer. But I think the real question you are asking is whether you should wait for Lord Mersey to come around and ask you to marry him. Do you want me to answer that one?"

Chapter Twelve

CADEN STARED OUT his window as rain struck the panes and fog obscured his view of the beautiful cove and its sparkling waters. The weather suited his foul temperament. Three days had passed since the assembly ball at the Kestrel Inn, and Ella had not come by to see him in all that time.

He was going out of his mind.

Nothing distracted him, not the grueling exercises that had Dr. Hewitt angrily telling him to take it easy or he was going to rip his stitches and damage his healing bones. Nor could hours spent with the wounded soldiers in the common wards take his mind off her. He also spent hours contemplating the speeches he would give while on his tour, but those thoughts always brought him back to Ella and the need to keep her out of the ugly battles certain to arise between his grandfather and him—not to mention those in the House of Lords who were lining their pockets along with his grandfather.

Lining their pockets with the blood of soldiers.

No matter what he did to occupy his mind, everything came back to Ella and how much he wanted her and missed her.

He turned at the sound of a knock at his open door, hoping it would be her. Instead, the hospital's commander, Major Brennan, strode in. "Ah, Fionn. What can I do for you?"

The major held out an envelope. "I just received this missive from your grandfather."

Caden arched an eyebrow. "He wrote to you and not me?"

Fionn nodded. "He already knows you are going to tell him to go to hell, so he thought to reason with me instead. He's coming here with a contingent of generals, government officials, and newspaper reporters. They'll be arriving tomorrow."

"Tomorrow?"

Bollocks.

This was not good. Caden still had unfinished business with Ella. Although he had no idea what he was going to say to her.

"Yes. I should have received this letter sooner, but the official pouch it was sent in somehow got delayed. It only reached me this morning. Perhaps it is better this way. Gives you less time to stew about it. Need I remind you how important it is for you to behave like a hero?"

"You mean, be reasonable?" Caden snorted. "No, I do not need the reminder. Where is Ella? Why has she not come to the hospital these past few days?"

"She has come by every day."

"What?"

"You heard me. She stops by here every day but does not want to see you. Or maybe she was hoping you would come in search of her, or bother to ask about her…which you did not."

"*Bollocks.* Now she must hate me."

Fionn sighed. "She doesn't hate you."

"But she is mightily disappointed in me." Caden crossed to the corner where he had left his crutches leaning against the wall. "I just assumed she would stay home because the weather has been so foul these past few days. Besides, I am asking about her now, aren't I? And why did Elmer not tell me? That boy blabs about everything."

"Well, it is too late now. She has returned to Westgate Hall already."

"Will she be here tomorrow?" Caden felt so frustrated—his own fault for waiting too long to ask about her. Another bloody misstep when dealing with Ella. How hurt she must be, thinking she was not in his thoughts at all when he could think of nothing but her to the point of obsession.

"Yes, to tend the garden. However, she can do little with the constant rain we've been having, so she spends extra time with the injured soldiers instead."

"So do I. Why haven't I seen her?"

Fionn shrugged. "She comes by early and leaves early."

"To purposely avoid me. She knows mornings are when I do my exercise regimen," Caden muttered, raking a hand through his hair.

He was the one at fault, for he could have asked anyone about her. He could have sent word to her at Westgate Hall. For all the thinking and writing he had done these past few days, he had not even bothered to write her a quick note.

Perhaps she was right about him, that he did not care for her as much as he claimed. But his heart immediately rebelled at the notion.

No, he loved her.

Truly and desperately.

But he had been too caught up in himself and what he needed to do, so he had ignored her feelings. "I must talk to Ella before my grandfather and his entourage show up." He still needed his crutches and could not simply walk over to Westgate Hall. "Can I borrow a horse?"

"No. First of all, I have no idea whether Ella returned directly home. She could be anywhere in town or off at Moonstone Cottage or St. Austell Grange. Second, the weather is miserable, and I will not have you running around in it just when you need to be at your fittest to undertake your tour."

"And what is your third reason? You are obviously not through giving me a piece of your mind."

"Ella is my third reason. You have already done a thorough job of breaking her heart." Fionn held up a hand when Caden meant to protest. "I know you did not do this on purpose. You made her no promises—she was quite adamant in defending you on this point. But it changes nothing. You need to leave her alone. Do not speak to her. Do not approach her unless it is to make that commitment and offer her marriage."

He knew Fionn was right.

So he spent the day brooding and scowling at everyone, even snapping at poor Elmer, who had the kindest soul of any person Caden had ever met.

His dreams were particularly fierce and unsettled that night.

Come morning, the sky was finally clear of those dark gray clouds. The sun shone, putting the sparkle back in the water. The oppressively wet air they had all had to endure these past few days was finally drying out.

Elmer came bounding in with his usual vigor. "Good morning, my lord."

"Morning, Elmer. Why did you not tell me Lady Ella had been coming here every day?"

The boy shrugged. "You did not ask me, my lord. Was it my place to mention it?"

"No, sorry. Is she here now?"

"No, it's much too early," he said with a shake of his head. "I expect she is just waking up, but she'll be along later."

Caden sighed. "Let's get to my exercises."

"Not today, my lord. I have been instructed to get you properly groomed for the guests you are to receive today." Elmer held up a strop and razor blade. "Shall we get to it, my lord? I have no idea when they will arrive, and you must look your best."

"All right. Elmer, you know I am going to be in need of a valet during my travels. Do you think your father would allow you to come with me on my tour?"

"No, m'lord. I am still in school. Not that it does me any good, but every once in a while, something sinks in. Besides, I am going to take over as constable from my father someday. If I leave with you now, he'll think I do not want the position or do not care to live in Moonstone Landing."

"I see."

"My place is here—at the hospital, that is. Those injured men are in desperate need of my assistance. All I would do for you is help you wash and shave. Now that you are mostly healed, you really don't need me for that. And I wouldn't know how to take care of your clothes. The hospital laundresses have been doing this for you all these weeks. I merely hand your clothes over to them. So, you see, I would not be a very good valet."

Caden smiled at him. "Elmer, I think you are going to be excellent at anything you do. All right, help me get ready now."

It was a good thing Fionn had sent Elmer earlier than usual. Caden was in his dress uniform, his boots shined to a bright polish, medals pinned to his jacket, and crutches propped beside his bed, when he heard a flurry of activity. He took his crutches, then considered setting them aside again. He could do without them…mostly. But he also wanted to remind everyone that he had been badly injured and was still recovering.

Better keep them. All part of the hero role he was undertaking.

Elmer was just gathering his nightshirt and washcloths when Caden's grandfather barged into his room. "Get out," he said to the boy, growling his order with typical, disdainful authority.

Oh, how Caden hated that superior tone.

He stared at the man he resembled more than he cared to admit. They had the same dark eyes. His grandfather's once-dark hair was now all gray, but he still had a full head of it. Caden was taller and broader in the shoulders, but his grandfather was still a vigorous man who held himself proudly.

"Thank you, Elmer," Caden said, knowing it would rile his grandfather, who believed servants were never to be thanked.

"You are most welcome, my lord," the boy replied as he scampered out of the room.

His grandfather waited until Elmer was out of sight to return his attention to Caden. "I see you haven't changed. Still willful and insolent."

Caden wanted to toss his crutches aside and stare down the man, show him he was no invalid and could stand on his own two feet. But that would completely ruin the image he needed to craft, not to mention he was still too unsteady on his feet. "You are wrong, Your Grace. I have changed most profoundly. Watching men die all around me, seeing them cut open and bleeding, is indelibly etched in my memory. Not that you care or will ever admit responsibility for your role. But make no mistake, *you* did this to them. You and the other greedy pigs feeding at the trough."

"Is this the welcome I am to receive from you? Insults and blame? How dare you!" His grandfather struck him with enough force to knock a weaker man over, but Caden kept a firm grip on his crutches and maintained his balance. He had taken much harder blows in battle, and knew his grandfather had not intended to lash out as hard as he had. The old man's ring had caught on his lip and cut it.

"Ah, I do love these warm family reunions," he said as little jolts of pain shot through his head to the spot where his skull had been crushed during the Ashanti battle. He momentarily saw stars before his eyes, but he would die before admitting to any pain.

Nor would he ever strike his grandfather, even if the old goat deserved it.

"Hit me all you want, but you cannot deny your responsibility for what happened. You and your business associates put Fulke in as governor to ensure your seizure of those gold mines. My regiment was wiped out because of your actions. Does it bother you at all that I narrowly escaped death? Or is your gold more important to you than your heir? If you think I am going to keep quiet about what happened out there, then you had better think again."

"Ungrateful bastard! I gave you everything."

He raised his hand and was about to strike Caden again when

a whirlwind with a broom raced in and began to smack the duke in the backside with it. Caden stifled a burst of laughter as he watched Ella. "Out, you old devil! Don't you dare touch any of our wounded soldiers!"

She gave his grandfather another solid whack to his backside.

"How dare you! I am the Duke of Seaton!" he roared.

Ella glowered at him. "And I am *Lady* Ella Stockwell. I will crack this broom over your head if you dare raise a hand to anyone in this hospital. Out! Out of this room at once!"

"Major Brennan will hear of this!"

She whacked him again on the backside. "And so will the newspaper reporters, I shall guarantee you that!"

Caden loved her—truly, he did.

He had been trying to keep her out of harm's way, and here she was leaping in with both feet, with a broom and an impudent mouth that he had not kissed often enough—but he would remedy that as soon as his tour was over.

She managed to chase his stunned grandfather out of the room and down the hall. Caden wasn't sure whether that was a smart idea, but he could no longer contain his laughter. Another man had been standing outside the door, one of the duke's entourage for certain. He was too slickly dressed for Moonstone Landing.

Who was he, exactly? Caden had never set eyes on this man before.

The slick gentleman walked in and offered Caden a handkerchief to wipe the blood off his mouth. "James Stafford, chief reporter for the *London Chronicler*. Don't worry about Lady Ella. He won't dare strike her, not while Major Brennan and five army generals are watching him. Not to mention the other reporters assigned to this story. Wouldn't look too good for him if the first headline is about him beating a young woman."

Caden nodded. Appearances were important to his grandfather.

"Every newspaper in London is eager to get your story, Lord

Mersey," Stafford continued.

"I am eager to tell it, not for myself but for the men who died. Their voices are silenced forever, so it falls on me to tell their stories, doesn't it?" Caden studied the man, who was obviously intelligent but not necessarily trustworthy. "Any other reporters follow you here?"

"No, they are all busy listening to Major Brennan as he leads them through the hospital wards. Your grandfather muttered some nonsense about being fatigued. I knew he was up to something and followed him. That man can outrun me, he is so fit. I fell back as the others moved on, and then found my way here. I suspected he would try to see you before the rest of us did. Not quite a tearful family reunion, was it? I did not expect him to hit you. Has he done it often before?"

"None of your business."

"Ah, you are a loyal fellow. Are you going to shield him from us?" Stafford asked.

"As to private matters between him and me, yes. As to what happened to my regiment in West Africa, no. Shall we join the others?"

"I was hoping for a little more information from you, perhaps an exclusive story."

"Maybe, Mr. Stafford. You'll have to earn my trust first."

"How about if I start now? I saw the way you were looking at Lady Ella. But I shall keep quiet about her for the moment. You needn't worry that I will include her in my story."

Caden's expression hardened. "You shall keep quiet about her now and forever. There is no negotiation on that. I don't know what you think you saw, but let me just say that all the women in Moonstone Landing are remarkable. Intelligent, talented, compassionate. You will not find better in all of England."

"But Lady Ella is not from Moonstone Landing. She is a *ton* diamond, raised in London. She made quite an impression on everyone last year. Obviously, she has made an impression on you. The public loves a romance. They would eat up one between England's hero and a diamond like her. We could not print enough newspapers—they would sell out too fast."

"Mr. Stafford, if there is a shred of decency in you, then do not print a word about Lady Ella. You saw what my grandfather did to me within five minutes of our heartwarming reunion. What do you think he and his business associates will do to her reputation the moment they decide to bring me down because I am damaging their interests?"

"Are you saying you intend to damage their interests?"

"I intend to shed light on government policies that are badly conceived and need to be addressed."

"Lord Mersey, put that way, you will have everyone snoring within five minutes of your getting started."

"Write it up however you wish," Caden said, truly hating the politics of it all. "Their policies killed my men, so if it grabs everyone's interest to call me an avenger, then do so. I want those culpable brought down. Say what you will about me, but do not let them hurt Lady Ella."

"You know, I did not get where I am by being decent."

"Try it. You might find it refreshing."

"Perhaps I will," Stafford said, laughing softly. "If I do, would you give me the exclusive story on how you managed to survive when all around you perished? You do not strike me as a coward who stands in the background and hides while your men take up the fight."

Caden wanted to grab the man and slam his head against the wall. Him, a coward?

"Battlefield commanders do not lead from the rear," he said with barely leashed rage. "Anyone who has ever fought alongside me will tell you I never ask more of my men than I am willing to give. Insult me like that again and I will knock your teeth out."

"Like your grandfather tried to do to you?"

"No, not like my grandfather. He would have already knocked out all your teeth." Caden walked out to find the generals and others in the entourage. Were all the reporters going to be as base as this fellow?

So much for his "I am a *bloody* hero" tour. It was going to completely implode before the day was out.

Stafford scurried after him, having to run to keep up, even though Caden was using his crutches. "Lord Mersey, I owe you an apology. It is my way to poke and prod, ruffle feathers and get enraged responses. This is how I get honest answers. The truth has a way of coming out in anger. But I've given you the wrong impression of me. I do respect decency and valor, and may I say, you reek of those traits. Your Lady Ella is safe from the ravages of my reporting. She will not be mentioned by me."

Caden was not sure he believed the man, but he was willing to give him the benefit of the doubt. "Thank you, Mr. Stafford."

They spotted Caden's grandfather and his entourage being escorted through the last of the wards by Major Brennan. As Caden strode in, the soldiers called out to him and in turn saluted him. Then one of them rose from his sickbed and began to clap, soon followed by others, until all the soldiers were applauding for him. Those able to get out of bed did so and stood at attention.

Caden was taken aback. Had someone orchestrated this little scene?

But he saw the truth in the eyes of those men and knew it had not been planned. It was just something that sprang from their hearts.

Instead of heading to the generals, he stopped by the bed of each man and acknowledged their compliments. The reporters among the group were scribbling furiously in their notepads. The generals and his grandfather did not know what to make of him.

They had come up with this bright idea of hailing him as a hero, but it had to be obvious they were not in control of him, or the public's response. Dealing with the generals was going to be easy, he now realized. However, because he truly was politically inept, it had taken him a while to figure out they were his natural allies, military men who needed to regain control of operations from the hands of politicians.

Of course, dealing with the politicians would be far more difficult. They were not about to concede their power, especially when many of them had their hands in the pie and were profiting from whatever bad rules and unworkable processes they had put in place.

Lord help him, he was not the right man for this task. How could he be? He had no tact or finesse.

He knew about tactical assaults and outflanking the enemy. But he also understood how easily the enemy could outflank him, starting with twisting the arms of these very reporters who thought to laud him as the next Wellington. But threats from a few powerful businessmen and government officials would have their editors slashing their stories and looking for all the dirt they could dig up on him.

Stafford was once again studying him closely.

Bollocks.

Were they all going to be sniffing up his arse like dogs on the scent?

His grandfather was standing in front of the delegation as Caden finished speaking to the wounded men and approached his visitors. Several ladies had been volunteering to read or write letters, but they had scooted off to the side while the adoring scene played out among the soldiers. The ladies were still off in a corner, Ella among them.

"Shall we try this again, Your Grace?" Caden said, hoping this time his grandfather's greeting would not end with punches thrown.

"Did you set up that mawkish scene just for me?"

Caden sighed, wishing his grandfather would stop being an arse for once. But that was hoping for too much. "Lying and scheming is not my style. Do not insult these men who risked their lives for England and will now be discarded by men like you because they have outlived their usefulness. Unlike the London politicians neatly tucked in your pocket, they cannot be bribed."

The generals gasped. The reporters once again scribbled

notes furiously. Fionn groaned.

Caden was not about to back down.

After glaring at him, the duke turned his gaze on Ella, who was still in the corner with the other ladies, broom in hand.

She smiled and irreverently tipped her broom at him.

Was it any wonder Caden loved her?

And was it also not eminently clear he had to protect her? His grandfather was not the sort to let insults slide, even if he was completely at fault and had brought the misery on himself. As the tour progressed from town to town, Caden hoped the old man would forget about Ella. Yes, she needed to become just a minor nuisance and not worth his trouble.

Unlike the other reporters, Stafford hadn't written down a bloody thing. What was he going to report?

Could he trust this man not to hurt Ella?

Chapter Thirteen

"CADEN WAS RIGHT to keep you at arm's length, Ella," Cormac said as he paced the carpet in front of her later that evening. They were in his study at Westgate Hall, now joined by Fionn and Cain, who had come over for the sole purpose of discussing her unladylike behavior at the hospital this morning.

Well, *discuss* was not the right word.

They lectured her. Admonished her. Had the gall to berate her.

After ten minutes of droning on about the ills of her impertinence, they went off in a corner to quietly talk among themselves. They were discussing what, if anything, was to be done with her. She was too old to be spanked and sent up to her room without supper. Besides, they all knew Imogen, her ever-loyal sister, would sneak a king's banquet up to her, so depriving her of food was never going to work.

Not that they ever seriously contemplated it.

For all their frowns and glowers, they were too soft-hearted to seriously punish her. In fact, they were probably going to dismiss her without any punishment at all.

But they felt she needed a bit more lecturing.

She waited patiently for them to finish before taking her turn.

"The Duke of Seaton *hit* his grandson," she argued, having

had enough of being told what to do. "Not a gentle slap, either. Closer to a *punch* in the face." She tipped her chin up in indignation. "Was I to let that ogre get away with it?"

"Yes," Cain said, emphasizing his response with a bearlike growl. "Caden is not a defenseless child. Do you have any idea how dangerous it was to get between them?"

"There was no risk to me. Even though Caden was not going to defend himself, he would have protected me to the death if his grandfather attempted to strike me. He is ridiculously honorable that way."

The three of them were groaning again.

"You would have done the same if you were there. Caden was not even trying to protect himself. Who knows what more damage his grandfather might have inflicted if I had not come to his rescue? How can the three of you stand there and frown at me? The duke is the one who needs to be taken to the woodshed and have his bottom spanked."

They struggled not to grin, but Ella knew they were not really furious with her. However, they were very concerned the duke might do something to retaliate for her smacking him on the backside with her broom...repeatedly.

She sighed. "Caden is leaving tomorrow morning and will forget all about me. His grandfather will forget me, too."

"That boy is in love with you, Ella," Fionn said. "I know exactly what he is feeling and how he is struggling, since I went through this same agony with Chloe. He is doing what he thinks is best for you now. We all agree with him. I will admit, I wasn't sure at first. But after meeting the duke, I am on board with his decision."

"And what do your wives say?"

Cormac frowned. "Do you think for a moment Phoebe would not be bursting in here to rail at us if she disagreed with our concerns?"

Ella slumped in her chair.

If the wives agreed, then all hope was lost.

Cormac raked a hand through his hair. "Ella, I wish things were different. Keep faith that he will return for you once his tour is over."

She shook her head. "I will melt away from his memory like snow in springtime. He will be so caught up in his work that he will forget about me. The real challenge for him is in making a change within the House of Lords. Once you lords are in, you are in for life, and your privilege of peerage leaves you practically untouchable. Why would his grandfather and his greedy associates ever agree to change anything? They are going to fight to keep the gold streaming into their pockets."

"We will do what we can to support Caden. He isn't in this battle alone. There are many of us who are incensed by the dirty dealings and corruption that has crept into our politics," Cain said.

"And because I am a mere woman, I will have no role in any of it," Ella muttered. "Soon, I will have no role in his life at all."

Fionn glanced at something on Cormac's desk.

Ella frowned. "What is that?"

"Nothing," Fionn shot back too quickly, so that she knew it was something quite important.

She went over to the desk and immediately recognized the rolled-up sketch paper. She did not need to see it unfurled to know it was the drawing of her and Caden that Imogen had made at the pirate cave. She stared at it, aghast.

Pain tore through her. "He is returning it to Imogen?"

"No, he wanted me to give it to you." Fionn's expression was indulgently sympathetic. "I'm so sorry, Ella. He did not want to keep it with him for fear his grandfather or one of those nosy reporters might see it."

Ella struggled to hold back tears. "So he has nothing of me now. Truly nothing. Not a ribbon. Not a note. Not even my book of poems that he tolerated only to be polite."

Cormac put his arm around her. "He will not forget you, Ella. I can assure you, this is not what men, even wretched ones like me, do. We hold on to your memory. We grasp it with all our heart and etch it into our soul."

"That may have worked for you, but you did not have every woman in England after you, even though you were quite full of yourself and thought you did."

Fionn and Cain burst out laughing.

"Ouch," Cormac said, although he was not really irritated, because he *had* been arrogant and rakish in his younger days. His meeting Phoebe had changed all that, and theirs was an achingly beautiful love match.

"They all want him, Uncle Cormac. At what point is he going to give up and just go along?"

"At no point, if he loves you," Cain replied.

"Well, that is the question, isn't it? How deeply does he love me?"

None of them could assure her with any certainty.

But Lord Fielding had spoken to her about this very thing on the night of the Kestrel Inn assembly ball. He had been staying at the inn, although he was good friends with Cain, and Cain had wanted him to stay with him and Henley at St. Austell Grange. But Lord Fielding enjoyed his privacy. He had come to Moonstone Landing specifically to visit Cain, but preferred to remain on his own in the village itself.

It struck Ella as odd, but perhaps that aloofness and desire for privacy was exactly why he had never married. Nor did he seem the sort to have any unusual preferences that required complete discretion. Uncle Cormac, an utter ape when it came to protecting her and Imogen, would have flung him across the ballroom when seeing her dance with Lord Fielding not once, but twice, if he thought the man less than above reproach.

Her ordeal now over, she went up to her bedchamber.

Imogen was already in the room they shared, obviously waiting for her report. "They just lectured me, Imogen. No punishment."

"Thank goodness." Imogen sat down on her bed and tucked

her legs under her bottom. "Why do you look so forlorn?"

"Because of this." Ella held out the sketch. "Caden gave it to Fionn with instructions to give it to me."

Imogen took it from her hands, unfurled it, and sighed. "I love this portrait of the two of you. I think it is among the best work I have ever done. But you shouldn't be sad, Ella. He wanted you to have it for safekeeping so it would not fall into the wrong hands."

"But he has nothing of me now."

"Oh, I think the memory of you chasing his grandfather around with your broom is embedded forever in his mind."

"Don't you start on me about that." Ella kicked off her slippers and sank onto her own bed. "I was thinking of talking to Lord Fielding. Cain, Fionn, and Uncle Cormac think of us as little girls, so I cannot talk to them about *womanly* feelings."

"I think they would choke and fall to their knees clutching their hearts if we tried," Imogen said with a laugh. "No, we could never talk to them about such things. But why Lord Fielding? Why not Aunt Phoebe? Or Chloe or Henley? I'm sure they will give you excellent advice."

"I will talk to them, too. But I also want a man's point of view. Lord Fielding told me that he never married because the woman he loved had not been available."

"So he never moved on? But he lost out on having a family, finding a good, intelligent woman with whom he could have a happy life."

Ella nodded. "This was precisely his point when talking to me the other night. He said he had wasted the best years of his life by remaining stuck in hope. The woman was now a widow, but the years had not been kind to her. She was almost unrecognizable. All these years, he had been pursuing nothing but a dream. The great love he imagined, the love that had sustained him through-out the years, had never existed."

"But he is not yet forty, certainly young enough to make a fresh start. It is not too late at all for him to begin a family."

Imogen's eyes rounded in horror. "Oh, Ella! Does he wish to pursue you for this reason?"

"No… He couldn't be thinking…"

Imogen rolled her eyes. "Honestly, you are the intelligent sister. I am the artistic scatterbrain. But even I can see what Lord Fielding is about. He intends to offer for you, but knows you will never be amenable unless you give up on Caden first."

Ella groaned and flopped back on her mattress. "Imogen, this is all getting too complicated."

"We have months yet before your next Season starts. I'm sure everything will be clearer by then. Even if not, you still have time. I am not suggesting you give up a decade of your life waiting for Caden, as Lord Fielding did for his lady love. But how will waiting another year or two hurt?"

Another *year or two*? Ella had yet to pass a single day and was already in agony.

Imogen scooted onto Ella's bed and flopped down beside her. "I'm glad he gave you back this portrait. I would have been devastated if it were left behind in some hotel room. Or worse, if his grandfather had gotten hold of it and ripped it up."

"Me too." Feeling exhausted and fighting off a headache, Ella retired early.

Her sister decided to retire, too. But this was Imogen, very soft-hearted and completely devoted to her big sister. Even when they were children, Ella barely four years old and Imogen only two, Imogen always followed her around, gazing up at her with big, worshipful eyes and certain her big sister could do no wrong.

But Ella felt so lost now.

Well, it was only one day.

The hurt felt worse because Caden did not want her writing to him, and nor did he intend to write to her. Once he left, it would be a complete break.

It felt so wrong.

What made it worse was that her family had gone along with his decision.

It was not fair. Would Aunt Phoebe not be howling and putting up a fuss if she were in Ella's situation? She would not have let Uncle Cormac get away with such a high-handed decision.

But it was pointless to argue about it. They still viewed her and Imogen as children, and always would.

Since Ella had fallen asleep early, she was up early the following morning. So was Imogen, who had appointed herself Ella's watchdog. What did her sister think she would do? Jump off one of the local cliffs in despair? That would be awfully stupid, wouldn't it? Caden had barely been gone an hour, and she was not nearly ready to give up hope.

But she did have to think of her future. Would she repeat Lord Fielding's mistake and lose out on a fulfilling life while waiting for something that could never be?

Yet again, she dismissed the concern. It was much too soon to worry about Caden and his romantic intentions.

Setting her thoughts aside, she and her sister washed up, helped each other to dress and style their hair, then went downstairs. Breakfast was already set out on gleaming silver salvers in the family's private dining room. Cormac and Phoebe had already eaten and were gone by the time Ella and Imogen sat down.

As much as Ella loved her aunt and uncle, she was relieved not to have to face them. They would ask questions, and she had no answers.

Ella did not eat much, for her stomach was still in knots. She nibbled on a scone and had a cup of mint tea.

Imogen, she noted, also ate sparingly, having picked up on Ella's misery, and was feeling sad herself. Once finished, they ran back upstairs to grab their pelisses, since the day was unusually cool for this time of the year. The sky was overcast, foretelling of rain.

Mr. Hawke was to take them into Moonstone Landing as he always did. He arrived at the stroke of nine, just as the clock in the entry hall began to bong. They hopped into his wagon, eager to head into the village. "Please take us straight to the hospital," Ella said.

"All right, lovies. Shall I pick you up from there as well?"

Ella shook her head. "No, we will keep to our regular routine and meet you by Mrs. Halsey's tea shop."

"She needs to drown her sorrows in lemon cake," Imogen added. "I shall commiserate and eat an entire cake of my own."

He cast Ella a pitying look, then snapped the reins to get his reliable mare moving.

They bounced and jounced in the rickety wagon all the way from Westgate Hall and down the high street. Ella loved this ride, and had such fond memories of traveling in Mr. Hawke's rattletrap over the years. They were lumbering past the Kestrel Inn when they saw Elmer running toward them and waving his arms. "Stop the wagon, Mr. Hawke," Ella cried. "I think Elmer Angel is trying to get our attention."

She hoped everything was all right. Her first thought was for Caden. He and his grandfather's entourage had intended to leave at first light. But had something soured their plans?

Was Caden hurt?

The lad was out of breath by the time he reached them. Ella reached out a hand to help him into the wagon. "What's wrong, Elmer?"

"Nothing, m'lady."

"Is it about Lord Mersey? Are he and his entourage still at the hospital?" Imogen asked, since she was obviously thinking the same as Ella.

Elmer shook his head. "No, they are gone."

Ella's stomach began to churn. Losing Caden now felt so final.

"But he gave me this packet and told me…" The boy handed it to Ella. "You had better hold on to it. I'm afraid to lose it. I've never seen so much money in all my life."

Now Ella was completely confused. "Lord Mersey gave you fistfuls of money?"

The boy nodded. "Piles of it, meant for you."

Ella frowned, for this did not sound right. She was secure financially. Why would Caden give her this?

Elmer regarded her in dismay. "He gave me instructions. But the jeweler's shop is not yet open, and I would not know what to choose." He shoved the packet into her hands.

She opened it carefully. If there were bank notes inside, she did not want them to fall out or fly off in the breeze. To her surprise, she counted over a hundred pounds. "Why in heaven's name did Lord Mersey give you this?"

Elmer pointed to the letter tucked in with it.

Imogen plucked it out and began to read aloud. "'Elmer, I am trusting you to purchase one item of jewelry or other gift Lady Ella might like each week that I am gone. Nothing extravagant or too ornate, because she will not wear it. A simple necklace with an opal. Small pearl earrings. A heart locket. A shawl for colder days. A cameo pin. Lace ribbons. Poetry books, because she loves them so much. Ask Lady Imogen's advice if you cannot choose. She knows Lady Ella's tastes better than anyone. Do not let on to Lady Ella what I have asked you to do. I want these gifts to be a surprise. Insert a note in each that says, *Always in my heart,* but do not include my name on the chance these notes fall into the wrong hands. I hope she will know they are from me.'"

"Oh." Elmer glanced at Ella. "I did not read that far down. I'm so sorry. I've ruined your surprise."

"No, you haven't at all." Ella shook with relief and then broke down in tears.

This was Caden's way of thinking of her, of showing her that he was not going to forget her. Writing the note itself was dangerous, for the reporters would have made much of it had they gotten their hands on it. His grandfather would have been apoplectic if he saw it.

She supposed this was the reason for requiring anonymity. But Caden knew he could trust Elmer with that letter, with the funds, and with his instructions written from the heart.

It was not the gifts or the ridiculous amount he meant Elmer to spend each week that had her in tears. It was that Caden was giving her a little of himself week by week.

Imogen put an arm around her. "Seems we have our answer, don't we? I knew he loved you. Now, all he has to do is tell you."

Ella had no idea when that would be.

It did not matter at the moment. Her heart was soaring.

There was one jewelry shop in Moonstone Landing, which had opened recently next to the Kestrel Inn. Ella had not been inside before. Instead of riding to the hospital, they hopped off Mr. Hawke's wagon, arranged to meet him at the usual hour in front of Mrs. Halsey's tea shop, then went into the inn's dining room and had a pot of tea while waiting for the jewelry shop to open.

Elmer was excited to make his first purchase. "You must come in with me once the shop opens, Lady Ella. I've ruined the surprise, but it all works out, since you can now choose exactly what you want."

"Yes," Imogen said, lightly clapping in approval.

"But please take the money," Elmer said quietly. "I dare not be responsible for it."

Imogen took the bank notes and the letter, tucking both in her reticule. "I will keep them, not Ella. Lord Mersey will be disappointed if he learns she had control. She would not buy things for herself, as is his wish."

"And what is wrong with spending it on others?" Ella remarked. "Is it not better to apply these funds on a greater need?"

"No, and stop being practical." Imogen frowned at her. "This is why Caden did not assign the task to you. He knows you are too logical and frugal. And do not think to return any of it to him unused. That is completely out of the question."

Ella rolled her eyes. "You are being ridiculous."

"No, you are the ridiculous one," her sister retorted. "I will not allow you to skimp. Caden will be disappointed and feel you did not appreciate his gallant gesture."

"I have every intention of using up his money," Ella insisted.

Imogen eyed her warily. "On yourself? That is entirely the point of his gesture. You cannot spend it on the soldiers or the villagers. It must be spent on yourself."

"But Imogen, they—"

"Need it more than you? I know that, but use your own funds for those concerns. This tidy sum is a gift fund for you. Stop fretting about it. You always think too hard."

After finishing their tea, they walked down to the jeweler's, Harrow & Sons. Ella thought the name misleading, since the owner was a young lady recently arrived in Moonstone Landing from York, or perhaps Edinburgh, and there were no sons, brothers, or any other males working in the business other than a giant of a man by the name of Amos Angel—yet another cousin of Elmer's—who guarded the merchandise.

"What do you know of her?" Ella asked Elmer as they were about to enter.

"Nothing other than Amos says she is a nice lady. But he's not sure if her real name is Miss Harrow. She comes from someplace far to the north, and Amos says she speaks with a refined English accent that sometime mingles with a light Scottish brogue."

"Yes, I've heard the gossip that she could be from Scotland. Now I'm curious to meet her."

"I've never been inside a jeweler's shop before," Elmer admitted.

That much was obvious to Ella the moment they walked in. The boy's eyes grew wide and his mouth gaped open as his gaze fell on the necklaces, rings, bracelets, and other sparkling pieces set out in the display cases.

Even Ella was awed by the quality of the merchandise. There were diamonds, sapphires, emeralds, and rubies twinkling through the glass.

"Good morning, Amos," Elmer said, tearing his gaze from the display cases long enough to toss his cousin a smile.

"Morning, Elmer," Amos replied. "What are you doing here?"

Elmer tipped his chin into the air, obviously proud of the task Caden had assigned him. "Escorting Lady Ella and Lady Imogen. They are here to buy something beautiful for Lady Ella."

Miss Harrow's ears perked. "I will gladly assist you with your selection," she said, revealing that light Scottish brogue everyone in town had been commenting upon. Her voice was pleasant and her accent refined. "Were you looking for something in particular? Or purchasing for a special occasion?"

"No special occasion," Ella said. "And nothing very sparkly."

"Ah, then you are not interested in diamonds?" The young woman appeared disappointed but recovered quickly and cast her a warm smile. "We have gold lockets. Or perhaps you might like this necklace with a lone pearl. It is beautiful and delicate, and will not overwhelm your slender neck."

Ella tried it on. It was beautiful, but she already had pearls that her father had given her for her debut Season.

Miss Harrow brought out another necklace, similar in design but having an opal at its center. Since the opal reminded her of moonstones, Ella chose it for her first gift. She would wear it tonight. Cormac and Phoebe were hosting a dinner party, and this necklace would go perfectly with the gown she intended to wear.

Miss Harrow mentioned she would wrap it up in a pretty box for her.

"No, wait," Elmer blurted.

Amos, who was easily the size of an ox, arched an eyebrow. "Elmer, what is the matter with you?"

"We need to add a note in the box." He turned to Imogen for support.

"Oh, yes," Imogen said. "We must include a note, and it must say, *Always in my heart*. Please do not ask what this is about. We are not permitted to say."

Miss Harrow nodded. "You need not worry. We are discreet here. I have some very pretty card stock in the back for just such a thing. Would you like me to write it for you? I assure you, my penmanship is quite excellent."

Elmer breathed a sigh of relief. "Yes, please. I'm not very good at my letters. My teacher says it is chicken scratch. I did not know how I was going to manage writing that note."

"You, Elmer?" his cousin remarked, once again regarding the lad dubiously.

"Yes, me. I am taking care of this delicate matter for a friend."

"A friend, you say?" Amos folded his arms across his chest. "Since when do you have wealthy friends? What is really going on?"

"None of your business. We didn't steal it. Lady Ella and Lady Imogen are heiresses, and you are just getting us angry now."

Miss Harrow cleared her throat. "That will be all, Amos. Thank you, Lady Ella. Lady Imogen. Please do come back soon. We have many beautiful items and are constantly getting in new stock."

Elmer cast his cousin a smug smirk, then turned to Miss Harrow. "Thank you, ma'am. We shall be back next week."

Although it seemed unnecessary to Ella, the gift was wrapped in a beautiful box, and the note was included in it. *Always in my heart.* She had felt so sad at the start of the day, but this cheered her up. These little notes were what she would truly treasure. She now looked forward to next week and the one she would find inside the next gift.

Lord Fielding happened to be walking out of the Kestrel Inn at the same moment they walked out of the jeweler's. He saw them and came over to greet them. "What a pretty box. A gift for you, Lady Ella?" he asked, since she was holding it and probably looking at it too lovingly.

"It is a surprise for a friend," Imogen said, completely believable in her lie.

Of course, Lord Fielding had only to question Miss Harrow or Amos and he would figure out the truth. Ella hoped he was too much of a gentleman to investigate this purchase.

Elmer coughed. "I had better get back to the hospital." He tore off without another word.

"We are due at the hospital as well," Ella said.

"How long will you be occupied?" Lord Fielding asked. "May I invite you both for lunch at the inn? I know I shall see you again tonight at your uncle's home, but I hope you will indulge me anyway."

Ella only needed to tend to the garden that was fairly well along and at this point mostly tended itself. She and Imogen were then going to spend the rest of the morning reading to the soldiers or helping them write letters. She was about to politely decline when Imogen surprised her by accepting the invitation for them.

Lord Fielding was delighted and accompanied them as they walked down the high street toward the hospital. However, he bade them farewell at the fort. "I have business with Major Brennan. Shouldn't take long. I will see you at the Kestrel Inn at noon."

She and Imogen walked on.

Once they were out of earshot, Ella turned to her sister. "Why did you accept his invitation? Now he is going to ask all sorts of questions about this gift box, not to mention ask about Caden—whom, as you pointed out to me last night, he views as a rival for my affections."

"Honestly, Ella. You have dozens of gentlemen interested in you. Yet you behave as though you just came out of a convent and have never spoken to a man before. The gift is none of his business. Caden is gone, and you have no idea where he is going next. If you are concerned about being questioned by Lord Fielding, then you ought to toss questions at him first. Ask about his racehorses. That will keep him talking throughout our meal."

"He doesn't own racehorses… At least, not that I am aware."

Imogen shook her head and laughed. "Must I teach you everything? All these peers own racehorses. Or used to own racehorses. Or wish they owned them. Or have good friends who own them. Or just purchased a rippingly handsome stallion he might try out at one of the smaller racecourses. Trust me, he will take the bait."

Ella joined in the laughter. "I don't know how you got so much wiser than me, and you are not even out in Society yet."

"I don't know very much," her sister said with a shrug, "but I do understand men. And before you gasp, let me assure you it is not from any actual experience. But I observe people. I notice their expressions, sense what they are feeling or what they are trying to hide. It is the artist in me that recognizes emotions."

"What does the artist in you say about Lord Fielding? Is he going to be a problem for Caden?"

Imogen pursed her lips as she contemplated her response. "I don't know enough about him yet. I'll tell you after we dine with him at the Kestrel Inn. I don't think he would ever do anything to harm Caden, at least not politically. However, he views Caden as a rival for your affections."

Ella nodded, nibbling her lip as she fretted over this very thing. "I wish you had not accepted his invitation."

"But this is the very reason why I thought it important to do so. The questions troubling both of us must be answered."

Ella did not think they needed to be answered this day, but she went along with it. "What can he possibly do to make me choose him over Caden?"

"I have no idea," Imogen said. "But I would also add...to what lengths will he go to ensure you choose him over Caden?"

Chapter Fourteen

CADEN PACED ACROSS the elegant suite he occupied in one of York's finest hotels, the Castle Hotel. Three weeks had passed since he had last seen Ella, and he missed her, ached for her every day. He and his hero tour entourage were to spend another two weeks riding north to Edinburgh before turning south again and heading to London just in time for Parliament to empty out. Most peers in the House of Lords went grouse hunting in Scotland.

He considered delaying their journey south and waiting for the lords to arrive in Scotland, but that would not work either. Most of them had their own private hunting lodges spread across the country, from Aberdeen in the east to Greenock in the west. He would merely talk himself hoarse going from lodge to lodge and repeating the same speech. No one would listen, anyway. They wanted to shoot grouse.

Besides, even if most peers were no longer in London and he had to wait for their return, his time would not be wasted. Ella would be back in London by then. Did he dare see her? Everyone was still watching his every move. The speculation would become frenzied if he were seen escorting Ella around London.

Yet it was not fair to ignore her. This would hurt her too much, to be in London together and he purposely avoiding her. Would it not be better to give in to his heart and openly court her? Well, this was certainly his desire, but was it wise?

He did not want all attention placed on their romance instead of the important work to be addressed once Parliament was back in session. Not to mention his concerns about his grandfather and his toadies doing anything to hurt Ella.

James Stafford stopped by to ask about his York speech, and watched him as he paced. "Your leg is much improved. Why don't you give up your crutches and use a cane instead? It will be just as effective in promoting sympathy among the masses, and your grandfather is already suspicious about your continued need for them."

"What does he have to be suspicious about? I am not using these crutches merely as props. That weakness in my leg is real. It will take time to repair the damage to the ligaments. But I suppose I could try using just a cane." Caden cast Stafford an arch glance. "Are you going to catch me if I fall?"

"Oh, no. You are far too big. However, I will report every detail of your tragic tumble and how valiantly you endured it."

Caden laughed.

He and Stafford had become friendly over the weeks, but Caden was never going to reveal anything truly personal to this man. As much as he liked him and respected his intelligence, Stafford was a reporter, and his loyalty was foremost to his newspaper. "What is on your mind, Lord Mersey? You are clearly fretting about something."

"Nothing out of the usual. I am still stewing because my grandfather has designed this tour so that we return to London just when Parliament is out of session."

"He is a wily fox, but there is still plenty important you can do once back in London. Use those weeks to gather information. Learn about the resources available to soldiers discharged from service."

Caden frowned. "What resources?"

Stafford regarded him impatiently. "There are some available, mostly through charitable organizations. Get to know which ones they are and who backs them. Point out what has been done right and how it can be duplicated across England. You must also talk to the clerks in the Home Office and Foreign Office. Those underlings know everything and will complain to you at your slightest urging."

"Sounds delightful."

"Fine, be sarcastic. I am only trying to help."

Caden sighed. "Sorry, I know."

"Learn all you can from these government clerks about the appointment process for these territorial governors. Who nominates them? Who interferes with those nominations? How is the ultimate decision made? Who is the real power behind these decisions? Then talk to the lords who have remained in Town. There are more than a few who will stay on because they cannot abide Scottish food or weather, and cannot stand grouse."

Caden grinned. "You are going to turn me into a crack reporter, aren't you?"

"Well, if your cause ultimately fails, you could always apply to the *London Chronicler* for a job. I'm sure they would hire you."

"No offense, but I think I will pass." He renewed his pacing, then stopped and turned to Stafford again. "How do I keep these issues fresh in the minds of the public until Parliament is back in session? You wouldn't happen to have any useful dirty secrets on my grandfather and his friends, would you?"

Stafford arched an eyebrow. "Are you asking me to do your investigation work for you? No, I don't have anything I can give you. Your grandfather's influence and that of his friends long ago got to all the major newspaper owners. Believe me, I have wanted to dig into their activities but got shot down every time I dared bring them up. What you need is an upstart reporter working for an upstart newspaper to shake things up."

Caden regarded him dubiously. "Do any exist?"

"Oh, yes. But they are small and struggling. They would leap at the chance to bring down a dishonest politician or two. I'm also sure they would love to smear the powerful establishment papers like the *London Chronicler* and call them out for being in bed with greedy peers like your grandfather. It is all about the bottom-line profit, isn't it? My bosses will relent if their earnings are being hurt because they are losing sales to a paper that is printing the truth."

"Printing the truth—what a refreshing idea," Caden said, not bothering to hide his sarcasm.

"Well, you could also shake things up by involving the Crown. You know, the king's silence on this tragic massacre is as good as condoning the injustices rampant in the appointment of these territorial governors."

"No, inciting anger against the Crown is not what I am trying to do. I've seen enough battles to last me a lifetime. I need the Crown on my side, exerting their royal influence to bring about these reforms."

Stafford had poured himself a drink and now made himself comfortable in one of the leather wing chairs by the hearth. "Will you be resigning your commission once this tour is over?"

"No. I can do more good if I remain in the Royal Marines. I just hope they don't ship me out on a new assignment to the other side of the world."

"That would silence you. But I doubt the public will stand for it, nor will your impressive allies. You know, all those dukes, marquesses, and earls in your corner. Not to mention the upstart reporters who will sell more newspapers because of you."

Caden settled into the wing chair beside his friend. "Do you happen to know any upstart reporters I can trust?"

"I do, but if I gave you their names, then I would be losing my chance at an exclusive story from you. I haven't quite forgiven you for not sharing that account of those mercenaries attacking the Ashanti chieftain's wife and daughters. I would have written up a very poignant article about it."

"I know. That story got out of hand fairly quickly. But you did do an excellent job of writing it up. Better than any of the other reporters, although even you made too much of it."

"Are you jesting? Why do you keep shrugging off your valiant accomplishments? You single-handedly bested those mercenaries. Saving women and children by threatening to blow the leader's brains out. It only enhanced your status as England's hero."

"And sold more newspapers."

"Yes, that too. But do not dismiss the power of what you did. Every woman saw you as their hero, and every man wished they were you, performing that heroic deed. What you did is much more than a romantic tale. It is at the heart of who you are as a person."

Caden laughed. "I have no idea who I am."

"Stop being dense, will you? You are hope for the future. You are honor and kindness. You are strength and compassion. Do you think we reporters have lost so much of our humanity that we cannot see it in others? Not all of us have. But that moment of valor… Is this not the essence of your heroism? *Your* humanity and the dignity with which you dealt with others?"

Stafford set aside his drink and continued. "Don't feel bad about not giving me that exclusive story. I would have been too philosophical if I had it all to myself. What that story needed was the lurid reporting it received."

Caden sighed again. "Perhaps."

"No perhaps about it. You know I'm right. Have you given more thought about you and Lady Ella?"

"She is always on my mind," Caden admitted. "Why are you asking?"

"*That* is the story I want."

Caden was surprised. Stafford was one of the most intelligent men he had ever met. "Is this not a more suitable topic for the scandal rags?"

"What is the *London Chronicler*, or any of the larger papers, other than a glorified gossip sheet? Oh, everyone will run this story. But I must have it first. Yes, this is the one I want."

"All right. But there will be nothing to report for weeks yet."

"I can wait," Stafford said with a nod. "Nothing has more

selling power than a love match between England's hero and the Society beauty he wishes to marry."

Caden rubbed the nape of his neck. "It could be months rather than weeks before I do anything about Ella. I am serious about protecting her."

"Don't keep her waiting too long. She is much in demand and will find someone else if you don't act soon."

"Not Ella. She is the sort who loves once and always."

"Then why are you prolonging her agony?"

"I am protecting her," Caden insisted.

"That girl is not afraid of a fight. I saw the way she dealt with your grandfather. When was the last time anyone dared swat him on the backside? I think he is still stunned by it." Stafford shook his head and chuckled, but sobered after a moment. "Your grandfather is going to realize you are in love with her, if he hasn't already."

"Doubtful. He is so caught up in himself that he does not see half of what goes on around him. I'm doing my best to keep it that way when it comes to Ella."

"Do not underestimate him or the toadies in his entourage. Why do you think he brings them along? It is to keep their eyes on you, and I can assure you they have noticed your bedroom activities. Or, should I say, your lack of them. Ladies are throwing themselves at you everywhere we go, yet you have taken none of them into your bed. This must have already been reported to your grandfather. Think about declaring your feelings for the girl. When you do, I want that exclusive."

"All right, upon my honor."

"Thank you." Stafford sat back and smiled at him. "You know, I am quite a romantic at heart."

"Is that so? You know, I never asked you… Are you married? Or have a sweetheart?"

"No to both, but I always hold out hope. Do you ever read poetry, Lord Mersey?"

"No. Lady Ella read some to me while I was recovering."

Caden chuckled. "I was bedridden and could not escape. But it was all right."

"She read you Shelley, didn't she? *And the sunlight clasps the earth. And the moonbeams kiss the sea.* All the young ladies swoon over that poem."

"Stafford, you are an extremely astute fellow. Why have you not run for office? The House of Commons could use a man as intelligent and wily as you."

"No, it isn't for me," Stafford said with a mock shudder. "Come on, I'm sure they are all waiting for you downstairs. Are you going to give the same speech you have been giving everywhere?"

"Actually, no. I think it is time I gave my grandfather and his smug friends an apoplectic fit."

"Naughty boy. What are you going to do?"

"York is a fully garrisoned city, and there will be plenty of officers in attendance. It is time to press the need for the military and not politicians to control the battlefield."

"Oh, that will have your grandfather turning purple."

"He brought along these generals thinking they are in his pocket, but he is about to have a rude awakening."

Stafford frowned. "Are you sure? They might be very comfortable sitting in his pocket."

"Then I will be the one to have the rude awakening, won't I?"

Stafford helped him up. "It is not your style to walk in unprepared. What have you done that I don't know about? And how did you manage to hide it from me?"

"That would be giving away my secrets, wouldn't it?"

ELLA PEERED THROUGH the display glass at the latest merchandise to arrive at Miss Harrow's elegant shop. "You say you have just received a supply of cameo brooches from Italy?"

Miss Harrow nodded. "They are stunning. You will love them. I have not had time to put them out yet, but I know the entire stock will sell out within hours when I do. In truth, I prefer this sort of merchandise. It appeals to everyone and is more affordable. A lady on holiday in Moonstone Landing will purchase a cameo not only for herself, but for her daughters, sisters, a gift for a friend. I expect most will leave here having bought more than one."

"Oh, I am eager to see them. Please do show us." Ella had been coming in here weekly for the past two months, and had collected eight *Always in my heart* notes so far. Elmer and Imogen always accompanied her on these weekly outings, for the lad took his responsibility quite seriously and was not going to shirk this important duty assigned to him by Caden.

But summer was coming to an end, and Ella's parents had arrived to pick them up. They were to spend one more week at Westgate Hall, then return to London. This would be their last visit to Miss Harrow's shop.

"Mama would love a cameo," Imogen said.

They both gasped when Miss Harrow opened up the black velvet boxes of neatly arrayed brooches. They were so delicately carved. Most were in the shape of a lady's face or depictions of Olympian goddesses and classical muses, every detail finely pronounced, even to the intricate curls on the subject's head. "Goodness, you were not exaggerating. They are exquisite," Ella said.

She chose one of Erato, the muse of love and love poetry, who was depicted from the shoulders up. The full-body carvings of the muses revealed too much of their voluptuous bodies, since the artisans crafting these beautiful designs did not see fit to provide them with more than a thin cloth that somehow never covered their ample breasts. Those etchings were beautiful, but her parents would never allow her to wear one of those, since she was young and not yet married.

Elmer paid for the brooch out of the funds Caden had provided. It was a bit of a ceremony they went through every week. Imogen was the keeper of the money and would hand the funds over to Elmer, who in turn would make the purchase, request the card be inserted, and then hand the gift box over to Ella, who was standing right beside him all the while.

She thought the whole thing silly and did not want to use any of Caden's money at all, but she was outvoted. Elmer took his responsibility very much to heart, and Ella could not disappoint him.

"Now, I will use my own funds to purchase a brooch for Imogen, another for Elmer's mother, and—"

Elmer gasped. "Oh, my lady! No, that is far too generous. Don't you agree, Amos?"

His cousin was standing guard quietly in the corner as always, his arms folded across his massive chest, saying nothing.

Imogen chimed in. "You have been so helpful to all of us, Elmer. Please let us do this for you. And I am sharing in that gift for her."

"But—"

Amos put a big hand on Elmer's slight shoulder. "It is a nice thing they are doing. Be quiet, Elmer. It is a sign of their respect for you. Appreciate it and just thank them."

The boy blushed. "All right. Thank you. My mother will love it."

Ella and Imogen then purchased cameos for their mother, Phoebe, Chloe, and Henley. The lovely shopkeeper was right— these brooches would sell out quickly.

Miss Harrow scurried into the back to wrap each gift. As they were waiting for her to finish, Lord Fielding walked in. "I thought I might find you here," he murmured, smiling as he tipped his hat to her and Imogen.

Ella tried to appear pleased to see him. "Ah, Lord Fielding. When did you return?"

He had stayed on in Moonstone Landing for several weeks after Caden departed with his grandfather and their entourage. It had felt like forever to Ella. Seeing Lord Fielding every day as he ingratiated himself with her family was wearying. Well, he, Cain, and Cormac were longtime friends and enjoyed each other's company.

But it was not only their company he sought. He wanted hers as well.

He was not openly courting her so much as trying to make her forget Caden. It was never going to work. She would never consider marrying him while her heart belonged to another. She had tried to be clear on that point.

She also thought he had returned to London after taking his leave of them. Why was he back now? She hoped it was not to pursue this unwanted courtship.

Nothing had changed for her. Caden still had her heart, and she was not ready to give up hope of marrying him. How could she when these weekly presents were a constant reminder of his affection for her?

"I arrived just last night and settled at the Kestrel Inn. I thought I would spend a few days here before returning to London," Lord Fielding explained. "My travels have taken me away for quite a while, and it will be good to return."

Ella frowned. "Were you not already in London?"

"No, I wasn't." He cast her a wry smile and said no more.

"Then where did you go?" Ella did not care if he thought the question rude.

"I had business up north."

"We are also returning at the end of the week," Imogen remarked, interrupting Ella before she could ask where precisely north he had gone.

"Ah, then perhaps I will wait and return to London with you. Which coaching inns will you be stopping at on the way home? I'm sure they are the same as mine. There are few along the way that are suitable."

To Ella's further dismay, Imogen told him.

"Excellent," he said. "Yes, they are the same as mine. I'll write ahead and push back my reservations." He tipped his hat to them again and was about to leave when he noticed the cameos on display on the counter. "Is this what you purchased?"

"Yes," Imogen interjected. "For ourselves and the ladies in our family."

He studied the brooches with a serious eye. "This one will be perfect for my mother."

When Miss Harrow returned, he asked for help in purchasing two brooches.

"One for your mother and the other…um, for a special young lady?" Miss Harrow asked.

He arched an eyebrow. "No, both for my mother."

"Oh, then they are perfect." She smiled brightly at him.

Ella could not quite figure out this young woman. She appeared to be in her mid-twenties, or possibly a few years older, but she had a youthful face and was quite pretty. Her speech was elegant, and so were her clothes. Not that she put on airs, for she did not at all. Her gowns were beautifully designed but modest, and the colors were soft shades, nothing garish.

"Yes, I thought they would suit my mother," Lord Fielding said, his manner polite and not as stuffy as he sometimes could be. Perhaps that was harsh. He really was a nice man, but Ella did not want him to waste his time courting her.

However, Ella noticed Miss Harrow staring at Lord Fielding and blushing slightly as he spoke to her. Of course, it was not likely that someone as elevated as Lord Fielding would deign to court a mere shopkeeper. If he liked her, he would likely propose another sort of arrangement.

Ella immediately dismissed that possibility. He was not a hound, as her Uncle Cormac and Cain had been. He would never be so crude as to suggest an improper arrangement with this young lady, would he?

She shook out of her rambling thoughts. If Lord Fielding had returned to Moonstone Landing for the purpose of courting her, then he would never cast his eye on another woman in the meanwhile. But could there be something between Miss Harrow and Lord Fielding?

She shook her head again and sighed. Imogen would accuse her of thinking too hard. But what was so wrong with pointing Lord Fielding in the direction of a charming young lady who actually liked him in *that* way?

They thanked Miss Harrow, bade good day to Lord Fielding, who was now asking the young woman to show him some other pieces, and walked out with their purchases. Elmer excused himself and hurried off to the hospital to assist the wounded. He was a favorite with the patients and staff, since he was always helpful and naturally cheerful, something much needed amid these depressing circumstances.

Before Ella and Imogen had gotten very far down the high street, Lord Fielding hurried out of Miss Harrow's shop and caught up to them. "May I invite you to tea at Mrs. Halsey's tea shop?"

"That is very kind of you," Ella said politely, "but we—"

"Would be delighted," Imogen cut in.

Ella nudged her sister's foot lightly with the toe of her walking boot. What was Imogen doing?

"Excellent." He escorted them across the street and greeted Mrs. Halsey as though she were an old friend. Was he trying to insinuate himself into the daily life in Moonstone Landing? Not that it was a bad idea. Was this not the perfect place to find love?

Just not with me, Ella prayed.

Her thoughts went back to Miss Harrow.

If three cousins in the Angel family managed to marry into the peerage, why couldn't Miss Harrow do the same? Not that Ella knew anything about the young woman, but she and Imogen could do a little investigating on their own. If they deemed her suitable for Lord Fielding, why not encourage a match? Miss Harrow obviously liked him—Ella could tell by the way she blushed and patted her hair while talking to him.

She would mention it to Imogen later.

The tea shop was busy, so Mrs. Halsey motioned for them to take any empty table. There was only one that was unoccupied, the lovely corner table by the window. It was slightly removed from the others and would offer them privacy as they spoke.

Mrs. Halsey's daughter bustled over to take their orders. Ella and Imogen, despite having finished an entire pot of tea at the Kestrel Inn less than an hour ago, ordered lemonades and the strawberry tarts that were always a favorite of Imogen's. Lord Fielding ordered a coffee for himself.

Once they were served, they began to chat.

"What really brings you back to Moonstone Landing?" Imogen asked, biting into her tart.

"To see Ella, if you must know."

Ella smothered a groan.

This was her worst fear.

But Lord Fielding leaned closer and grinned. "Not for myself, Ella. I am not blind to your feelings. As lovely as you are, I think you are too young for me…or perhaps I am too old for you. I would rather not think about it that way, since I am hardly gray-haired yet. However, I happened to be in York and saw Lord Mersey."

Ella gasped at the mention of Caden. "You did?"

"I came back here to give you a message from him."

She held her breath. Was it to say he loved her?

Oh, but she wanted to hear it from Caden himself. But any indication that he still thought about her and cared for her was welcome. "What did he say to you?"

"That he misses your broom."

Ella had just taken a sip of her lemonade and choked it down the wrong pipe as she laughed.

Lord, why did Caden have to be such a clot? "Did he have anything else to say to me?" she managed to ask between coughs.

Fielding regarded her with concern. "Are you all right?"

She nodded and took several deep breaths. "Quite. Please go on."

"That was all the message he wished me to deliver. I assume it is a private jest between the two of you. Care to share it with us? After all, I did come all the way down from York at his behest."

"I suppose it is all right to tell you now." She sighed. "I hit his grandfather with a broom."

Lord Fielding laughed. "Seriously? Accidentally or on purpose?"

"On purpose," she admitted. "Believe me, he deserved it. I dare not say any more about the incident, only that you would have hit the Duke of Seaton, too, if you had seen what he was doing."

"I have no doubt. He's a tough old bas—" He shook his head. "Ah, forgive my language. The old man is not one to be crossed."

"How was Lord Mersey's speech? Did you hear him give it?"

"Heard it. Was inspired by it. Stood up and cheered along with everyone else in the audience. The hall was packed to the rafters with lords, soldiers, and ordinary citizens. He was marvelous, and his popularity continues to grow. His grandfather is not happy about it."

Ella nodded, understanding just how controlling the duke hoped to be over his grandson. "This hero tour was his grandfather's idea. I am glad to hear it is not going according to his devious plans."

"That would be an understatement. The Duke of Seaton has even lost the support of those generals he brought along, thinking they were going to keep his grandson contained. Instead, they were among the loudest voices cheering him on."

Ella was delighted. "What did he say that has everyone so inspired?"

"It is hard to repeat, for I do not have his eloquence. But I hope you have the chance to hear him talk when you return to London. All hell is likely to break loose once Lord Mersey arrives there. This is his grandfather's territory. He will gather his powerful allies in the hope of putting an end to his grandson's popularity."

"I don't think it is possible to stop him now," Ella said, for she understood Caden's devastating appeal whenever he applied his charm. Was any girl's heart safe? Hers certainly wasn't.

But it was not only the women who had succumbed to his charms. Caden knew how to inspire and motivate everyone. She'd seen the impact he had on the injured soldiers in Moonstone Landing's hospital. He must have had a similar impact everywhere he went, at every hospital he visited and on every soldier he encountered who was still serving or had been discharged from service. His influence would also have extended to their families, for almost everyone had a family member or sweetheart in the military.

The point was, Caden knew how to touch everyone's heart, while his grandfather only knew how to crush hearts.

"Lord Mersey is smart and has been in control of his audiences all along," Lord Fielding said. "Even the reporters are persuaded by his message, and they are a hard lot to convince. Most would betray their own grandmothers in order to capture an exclusive story."

Ella thought that was quite a cynical comment, but she did not say more about it. What she wanted to hear about was Caden. "Tell me about his speech. Please, Lord Fielding."

"He is pushing for control of military operations to be wrested from the hands of politicians and restored to the military. He tore into Governor Fulke, sparing nothing as he spoke of the man's greed, and how he betrayed Crown interests to enrich himself and his friends. He did not mention who those friends were, but obviously his grandfather was one of them."

"Did Lord Mersey speak more about how he got injured?"

"It is very hard for a man as proud as he is to speak of that massacre. He did not go into detail about it. But he mentioned his injuries and the fact that no one else in his regiment survived. His anguish was sincere."

Ella nodded. "I think it will haunt him for the rest of his life."

"It is not something one ever forgets. I dared not press him about it when we met privately afterward. These speeches take a lot out of him. He was in agony and could not bear to discuss it. However, more reports of that battle are starting to come out in the daily newspaper accounts."

"How much of what they print is true?"

Lord Fielding's expression turned solemn. "It depends on which papers you are reading. The *London Chronicler*'s reporting has been excellent. Much more insightful and detailed than reports in the other newspapers."

Imogen had been listening quietly and now spoke up. "We get the papers several days after they come out in London, so we are always behind on the news."

"What Lord Mersey experienced was horrific. I would caution you against reading the more explicit accounts, but I know you will not listen to me. No one can remain unaffected by his ordeal and the tragic fate of his regiment. I sat in on the conversation Lord Mersey had with the men in your family and the Duke of Claymore before he started on his tour. He was restrained in what he revealed to us. I wish he had been more forthcoming."

"But he has your support anyway?" Imogen asked.

"Yes, without question. We are more and more horrified as these reports come out. I think he will have almost unanimous support in the House of Commons. Many in the House of Lords will support him, too. But there are those who are not eager to make changes."

Ella wished she could stand by Caden as he campaigned for these reforms. Did those slain not deserve justice?

Lord Fielding absently stirred the coffee in his cup as he spoke. "Whether the territorial governors will be stripped of control over the military, I don't know. But I think some changes must occur. Most will agree to get rid of men like Fulke and enact new rules regarding these high-level appointments."

Ella nodded. "That is something."

"Yes, that alone would be a major accomplishment. However…"

"Why the hesitation, Lord Fielding?" she asked.

"If you know Lord Mersey as well as I suspect you do, then you will know he is not one to stop at half measures."

This was what Ella feared most—that there would always be another wrong to right, another important cause to champion, and she would eventually be forgotten.

He slapped his hands to his thighs. "This talk is dry, and I do not wish to bore you with more of it. Just know that Lord Mersey has months of fighting ahead of him now that he has directly challenged his grandfather's powerful crowd."

"I wish we could help in some way," Ella said.

"You'd help best by keeping out of this fight between him and his grandfather. This was the other message he wanted me to deliver to you, Ella. Stay out, because it is going to get intense, and he does not want you in the crossfire."

She frowned. "I hate when men do this, try to shield us when we are just as willing as they are to fight."

Lord Fielding regarded her closely. "Do not even attempt it. The ways they can hurt a sweet girl like you are not pretty. I assure you, men like that will stoop low indeed to get what they want. Do not be naïve, Ella. There is a reason Mersey wanted you out of his way."

"How long does he expect me to hide?"

"He did not tell me. I cannot say. We will know better once Parliament is back in session."

ELLA HAD A lot to think about over the next few days.

While sad to leave Moonstone Landing, she was eager to return to London and be closer to the gladiatorial arena that Caden would be tossed into once he addressed Parliament. She was not certain yet how much she should trust Lord Fielding or whether she should consider him a friend. He claimed he had given up pursuing her, but she sensed this was not quite true.

As the days passed, she had tried to steer him into Miss Harrow's shop a time or two. But he did not appear receptive to her hints...for now.

And just how reliable was Lord Fielding? Ella knew he was honorable, but the Marriage Mart seemed to have few rules when it came to securing the object of one's desire. Some men deemed anything fair.

Women were no better, for she had encountered plenty of schemers in her first year out. This was precisely the reason Caden had been so distrustful of her at their first meeting. Every time they shared a dance or a conversation, he goaded and tested her.

In truth, he was *so* cynical and distrustful, she was surprised he was capable of believing in her as confidently as he did now.

Her head began to pound. She silently berated herself for dwelling on things that were not in her control.

Caden's ordeal, for one. His grandfather for another. How far would he and his confederates go to stop Caden? Would they hurt her if they knew he cared for her?

Would Lord Fielding betray Caden because he wanted her?

Chapter Fifteen

RETURNING TO LONDON was quite a jolt for Ella. Even though many peers had gone off to Scotland or back to their estates, almost as many had remained. Ella's suitors, Lord Harvey and Lord Eckleston, immediately sought her out, bringing her flowers and sweet confections when they visited her on her designated at-home day.

Nor was there a lull in social events, despite it being a quieter time of the year. She and her parents received invitations to soirees, musicales, dinner parties, and balls, piles of them. She left it up to her parents to accept or decline those they wished.

"Ella, stop fretting," Imogen said when they returned to their bedchamber after their visiting hours were over and all the guests had gone.

"I cannot help it. Lord Eckleston mentioned that Caden was expected back in London next week."

Imogen regarded her with some surprise. "Has his tour been cut short? The newspaper accounts claimed he was still in the north, probably in Edinburgh now."

"The accounts are several days behind."

"Let's keep an ear to the ground," Imogen said. "I'm sure we'll hear something more about Caden. He is all anyone talks about. Who else will be at Lady Fielding's supper party this evening? I'm so pleased she included me in the invitation. No doubt at her son's request. I wish I could attend more of these affairs."

"Papa won't ever allow it, since you are not out officially yet. This was his one concession."

Imogen tipped her chin up and sniffed. "I think I am quite mature for my age."

Ella laughed.

So did Imogen. "Well, I suppose you do not need your little sister underfoot. You have been managing quite well without me."

Ella hugged her. "Never say that. I cannot wait until you have your come-out. It will be so much fun to attend these functions together."

"You will be married by then and off talking with other married ladies about managing houses, husbands, and children, while I will be left on my own to fend off all the love-struck bachelors courting my purse strings."

Ella gave her another hug. "They will be lined up outside our door for *you*. How could they not adore you?"

"I know, I am wonderful. Now turn around and let me help you out of your gown."

Ella raised her arms so that her sister had easier access to her laces. "I doubt a wedding is in the plans for me this year. It would only happen if Caden were ever to ask me, and who knows when that might be, if ever?"

"We'll know more when he arrives in London. I'm sure he will try to see you."

"No, he won't." This was what hurt Ella most, knowing he would be here and not available to her. What also made her ache were the gossip rag stories that had recently been circulating about his rakish behavior while on his hero tour. "He was seen in the company of other ladies."

"And you believe those lies?" Imogen untied the last of the laces and regarded her incredulously. "His grandfather is obviously planting these stories. Did we not worry about this very thing? This is the start of the campaign to destroy him in the eyes of his adoring public."

"Imogen, no one is going to think less of a handsome bachelor being seen escorting elegant young ladies around Town. In fact, it will enhance his appeal. The dashing marquess, flocked to by adoring women. Will he fall in love? How does this help his grandfather's plans to crush him? Here, your turn. Lift up your arm so I can undo your laces."

Imogen sighed as she complied. "Perhaps his grandfather planted those stories because he is hoping to hurt *you*."

"Me? How would he even know who I am when Caden is doing everything he can to keep my name out of any association with him?"

Imogen slipped out of her gown. "Who else would have gone after him with a broom? But even if he does not remember who you are, he has to know there is a young lady who has stolen his grandson's heart. Caden will have given himself away by being as celibate as a monk. We know that ladies by the dozens must have been offering themselves to him at every stop."

Ella picked up a washcloth and soap. After dipping the cloth in fresh water, she began to lather the soap on it. "What if he has not been celibate and the reports are true?"

Imogen pushed her lightly.

Ella almost dropped the soap and cloth, not to mention almost spilling the water. "Imogen!" she said, emitting a startled laugh.

"I will dump that water over your head if you utter anything so foolish again. Are you not playing into the hands of that mean old man? How can you think Caden has strayed?"

"I don't really think it. Even if he did—Ow! Why did you pinch me?"

"Because there is no question of his loyalty."

"Good grief, Imogen. Stop being such a moon-eyed romantic."

"I am not. I am merely stating the obvious."

"Well, if there is anything I have learned in my first year out, it is that men and women play by different rules. An unattached gentleman can do just about anything he pleases, short of ruining a lady of good breeding, and even that can be brushed aside in time. We, on the other hand, are ruined at the mere perception of misbehaving. We don't have to actually do anything wrong to be reviled and snubbed."

Imogen cast her a stubborn look. "I am going to pinch you again if you suggest Caden has not been loyal to you."

"Loyal? He has done nothing but push me away. And the galling part about it is how everyone agrees with him. They are going to agree him straight into the arms of a horrid debutante of his grandfather's choosing."

"It will never happen, because he loves you."

"Oh, Imogen. Get away from me and go pick out our gowns for this evening. Honestly, you are a pain for a little sister."

"And you are remarkably irritating for an older sister. I will pinch you again if you dare feel sorry for yourself and cry. Caden loves you. I know what I saw in his eyes while I was drawing his portrait."

They stared at each other, made faces at each other, then laughed and hugged each other.

"Just behave yourself at Lady Fielding's supper party," Ella affectionately warned her sister. "I'm glad she extended the invitation to all of us. As you said, no doubt this was at the behest of her son. I must say, it was surprisingly pleasant having his company on the journey back to London. It wasn't nearly as awkward as I was dreading."

Imogen went to their armoire to select gowns for each of them. "I hear his mother is very nice."

"Yes, Cain and Henley spoke very highly of her. Oh, have you chosen the pale blue silk for me?"

"Yes," Imogen said. "It is very becoming on you. I'll wear this tea rose one. It has a lovely band that goes around just below my bosom and fills me out. I could do with some enhancement in that area."

Ella laughed. "You are young still, Imogen. I was a scarecrow at your age."

"And now you are a gloriously large-breasted diamond."

"Imogen! Goodness, you are wicked. I am not all that well endowed, as must be obvious. And do stop referring to me as a diamond. I hate being called that."

But Ella was in good spirits by the time she, Imogen, and their parents rode to the Fielding residence in their sleek carriage.

Their mother was all smiles. "I missed you girls so much while you were off in Moonstone Landing. It is nice to be back home and have you with us again."

Their father agreed. "Indeed, it is good to have my darling daughters back."

Ella and Imogen exchanged guilty looks.

Yes, they loved their parents, but had missed them only occasionally while in Moonstone Landing. Nothing could compare to the summers spent with Cormac and Phoebe. Ella and Imogen always had so much fun with them.

As for the social life in Moonstone Landing, it was quieter, but not at all dull. There were advantages to life in a quaint Cornwall village. Ella and Imogen were given greater freedom to walk to most places on their own. Now that the hospital was built and taking in patients, they also had a useful purpose to their days in helping the wounded.

None of this was possible in London. They required chaperones everywhere they went and were not permitted to do more than pay social calls on their friends or go shopping.

As it turned out, Lady Fielding's supper party was a much grander affair than expected. Over fifty guests were in attendance. Many of them were Lady Fielding's elderly friends, and there was only a sprinkling of eligible bachelors or other debutantes. Ella found the company delightful, since she did not have to worry about unwanted suitors clamoring for her attention.

Imogen charmed everyone with her youthful ebullience.

"I thought we were to dine at eight," she whispered as the hour approached nine o'clock and they had yet to be called into the dining room.

"I thought so too. Something must be going on." Ella glanced at Lord Fielding and his mother, who were quietly consulting in a corner of the parlor. Lady Fielding appeared ready to order her butler to summon them in to supper when a buzz suddenly swept through the room.

All eyes turned toward the entry hall.

Ella's legs almost buckled out from under her. "Dear heaven."

Caden walked in.

He was out of uniform and looked magnificent in black tie and tails, his shoulders broad and his body lean and muscled. He relied on a cane to assist him in walking. Her heart tightened as she watched him make his way toward their host and hostess, his limp slight but obvious.

This only enhanced his appeal.

"Imogen, am I dreaming? How is it possible?"

Her ever-faithful sister was by her side, holding her up as they both watched Caden. "He must have hopped on a mail coach and escaped his grandfather, the reporters, and the rest of his entourage. It is the only explanation."

Ella was delighted, for it meant she would have a few days alone with Caden before his grandfather stormed back to London, mad as a raging bull.

All Ella wanted was a precious moment in Caden's company. Would he seek her out now? Had he accepted Lady Fielding's invitation knowing she would be here tonight?

Lord Fielding noticed her staring and winked at her.

Dear heaven.

Had *he* arranged this? She owed him a sincere apology for ever doubting his honor.

Caden's gaze swept the room, those dark eyes of his taking everything in like he were a savage jungle cat on the prowl.

Then he saw her.

Ella's breath caught.

He smiled.

Her heart melted and she smiled back.

She wanted to run into his arms, but Imogen had a hand on her elbow and was holding her back. "Do not be a ninny, Ella. Wait for him to come to you."

It felt like an eternity before he finally got around to greeting her and her family.

"Lord Stockwell. Lady Stockwell. It is a pleasure to finally meet you." He bowed politely over their mother's extended hand.

"We have heard so much about you from our daughters, Lord Mersey," their father said. "Of course, we have also avidly read the newspaper accounts of your exploits. It is an honor to meet you, too."

"The honor is all mine." Caden sounded so polished as he engaged their father in brief conversation. His voice was deep and utterly divine.

He greeted Imogen politely next, which was a *faux pas*, since she was the younger sister and not even out in Society yet.

But Ella knew he meant to save the best for last.

Lightning bolts coursed through her when he took her hand. Instead of merely bowing politely over it, as he had done with all the other ladies, he pressed a kiss to it—a deep, gloriously burning kiss that everyone noticed because all eyes were upon him.

"Ella, I missed you so much," he whispered.

Tears threatened to cloud her eyes. "I missed you too. Oh, Caden, I am shaking. There is so much I wish to say to you."

"Me too. When can I see you?"

She laughed softly. "Any time. I'll be waiting."

"I'll call on you first thing tomorrow. It will have to be un-fashionably early because of my other obligations. Or may I see you tonight, after this supper party?"

"Both, if you wish. I am hungry for time with you."

He laughed. "Is that a pun?"

She grinned. "Unintended, but yes. Dinner was held up by the Fieldings in order to wait for you, so I expect everyone here is famished. It is so good to see you."

"Same here. You look beautiful." He moved on to the next guests, leaving Ella elated and at the same time bereft. Was this all they were to have of each other? Fleeting moments at various affairs?

But he said he would call upon her.

What did that mean? Was he through hiding his feelings for her? Kissing her hand had been an obvious and dangerous gesture. Everyone noticed and were still whispering about it. The news would be reported in the gossip rags tomorrow.

Not that she minded. She loved him and did not want to hide her feelings. Nor had she ever been afraid of his grandfather. Not that she would ever let her guard down around the old man—she wasn't that foolish. But what could he do once she and Caden were married?

Oh, dear.

Did Caden want to marry her?

She clutched her stomach as it began to churn with doubt. She tried to shake off the feeling, for Caden would not have kissed her hand if he were not serious in his intentions. Or was she merely being used as a tactical weapon? A budding romance to keep the public interested in him until Parliament returned to session?

No, Caden did not use people. He would never treat her like that.

Suddenly, he was back by her side. "You are thinking too hard, Ella."

She winced. "Does it show?"

"Yes, love."

Ella was sure her parents had heard him utter that endearment, for her mother gasped and her father furrowed his brow. His expression darkened as he stared at Caden. "Is there something you wish to say to me, Lord Mersey?"

"No, Papa. He did not—"

But Caden took her hand and gave it a light squeeze before releasing it. "Yes, my lord. May I stop by your home tomorrow morning? It will have to be early, for my day is already filled with appointments. Or I could follow you home this evening. Perhaps that is better, since I would prefer to have the matter resolved as soon as possible."

Gasps and whispers could be heard around the room. Everyone was listening in.

"Tonight would be perfect," Ella said before her father had the chance to respond. In truth, she wished they could return home right now.

"Seems my daughter has a decided opinion." He let out a breath. "Tonight, then. If you are amenable, my lord?"

Caden nodded. "Eager for it."

All eyes remained on them as Caden escorted Lady Fielding into the dining room. Lord Fielding added to the whispers by escorting Ella in, even though there were ladies above her rank who should have been accorded the privilege.

She expected it was done on purpose to send a message to their guests that she would soon be married to Caden, the Marquess of Mersey.

"Surprised?" Lord Fielding asked, leading her to her seat, which was beside his.

Caden's place was at the opposite end of the table, for he had been assigned the seat of honor beside Lady Fielding.

Ella turned to Lord Fielding. "Yes, I am quite astounded. Why did you not tell me he would be here?"

"I was afraid to raise your hopes only to have them dashed if he did not make it back to London in time. But I am not surprised he moved heaven and earth to be here."

"Lord Fielding, did you do this for me?"

He nodded. "I will not deny having seriously considered you for myself. But seeing the two of you together... Well, it was quite a revelation for me. You and I do not have this feeling. At best, we check off items on a list of suitability. We do not combust upon seeing each other."

"Sadly, that is true. However, I do value your friendship. You are a good, kind man."

"Oh, no. Don't say that. Perhaps we might have suited if Lord Mersey had not come along."

She nodded. "I think we might have."

"Well, I shall settle for that," he said with a wistful smile. "I am truly happy for you, Ella. You have found your love match. Two hearts eternally united. Two flames eternally burning. This is the power of love."

"Dare I hope you now want this for yourself?"

He laughed. "Desperately, but I don't know if I will find it here."

"Come back to Moonstone Landing next summer, Lord Fielding. Set aside your *ton* rules and keep yourself open to whatever may transpire. Look to the heart of a person, not rank or wealth or business advantage. You are in a fortunate position to do this… At least, I think you are. There is no talk of your dodging creditors."

"Heaven forbid." He laughed again. "I am quite secure in my fortune."

As all the guests settled in their seats, the footmen brought out the elaborate meal—starting with the soup course, a traditional white soup that was rather tasty, although Ella's stomach was in such a flutter that she merely took a few sips before setting her spoon aside. She did the same with the other courses, for she was barely able to swallow more than a bite or two.

She hardly touched her game fowl or the fish that was swimming in butter and capers. The potato, artichoke, and peas accompaniments were plentiful, but she mostly moved them around on her plate rather than eating any.

All the while, Caden was holding forth at the other end of the table. All the guests at that end were leaning in, hanging on his every word. Even those at her end were straining to hear him speak.

There was no denying the man was magnificent in every way.

It was around midnight by the time the ladies rose from the table and left the men to their cigars and port. It would be perhaps another hour before the men joined the ladies in the parlor. Ella was not sure her heart, which beat rapidly every time she glanced at Caden, would hold up much longer.

As soon as the ladies entered the parlor, they surrounded her and began to toss questions at her. When did she meet Caden? Did she know how he felt about her? Had they been secretly engaged all the while? When were they to be married?

Lady Lothbridge, an elderly but quite sharp friend of Lady Fielding's, finally asked the most important question. "Does the Duke of Seaton know about his grandson's feelings for you? Will he approve of this marriage?"

Ella strove to keep her answers honest, but she truly had no answer to provide about Caden's grandfather. She expected the old man would not approve of her because she was not biddable and he could not manipulate her to gain his way. "I have not spoken to the Duke of Seaton, but I expect he will make his feelings known to us as soon as he arrives in London."

"Mersey will deal with him handily enough," Lady Lothbridge intoned. "His grandfather has little hold on him, since he is independently wealthy and not reliant on an allowance at all. Nor can the duke alter the bloodline. Mersey will inherit the title once his grandfather dies."

Ella had not thought about Caden's financial circumstances at all. She had a significant dowry, and had just assumed they would live off it after they were married. Caden earned a steady wage due to his rank in the Royal Marines. But it was hardly adequate to maintain them in their current standard of living. Not that she cared, for she assumed they would reside outside of London.

Perhaps in Moonstone Landing.

However, that was a foolhardy notion.

Caden was a forceful presence, and everyone would want him to remain in London, take on a major role in government, perhaps a leadership role. He might also be asked to travel extensively on behalf of the Crown, visiting every country brought into the British Empire.

In truth, Caden was so special, he would belong to all of England and never to her alone.

"Thinking too hard again," Imogen whispered in her ear.

Ella smiled. "Yes. Ah, here come the men to join us."

The ladies fluttered around Caden the moment he walked in alongside Lord Fielding. But he spent no more than a minute before breaking away and coming toward her. Once again, her legs threatened to buckle. Her heart was overwhelmed as she watched him approach with his proud but limping stride.

He was all male, devastatingly handsome, and yet had just that touch of vulnerability to make him irresistible to women.

He made her swoon.

His smile broadened as he reached her side. "That's a pretty necklace you are wearing."

She placed a hand lightly on the opal. "I'm glad you like it. Elmer purchased it for me. He wrote the loveliest note with it. *Always in my heart.* I received eight more gifts and notes from him after that. Are you jealous?" she teased.

"Should I be? Well, he is a cheerful boy."

"Imogen, Elmer, and I went together each week to pick out a gift for me. You needn't have done it, Caden. But I will admit to loving the generous gesture. Elmer was quite the tyrant about it. He would not allow me to spend the weekly allotment on anyone but myself. I'll show you the other purchases another time. But they are all beautiful memories of you."

"As you are beautiful," he said in a whisper for her ears alone. "Ella, I will burst if I don't kiss you soon. What do you think? Shall I kiss you right here and now?"

Her face turned to flames.

He laughed. "Bollocks, I forgot how shy you are. Sorry, love. Forget I said that."

Of course, she could not possibly.

Nor could she quite reconcile herself to this change in Caden. "Are you sure about this?" she asked.

"What? Declaring to the world I am courting you?"

She nodded. "Why the drastic turnabout?"

"Because I love you, and denying it was too hard for me and no longer felt right." He took her hand in his, ignoring the buzz once again caused by his actions. "I was hoping for a little privacy, but that will not happen, since I am followed and watched everywhere I go."

"I'm sorry. It must be so draining for you."

"It is, Ella. But I brought this on myself, didn't I?"

She nodded. "For a good cause."

"That cause is still important to me, but so are you. I should have told you how I felt before leaving Moonstone Landing. I considered riding over to Westgate Hall that last night before my departure. I wanted to take you down to the beach. I did not care that the moon was not full. I did not care that the tide might not be out or that there might be fog upon the water. I knew those moonstones would shine for us no matter the conditions. I knew it because I love you, Ella."

The declaration rang in her ears like a chorus of angels.

Had she heard right? Had she fainted and this was all a dream? If so, she did not want to wake up from it.

"I love you too. So very much, Caden."

He smiled affectionately. "I'm sure I loved you first. I knew it even before my regiment shipped out of England. My feelings were confirmed the moment I saw you again in the Moonstone Landing hospital. I will love you forever, Ella."

She brushed aside a tear as it fell onto her cheek. "I want to throw my arms around you and kiss you with every ounce of my being."

"I won't complain," Caden said.

Imogen sidled up to her and poked her in the ribs. "Honestly, you two. You are turning the temperature up in this room, and it is becoming unbearably hot. If I wore spectacles, they would be completely steamed. Everyone is looking at you, especially Papa, who does not know whether to shake Caden's hand and welcome him as a son or punch him for ogling you like a lion about to devour its prey."

Ella groaned. "I know they are looking, but do you think they heard what we said?"

"No," Imogen said with a shake of her head. "But they did not need to hear a word, since the flaming looks you are tossing each other say it all."

Ella looked up at Caden in dismay. He chuckled. "Stop looking so horrified. Do you think every woman here is not jealous?"

"My father is going to give me a stern lecture."

"Fine, we'll save our cooing and inane love words for later. Wait up for me when you return to your townhouse. I intend to speak to your father."

Imogen squealed and began to hop up and down. "I'm going to wait up, too."

The remark had Caden grinning again. "Which reminds me… I haven't officially asked you yet, have I?"

Imogen squealed again and continued to hop up and down.

Caden's expression softened as his gaze fixed on Ella. "Will you marry me?"

Everyone in the parlor heard the question. Their gazes had already been on her and Caden, not only because Caden had gone straight to her the moment the men joined the ladies, but because Imogen was now bouncing up and down and making noises like an excited chicken.

The room erupted in cheers and clapping.

Ella had not given her answer yet—not that anyone had a doubt what it would be. She threw herself into Caden's arms, no longer caring what anyone thought. "Yes, I will. But are you sure about this?" He had wanted to keep her as far away from him as possible.

He wrapped his arms around her in a heartfelt embrace. "I couldn't bear to be apart from you any longer. When I read those lies printed in the gossip rags about my consorting with other women, I knew this was my grandfather's delightful touch. He meant to hurt your feelings, make you doubt me. I had not protected you from anything."

"I knew they were lies," she assured him. "Even if they weren't, you had made me no promises."

"They were complete fabrications," he said with a soft growl. "I'm sorry I waited so long to declare my feelings for you. But I was truly concerned they meant to hurt you while I was off on my tour."

"Well, you are here now. Elmer's gifts and notes kept you foremost in my heart."

He caressed her cheek. "I want you as my wife, Ella. The sooner we marry, the happier I will be."

He released her, and they spent the next few minutes accepting congratulations from all the well-wishers. Indeed, they spoke no more about his grandfather or his own intentions now that he was back in London.

Lord Fielding appeared wistful but otherwise genuinely happy for them. He ordered champagne brought out and served all around. His mother was thrilled, for this was certainly a coup for her—England's most eligible bachelor proposing to his lady love at her party. Every family with an unmarried daughter would be seeking an invitation to one of Lady Fielding's dinner parties.

With the evening now at an end, Ella and her family returned to their townhouse to await Caden. He arrived soon after, bringing along a gentleman Ella recognized as one of the reporters who had come to Moonstone Landing along with his grandfather.

What was going on?

Caden introduced the man as James Stafford, reporter for the

London Chronicler. Neither she nor her father were pleased to have him in their home.

Caden apologized and began to explain. "Mr. Stafford has been honest in his reporting throughout my tour. In return, I promised him an exclusive story about Ella and me."

Ella did not like this one bit. "You had to bribe him to be honest? What assurances do we have that he won't print lies now that he will have his story?"

Mr. Stafford cleared his throat. "You have my word of honor, Lady Ella. I am not a liar or a cheat."

"But you are someone under pressure to sell newspapers."

Caden groaned. "Ella, it is all right. He can be trusted."

She wished she could be as confident as Caden. She did not know this man at all and did not want him here. But Caden did, so she respected his wishes and said nothing further.

But so many questions leaped to mind as Caden and her father disappeared into the study to discuss betrothal terms. Ella, Imogen, and Mr. Stafford settled in the parlor while their mother ran off to wake their cook and head butler in order to arrange for refreshments to be brought in.

Not that any of them were in the least hungry after the feast they'd had, but Mr. Stafford had not been invited and perhaps needed to be fed more than just information.

"Lady Ella," he said gently, "you have concerns. Tell me what they are and I will address them."

"Very well." Since he had asked, she decided not to hold back. Caden trusted him, and he was not one to trust anybody lightly. Perhaps the man had proven himself in their weeks on the road. "I am not certain what is really going on here, Mr. Stafford. How is Lord Mersey and my betrothal to be handled? The more I think on it, the more surprised I am that we are even betrothed, for he was so much against it when he left Moonstone Landing. How will your reporting of our wedding plans help him? Will it not disappoint the ladies who adore and worship him? Will it not make things more difficult between him and his grandfather? And why this sudden change of heart? Just because his grandfather now suspects he cares for someone? It all feels odd to me."

"I know, but it simply comes down to the fact he loves you and cannot bear to be without you any longer."

"That is so romantic." Imogen emitted a dreamy sigh. "I told my sister, but she wouldn't believe me."

Ella needed to be practical about this, because the betrothal would bring great changes to her life. Her every word and action would now be scrutinized. How did someone as private as Caden manage under all this attention? "What does he expect my role to be now, Mr. Stafford?"

"He will leave it up to you. It shall be no more than you want it to be."

Ella shook her head. "No, that will not do. Now that we are betrothed, I must support him in every way I can. He will never ask for that support, but we all know he needs it, and everyone will expect it of me. If he visits a local hospital, then I ought to go with him. If he gives a speech, I ought to stand by his side. Don't you think?"

"Yes, Lady Ella. I do."

"Most important—and I think this is where the real problem lies—what if his grandfather tries to damage Caden's reputation?"

"You know Lord Mersey is not worried about himself," Mr. Stafford said. "It is you he worries will be damaged by his grandfather. This is why he will ask your father's permission for a quick wedding."

Ella glanced toward the closed study door. "A quick wedding? I doubt my father will agree to it. Everyone will believe rushing it was necessary, and that will tarnish my reputation. I long to marry him, but a scramble to the altar might do more harm than good, I think."

Mr. Stafford chuckled. "I suggested as much, but he ignored me."

Imogen did not look pleased. "But not being married leaves you vulnerable, Ella. This is why Caden wants the two of you wed as soon as possible."

They spoke no more of the potential hazards, as their mother returned, and Ella did not want to upset her with such talk. For several years now she had been in delicate health, suffering from bouts of ague that left her physically weak. Much of the time she was fine, but she relapsed easily, especially when under stress.

For this reason, Ella kept the conversation light and spoke only of her love for Caden, emphasizing the romance and minimizing any concerns. Mr. Stafford seemed quite pleased with their conversation, but Ella hoped he would not twist whatever she had told him into something sensational and tawdry.

When Caden and her father finally joined them, both were frowning.

This could not be good. Had her father refused Caden's offer of marriage?

The possibility had her heart lurching, but Caden seemed to read her thoughts and immediately calmed her. "Ella, he has given his consent."

"Thank goodness," Imogen murmured.

Ella looked from her father to Caden. "Then why do you both look so miserable?"

Chapter Sixteen

CADEN WAS NOT happy with Lord Stockwell's terms. However, he had no choice but to agree to them, since he wanted to marry Ella. His requirement that it be a Christmas wedding did not sit well at all.

He ached to make Ella his wife immediately.

But as the weeks passed, Caden became resolved to the idea of waiting. He was not a patient man, and this delay tore him apart inside. However, the constant mentions of their romance in the newspapers, and the public's eagerness to learn of their wedding plans, proved quite helpful in keeping his own political goals fresh in everyone's mind.

The wounded soldiers were not forgotten. The questions regarding who ought to control the battlefield and what was to be done to root out corruption in the Crown's political appointments would be addressed now that Parliament was coming back in session.

He was scheduled to visit the Royal Army Hospital today. As usual, Ella had insisted on accompanying him. Not that he minded, for she made each day bearable. The nights were another matter, because this was when he missed her most. His sleep was always restless, and he longed to have her soft body next to him. He longed to breathe in her scent and wake to her fairy-pool eyes and her smile each morning.

It was now late November, and the weather had turned decidedly cool and blustery. Caden's cloak swirled around his legs as he walked up to Ella's residence on the now-familiar square of elegant townhouses in Belgravia.

"Good morning, my lord," the Stockwell butler intoned, and immediately allowed him in.

"Good morning, Merrick. It is colder than usual today. Seems winter will soon be upon us." Caden had just stepped inside and was standing in the entry hall exchanging a few more words with the butler when Ella breezed downstairs.

"Oh, that is a chill wind," she said, giving a little shiver as she walked toward him.

"Good morning, love." He gave her a respectful kiss on the cheek, although his thoughts were not at all respectful. That little shiver of hers made him ache to have her in his bed. He thought of her response to the intimacy they would share, and the things he would teach her. He longed to make her shiver with pleasure and moan his name.

The day was cold, but his body began to heat.

He shook out of his thoughts that would have Ella blushing if she had any idea what was going through his mind. "We ought to hurry, or we'll be late."

"I won't be a moment. Oh, and Imogen wanted to join us. You don't mind, do you?"

He groaned. "Doesn't she have an art lesson or something?"

Imogen skipped downstairs, carrying her cloak and gloves. She was sporting a jaunty hat atop her head that resembled a Scottish tam. "No, I don't have an art lesson or something. I'm coming with you. You'll just have to endure my company."

Ella cast him a helpless look. "Papa insisted on it."

"As he always does," Caden muttered, not used to being so restrained and not liking it at all. Well, it really was Ella under restraint, and considering all the things he ached to do to her, he supposed it was warranted. "What's in the bag, Imogen?"

Ella's sister was dangling a cloth pouch on her arm. "Ella

mentioned the soldiers we are visiting belong to a Scottish regiment. She thought it would be a nice gesture if we wore these traditional Highlands shawls while going around the ward."

"I hope they take it as a sign of respect," Ella added. "We weren't sure which clans these tartans represented, if any. We may set off an uproar if we've chosen the wrong ones."

Caden arched an eyebrow, but he was pleased. "The clans are intermingled in the Scots regiments. They will appreciate the gesture."

She cast him one of her beautiful smiles. "Well, we're wearing our sturdy walking boots and can make a run for it if we are wrong."

He laughed. "I think you and Imogen will be quite safe."

He marveled at Ella's considerate nature, for that feminine touch would mean so much to the homesick, injured soldiers. She had a genuine kindness that just flowed out of her. She still did not understand how special she was, how effortlessly she touched the heart of every injured soldier with her smile.

He helped Imogen into his carriage and then assisted Ella, holding on to her far longer than was necessary because he could not get enough of holding her. She knew what he was doing and glanced back at him, smiling. "Merrick is going to tattle on you to my father," she teased.

The sun shone on her golden hair and her eyes sparkled in amusement as he helped her into his carriage and then settled beside her.

She looked up at him.

Those glorious fairy eyes.

"I am going to kiss you senseless if you do not stop looking at me that way," he said.

Imogen gasped and then giggled.

Ella poked Caden's arm lightly. "Now she is going to tattle on you to my father."

Imogen did not realize her sister was jesting, and her expression turned to one of dismay. "Oh, Ella. I never would!"

After assuring her sister she was only teasing, they turned to the more serious topic of their hospital visit. It seemed the brisk weather also made everyone move briskly, and it was not very long before they arrived at their destination. Caden's grandfather and a group of men he recognized as low-level politicians were already at the hospital awaiting them. Also present were a horde of reporters. "Bollocks. What are they doing here?"

A small, priggish man approached them as they entered. "I am sorry, my lord. But someone should have told you. No ladies allowed."

"That is nonsense." Caden had been clear when making arrangements that Ella would accompany him. By the smug look on his grandfather's face, he realized the old man had gotten to the little prig and bribed him. "Who are you?"

The man introduced himself as the commanding officer in charge of the hospital, Major Crayapple.

"Are the soldiers in your wards carrying a contagion?" Ella asked, stepping forward.

"Yes," the man responded, tossing her a smug look.

Ella, ever the lady, ignored his rudeness. "Then just tell us which are the quarantined wards and we shall keep away from them."

"That isn't possible. All our wards are contaminated. You may not enter any of them."

"Do you mean to say you are keeping contagious soldiers in with the healthy men in the regular wards instead of putting them in quarantine? That is clearly in contravention of hospital procedure." She then turned to the reporters, smiling as she recognized a friendly face. "Ah, Mr. Stafford—I hope you are making note of this deplorable lapse in the safety protocols for our soldiers. May I count on you to mention it in your daily reporting? And you did catch the commanding officer's name, didn't you? That's Major Crayapple. C-R-A-"

Stafford burst out laughing. "Yes, Lady Ella. I have his name and shall make certain it is posted on the front page."

Several other reporters assured her of the same.

Whether their editors would ever permit such a story to run in their papers was another matter, but the hospital commander got the message. "We do not violate protocols. There are no infected men in the common wards."

"Glad to hear it," Ella said. She and Imogen marched straight into the nearest ward.

"Now see here, Lord Mersey," the weaselly commander said. "Your lady friends cannot traipse in here and disrupt our hospital routine."

Caden had dealt with officious buffoons like him often enough during his tour. "Lady Ella and her sister have been volunteering at army hospitals for years. In fact, they are likely better trained, and certainly more compassionate, than most of your staff, so do not condescend to them. They have done more to help injured soldiers than this delegation of politicians standing beside us." He turned to his grandfather. "Your Grace, utter a word against them and I shall toss you out of here on your arse."

He probably should not have said that, but he was so tired of the duke attempting to manipulate every situation and undermine him at every turn.

"I'll see that impudent little fortune hunter brought low," his grandfather threatened.

"Fortune hunter?" Caden shook his head and laughed. "She is wealthier than me."

He followed Ella and Imogen, concerned they had marched too far ahead of him and been left alone in a ward of Highlanders. But he need not have worried. The men were like lambs around the pair of them. He noticed Imogen and Ella had shed their cloaks and now wore the tartan shawls they had brought along with them.

What were they saying to these men?

"Oh, yes. We can dance a Highland fling," Ella remarked in response to a question Caden had not heard, for the man who had asked it was lying flat in his cot and was too injured to speak up. "My sister and I shall show you."

Ella took Imogen's hand and positioned them in the center of the ward, making certain the badly injured soldier could see them.

One of the other soldiers took out a bagpipe. Blessed saints, how did he sneak that thing in here?

The shrill wheeze as he pumped air into it made everyone wince except for the Highlanders, Ella, and Imogen. The piper began to play a Scottish lilt. Within minutes, the men were clapping and stomping their feet—those who were able—while Ella and Imogen were gracefully leaping and twirling, clearly having mastered the intricate steps.

Where did they learn this dance?

Two of the reporters happened to be Scottish and were now misty-eyed as they clapped along.

Caden glanced at his grandfather, who had to be mad as a hornet now that his scheme to discredit Ella had failed. *Ah, yes.* His face was purple.

The officer in charge of the hospital began to push himself forward, but one of the beefy Highlanders realized what he intended to do and grabbed him by the scruff of his neck. "Ye're no' going to interfere, Crabapple."

"That is Major Crayapple to you," he grumbled. "Let go of me, or I—"

"What? Report me to my superiors? What do ye think they'll do to ye when they hear how ye deprived their soldiers of a taste of home? Not to mention yer rudeness to Lord Stockwell's daughters or the affront to Lord Mersey."

Crayapple looked like he wanted to hide under one of the cots.

Stafford sidled over to Caden. "If Lady Ella weren't already taken, I would marry her myself. She surprises me at every turn, but I suppose you knew how special she was."

Caden nodded. "Lord Harvey and Lord Eckleston are still licking their wounds. They are decent men, and I think they truly cared for her."

"And not her dowry?"

Caden shrugged. "Perhaps there was a little of that, but they are not paupers. As for me, I would have proposed to her whether or not she had a shilling to her name. They might not have, though."

Stafford returned his gaze to the ladies. "Well, the point is irrelevant, since her heart belongs to you."

Caden looked over and smiled at her.

She smiled back.

His heart desperately needed her.

When the dancing was done, Ella and Imogen split up and made their way to each seriously injured soldier's bedside to ask how they felt and whether they needed a letter sent to their wives or sweethearts. Caden knew they would stay into the evening to write those letters rather than disappoint any of these men. But they had a musicale to attend this evening, so he needed to make certain they left in plenty of time to prepare for it.

With Ella and Imogen quietly talking to the most severely injured, Caden now claimed the attention of the others. He gave a brief speech and then made note of their complaints.

Three hours later, they left the hospital to return to the Stockwell townhouse. Ella and Imogen were tired but invigorated. "That went well. Don't you think so, Caden?" Ella asked.

"Yes, the two of you easily won every soldier's heart."

"But you look worried." Ella had been leaning her head against his shoulder as they relaxed on the ride home, but she now sat up and studied him.

"I am worried," he admitted. "I have no idea what those reporters are going to write. My grandfather may still get to them."

Imogen regarded him in dismay. "I hope not. I am too young to be disillusioned by men and their petty behaviors."

Ella invited him in when his carriage drew up in front of the Stockwell home, but he declined. "I'll see you tonight at Lady

Mayberry's musicale. There's to be dancing afterward. Save the supper dance for me."

Ella laughed. "You ask this of me at every affair. Who else am I going to accept but you?"

He tipped a finger under her chin and gave her a light kiss on the mouth. "Just hoping to keep my spot secure."

After kissing her again—a deeper kiss on those soft lips that tasted like mint tea and raisin scones—he saw them to the door, then returned to his carriage and headed off to his next appointment.

He had much to get through before this evening and Lady Mayberry's affair.

ELLA AND HER parents were already at the Mayberry townhouse when Caden arrived later that evening. He spotted them speaking to some elderly friends of Lord Stockwell and began to make his way through the crowd toward them.

But Caden had barely taken two steps forward when he began to hear whispers about Ella. What in blazes?

Lord Fielding came over and drew him aside. "Mersey, you need to be made aware of what is going on."

"Tell me. I'm already noticing everyone's stares and hasty exchange of comments. What has happened?"

Fielding told him of the lies being spread about Ella's visit to the Scottish regiment this morning. "I'm doing my best to dispel the gossip, but I wasn't there and no one will listen to me."

Caden was not surprised his grandfather and ever-present toadies were describing Ella's visit in the most unflattering terms. He could also see the change in her expression as the unkind whispers reached her ears. Since she was standing beside her parents, they got an earful as well.

Caden could see they were distraught, especially her father, who wanted to protect his little girl.

"They are calling me brazen and a shameless flirt!" Ella cried as he approached.

He took her hands in his. "Ignore the comments. This is what the *ton* is all about, humiliating and bringing down their own. They are nothing but jackals. It is only a few jealous dolts who are trying to cause mischief. I was there. I saw your magical influence on those soldiers."

"It is horrible how everyone prefers to believe the worst. Oh, Caden. This is so hard for me."

"I know, love. It is all my fault. Perhaps I should have continued to keep away from you."

"No. It is the last thing I ever wanted."

He nodded. "Same for me. Being apart from you was more than I could bear. But this prolonged betrothal is also creating an impossible situation. This is why I wanted us to marry right away. No one would dare insult you if you were my wife. Care to elope?"

She looked up at him with pained eyes. "I am seriously considering it."

"Good. Just say the word and I'll take you to Gretna Green."

She laughed. "Or we could just ask my father to give his consent and let us marry quietly here and now. What do you think?"

He was about to respond when he heard a violent crash. "What the...?"

All eyes turned toward the pianoforte at the front of Lady Mayberry's music room. Two men in kilts stood on the dais beside the pianoforte while shattered glass lay strewn all around them. Sprawled on the ground beside them was one of the politicians who had been at the hospital earlier today. He was cursing at the two men and holding a hand over his eye.

"What is going on?" Ella asked, craning her neck to see.

Caden was taller than most people in attendance and had no trouble getting a clear view. "One of those kilted men must have punched Lord Abbott."

"Abbott? That same unpleasant man who joined your grand-father today and kept making noises to have Crayapple kick us out?"

"Yes. Blessed saints, I think the Duke of Solway is the one who hit him. He's the Scot standing on the right. The other one is the Duke of Mar."

Ella's eyes widened. "Do you know them?"

He nodded. "I've met Cheyne Lyon, the Duke of Mar, and his brothers a time or two. They are good men, although I do not know them well enough to call them friends."

"And the Duke of Solway?"

"Never met the man, but I think that is about to change. He's staring at you."

The Duke of Solway was a big, red-haired brute of a man, while the dark-haired Duke of Mar was much more elegant, although he was also a big, stern man who tolerated few people except for his wife, whom he adored. Each man had a brandy in hand and now raised his glass in toast to Ella.

She was uncertain what to do, so she smiled back. But in the next moment, she burrowed into Caden. "Oh, no. They are coming toward us. What shall we do?"

He placed an arm around her shoulder. "It's all right, love. They do not mean to hurt you."

"How can you be sure? Is it too late to run?"

He chuckled. "Yes, and there is no reason to run. Anyone who hits that insufferable toady Abbott will earn my favor. Just be your beautiful self and smile."

The Duke of Solway did not bother with polite introductions when he reached them. The man had no *ton* grace, which Caden preferred at the moment, since so many around them, despite being considered elegant, were actually graceless curs who deserved none of his respect.

Solway gave a quick bow of his head, and then spoke in a booming voice that all could hear. Not that he needed to shout, for everyone had turned quiet as a mouse once this big Scot knocked Abbott to the ground. "Lass, I visited my men this afternoon in the hospital and heard what went on. So, it was with much dismay to learn of the shabby way that weasel Abbott is spreading lies about ye. Mar and I had no choice but to defend yer honor."

Ella blushed. "Thank you, Your Grace. May I say, I was honored to spend time with your injured men. I hope to visit them again in the coming weeks."

"I can see why they dubbed ye their angel. So I raise my glass in toast to ye again, with profound gratitude for yer kindness and caring. Ye lightened their heavy hearts. Ye showed that ye cared for their health, unlike the vipers in this room, who have not done a worthwhile thing in their entire lives. And yet they would sneer at ye unfairly. Ye are a lady through and through, and I mean to let His Majesty know about this unpleasant incident."

The room remained quiet as a tomb while the Duke of Mar had his turn addressing her. "Do not let the petty liars and cheats get to ye, Lady Ella. We shall stand up for ye and for Lord Mersey in Parliament when the time comes. As for here and now, I shall call out any man who utters a snide comment about ye. Had they been to the hospital and listened to our valiant wounded give the *true* account, they would not be saying any such thing. As for the ladies, what is it ye Sassenachs like to do? Give one the cut direct? Well, this is what they shall receive from me, my wife, and all our kinsmen if they dare besmirch yer reputation."

Ella was stunned.

Her parents stared at her in amazement.

"Thank you," Caden said, more appreciative for their support than he could ever convey with mere words.

Ella nodded. "Indeed, you have my gratitude. I felt gutted as I heard those horrid lies being told about me."

"They can be a mean lot, both lords and ladies," Solway remarked. "I canna stand to be among them, but there is important work to be done in the upcoming session of Parliament. Mersey, I think we need to meet with ye to discuss all that needs fixing."

"With pleasure, Your Grace." Caden's reception when in Edinburgh had been welcoming but did not yield any meaningful support. These Scots did not trust his grandfather, but they also viewed him as a Sassenach and were not ready to leap to support his cause. But Ella and Imogen with their Scottish shawls proudly wrapped around their shoulders and their mastery of the Highland fling had changed all that in a morning.

"Och, yer grandfather is glaring at us," Solway said. "Time to give him a piece of my mind."

The Duke of Mar nodded to Ella. "I shall join Solway, just to be sure a piece of his mind does not also include a piece of his fist. By the way, Jenny and I will be happy to have ye visit us in Stonehaven, should ye ever be up that way."

Caden stared at the two Scots as they crossed the room to confront his grandfather. "I ought to join them," he said, worried that his grandfather might incite even the usually calm and composed Mar to violence because he was such a provoking old goat. "Will you be all right?"

She nodded. "I don't think anything can ruin my evening now."

Caden hoped the worst had passed, but he was worried. What his grandfather had been plotting up to now were minor annoyances. With this latest attempt to discredit Caden and insult Ella having failed, Caden was now concerned he would turn to more sinister options. The old man had been thwarted at every turn and had to be enraged.

Caden also knew he had to speak to Ella's father this very evening and have the wedding moved up. There would be speculation about the necessity of marrying in haste, but any gossip would soon die down once it became clear Ella was not with child and there would be no "early" arrival.

To his relief, the Duke of Mar maintained his composure and held Solway back as his grandfather unloaded a string of invectives, cursing Caden—as usual—and every Scot who dared support his cause. His grandfather was always private with these outbursts, reserving his ire for moments he and Caden were alone. Appearances were always important to the old man.

But something had changed, and Caden was concerned about it.

After the way his grandfather had treated him for much of his life, Caden should not have felt any mercy toward him. He had always been a stern, bitter person. Yet he had always done his duty to Caden, taking him in when he was orphaned, feeding and clothing him, and seeing to his education. Caden had no one else to call family. As much as he disagreed with many things his grandfather stood for, he could not ignore this disturbing change in him, this lack of control when in public.

No, he could not abandon him when something obviously was not right with him.

"Grandfather, let me take you home."

The duke pushed Caden away. "You? After what you have done to me?"

Caden had always challenged him, bridling when his grandfather attempted to control him. But his causes had never been as serious as the ones he was now championing, which threatened his grandfather's ownership of those Ashanti gold mines—those gold mines he seemed to cherish more than his own grandson. This was another thing that struck Caden as worrisome, the inability of his grandfather to connect the massacre of the regiment and Caden's own near-death to the greedy actions on his part.

Caden had attributed that behavior to sheer stubbornness, but what if there was something more going on that affected his grandfather's mental acuity?

When the duke suddenly curled his hand into a fist and raised his arm to take a swipe at Solway, Caden grabbed him and held him with gentle restraint. "Grandfather, please. Let me take you home."

"I never want to see you again! Get your hands off me." The

old man's face distorted with rage.

Caden had never seen him as bad as this. "I won't. Stop fighting me. I am not going to leave you. I am your grandson. Who else but me should look after you?"

"The very grandson who seeks to destroy me?" The duke struggled against Caden, now trying to punch him, but Caden would not release his arms.

"Losing a gold mine that you never paid for in the first place is hardly going to destroy you or put a dent in your wealth," he said, speaking calmly in the hope of quieting the obviously agitated old man. "Grandfather, this outburst cannot be good for your heart."

"There is not a thing wrong with my heart."

Other than its being icy and devoid of all compassion.

Caden kept the thought to himself.

His grandfather finally calmed down, but not before he shocked everyone by letting loose another string of invectives that had men gasping and women covering their ears.

He then left with his toady, Abbott, which did not give Caden much comfort at all.

"Ye were gentle with him," Solway remarked as he and Mar stood beside Caden, watching the two storm out.

"He is family. Much as I sometimes detest him, I have to protect him."

"Is that so?" Solway cast him a wry smile. "Och, ye sure think like a Scot. Are ye sure ye were no' born one?"

Chapter Seventeen

"NO, ELLA. NOT only am I forbidding you to marry Lord Mersey, I want this betrothal ended right now!" Ella's father was agitated and pacing like a caged tiger.

"But Papa—"

"No!" He frowned at her, as well as Imogen, and even their dear mother. They were all in his study, the ladies summoned by him for a conference immediately upon their return from Lady Mayberry's musicale.

What a disastrous affair that turned out to be.

First to be called an immoral harlot, then to watch a fight almost break out between Caden's grandfather and those Scottish dukes. But it hadn't ended there, and Ella quickly related to Imogen all that had gone on. "Then Caden's grandfather turned on him and spouted the foulest invectives."

"What a show that must have been," Imogen muttered.

"The young ladies who were giving their recital were so rattled, they could not sing a single note in tune. Not one of them. It was painful to watch."

"And how was Caden through it all?"

"I hardly saw him afterward. He disappeared with Solway and Mar, and only turned up at the very end of the evening. That did not sit well with Papa, hence his ranting at me now."

"Ella, that is so unfair."

Their father heard the comment. "Unfair? Am I supposed to laugh off the insults hurled at Ella?"

Imogen stared down at her toes. "No, Papa."

Ella cleared her throat. "They were whispers. No one dared say anything to my face."

"And is that not worse? Lying, scorning, and belittling you behind your back?" He turned to their mother in chagrin. "Charlotte, am I wrong in wanting to protect our daughter?"

Ella groaned inwardly because she already knew what their mother's answer would be. She had never disagreed with anything their father had said during the entire course of the marriage. It was quite frustrating oftentimes, because she was so steadfast in her support of him. She was no simpleton who merely nodded on command and deferred to all his opinions. In her eyes, their father was the most brilliant man who ever existed. It was as simple as that.

"No, my love. You are not wrong," she said.

Her husband gave a satisfied grumble. "You see, Ella? We are only thinking of your well-being."

Ella stood to face her father. "No, Papa. You are thinking like a father wanting to protect his child. But I am not a child anymore. I am old enough to be married, and my heart wants Caden. I could never accept anyone else. So do not think to have us end the betrothal. Let us marry quietly now. We can still hold the wedding breakfast as originally planned. We can even go through with a second wedding ceremony as originally planned, if you wish. But do not ask me and Caden to separate."

Her father cast her a stubborn scowl. She had never seen him look so put out before. "What you experienced this evening will be nothing to the dirty tricks the Duke of Seaton will play while trying to stop Lord Mersey from swaying the House of Lords. I appreciate that Caden is fighting for justice, but his grandfather and his business associates are fighting for a king's ransom wrapped up in those gold mines."

"Which Fulke unlawfully seized for *them*, and not the Crown, at the cost of the lives of hundreds of men. Caden is not suggesting we do anything but return those properties to their rightful owners and strike our deals with them, whether it be to purchase those mines outright or operate in partnership, or merely contract for the mineral rights."

"I don't care what his reasons are. I will not have you caught between two raging bulls. Mersey was right to keep you out of it. I'm sorry he changed his mind, and even sorrier I agreed."

Ella was now on the verge of tears. "So you would humiliate me further by making me break off the betrothal? Tear us apart? I will be ruined if you make me do this."

Her father caressed her cheek. "I am not saying you cannot ever marry him. You would only have to wait until this matter is resolved in Parliament."

"But it could take years!" What if Caden got tired of waiting for her? She was two years away from being of age to marry without her father's consent. While she and Caden could run off to Gretna Green, when would they do this? He was going to be caught up in political haggling for the foreseeable future. If he left London now, it would set his cause back, perhaps irrevocably.

Her father was unmoved. "He will understand. If he loves you, he will wait forever."

"Can you promise me this?"

"You know I cannot, my child. But perhaps Lord Mersey can give you some assurance." He glanced over her head toward the door, where their butler and Caden were standing.

Ella was surprised to see him quietly waiting there. How long had he been listening in?

"Never mind announcing him, Merrick." Her father waved Caden in. "Join us, lad. We have a lot to discuss."

"So I gather. Ella..." Caden opened his arms to her, and she ran to him.

"He wants me to break off our betrothal. Tell him it is a terrible idea and he is wrong."

But Caden just held her and remained silent.

She looked up at him, searching his face. "No! Don't you dare agree with him. The scandal of my ending our betrothal will be worse than anything I would ever have to endure from your grandfather and his friends. I refuse to end it. Don't you dare think of ending it, either. Weren't you the one who suggested moving up the wedding date?"

He nodded. "I did, but perhaps I was hasty in—"

"No!"

"Ella, we don't have to decide anything tonight. Let's sleep on it, and I will stop by in the morning once we have all had a chance to clear our heads. It isn't about those stupid whispers. Solway and Mar shot those down fast. Nor is it about the politics."

"Then why the change of heart about our marrying sooner?"

"My grandfather's behavior tonight," he said. "That public outburst… It isn't like him. Taking a swipe at Solway and then at me in front of the *ton* elite. Cursing like a madman. This is something new and worrisome."

"But you were always afraid he would do something cruel."

"Not like this, Ella. He has hit me before…firmly believed I was insolent and had to beat sense into me for my own good. But I am strong and can endure his nonsense. Tonight, I feared he might do the same to you. He would physically hurt you if ever he got his hands on you."

"Caden, he cannot be *that* mad."

"What if he is? What if his months of anger and outrage, coupled with Abbott's whispers in his ear, affected his mind? This goes beyond creating stupid rumors or attempting to ruin your reputation. My trust in you is unshakable," Caden said. "I could find you naked in bed with another man and know you had been set up."

"Now see here, Mersey!" her father retorted, leaping to his feet.

"Oh, Papa, do sit down. Caden was just making a point that he knows I will always be faithful to him. You should be pleased he has such trust in me."

Caden nodded. "I would not put it past my grandfather and his cohorts to attempt something heinous. Trying to set you up in a compromising situation or doing the same to me. Would you have the same faith in me, Ella?"

"What do you mean?"

"If there were rumors of my being found in bed with another woman?" He raked a hand through his hair. "I would never do this. All I want to do is marry you and build a life with you."

"Then let us do so."

"Will our marriage make it through a first year with my grandfather's constant dirty tricks? But it is more serious than that. For the first time in all my years, I saw something truly dark in my grandfather's eyes. I think he may be losing his reason. With that loss of reason may come loss of restraint. I cannot allow him to harm you, Ella."

He sighed heavily and turned to her father. "For this reason, I am in agreement with you, Lord Stockwell. Perhaps it is for the best we end the betrothal."

Ella tore out of Caden's arms and sank down in a chair. She lowered her head into her hands and tried not to burst into tears. "So this is it? We are done?"

Caden groaned. "No, love. We are not done, just postponed for the moment."

"Which could stretch into years, and you will forget me."

"I did not forget you when I left Moonstone Landing and will not forget you now." He knelt beside her and slipped her hands off her face, then tucked a finger under chin and tilted her face up to meet his gaze. "Do you hear me, Ella? I will never forget you. Every moment I am away from you is torture for me. There is no one else for me and will never be."

"Then why change our plans? Your grandfather wins if we break off the betrothal. How does this help anything? Not to mention the stir it will cause. Your grandfather can so easily use this against you. You are inconstant. You are a heartbreaker. You are unreliable."

Her father groaned. "Ella, enough. I think we are all best served by sleeping on the matter. We will discuss it tomorrow. No hasty decisions will be made tonight. Lord Mersey, will you join us for breakfast?"

Caden nodded. "I'll be here."

"Good," Ella's mother said, taking her husband's arm. "Imogen, go on up to bed."

Imogen grumbled. "And miss all the excitement?"

"There is no more to be had. Consider the matter adjourned until tomorrow." Their mother turned to her husband. "My love, let us retire as well. It has been a long and unpleasant night, and I am quite weary."

"I will, as soon as Lord Mersey leaves."

"No, he and Ella will have more to say to each other. They are still betrothed and have the right to some privacy." She then surprised Ella by nudging her father out of his study. He was not happy about it, but this was how their marriage worked. She supported him in every way, and in turn, he denied her nothing because she demanded so little of him.

Also, her father had to realize that everyone already believed she and Caden had shared some intimate moments. He was a gorgeous man and a war hero. Who was going to resist him? She was certain to be accused of giving herself to him, so why should she not be permitted something out of it?

"Keep this door open, Ella," her father warned. "Merrick is going to be standing right outside and will hear everything that goes on."

"Yes, Papa."

"I won't stay long," Caden assured him. "Your butler is eager to close up the house and return to his bed."

The moment her parents and Imogen went upstairs, Caden drew Ella out of view of the doorway and lightly pinned her against the bookshelves lining the back wall. He placed a finger to her lips to warn her to keep quiet, then replaced his finger with the exquisite touch of his lips.

His mouth was so beautifully shaped and fit against hers perfectly.

"Ella. My sweet, lovely Ella." He deepened the kiss, turning it fiery. At the same time, he took her hands and held them above her head in an unmistakable gesture of possession.

Yes, he possessed her heart. This man overwhelmed her, and she burned for him. How could she ever desire anyone else?

She inhaled the manly scent of him, the sandalwood on his skin and the hint of brandy on his breath.

"Don't move, love," he whispered as she squirmed against him, trying to get closer. He kissed her again, then moved lower, kissing her throat, her neck, the swell of her bosom. "Mercy, Ella," he said with a soft chuckle, "you will push me over the edge if you keep wriggling against me."

He licked along her throat.

Oh, that tongue of his…so hot and teasing.

She melted against him, no longer able to hold herself up. He held both of her hands in one of his so the other would be free to trace the curves of her body. She shivered with pleasure as his calloused fingers stroked and glided along the silk fabric and then slid into her bosom to caress her warm skin.

Her eyes flew wide open. "Caden…"

"Hush, love. I want to memorize you." He kissed her on the lips again. "No matter what is decided tomorrow, I want this remembrance of you."

He then shocked her by nudging down the bodice of her gown. Her eyes widened further, and she stared at him as he put his mouth to her breast and turned her body molten with the suckle of his lips and the flick of his tongue. An intense heat suddenly formed between her legs, an ache to have him touch her *there*. But he did not move his hand lower, and instead eased off her with a groan, then lovingly readjusted her bodice.

She moaned softly and closed her eyes. "Oh, sweet heaven, Caden."

He groaned. "I had better stop."

"Don't."

He shuddered. "Ella, I am never going to walk away from you. *Never.* We will be married. Whether it happens at Christmastide or later, it *will* happen."

"Sooner is also a choice. Tomorrow, if you are willing, because delaying the wedding only places me more at risk."

"Yes, tomorrow. If your father agrees to it. Upon my word of honor. Now close your eyes. I want to kiss you again before I leave," he whispered, and then seared her with a farewell kiss that left her shattered, because she sensed he had already made up his mind. He was going to insist on breaking off their betrothal, just as her father wished.

She whispered his name and buried her fingers in his hair. "Don't leave me, Caden. Please. I don't mean just for tonight. If you love me, then fight for us. Don't let others tear us apart, even my own well-meaning father."

How could he abandon her when he loved her and his touch was so exquisite?

"Ella, love," he said with a whispered ache, "don't make this more difficult than it needs to be."

"Difficult, Caden? Dear heaven." She wasn't certain, but a book might have fallen off a shelf as she began to cry. The soft thud as it hit the floor must have brought him back to his senses. He drew off her with an aching groan, his eyes dark and wild as he stared at her body. He kissed her again, the touch of his lips light and reverential.

"Don't cry, sweetheart. Please, it will all turn out right. I give you my word of honor. Do you think this is any easier for me?" He released her and eased away. "Your hair has come undone."

All of her had come undone, not just a few wayward strands of hair.

She stood there feeling so helpless.

His gaze did not leave hers as he ran his fingers through the tumble of curls. "Gold silk."

She could see by the flare of desire in his eyes that he wanted to remove all the pins and let her hair fall over her shoulders in sinuous waves.

"One more touch, and then I really must go." He closed his eyes as he traced his knuckles ever so lightly along the line of her jaw. After placing another feather-soft kiss on her lips, he gathered her in his arms and leaned his forehead against hers.

"Caden…"

"I know, love. We all need to think this through."

There was nothing for her to think about. "Goodnight, Caden. I'll see you in the morning."

He nodded, gave her a final, fiery kiss, and then strode out.

She stood at the study door and watched him as he crossed the entry hall.

Merrick, the dear man, had been standing by the front door all the while, probably with his hands over his ears so as not to hear whatever was going on in the study. Not that they made any noise beyond a few soft groans and breathy moans that should have been swallowed up by their kisses.

"Goodnight, Merrick," Caden said, his expression giving away nothing as he walked out into the cool night air.

"And to you, my lord," the butler replied, no doubt eager to leap back into his bed. He shut the door and bolted it.

"Goodnight, Merrick," Ella said as she ran upstairs struggling to hold back more tears. She managed until she reached her bedchamber.

Imogen had changed into her nightgown and was seated on her bed, waiting for Ella to return. She had her hands clasped and a worried expression on her face. "Oh, Ella. Are you all right?"

"No." Ella threw herself onto her bed and burst into tears.

After having a good cry, she dried her tears and kicked off her slippers. Imogen helped her out of her elegant gown and into her far more practical nightclothes, then removed the last of the pins from her hair and carefully unwound the strand of seed pearls that had been threaded through her tresses. She placed the delicate strand back in Ella's jewelry box, then turned to her sister. "It will all work out," she said, her voice wobbly, as though she was going to burst into tears herself.

Well, this was Imogen, always sensitive to the feelings of others.

"I'm sure it will." Ella cast her a smile, wanting to reassure herself as much as her sister.

COME MORNING, THE family assembled at the breakfast table to await Caden's arrival. As the minutes ticked by, her father began to grumble. "He's late."

"He will be here," Ella insisted. "His grandfather might have delayed him."

Caden had taken rooms at one of his clubs rather than reside with his grandfather in the magnificent Seaton townhouse while the two of them remained at odds. However, knowing Caden, she expected he had gone to look in on his grandfather before coming over here. He had been worried about the old man after last night's incident. Despite everything, Caden had an unwavering loyalty to his grandfather.

"I am all the family he has left," he had explained to Ella when recovering in the Moonstone Landing hospital months ago.

But this also applied in reverse. The Duke of Seaton was the only family Caden had left. Did he not owe him some kindness?

How awful that the two of them were in all-out war. At least, his grandfather perceived it to be this way.

Caden was hoping to make him see reason, but his grandfather was never going to accept that his greed had anything to do with Caden's injuries or the massacre of the regiment. Nor was he likely to forgive his grandson for taking him on regarding this matter.

Caden believed that, as Duke of Seaton, his grandfather was

protected from any severe repercussions if changes were ever adopted in the Houses of Parliament. In truth, he was protected because Caden would intercede if the Crown ever thought to punish the duke. Not that the Crown would ever want to take on its most powerful peers. Territorial governors might be recalled, a few government officials might be dismissed, but the dukes would remain untouched. Perhaps a fine might be assessed, or a property here or there forfeited.

But this reconciliation Caden hoped would occur between him and his grandfather? That was never going to happen.

"He is half an hour late, Ella," her father grumbled, shaking her out of her musings.

"I know, Papa. This isn't like Caden. I am starting to worry. Will you take me to his club if he is not here within the hour?"

"Out of the question. You walking into a gentlemen's club? I will not hear of it. Besides, I must get to my office. While I am gone, I do not want you going anywhere near the place."

"I'm sure he will send word as soon as he can," her mother said gently.

Ella felt so frustrated.

"Let's eat." Her father held up his cup for one of the footmen to fill it. As the aroma of hot coffee filled the air, Ella and Imogen went to the salvers set out on the buffet to fill their plates with the usual eggs, kippers, and sausages.

Ella hardly ate a thing. She was now seriously worried, because Caden was over an hour late and had not sent a messenger to them.

When breakfast was over, they all walked out of the dining room. Her father grabbed his cloak and hat, for the family carriage had been brought around and was waiting for him in front of the house. "Ella, I am not angry with Lord Mersey. I know he is a responsible fellow. He is also someone much in demand and dealing with many important matters."

"Perhaps he was summoned by the king," Imogen suggested.

"Doubtful," their father replied. "It could be that he is not certain what to do about your betrothal yet and decided to wait until later to address it."

"No, Papa. He would have sent word. This feels very wrong," Ella replied.

He kissed her on the forehead. "I forbid you to go anywhere near his club or the Seaton townhouse, Ella. If something serious is going on, I do not want you anywhere near Mersey or his grandfather. We will speak more on the matter tonight."

Their mother had a modiste appointment later that morning. Their driver had returned with the carriage to take her to Madame de Bressard's shop. "Do not do anything foolish while I am out, girls."

"No, Mama," Imogen assured their mother as she marched out the door.

Ella and Imogen raced upstairs, grabbed their cloaks and reticules, and hurried out not five minutes later. They grabbed a hack on the corner and instructed the driver to stop at Caden's club.

"Lady Ella," the steward guarding the front door said, casting her a look of reproof for being so bold as to come to a gentleman's domain, "he left quite early this morning and hasn't returned."

"Oh, I see."

They tried two other gentlemen's clubs he was known to frequent.

The response was the same, as were the reproving looks. "He has not come by today."

She instructed their driver to take them to the Seaton townhouse.

Imogen's eyes widened in surprise. "No, Ella. We promised Papa."

"I won't go in. I'll have the driver inquire for us while we wait in the hack."

Imogen did not seem thrilled by the idea, but she went along with it.

The driver had gotten no closer than the front gate when one of the footmen, a large, barking dog at his side, chased him away.

"Sorry, Lady Ella," the driver said. "Couldn't get nothing out of that bloke."

"Thank you for trying. Are you all right?"

The man nodded. "Yes, I'm sure that dog is trained not to bite unless given the instruction. If your Lord Mersey was in there, he must have heard the commotion. Let's give it a few minutes. Where shall I take you next if he doesn't poke his head out?"

"To the Duke of Solway's residence." The duke had seemed particularly impressed with Caden and was just the bull of a man needed to accompany them back here. The footman and his big dog would not dare toss him out.

Yes, she was defying her father's wishes. But was it not more important to make certain Caden was unharmed? Fortunately, Imogen was just as worried and eager to find him.

"Papa is wrong," she said as the hack took off for the Duke of Solway's residence. They had been crisscrossing the park, riding back and forth between Belgravia and Mayfair for what felt like almost two hours.

It was approaching noon by the time they reached the Duke of Solway's home. Fortunately, he was accepting visitors and willing to receive them. His butler, another red-haired Scot who was almost as big as the duke, led them into his study. "Yer Grace," he said. "Lady Ella Stockwell and her sister, Lady Imogen."

The duke was seated behind his desk attending to the documents piled upon it. He rose as soon as they walked in and motioned for them to sit in the elegant chairs in front of his desk. "To what do I owe the honor of yer visit?"

Ella quickly told him. "Do you know where he might be? We came to you for help because our father will not allow us to go near the Seaton townhouse…although we did drive up to it, and the driver of our hack was kind enough to make inquiries. They chased him off the premises. So, I was hoping perhaps you might call on the Duke of Seaton. We would accompany you but wait in the carriage."

"Because we promised our father we would not enter the Seaton home," Imogen added, as though traipsing around London from one gentlemen's club to another and barging in on dukes was not just as bad.

"Ye've had a busy morning. But I'm glad ye came to me." He sighed. "By chance, Lord Mersey is to meet me here at noon."

"He is? How wonderful." Ella glanced at the large clock standing in a corner of his study. "It is coming upon the hour now."

Solway nodded. "He and the Duke of Mar are meeting me here for a working lunch."

He did not invite them to stay for this meeting, nor did Ella expect he would, since it was not meant to be a social occasion. "We will leave when he shows up. I just want to know that he is all right. After the state his grandfather was in last night, I'm afraid he might have done something to harm his grandson."

"Harm his heir?" Solway frowned. "The man would have to be deranged."

"And you call his behavior normal last night?"

Solway raked a beefy hand through his bright shock of hair. "No, but…the lad knows how to defend himself."

"Not when it comes to his grandfather," Ella said, her unease growing by the moment. "He will never strike him. This is what I fear most, that he will not properly protect himself because he loves that old man."

"Aye, I noticed how gentle he was with him last night. We'll know soon enough if there is something of concern going on. Would ye lassies care for tea while we wait?"

"No, thank you," Imogen said. "Our stomachs are too unsettled."

They all leaped to their feet when a carriage drew up in front of Solway's residence, but hopes were dashed when the Duke of Mar strode in.

Ella groaned in disappointment. "Oh."

Mar chuckled as he bowed over her hand. "A pleasure to see ye, Lady Ella. Although I am not too sure the sentiment is returned."

"Do forgive me." Ella quickly explained the situation.

"Och, I'm sorry. Well, I am confident he will arrive at any moment and resolve this for ye."

But the minutes ticked by.

When the clock chimed the half-hour, tears began to fill Ella's eyes. "I knew something was wrong. And now all these hours have been wasted. Is it possible he went to see his grandfather after he left our house last night? It would have been quite late, after two o'clock in the morning. Anything might have happened to him. Footpads. Cutpurses. Even his grandfather's own villainy."

Solway was insistent. "No, lass. No matter how outraged Seaton is right now, he would not purposely harm his heir."

"Perhaps one of his business associates, then," Ella added. "There is nothing to keep one of them from hurting Lord Mersey to protect his own interests. Last night's outburst between the Duke of Seaton and Caden might have been taken as a sign he would permit Caden to be harmed."

"Aye, that's a possibility," Solway admitted. "Ye lassies had better wait here while Mar and I pay a call on old Seaton."

Ella would go mad if she were left behind. "We're coming with you. You may as well bring us along, because we will get there even if we have hire another hack."

Mar stared at her. "All right. But ye are to remain in my carriage and not follow us in. I want your promise on this, Lady Ella."

"You have it."

He turned to her sister. "Lady Imogen?"

"Yes, you have my promise. Please, let's hurry."

Ella knew her father would be livid, but he was a reasonable man and would understand the necessity of their actions. Would he not move heaven and earth to save their mother?

To Ella's surprise, Mr. Stafford was standing outside the Seaton townhouse when they drew up. She leaped out and ran to him. "Mr. Stafford, where is Lord Mersey?"

"I was hoping you might tell me. I was supposed to meet him at his club this morning at ten o'clock, but he never showed up. He had arranged to have breakfast with you and your family first."

"He never showed up for that, either." Ella dragged him over to the Duke of Mar's carriage and quickly introduced him to Solway and Mar, although she expected they all knew each other. A quick exchange of information revealed Caden had not shown up anywhere today.

"Stay with the ladies, Stafford," Mar said, a frown revealing his heightened concern.

Ella shook her head. "We are not in need of a nanny to watch us. He must go in with you. He's very clever and will know how to speak to the servants to pry information out of them. Is that not right, Mr. Stafford?"

"I like to think so."

She nodded and continued. "Also, Mr. Stafford might spot something amiss that you would overlook because he has been traveling with Lord Mersey and his grandfather, not to mention their entire entourage, for months."

"Aye, lass. Ye have a point," Solway said. "Stafford, we'll knock at the front door while ye go in through the back."

Ella watched the three men move into action.

"If Caden's grandfather does not kill us," Imogen murmured now that it was just the two of them seated in the elegant carriage. "Papa is going to do it."

Ella emitted a nervous laugh to break the tension. "I know, but I am not going to worry about that now. Oh, Imogen, what if Caden is hurt? I cannot stand the not knowing."

Her sister rested her hand on Ella's. "There is nothing we can do that is not already being done by Solway, Mar, and Stafford."

As more time passed, the wait became even more oppressive, and Ella felt as though she were suffocating. She opened the carriage door and peered out. "What is taking them so long? What if Caden's grandfather is mad as a hatter and has now shot Solway and Mar?"

"We would have heard shots fired. Don't even suggest such a thing."

Ella's stomach was twisted in a thousand knots and her heart skipped beats all over the place. "Oh, Imogen, I pray you are right and he won't hurt anybody. But what if we are wrong and he has already shot Caden?"

Chapter Eighteen

CADEN WAS SEATED beside his grandfather's bed, holding on to the old man's limp hand, when Solway and Mar burst in. He and the doctor immediately turned toward them, surprised by the commotion.

"What the…?" Caden shot to his feet, his every instinct to protect his grandfather, who was no longer conscious and could not defend himself. His tension eased the moment he recognized the men who had burst in. "What are you doing here?"

"We were afraid something bad had happened to ye, lad. Why did ye not send word to us?" Solway asked.

"But I did. I sent one of my grandfather's footmen off hours ago to everyone I was to meet this morning."

"Ye had better see if this footman is all right, because he never reached anyone. Yer betrothed and her sister are waiting outside in my carriage as we speak. The lass is certain ye've been killed."

"Bollocks, none of you knew?" He glanced at the trusted doctor he had personally run to fetch this morning. Dr. George Farthingale was considered the best in London, and Caden would allow no one else to attend his grandfather. "Ella must be scared out of her wits. I had better go to her."

"Aye, but give us a minute and first tell us what happened," Mar said. "Stafford is also here, and who knows what he is going to write about this?"

"He's all right. He can be trusted. Grandfather suffered a heart attack sometime in the wee hours of the morning," Caden said, his voice as broken as his own heart. "I knew something was off with him after his behavior at the musicale and should have insisted on staying with him."

Solway approached and gave him a kindly pat on the shoulder. "How could ye, lad? The stubborn old dog was at your throat the entire time."

Caden nodded numbly, for this was true. But this did not make him feel any better or absolve him from responsibility in bringing on his grandfather's attack. What could he have done differently to prevent this? In all the weeks they had toured the country together, they had been so at odds with each other. Never in public—but privately was another matter. They were two wild dogs constantly growling and snapping at each other.

"I was at fault, too. I should have gone easier on him." He raked a hand through his hair. "I was to have breakfast with Lady Ella and her family this morning but left my club early to look in on him. His valet found him unconscious on the floor. But Ella… I must assure her that I am unharmed."

He escorted Mar and Solway into the parlor, leaving Dr. Farthingale to do what he did best, and that was to work medical miracles.

Caden was not a praying man, but he had been silently praying all morning that his grandfather would recover.

"Swindon," he said to the head butler, who hurried toward him, obviously quite distressed, "have tea and refreshments brought into the parlor. And I believe a Mr. Stafford is in the kitchen. Have him join us in the parlor as well."

"At once, my lord." But Swindon hesitated a moment. "Might I ask…how is His Grace?"

"Holding his own." Caden had known the head butler almost all of his life, ever since his parents had died when he was only six. His grandfather had taken him in then, and it had been quite a change from his mother's delicate touch and his father's patient ways to the stern training his grandfather had thought it important to pound into him. "We'll know more as the day wears on."

After giving a nod of encouragement to the butler, he strode out of the house toward Mar's waiting carriage. The door flew open as he approached, and Ella flung herself into his arms. "I thought he had killed you."

Before he had the chance to utter a word, she drew his head down and began to kiss him everywhere on his face. Her kisses were a balm to him, her lips so soft and sweet as she kissed his cheeks, jaw, nose, and, urgently, his mouth. "I am very much alive and in health, Ella," he said with a light, groaning laugh.

She looked up at him, her luminescent eyes tearful. "I was so worried."

"I know, love. I'm so sorry about the confusion. I sent a footman off with messages to you, Stafford, and the two dukes, but it seems he never made it to anyone's home. We're looking into the matter now. The doctor is here. I think you know Dr. Farthingale."

"Yes, we know him well. He treated Uncle Cormac years ago and tried to save his arm. If anyone could have succeeded, it would have been him. But too much time had elapsed between Cormac's getting shot and his return to England. There was no chance to save the arm, but he certainly saved my uncle's life. We are forever in his debt." She frowned. "Why is he here? Has something happened to your grandfather?"

He nodded. "Come inside and I will tell everyone. Ah, Imogen is with you. I might have known."

Imogen had popped her head out to listen as they spoke. "I'm glad you are unharmed, Caden. But I'm very sorry your grandfather is ailing."

"Thank you, Imogen. His heart gave out sometime in the middle of the night. We can only wait and see whether he will recover."

"But you have the best man on the task," Ella assured him.

He led the two of them into the house, intending to allay their fears, allow them to ask their questions, and then have Stafford escort them home. Ella would know not to press him. He would visit her later. Attending to his grandfather and meeting with Solway and Mar were his priorities today.

In fact, he and the Scots could meet in the privacy of his grandfather's study. The irony would be lost on no one, for he was plotting how to defeat the old man under his very roof.

That was another thing. It was time he moved back in with his grandfather and claimed his rightful status as heir. He should not have set up residence at his club in the first place. This was him being stubborn, for his grandfather had demanded Caden stay with him now that they were back in London. "You are a Seaton and all should know it," he had declared, but Caden could not understand how they could be so opposed on so many matters and yet live amicably under the same roof.

He was worried they would constantly be at each other's throats. No doubt they would have been, and would be fighting again once his grandfather regained his health. But the old man had been right. They were family, and it was time they learned to deal with each other without their tempers flaring.

He was pleased to see Stafford waiting for him in the parlor, along with Solway and Mar, when he walked back inside with the ladies.

"You can blame this uproar on your grandfather's toady, Abbott," Stafford said. "Mrs. Nance, your grandfather's house-keeper, told me that he arrived moments after you rushed off to summon Dr. Farthingale. He stopped the footman, had the audacity to countermand your orders, and took the notes you had written to each of us. He assured the footman he was going to deliver them personally, but walked off and must have dumped the lot somewhere along the way."

"Or is still holding them in his pocket and laughing about it," Caden muttered.

"The footman is now trembling in the kitchen, certain you are going to sack him."

"I have no authority to sack him," Caden said. "Nor would I do so if I did. How can I blame him for obeying Abbott when I have not been around to exert my presence, as I should have been? I allowed that toady to gain importance in my grandfather's household and in his life."

Ella cast him a gentle look. "You have the opportunity to change this now."

"I know. I have already given it thought."

"Don't think too hard," Imogen interjected. "There is much to be said for just following one's heart."

Caden settled into a chair beside Ella, who was seated on the sofa with her sister. "Well, you are all conveniently here, so this saves my having to run from appointment to appointment. This will also give me time to write my speech for Parliament. In truth, I have been struggling with it."

Ella looked up at him in surprise. "But you have been making wonderful speeches across the country. No one doubts your eloquence or how inspiring you are to all who hear you. Can you not adapt one of them for your Parliament speech?"

He shook his head. "No, this one must be an oration for the ages. It must touch the hearts of peers and politicians. Many would argue these men do not have hearts."

That earned him several chuckles.

"Aye, laddie," Solway said. "But many of us do and will care."

"You will be wonderful," Imogen said, smiling at him. "We hope to be in the spectators' gallery and hear you speak. Papa has already agreed to accompany us."

Caden grinned. "Thank you, Imogen." He turned serious in the next moment. "I hope my grandfather will be well enough to attend, too. Dr. Farthingale is giving him the best care, but even his skill might not be enough. The speech is next week. I don't know if my grandfather will have the strength to open his eyes by then."

"Is it that bad?" Mar asked.

"It looks that way, but I am no medical man. He could be hopping about by tomorrow and cursing my existence. I would rejoice in that." Caden's voice broke, as it had several times already. His grandfather's illness was hitting him quite hard. For all his oration and the standing ovations he had received, he had been thinking outwardly, criticizing others for their actions or inactions, talking about how they needed to change their attitude—but when had he ever looked inwardly and examined his own shortcomings?

Who *was* he? What did he stand for as a man? What was he willing to take on for the sake of others? What did he need to change in himself to become a better man?

Ella was staring at him.

What did she see in him now?

They finished their refreshments, then Stafford escorted Ella and her sister back to their home in Mar's carriage. The driver would return for Mar and Solway later. "We can put off our meeting for another day," Mar offered as the ladies were being escorted to his carriage.

Caden shook his head. "If you don't mind, I would prefer to work now. Dr. Farthingale is with my grandfather and knows to summon me if he wakes up. I've been by his side all morning and he has not blinked, not even once. Nor has he responded to the light squeeze of my hand. I don't think he hears my voice, but Dr. Farthingale suggests I read to him or talk to him whenever I am at his bedside. He is convinced it helps."

"Well, let's get to work, then," Solway said with a nod. "What changes are ye hoping to bring about, and what support do ye need from us?"

They spent the next hour in discussion.

Caden was interested in hearing what was of greatest importance to them and what mattered least. He had been looking at this as a soldier and not a politician when he first started his hero tour. But Stafford's wisdom had been invaluable in making him understand give-and-take. A soldier was trained to fight to the death for an objective. There was no give-and-take, only conquest. It was up to the other side to surrender and plead for a truce. However, a smart politician was trained to barter and avoid fights. That bartering involved trading on matters of lesser significance in order to gain support for those of importance to him.

He listened in all earnestness to these dukes, who were good men and truly cared for their soldiers.

Once they had departed, Caden returned upstairs to see his grandfather. Dr. Farthingale was at his bedside issuing instructions to two sturdy-looking ladies in uniform about proper care. Those uniforms consisted of modest dove-gray gowns, crisp white aprons, and white caps without any frills. Earlier this morning, Caden had sent word to an agency highly recommended by Dr. Farthingale for attendants trained in medical care. The ladies appeared to be the no-nonsense, earnest sort. The few questions they asked were intelligent and showed them to be experienced.

His grandfather's longtime valet, Cranford, stood quietly in a corner and was straining to hear Dr. Farthingale's every word. However, as devoted as Cranford was to his employer, he did not possess even the most rudimentary medical knowledge necessary to be of much use at the moment.

No, the duke's survival was now in the hands of Dr. Farthingale and these ladies of mercy.

Caden waited beside the valet, not wanting to interfere with the doctor's instructions. But once he was done, Caden called for Mrs. Nance to show the ladies to their quarters and offer them a meal before one rejoined them to watch over his grandfather. They were to reside here and work in shifts for the next few days until his condition could be better assessed.

Caden resumed his seat beside his grandfather's massive bed and took his hand. This once fierce and vital man looked so small and pale right now, so lost amid the bedding. "Come on, you old goat. Open your eyes and shout at me."

There was no response.

Sighing, he listened with half an ear as the doctor walked over to Cranford and issued him instructions. "What did you tell him?" he asked when Cranford rushed out.

Dr. Farthingale arched an eyebrow and grinned. "I gave him chores. Otherwise, he will be fussing and fretting, and irritating the ladies to no end while he remains underfoot."

"Clever idea. I'm going to move back in here today. I'll keep Cranford busy acting as my valet in the meanwhile. I haven't used one in quite some time, so he ought to have plenty to do to put me back in fashionable shape. I'll have him start with polishing my boots and freshening my uniforms. Perhaps I'll rip a seam or pull a button or two—that ought to keep him fussing."

"That should work." The doctor's grin broadened, but only for a moment before he quickly sobered. "I have other patients requiring my attention, but will stop in as often as I can through-out the day. He is resting peacefully now, and his condition is stable. There is nothing any of us can do but wait. If you have matters that require your attention, then go about your day and do them."

"Thank you, doctor."

Momentarily alone with his grandfather, Caden stared down at an ashen face so devoid of vitality. He ran a hand gently across the old man's forehead and then along his cheek, his touch remaining soft as a caress. "I love you, Grandfather."

He knew this was something he should have told him sooner.

There was not the slightest twinge in response.

Well, he had waited too long to say it. And his grandfather had never said it to him. All that seemingly mattered to the old man was maintaining tradition and holding on to power. Caden's near-death at the hands of the Ashanti had not troubled him—or if it had, he had certainly hidden his anguish well.

Perhaps the love Caden felt for his grandfather only went one way.

"Bah," he muttered, setting that hurt aside.

But a thought struck him—that feelings had an important place in the speech he was to give the members of Parliament. Most of his speeches had been about duty, honor, service, and sacrifice of soldiers, and the duty now owed to them in return by England. He was a soldier, not a philosopher, yet philosophy was at the very heart of what England was to be and what it ought to represent to the world.

In this, he and his grandfather had opposing views, his grandfather believing that to prove one's might, one had to grab and oppress, while Caden, having seen the damage caused by this attitude, preferred a more reasoned approach.

What argument could the old man possibly make in support of his position when he had been using government appointees like Fulke to "grab and oppress" for his own personal gain and did not care about Crown interests or the life of his own grandson?

Caden grunted in frustration. The world was not going to change. Men were always going to be greedy and seek personal gain above the interests of others. Men were always going to thirst for power—or desire what their neighbor had and try to steal it for themselves. Thousands of years of fighting had proven this. He was never one to back down from a fight himself. But so many of these battles were senseless, and often destroyed the very thing coveted in the first place.

Knowing his grandfather was in competent hands, and not wishing to remain underfoot while the ladies tended to him, Caden went downstairs. It was time he attended to the running of the Seaton holdings and household. His first priority was to kick out Abbott. That worm would never give a blessed order to anyone in the Seaton employ or enter this house again.

He summoned the head staff and his father's secretary to the study. Once they were all gathered, he chose to address them while standing in front of the massive mahogany desk rather than usurp his grandfather's position by sitting behind it. "Swindon," he said, turning to the head butler, "my belongings are to be brought here. I'll have Mr. Talbott write instructions for the club steward. Have one of your footmen deliver it. He is to take the Seaton carriage. I don't have much other than clothes at the club, and it can all fit easily in there."

"Would a wagon not suit better, my lord?"

"No." He wanted everyone to know—as if they didn't already—that he was the duke's heir. It could not hurt to reinforce this.

He next turned to his grandfather's personal secretary. "Mr. Talbott, I shall dictate notes to be sent to various persons. Plain sheets. I will not use His Grace's stationery."

"Very good, my lord." The gangly young man immediately hopped to a small desk in the corner and took out quill pen, inkpot, and writing paper.

With a satisfied nod, Caden turned to Mrs. Nance. "Please have my old bedchamber prepared. I shall settle in there."

"At once, my lord." She bustled out, seeming quite pleased.

He had called in his grandfather's valet as well. "Cranford, I have not been home in a while, but I do have an entire wardrobe moldering in the armoire that must be badly in need of attention by now. In addition, I have my uniforms that will soon be brought over from my club. Sort through all of it and decide on what is to be kept, what is to be cleaned and mended, and what cannot be brought up to fashion. Those articles of attire can be donated to any charity His Grace sponsors."

Cranford cleared his throat. "Um, I do not believe His Grace personally sponsors any."

Caden suppressed a sigh of exasperation. He should have known his grandfather was all about acquiring things, never about giving things away, even if they no longer served a useful purpose. "Obviously, my uniforms are to be cleaned and mended. Those are not to be discarded for any reason. I am still serving in the Royal Marines. Also, my medals are to be handled with utmost care and stored in a velvet-lined box in the top drawer of my bureau."

He turned back to Talbott and dictated more notes, the first for the head steward at his club, since he wanted to get himself moved in here as soon as possible. The next notes were for his grandfather's financial advisors. The last, and probably most important, was for his grandfather's estate manager. There were several estate managers employed by the old man, since the Seaton holdings were vast, but only one held seniority and oversaw the other managers. "I believe Mr. Randall is in Town now. Have him come here at eleven o'clock tomorrow morning."

Talbott nodded. "Very good, my lord."

If he was offended by Caden's apparent move to take over, he did not show it. Caden supposed this was because his grandfather merely regarded his staff as useful but easily replaceable. He had done little to win their devotion or loyalty over the years.

Not that it mattered here and now. In truth, this distance between servant and master his grandfather had always maintained served Caden well at the moment. He met with no resistance to his edicts. In fact, they seemed relieved that he, and not Abbott, had taken charge.

Once all messages were properly sent off, he looked in on his grandfather again. Seeing he was resting comfortably, Caden rode off to call on Ella.

She was anxiously awaiting him, and rushed to the front door as soon as she heard Merrick greet him. "Come into the parlor," she said, pulling him toward it before he'd had the chance to remove his cloak.

Merrick managed to catch it, along with his gloves and hat, as Caden quickly took them off and tossed them to the butler, who had scampered after them.

"Lady Ella, shall I bring in tea and refreshments?"

"An excellent idea. Thank you, Merrick." She turned to Caden. "Would you like something stronger than tea?"

"No, I'll save the stiff drinks for later."

When Ella settled on the settee, he sat beside her and quickly brought her up to date on his grandfather's condition, including all that had been arranged for his care.

"Yes, his care is most important," she replied. "The ladies must keep him clean and shift his position from time to time, or he will develop bedsores."

"How do you know this? Oh, from your time at the hospital in Moonstone Landing."

She nodded. "Imogen and I were never permitted to do this sort of work, but it did not stop us from watching others and learning."

"There is much I have to learn, as well. Not only medical, but about running a dukedom. My grandfather was so vibrant that I thought I still had years to address this. Now, I will have to cram quite a bit of study over the next few days. I intend to meet with my grandfather's estate manager and financial men next, assure them I will be handling Seaton affairs while my grandfather cannot. In this, I fear I am going to be as tough as him."

"Not everything he did was wrong," Ella pointed out.

"I suppose not. He did beat quite a bit of business sense into me."

"You were always strong, smart, and sensible. I do not think he needed to beat anything into you. But Caden...the way he used his fist on you," she said haltingly and with sudden distress, "you would not beat our children, would you?"

The question surprised him, although it should not have, considering the combative relations between him and his grandfather. "No, Ella. Not even an occasional trip to the woodshed if they severely misbehave. Being beaten never worked on me. It only made me more willful and defiant."

"I am not surprised. I don't think anyone could ever beat you into submission."

"I am as thickheaded as my grandfather," he said with a nod. "But I learned some important lessons while serving in the Royal Marines. Men follow out of duty, but they will fight to the death for friendship and brotherhood. Trust must be earned. It is something every good battlefield commander understands. Men will fight for you and follow you unfailingly if they believe in you. It is all about leadership and loyalty. Beating fear into others never works in the long run. It has helped me to understand what I need to convey in my speech to Parliament."

Ella leaned forward, obviously eager to hear more. "I know it will be wonderful and inspirational."

He chuckled. "We'll see."

"My mother dotes on my father. She thinks the sun and moon revolve around him. I never understood how she could feel this way about him. We love him, of course. But now, I find myself thinking of you in this same way. Every time I see you, I am filled with pride and wonder. I know you will be magnificent in everything you do."

"Don't put me up on that high a pedestal, Ella."

She shook her head. "I'm not. Nor will I be as docile as my mother in voicing opinions. You know you are going to hear an earful from me."

He cast her an affectionate smile. "I hope so."

"You do?"

He nodded. "I value your judgment."

She leaned forward and kissed him, deliciously pressing her mouth to his, an action he prolonged by cupping the back of her head to keep her from drawing away while he deepened the kiss and took pleasure in the sweet taste of her. He released her abruptly when he heard the tea cart rattling down the hall. "Merrick's approaching."

"Oh, yes. Mustn't shock the dear man." Ella gave him one of her typically radiant smiles. "Perhaps I will be as docile as my mother after all. You have a way of making me swoon."

"And you have a way of stealing my breath away."

"I'm glad I do. In truth, I have such difficulty understanding what makes me so special to you."

"Everything about you draws me to you," he responded earnestly. "Your smile, your beauty, your thoughtfulness and kindness. I trust you with my heart and also with my innermost thoughts. You are my safe harbor, I suppose. A lovely harbor."

"You say this as though you have need of me now. How can I help?"

He winced. "Ella, my grandfather and I were so often at odds, but despite it all, I loved him. I waited until now to tell him, waited until he was unconscious and could not hear me."

"He did not make it easy for you, Caden. In fact, he probably made you feel as though he would beat you for your softness. But I'm glad you told him now. It is right that you did, and hopefully he heard it. Whether he wanted to leap out of bed and rail at you for saying it is another matter," she admitted, laughing softly.

He smiled back. "I will never make that mistake with you. I love you, Ella. I will tell you so every day of my life."

"Caden," she whispered, and kissed him again—a swift, brief kiss—then drew away quickly, as Merrick was now at the threshold with the tea cart. "You know I feel the same about you. I love you so dearly. Have you given consideration to our wedding? Do we move it up? Postpone it? Keep to the original plan?"

"I don't know. Everything has changed since yesterday. I haven't had a chance to think about these new circumstances."

She was obviously disappointed, but made no fuss. "I understand. Papa will also have to reconsider. That is a good thing, because I don't think he has changed his mind about wanting it postponed. What he really wants is for it to be broken off, but I will never agree to such a thing. Postponement it shall be if you and my father wish it. But that discussion is better left for another day. As you said, you have too much on your mind now."

She turned toward Merrick as he set the cart beside them. "Is there anything more you need, Lady Ella?" he asked.

"No, thank you. It is all perfect."

He nodded and returned to his post by the front door.

Ella poured tea into each cup with graceful efficiency and set a slice of lemon cake on each plate. But neither of them were hungry, and the cake went untouched while they spoke. "Caden, I know we just agreed not to discuss the wedding. But plans have been underway for weeks now. Any changes will not only impact us, but our guests and everyone hired for the occasion. The invitations are about to go out. Everything has been ordered. I am not asking for a decision today. But it cannot be put off beyond the end of this week, or we won't be able to alert our guests in time."

"Nor is it fair to the orchestra hired or anyone else involved." He raked a hand through his hair. "I understand. Don't change anything yet. We'll see what happens over the next few days. It is very possible you will be marrying a duke, not just some soldier with the courtesy title of marquess."

Her expression turned pained. "If you do come into the title, then it is likely we shall not be able to marry as planned. It would not be right to proceed with a grand wedding while you are in mourning. I hope it does not come to pass, because I wish only good health for your grandfather. You know I never cared about titles. You were all that mattered to me."

"I know, love." Caden regarded her, realizing suddenly how dense he was. Ella was right. Their wedding could never go ahead as planned if he lost his grandfather. But postponing it was the last thing he wanted to do.

In truth, he would need Ella more than ever. Without her gentle touch and guidance, what sort of man would he become once he became Duke of Seaton? He had so much of the old man's stubborn and combative ways in him already.

Indeed, they were two peas in a pod.

He took Ella's hand and held on to it dearly.

She glanced at their clasped hands, then looked up at him. "You are not your grandfather, Caden."

He gave a mirthless laugh. "Can you promise me this?"

She smiled at him. "I'll chase you around with a broom if you ever behave like him. Is this what has you so worried?"

He nodded.

Would he turn into a greedy beast just like his grandfather?

Chapter Nineteen

CADEN STARED DOWN at his grandfather, seriously worried.

Two days had passed since his heart attack, and the old man had yet to wake up. In another few days, there would be no chance of his recovery. Without water, a person could last no more than four or five days.

Caden took a damp cloth and dabbed drops of water onto his grandfather's lips to moisten them, but it was not the same as swallowing liquids, which he had not yet done. Nor was he capable of swallowing anything while lying unconscious.

Frustrated, Caden set the cloth aside as Dr. Farthingale walked in shortly before noon. To his surprise, Ella followed close on his heels. He was pleased to see her and rose to cross the bedchamber to greet her. "Ella, is everything all right at home? I did not expect your visit."

She looked like an angel, her golden hair soft and shining, and her eyes filled with concern. Her gown, a dark green merino wool, was elegant and understated in its style. She looked exquisite. Perhaps it was just him responding with heat every time he set eyes on her. The lace about the collar and sleeve cuffs, and the prim way the gown buttoned to her slender throat, never failed to get his heart pounding and turn his blood hot.

"It is terribly forward of me, I know," she said as though worried he might toss her out. Lord, he just wanted to pull her into his arms and hold on to her forever. "I had to see how you were doing. Have you eaten? Or slept at all? You help no one, least of all your grandfather, by wearing yourself down."

"I know. But I have no appetite."

"Maybe something light will do, a broth and a little bread. I asked Mrs. Nance to bring up a bowl for you when she mentioned that you hadn't been taking anything."

He cast her an affectionate grin. "I don't need you mothering me."

"I'm sorry."

"Don't be—it's nice." He took her hands in his. "I haven't thanked you for taking over my hospital visits."

"None required. Imogen and I are happy to help out. She and Mr. Stafford are waiting in the carriage for me now. We are off to that new seamen's home just opened in Southwark. We'll be fine. Do not fret."

He frowned. "Don't stay too long. You mustn't be in that part of London after dark."

She nodded. "I have received this same lecture from my father and have every intention of obeying. Unlike you, I do not bridle at instruction from others, especially when it is sensible. Is there anything in particular you wish me to convey to the seamen?"

"No, just good wishes from me and that I will come by as soon as I can. I don't think they will miss my presence once they set eyes on you and Imogen. But do make note of their needs, write down what they deem most important to them and what is least important."

"All right. I took copious notes on yesterday's visits and will do the same today. What should I do with these notes once I have them in coherent order? Send them over to you?"

"No, love. I'll come by your home before supper this evening. But I won't stay long. Please tell your mother not to set out a place for me. I wouldn't be good company even if I were to stay."

"Oh."

He could see she was disappointed, not only because he was brushing off the dinner invitation. They had yet to speak about their wedding plans, and he still was not ready to discuss them. No doubt this was troubling Ella, although she was too sweet ever to raise the matter.

He knew for a certainty it was irritating her father.

Well, it could not be helped. How was Caden to know what might be required of him while his grandfather was in a coma and on the verge of taking his last breath? All would be clarified within the next two or three days.

"Well, see that you take a little sustenance," she said, glancing at the bowl of broth Mrs. Nance had just brought up and quietly set beside him. "I had better be on my way."

"I'll walk you out." But he took his time leading her down the long hall toward the stairs. He liked being with her and was reluctant to see her go.

"I meant to ask," she said, breaking into his thoughts, "how did the meetings go with your grandfather's advisors?"

"Quite well. I certainly cannot fault the old man in his attention to the family interests. I've gone through dozens of reports regarding the Seaton assets, and there is very little to trim away. They are all operating at a profit."

"I am not surprised. Your grandfather seemed sharp as a hawk and very much needing to be in control of everything."

"Including whom I marry," Caden said with a sigh, but dismissed that concern, since he was now betrothed to Ella and there was nothing and no one ever going to dissuade him from marrying her. All that was in doubt was the timing. "As for the Seaton assets, I was relieved to see he hadn't gotten much into 'the steal from others to enrich myself' business yet."

"Oh, I'm glad."

"Those Ashanti gold mines are all that were taken by him and his so-called business partners. Perhaps more of these shady dealings will turn up as I dig deeper, but it appears most of our holdings are in England and inherited from the former Duke of

Seaton. There's no question my grandfather improved on them, but they were gained by legitimate means, assuming our early ancestors were not scoundrels and cutthroats."

"England's history is so filled with wars and brutal grabs for power," Ella said. "I cannot imagine any of today's powerful families having reached their status because their forefathers were pious."

"I suppose not," Caden admitted. "Was I too hard on my grandfather? Am I a fool to be enraged and blaming him and that worm, Abbott, because of what happened to my men?"

She shook her head. "No. Absolutely not. What they allowed Fulke to do was heinous. There is a difference between fighting for our country because we are at risk of being attacked, and our marching in and grabbing whatever we want from others who never had any intention of harming us. I see that clearly. So do many of your peers, particularly Solway and Mar. I think the Scottish lords are most sympathetic because this is what the English did to them on their lands, and it is still quite fresh in their minds."

He gave her a soft kiss. "I think *you* ought to make the speech to Parliament. You will be far more persuasive."

Her eyes rounded in mock horror. "Dear heaven, no. But I shall cheer for you loudly from my high perch in the gallery."

He gave her cheek a light caress. "I love you, Ella."

She melted into his embrace. "I love you too."

He realized by her tone that his words came as a relief for her.

Idiot!

He had not properly considered what his reluctance in firming their wedding plans was doing to her. And Ella was not the sort ever to say something to him about it. But it had to be worrying her. Would he back out? Would things change if he became duke?

"Ella, I am going to marry you." This was all he could say, and he would keep telling her until he knew more about his grandfather's condition.

"I know."

But she didn't really. Caden could hear the false bravado in her words. "I will, Ella. Even though we are not in Moonstone Landing, I do not need to see those moonstones to know they are shining for us. Have faith, love."

He walked her out to the waiting carriage, greeted Stafford and Imogen, and remained on the street to watch them as their carriage disappeared around the corner.

He strode back inside to speak to Dr. Farthingale. "Do you detect any change?"

"No," the doctor said. "Tomorrow will be a turning point, I fear."

Caden's heart tightened. "I suppose I had better pray harder for that miracle."

He spent the rest of the day by his grandfather's side, talking to him and reading to him. He even read the Shelley poem Ella loved so much. "I know, Grandfather. I cringed too when she first read it to me. But it helped pull me out of the depths of my despair. Well, seeing Ella's beautiful face again probably did most of that for me. The poem helped, too. It reminded me that beauty does still exist. Not everything in life is about cruelty and greed."

He sighed and continued. "Do not take that as an accusation against you. It is just a general comment on the nature of man."

Caden left his grandfather's side only occasionally to meet with the estate manager and financial advisors. He had several very smart money men, but the one who stood out as best among them was Finn Brayden. For this reason, Caden had asked to meet with him privately today.

"Lord Mersey, you look as though you have something specific on your mind. What is it you wish to ask me?"

Finn settled into one of the chairs opposite the desk, obviously comfortable with their meeting, and perhaps relieved to be meeting with Caden and not Abbott. Caden took the chair beside his, preferring a more casual chat to sitting behind that big desk, which only served as a barrier between them. "There is something that worries me, Mr. Brayden. It has nothing to do with the Seaton investments under your management. It is those he has with Lord Horace Abbott. Do you know anything about them?"

"Yes, I make it my business to know what else my clients are investing in. Are we to be honest here?"

"Absolutely. This is why I invited you here alone. If I could strangle Abbott and get away with it, I would. I do not like his influence over my grandfather at all."

Finn nodded. "Nor do I. But I have somehow been relegated to managing the England investments and a few on the Continent, while Abbott has somehow placed himself in charge of all your grandfather's investments in the far reaches. I think he has your grandfather involved in African ventures other than those Ashanti mines, as well as a few endeavors in India and the Caribbean islands."

"Tea plantations? Rum and sorghum? Sugarcane?"

"Yes, some of that," Finn said. "I am not too concerned about the sugarcane and rum investments in the Caribbean. Those were acquired legitimately. What troubles me most are the mining interests. Diamonds and gold from Africa. Emeralds, sapphires, and rubies from Asia. Abbott will not show me his contracts on those, which indicates they were gained by other means. Watch out for him, my lord. I think he is making deals with mercenary armies, especially in these mining regions."

"Do you think he is quietly amassing his own private army right here in England?"

Finn appeared surprised by the notion. "No, my lord. Surely someone would have noticed. I have been keeping an eye on him. I suppose the risk is small as to that sort of activity in England, for the king himself would come down hard on him. Abbott has too much to lose by bringing his mercenaries here."

Caden nodded. "I suppose you are right. Have you discussed your concerns about Abbott's investments with anyone else?"

Finn shook his head. "Not yet. I would need hard proof before making any serious accusations. However, I have been trying to steer my other clients away from investing with him. Some are like your grandfather, too tempted by the easy profits to understand the risks involved. Well, I suppose they must understand, but still turn a blind eye. Unsanctioned land grabs are never a wise investment. Those lands are inevitably grabbed back, and the investors will lose everything."

"I am not in a position to undo those Abbott investments, but my grandfather is in no condition to undertake any new ventures with him. I have barred Abbott from this house for now. Of course, my grandfather can countermand my orders should he…" Caden emitted a ragged sigh. "Should he ever return to alertness. Dr. Farthingale has been doing his best."

Finn smiled. "I am married to a Farthingale myself, so I know the family very well. Your grandfather is in the most capable hands with George."

They quickly finished the rest of their business, and Caden returned to his grandfather's bedchamber. To his amazement, the duke's eyes were open. "Thank heaven!"

Caden rushed to his side, but looked to Dr. Farthingale for guidance when his grandfather did not appear to respond.

He shook his head, and his expression was quite devoid of glee. "I'm not sure he is awake, my lord. Yes, his eyes are open, but he remains unresponsive."

"Does this mean he still has not been able to drink?"

"Not a drop yet."

Caden knelt beside his grandfather's bed and spoke gently. "Can you hear me, Grandfather? Just give me a sign, any sign. We need to get some water into you. Do you think you can drink? Just a sip to hold you over."

Caden received a blank stare back.

"It's all right," he muttered, caressing the old man's brow. "Maybe later. We'll give it a try later." He smothered his disappointment when his grandfather remained unresponsive. "I love you. Do not give up the fight."

At some point, the old curmudgeon might hear him.

Caden remained by his grandfather's bed as the hours passed, watching his vacant stare and thinking very hard about his own future. His muscles ached and his throat was a little dry from talking to him all the while, but he rose and stretched when Swindon appeared at the bedchamber door. "My lord, you have visitors."

"Send them away."

"It is Lady Melinda and her father."

The last people he wanted to see were Melinda Wycliff and her surly bull of a father. What did they want? Well, he supposed he owed them the courtesy, since Wycliff and his grandfather had been talking of a match between him and Melinda ever since they were born.

"Bollocks." He sighed. "Show them into the parlor. I'll be down in a moment."

"WE HEAR YOUR grandfather is at death's door," Melinda's father remarked the moment he strode in.

"What do you want?" Caden did not bother with any courtesies, since they were showing none to him or his grandfather. Neither of them asked how his grandfather was doing, nor did they seem to particularly care.

Melinda just looked at him, not even considering the mumble of a "so sorry" or a tender expression of remorse.

Well, why should *she* be sad? Her only interest in the Seaton family was the possibility of her becoming a duchess. Was this why they were here? Hoping to renew discussions of a marriage between them?

Her father confirmed it with his next words. "Your grandfather and I had an agreement. You were to marry Melinda."

Caden stared him down. "I never agreed to it. I am betrothed now, as you well know. And so is Melinda, is she not? What happened to Jeremy Flint?"

Melinda's mouth curled in distaste. "I did not like him. I broke off the engagement."

"*You* broke it off?" Caden noted the flicker in her eyes and knew she was lying to him. "Or was it the other way around?" Good for Flint—took him long enough to realize that a whopping fortune was not enough to offset the misery he would have to endure while married to this girl. Not that Flint was any prize either.

She shot to her feet and slapped him. "How dare you!"

That slap awakened Caden to what was important…and what he had been taking for granted all these weeks. Love. Happiness. A wife who would challenge him but never demean him. Ella would never have struck him, not in a million years.

"We will battle this out in the press, if we must," her father threatened, just as he had done the last time. Why did Wycliff think threats would force Caden into submission now, when they hadn't worked while his grandfather was healthy and pressing for the marriage as well?

"You still haven't learned, have you? All this will accomplish is making your daughter look the fool." How many times were they to have this discussion before the pair slithered away like snakes in the grass? "The only reason to go to the press is because you have not a prayer of winning in the courts. Even if you produce a betrothal agreement, Melinda's betrothal to Flint—as doomed as it was bound to be—will have made that earlier document irrelevant."

"My wealth will insulate her from any damage," her father insisted. "But your reputation will be destroyed. You will be no one's hero, but branded a cad and a coward."

"Do whatever you feel you must, but I will *never* marry your daughter. Save yourself the embarrassment and buy some other toady who is easier to manage than Flint turned out to be." He rang for Swindon. "Please show my guests to the door."

"This isn't over, Mersey. You are not duke yet, and I will make you suffer!" The pair stormed out.

Swindon returned to look in on him. "My lord, I am so sorry. Your grandfather never refused his visits. I did not know what to do. I ought to have kept them out."

"It is all right, Swindon. You did the right thing." Caden gave the man an encouraging nod. "And now *I* must do the right thing."

He had to talk to Ella.

He rode over to the Stockwell townhouse. It was early evening, and the family would soon gather for the supper meal. The family now included the Marquess of Burness, who had arrived for the purpose of participating in the upcoming sessions of Parliament.

Caden dismounted and was greeted at the door by the ever-reliable Merrick, then shown into the parlor, where the marquess and Ella's parents were having a drink before they sat down to dine.

He had yet to greet them when Ella hurried in just behind him.

"Caden, I wasn't sure we would see you this evening." She was breathless and appeared happy as she bustled in with papers in hand. "I've made notes on all the places I visited yesterday and today, just as you asked. I hope you find them useful."

He took them from her hands and quickly perused the neatly written lists. Everything he'd asked for was set out in an organized fashion and helpfully outlined. "Thank you, this is excellent. Your efforts are much appreciated."

She gazed up at him with big, hopeful eyes. "I can tell you a little about my findings, if you wish to hear them now."

He smiled, knowing how proud she must be of her work. But he glanced at the elders, especially her father, who did not particularly care about anything other than when Caden would marry his daughter. "Perhaps now is not the best time, Ella," he said, setting the notes aside for the moment, since her father was glowering at him and showing marked impatience.

"But it won't take long. Papa, you don't mind, do you?"

"In fact, I do mind." Lord Stockwell, not pleased with the idea of Caden's hero tour and the frenzy of adulation surrounding him, had been the one to push for a delay. So why was he frowning now when he and Ella had been going along with his wishes? He could not have been too pleased about Ella making those hospital appearances in Caden's stead.

Fortunately, the marquess seemed to be more tolerant of their situation. "Come on, John. Charlotte. What your daughter is doing is important, and she obviously enjoys the work. Give them a few minutes alone."

Caden meant to express his gratitude, but the marquess patted him on the shoulder and cast him a warning look. "This does not mean you have my permission to kiss her. You have my blessing to talk…just talk."

Ella tilted her chin up in indignation. "Well, I never. You are the last person who should level that threat. When have you ever—"

"Ella!" her father said sharply. "It is not at all the same thing."

Ella merely harrumphed.

Caden knew she was going to grab him and kiss him just to be contrary. Not that he minded. He liked that she had her own convictions and knew how to think for herself. Of course, he would probably like it less if she were arguing with him instead of her father.

"Before you all leave, there is something I need to say," he announced. "It is about Ella and me. Lord Stockwell, you have not been happy about my betrothal to your daughter. I have been giving it a lot of thought, and I see your point. What she has had to endure is unforgivable."

Ella's mother had a fan in hand and now began to flutter it in front of her face. "Oh, John. This is what you feared."

Her father's face turned red in anger. "I knew it. You are going to put off the wedding."

Ella immediately assumed her protective Valkyrie stance. "And whose fault is that? You are the one who raised the possibility of a postponement first, Papa. We wanted to marry sooner. You insisted we wait. Then you wanted us to break it off. Then postpone it. I understand that you cannot bear to lose me, your little girl. You and Mama will never lose me. You are overset, but how dare you be angry that Caden is now taking you up on your suggestion."

"I am not taking him up on it," Caden started. "I—"

Her mother emitted another soft cry and sank into a chair. "You are breaking off the betrothal altogether? How could you?"

Everyone now started arguing at once.

Lord in heaven, no wonder the world was such a mess. Not even Ella's family had the sense to simply hear Caden out. He silenced everyone by lifting Ella in his arms and carrying her out of the parlor. He did not care where else they talked, just as long as they were alone.

They all chased after him.

He sighed and set her down in the center of the entry hall. "Yes, I wish to end this betrothal, but only because—"

Everyone began to shout at him again.

"Because I wish to marry Ella tomorrow!" he shouted back.

"Tomorrow?" Her father's eyes narrowed.

"Yes, tomorrow. Assuming I can obtain the special license."

"Why do you need a special license when a common license will do?" he asked.

"Because it will *not* do. I want my grandfather in attendance. The only way we can marry outside of the church and in the Seaton townhouse is with that special license. Will you help me, Lord Stockwell? My hero tour is almost over, and all I have left of importance is addressing the Houses of Parliament this week."

Ella placed her soft hand on his arm. "The truly important work will begin after that."

"Yes, I suppose. But I want you by my side as I undertake it, Ella. If I have to travel throughout England again, I want you with me. I should not have left you behind in Moonstone Landing this first time. I thought I was doing the right thing and protecting you."

"You were," the marquess said. "There was no telling what your grandfather and his friends might have done."

"That is true, but I think the threat is no longer. My grandfather is in no condition to continue the fight. Even if he were, I do not think he would ever do anything to harm Ella now." Caden turned to Ella. "You are wonderful, you know."

She grinned. "You are not so bad yourself."

"I am an arse, but one who loves you deeply and sincerely. Will you marry me tomorrow, Ella?"

She nodded. "Anytime, anywhere."

"I'm sorry if I ever made you feel second to anyone or anything. You are not." He kissed her lightly on the mouth. "You are the best thing in my life."

"As you are in mine."

Imogen must have been watching from the top of the stairs, and now caught their attention by clapping and cheering. "It's about time! Papa, what are you standing around for? Is there not an archbishop for you to track down?"

The Marquess of Burness laughed. "I'm coming with you. Phoebe will never forgive me if I choose to dine rather than get Ella married off to her true love."

"True love," Caden whispered, smiling at Ella. He did not need moonstones to confirm what he felt in his heart. "Yes, how can it be anything else?"

Chapter Twenty

STAFFORD CAUGHT UP to Caden as he, Lord Stockwell, and the Marquess of Burness were about to climb into his carriage, their mission to call upon the Archbishop of London for the grant of that special license. "You will never get it," Stafford said. "The archbishop is not in London at the moment."

Ella's father turned to Caden with a scowl. "Did you know this? Were you just putting on a show for my daughter?"

"No, I had no idea. I will still marry her tomorrow under a common license, but it will have to be in church without my grandfather present, won't it?" In truth, Caden was so tired of all the back-and-forth, and he did not care about wedding plans. He just wanted it done, be told when and where to show up.

He just wanted Ella.

"My wife has been working hard to put all the wedding preparations in order," Lord Stockwell protested. "What is the point of marrying Ella tomorrow if everything is already arranged for next month? I don't know if I approve of your inconstancy."

The Marquess of Burness groaned. "John, calm down. I have never seen you in such a stir. Your little girl loves him, and he loves her. There is nothing inconstant about their desire to marry or your inability to accept it. Just let them do what they must. There's nothing wrong with having a private ceremony tomorrow. Short. Sweet. Just the immediate family."

He turned to Caden. "I'm sorry it will take place without your grandfather. I can see how important he is to you. Despite the friction between the two of you, he is your closest family. We can keep this first ceremony quiet, and you'll simply have a second ceremony along with the wedding breakfast next month as originally planned. Hopefully, your grandfather will be recovered by then and can join us for those festivities."

Ella's father frowned. "Since when have you been the reasonable one? Do not tell us what to do, Cormac."

"Since when have you been the arse in the family?" Cormac shot back. "That is my role, and I am not about to cede it to you."

Caden raked a hand through his hair.

Now these two brothers were fighting over him and Ella.

He was never going to win an argument with Lord Stockwell, since the man obviously adored the idyllic home life he had made with his wife and little girls—but he was about to lose one of those precious girls to Caden, and he could not bear it.

Caden understood his turmoil and hoped he would eventually get over it, mostly for Ella's sake. They were a close family, it was obvious to see.

He also realized Stafford must have shown up for a reason. "What brought you here? Were you looking for me?"

"Everyone is looking for you. Have you not heard? Fulke is dead."

Caden's eyes widened. "How? What happened? When did it happen?"

"Must have been a few weeks after you were shipped home, but news only reached the Foreign Office a short while ago. The Ashanti raided his home and killed him. Dismembered him, I am told."

Caden's expression turned hard as steel. "I cannot say I am sorry for this loss. That man caused so much damage. It was only a matter of time before he met his own end, although it is indeed an awful one. Was it a general uprising, or did they just come after him?"

"I don't know. Lord Palmerston wants you to report to him at the Foreign Office immediately."

The Marquess of Burness arched an eyebrow. "Lord Palmerston? The foreign secretary himself?"

"Yes," Caden said, not pleased to be drawn away but knowing it was important.

Stafford nodded. "I'm sure he will have more to tell us. Mind if I come along?"

Caden turned to Ella's father. "I do not know what this will mean for tomorrow."

"Do you not? I highly doubt that. You are a weasel and have no intention of ever marrying my daughter."

"Lord in heaven," he muttered. "I'll return as soon as my meeting is over."

Ella had been standing on the front steps all the while and must have heard their exchange. He started toward her, but she fled inside.

"Ella!" He wanted to go after her.

Stafford held him back. "The matter is urgent. I think the Duke of Wellington and Earl Grey are also heading over to the Foreign Office. You cannot keep them waiting."

The marquess clapped him on the shoulder. "Ella will understand…even if her stubborn father does not. I will talk to her."

"Thank you." Caden nodded and walked off, his stomach churning as he heard the two brothers arguing again. But his main concern was for Ella. She had to be raw and hurting for the way he was treating her. Wanting to marry right away. Delaying. Then back to their original plan of a December wedding. Postponement. Rushing it forward again, only to have it upended minutes later.

He was overwhelmed himself, feeling tugged in a thousand directions. Pulled one way by his duty to the men who had served and died under his command, another by his duty to ensure the welfare of all soldiers who returned to England after serving. A third direction was his duty to his grandfather and the Seaton dukedom. And now the Foreign Office wanted him.

Ella, in the meanwhile, was shoved and buffeted about like driftwood on a stormy ocean, left to fend for herself as though she mattered least.

Did his duty to her not matter above all else?

The carriage rolled away from the Stockwell residence as soon as he and Stafford climbed in. He considered turning it around, but Stafford stopped him. "This is serious, my lord. Lady Ella will be fine. She is resilient and she loves you."

"She'll tire of me if I continue to tread on her feelings."

"She understands what you are going through. Let's find out why the foreign secretary is so desperate to see you."

"They're not going to let you into the meeting, Stafford."

His friend shrugged. "I never expected they would. I'll wait outside. You'll tell me whatever it is they allow you to tell me. Do you think they are going to ask you to take over as governor in Fulke's stead?"

"It was the first thing that crossed my mind. I'm not going back there, at least not now. There is too much of importance to be done here."

"Marrying Lady Ella, for one," Stafford muttered.

Caden nodded. "She is at the top of my list, although I seem to set her aside too often. No more, Stafford. I am marrying her tomorrow, even if it has to be done at the crack of dawn."

"You do realize the government is in turmoil, don't you? New king. Wellington has just stepped down as prime minister and Earl Grey has yet to officially take his place. You are England's hero. Everyone loves you. They are going to rely on you heavily."

"Let them find another hero."

"It is not that easy," Stafford replied. "I doubt there is anyone in England at the moment who outshines you."

They rode on and arrived apace at the Foreign Office.

As expected, Caden was ushered into a small meeting room while Stafford was told to wait outside.

Lord in heaven.

He came face to face with Wellington and Earl Grey. Also present was the Duke of Wooton, known as the Duke of Ice and legendary among the agents of the Home Office. It calmed Caden to know Wooton was participating in the discussions, for he had been home secretary for years and provided much-needed continuity in the affairs of government.

Finally, Viscount Palmerston entered carrying maps of West Africa in his fisted hands, and set them on the table as he began to bark questions at Caden. "This is an unholy mess, Mersey. What do you know of Fulke's activities? Is it true he had mercenary soldiers under his private hire? Did he claim Ashanti gold mines for himself? I've heard about your speeches and how you are railing about the way territorial governors are appointed and the powers they are given. Talk to us now. What is wrong with our system?"

Caden was surprised by the urgency when he had been trying to gain Lord Palmerston's attention for weeks now. His stomach began to roil, for this meant something terrible had happened beyond the loss of his entire regiment several months ago.

"Fulke was a greedy arse who purposely stirred up rebellion for his own aims," he said, taking a seat at the table as the others did. "He cared not a whit for the good of the Crown. If anything, he was subverting Crown goals for the purpose of enriching himself and his friends. I suggest you bring Lord Abbott in for questioning, for he appears to be at the heart of this matter."

"What do you mean?" Wellington asked. "I've heard he has been putting together investor groups to explore opportunities in various areas of the world. I see nothing wrong with that. Does it not bolster our ties to those countries?"

"Not if we are outright stealing their richest assets, which is what Abbott does. He finds the crooked territorial governors, has them stir up trouble, and then has them send in British soldiers to quiet the unrest. But it does not stop there. Those governors then seize the properties of these supposed rebels, claiming it is done on behalf of the Crown."

"Should these properties not be taken? After all, we must protect our interests," Earl Grey intoned.

"Yes, if ever they were Crown interests. However, the Crown never acquires control, nor does it see a shilling of profit. Those seized properties are turned over to Abbott and his investors. The crooked governor is given a cut for himself. This is where Abbott's mercenaries come in, for they are tasked with guarding the properties so they are not reclaimed by the original owners or the Crown."

"This sounds quite wild," Wooton muttered. "Do you really expect us to believe that Abbott has mercenaries?"

"Who do you think Fulke used to protect himself?" Caden shot back.

Palmerston frowned. "Was this not your duty?"

"Yes, but he would not allow me or my men near him. Because of the unlimited powers granted to him, as with all territorial governors, I had no authority to override his decisions. You made it very simple for him to shut me out and prevent me from acting on behalf of the Crown. *Me.* A commanding officer in the Royal Marines, and you had me taking orders from that oaf."

Caden could see Lord Palmerston's face getting red with anger, but he had no intention of stopping now that he had everyone's ear.

"As far as I know, Abbott has not dared bring his mercenaries onto English soil. I don't know the exact arrangement between Abbott and other governors like Fulke, or between him and his mercenaries, but they all played a role in cheating the Crown. Get rid of these crooked governors and you will fix most of the problem. Remove their authority over British troops and more of the problem will be solved."

"You are familiar with Fulke, but do you have the names of other such governors for us to start our investigation?" Palmerston asked.

"Not offhand, but I know exactly where to look first. The

areas with recent rebellions against the British. Focus your attention on those regions known for their gold, diamonds, and other precious stones. I would not rule out those with profitable trades in salt, cocoa, vanilla beans, tea, or pepper. You will find Abbott's influence wherever there are riches to be made."

"You would have us look at every country in the world," Wellington said, dismissing the notion out of hand.

"No, Your Grace. Only those spots where you are seeing unexpected uprisings against the British. Do not tell me the Ashanti are the only ones in rebellion. Take a closer look at those governors. Question the injured soldiers as they return to England. You must do this."

Wellington arched an eyebrow. "You are telling us what to do?"

"I am *pleading* for you to do this. Your Grace, you are England's hero who led us to victory against Napoleon. Would you not be outraged if your own countrymen were feeding you false information about enemy battle strengths? Refusing to allow your own scouts to get the lie of the land for themselves? Purposely ordering your men into a massacre? Colluding with the Dutch, French, or Portuguese for the goal of seizing profitable mines or plantations for yourself?"

"Are you accusing Fulke of colluding with other countries?"

"He did collude, whenever it served his purpose. I sent off my reports addressing this very concern. Where did they go? Has anyone read them? What will it take to make you understand? You set him up like a potentate, with unrestricted authority to do as he pleased. Need I repeat, you left me helpless to stop him. So he tore up the existing treaties and ordered me and my men into a massacre. Has he done the same again? Was he the only one the Ashanti killed, or were other lives lost because of his venal actions? What else are you not telling me, Lord Palmerston? This outrage cannot be only about Fulke."

"It isn't," Palmerston admitted. "Those mercenaries you mentioned… They were all killed as well."

Caden inhaled sharply. "Where were the Royal Marines in all this? I know my regiment was replaced by fresh forces. Were they harmed, too?"

"No," Lord Palmerston quickly assured him. "This is what had me confused. But if what you say is true, then everything starts to make sense. Fulke surrounded himself with his mercenaries and sent the regiment off on some wild goose chase."

"Thank goodness for that." Caden shook his head and sighed. "Fulke must have wanted them out of the way while he conducted some other private dealings designed to enrich himself and cheat the Crown. The Ashanti are the most powerful tribe in the region. They were not going to put up with Fulke and his greed."

He paused to gauge their interest in what he was saying. They all appeared to be listening avidly.

"I'm sure Fulke thought the Fanta and other local tribes would serve as another layer of protection for him, since they are natural enemies of the Ashanti. But they never had the disciplined military strength of the Ashanti. He was an idiot and bound to fail. Which brings me to another point. What training do any of these governors have? Was Fulke told anything of the area's history? Taught the language? Tested in any way? How did he qualify for his position? Merciful heaven. How was such a man ever selected?"

Palmerston cleared his throat. "That is something to be looked into. I'm sure we did not send Fulke off into Ashanti territory without any briefings."

"You just gave him free rein to shut us out and do as he pleased. And off he went, with his hand out, ready to take all the bribes offered, and no one in place to look over his shoulder and restrain him. How could you hand him control of the Royal Marines? Was anyone even aware he had torn up the hard-fought treaties we had in place? This is just one spot around the world. Who else have you put in power in our colonies?"

"Indeed, how many crooks have we put in place?" Earl Grey muttered.

All eyes were on Palmerston now. He frowned. "We are the greatest power in the world. Obviously, we are doing many things right."

"But there is much room for improvement," Wooton commented. "And the fixes seem rather simple."

"I could not have been the only commanding officer who expressed concerns. How many others were reporting similar problems?" Caden asked. "Where were our complaints going? Did any of mine ever reach your desk, Lord Palmerston?"

Palmerston sighed. "No, they did not."

Wellington pounded his fist on the table. "What a bloody mess. Has our chain of command been so badly degraded? And why are there no generals or admirals at this meeting? What is their responsibility in all this?"

"This is part of the problem," Caden insisted. "You have shut them out here and around the world. Can you not see this?"

He wound up speaking to these high-ranking officials for hours. They had more questions, and then brought in their underlings, who asked more questions. Caden did not know if they would ultimately act upon any of his suggestions.

Would Abbott's activities fall under closer scrutiny? There had to be other businessmen doing the same. For all he knew, that weasel could be but one among a wider circle of privateers sowing discord for their own profit. It required a large purse to fund mercenaries, and he did not think Abbott had the wealth to do it on his own.

Caden personally viewed men like Abbott as snakes. Cut off their ability to bribe territorial governors, and you effectively cut off the head of the snake.

His own role was to protect the Crown interests on the battlefield and secure its peaceful operations. No commanding officer wanted to operate with his hands tied behind his back, as he had been forced to do while Fulke held all the power.

It was the wee hours of the morning by the time the meeting broke up. To Caden's surprise, Stafford was still waiting for him.

"What did you tell them? What did they ask you? What was decided?"

Caden's voice was hoarse as he began to fill Stafford in. "You had better clear everything through Palmerston before you print a single word of what I am about to tell you."

"Why? Did he demand confidentiality?"

Caden grunted. "No, I wouldn't tell you anything if he had asked me to keep it quiet. But I don't want the villains alerted, especially if Palmerston and Wooton plan on acting on the information fast. They'll want the element of surprise on their side."

Stafford rolled his eyes. "Nothing moves fast in government. Besides, you have been giving speeches about these ills for the past two months. It does not matter whether or not you named anyone specifically. The bad players know who they are and have been scrambling to hide their involvement."

"I suppose. Gad, what time is it?"

"Late. About three o'clock in the morning."

"No wonder I'm exhausted." Caden climbed into the Seaton carriage after Stafford, then laid his head back against the squabs and groaned. "Where shall I drop you?"

"I live in Bloomsbury along with the hungry students. A hole-in-the-wall apartment on Southampton Row, near the university. It is out of your way. I can see my own way home."

"How? On foot? Do not be absurd. Some cutpurse will carve out your entrails before you get ten steps around the corner." Caden knocked on the roof of the carriage. "Southampton Row, Danvers."

"As ye wish, my lord." The driver turned the carriage around and set the horses at a trot for Stafford's residence. Because of the late hour, there was no one on the streets, and they made fast time.

"Where do you plan to be tomorrow?" Stafford asked. "I thought I might put my article past you before I hand it over to my editor."

Caden nodded. "I am flattered you would do so. I'll be mostly at my grandfather's bedside, but first thing in the morning, you will find me with Ella. I am serious about marrying her tomorrow...this morning..." He rubbed his eyes. "Lord, I am exhausted. How do you manage to keep alert?"

"I sleep whenever I can," Stafford replied. "In fact, I stretched out on the chairs and napped for several hours while you were holed up with England's finest. I had supper, too. Do you know they have a private dining room in the Foreign Office? They must have a luncheon banquet planned for tomorrow. I ate one of the meals. Delicious."

Caden laughed. "I'll scrounge something in the kitchen when I return to my grandfather's place. Cook will have something left out for me, I'm sure."

"His staff likes you."

Caden shrugged. "Better than hating me, I suppose. Most of them have been with my grandfather since before I was born. They've known me a long time, ever since I came to live with the old man. I was six years old. Feels like three lifetimes ago."

The carriage drew up in front of an elegant building on Southampton Row. Caden peered out. "Doesn't look like a hovel. You must be doing better than you let on."

"I'm not quite a pauper. But a reporter's wages will never make me rich." Stafford hopped down and waved to Caden before entering the building. In truth, it looked like an impressive residence from the outside, but he supposed the rooms had been carved up to fit as many apartments as possible.

He gave this no more thought as he reached the Seaton townhouse and rang for Swindon to unlock the door. He thought he would have a few minutes to wait, but the reliable butler must have been awake and pacing the entry hall, for he opened the door almost immediately. "Thank goodness you are home. I have been beside myself, not knowing what to do."

Caden's heart shot into his throat. "Is it my grandfather?"

Swindon nodded.

Bollocks.

"Has he taken a turn for the worse?"

"No, my lord. He is alert and has been asking for you."

"Thank the Graces," Caden muttered, his heart now soaring with elation. "Has he been able to eat? More important, has he been able to drink?"

"Yes, he's had two helpings of Cook's broth. No solid foods, however. Dr. Farthingale would not allow it. The doctor was here but left several hours ago."

"Is His Grace awake now?"

"No, my lord. He fell back to sleep. You could use some sleep yourself. You look dead on your feet, if I might be so bold as to comment. A few hours' rest won't hurt you. Mrs. Nance brought a tray of fruit and cheese up to your room, knowing you might be late and not have eaten. There's also a pot of tea, but I'm sure it has grown cold by now. She also left you a bottle of wine from His Grace's cellar."

"Fruit, cheese, and wine sound perfect."

He climbed the stairs and quietly looked in on his grandfather, but did not stay because he saw the old man was comfortably sleeping. The night attendant was awake and nodded to him. He nodded back, pleased she was alert and on duty instead of snoring off in a corner.

He undressed, popped a few grapes in his mouth, quickly washed the day's grime off himself, then climbed into bed. A few hours' rest was all he intended, but he fell into a dead sleep before his head ever hit the pillow.

THE SUN WAS high in the sky by the time Cranford entered and began to fuss about his bedchamber. "Oh, my lord. You are finally awake. I was beginning to grow concerned." He drew the drapes aside to allow the sunlight to stream in.

"Bollocks, what time is it?"

"Almost noon, my lord." He scurried to the armoire and withdrew Caden's robe. "I have taken the liberty of ordering you a bath. You'll need a shave, too. Your uniform is refreshed and neatly pressed, and your boots are polished to a shine. I just assumed you would be wearing your uniform today. Or shall I set out…"

Caden ignored Cranford as he babbled on.

He groaned and rolled out of bed, grabbing his robe in the same motion, for he hadn't a stitch on. He was in the habit of sleeping in the nude. Cranford was used to this, but Caden had no wish to be on display for others of the staff who would soon be at his door, wheeling in the tub and pails of water.

Of greater concern was Ella and the fact he had not shown up this morning as promised. Not showing up for a tea party might be excused. Not showing up for one's own wedding was a cardinal sin that might never be forgiven.

She was never going to speak to him again.

He rubbed his stubble. "Crack of dawn, I told her."

"Did you say something, my lord?"

"No." He blinked to accustom himself to the sun's bright glare.

Cranford was now at the armoire, fussing over clothes. There was no need for him to be burrowing through the neatly laid-out garments. Caden was going to wear his uniform, as he always did.

"How is my grandfather, Cranford? Have you seen him this morning?"

"Indeed, several times throughout the morning. He is asking for you. He wants to speak to you as soon as possible."

"All right. Help me to wash and dress," he said as the tub and buckets of water were brought in.

"You'll need a shave, too."

"Fine. And have my breakfast brought up here. I'm starving." He noted the tray from last night had been taken away.

It did not take him long to get ready, after which he eagerly went to see his grandfather. He found the old man sitting up in his bed, his color much returned, although he still appeared a little wan. "Grandfather, how do you feel?"

"Better than you, by the look of it," the duke grumbled. "Where were you all evening?"

Caden was reluctant to tell him, but nor did he wish to withhold the truth. He settled in the chair beside his grandfather's bed. "I met with Palmerston, Wooton, Wellington, and Grey."

"Bloody blazes, all four of them in a room together? What happened? Is England at war?"

"No...hopefully not." He then told him about Fulke's death and that of his mercenaries. "The Ashanti have reclaimed the gold mines."

"Go ahead, say it."

"Say what?"

"That 'I told you so' is on the tip of your tongue, is it not?"

"Not at all. I don't care about those damn gold mines or about shoving the loss of them in your face. I'm just relieved you are on the mend. I was so worried about you."

"I know, Grandson." The duke cleared his throat as it turned raspy. "I heard you by my bedside. I wanted to respond but couldn't. My eyes refused to open. I had no voice and I could not get my limbs to move. But I was awake and heard your every word...appreciated all you said." His eyes turned misty, but the old man quickly wiped away his tears as they fell upon his pale cheeks. "What's to be done about those mines?"

"Nothing at the moment," Caden said. "An envoy is to be sent to the Ashanti with an offer to restore the treaty that was in place before Fulke arrived and tore everything up. However, I won't be that envoy. I will be on my honeymoon, hopefully... That is, if Ella has not given up on me. I'm not sure she will still have me."

"Why would she not have you? You are going to be a duke."

Caden emitted a soft growl as he rubbed the nape of his neck. "She does not care about that. And neither of us wish to see your demise anytime soon. I was supposed to marry her today."

"I thought the wedding was set for next month?"

"Yes, it is. But I could not bear to wait that long." Caden emitted a wrenching groan. "Grandfather, what have I done? I promised Ella we would exchange vows this morning. Instead, I've slept half the day away. How could I do this horrible thing?"

"Perhaps it is no coincidence. Are you certain you want to marry her?"

"Not marry that angel?" He shook his head and laughed. "It is the only thing I have wanted to do for months now. In truth, longer. I fell in love with her the moment I set eyes on her. And now she will never believe me. Why should she? I have been nothing but an arse to her, putting everything and everyone else ahead of her."

"Your causes were valid and very important, Caden," his grandfather said with surprising sincerity.

But this did not make Caden feel any better. How was he ever to make it up to Ella? "Oh, so *now* you admit I might have been right? Never mind, Grandfather. I don't want to argue with you. In truth, I may need your help to win back Ella."

"You are asking for my help?" The duke appeared stunned. And why would he not? When had Caden ever relied on anyone but himself? He had often spurned the old man's offers of advice.

Caden let out a breath. "I'm sure you never thought the day would come."

His grandfather nodded. "I'm sure neither of us did. What do you need from me?"

"Your support. Perhaps having you talk to Ella if she refuses to see me. She's wonderful, Grandfather. I cannot lose her. I wanted to get a special license so she and I could marry right here instead of in church."

"Why here, Caden? Would it not be simpler to have the ceremony take place in church?"

"Yes, but I wanted you with me. You may not believe it, but I love you. It mattered to me to have you by my side. Well, within hearing, even if you were unable to get out of bed. Not that I expect you to believe me when I have been an arse to you as well as to Ella. I cannot seem to get out of my own way. I've hurt the two people I love most."

"I have been no prize, either. Angry with you for staying with the Royal Marines when I wanted you here. But I chased you away with that iron grip I tried to keep on you. Then to almost lose you in that massacre because of my stubborn pride and foolish decisions…"

Caden cast him a wry smile. "We are too much alike, Grandfather. But I never stopped caring about you. If there is any way possible, I want you at my wedding. Assuming there is to be one. But I've botched it so badly. The Archbishop of London is away, and I will not be able to obtain the special license. Now, Ella's father is convinced this was just another ploy and I will break his daughter's heart."

"Did you know the archbishop was not in London?"

"Of course not!"

"Then your Ella will believe you in time," the duke said, his expression softer than Caden had ever seen before.

"How? All I have given her is disappointment. I've been no *hero* to her. And now she is going to hear vile rumors that will add to her distrust of me."

"What rumors? Have there been other women, Caden?"

"No, Grandfather! You know there haven't been any. Were you not with me throughout our tour of England? But that arse, Wycliff, and his daughter came to see me yesterday. They are attempting to revive the matter of a betrothal between me and Melinda. Rumors of our getting back together—when we were never together in the first place—are bound to show up in the gossip rags."

"Planted by them?"

"Yes. They think to force my hand. Failing that, they hope to damage my reputation."

"I see. Are you going to blame me for this, too?"

"No, you were only doing what you thought was best for

me," Caden replied. "But your matchmaking skills leave much to be desired. In fact, they are abominable. That girl is a cold-hearted witch, and I would sooner marry a frog than her. The only woman I want or shall ever want is Ella."

"Then just tell her, Caden. If she loves you, she will understand."

"No, this mistake is even too much for her to forgive."

"Grandson, just talk to her."

Caden nodded. "I plan to, but I needed to see you first."

"Maybe you can talk to us both." His grandfather peered over Caden's head toward the door and winked.

Who was he winking at?

And since when did the duke *wink*?

It took Caden a moment to turn around to see who was at the door. "Ella," he said in a strangled whisper of surprise, and immediately strode toward her. "I'm so sorry."

She looked up at him, casting him a radiant, angelic smile that never failed to steal his breath. "I knew something important had to be going on when you did not show up this morning."

"It was." Caden groaned. "But that is no excuse. I will never forgive myself."

She shook her head. "I won't lie and say it did not hurt, but I never doubted you. I was just sorry I wasn't at the top of your list of importance."

"But you are, Ella. Not that I have ever properly shown it. Quite the opposite—I've taken unfair advantage of your sweetness, and you have been an angel about it. It wasn't intentional. I am pulled in a thousand directions and do not know where to turn first. Everyone tugs at me, but you never do…so I always seem to leave you for last."

"I know how heavily burdened you are, Caden. You don't need me adding to your load by demanding your attention. Besides, I never want to force you to come to me."

He laughed. "I am such a stupid clot. All I ever wanted was to be with you, and yet I allowed everyone else to lead me away.

We'll try this again tomorrow."

"No, Caden. My father is livid, and it will take quite some convincing before he calms down."

"Lord, what he must think of me."

"Well, you are not his favorite at the moment." She winced. "He will grow to like you in time."

Caden took her in his arms. "And you, Ella. Will you like me?"

"Yes, I will like you. I will love you. I *do* love you, now and forever."

"Same here." He kissed her, an urgent kiss he hoped would convey the depth of his love. "I don't deserve you."

"Indeed, you don't," his grandfather interjected. "Nor do you deserve a good grandfather like me. Who do you think sent word to Ella and brought her here?"

Ella nodded. "I was heartbroken when you did not show up this morning," she admitted. "Then I received your grandfather's note and came over. We sat and chatted while you slept. We knew something important must have happened, since you returned home so late last night. Swindon reported it to your grandfather. Sharing you with everyone comes with the territory, doesn't it? It is something I am going to have to accept if I marry you. And I do want to marry you, Caden."

He gave her a weary smile. "I won't always be England's hero."

"I'm sure someone else will come along in time, but not for quite a while yet." She reached up and kissed him on the cheek. "It is all right. You are a very special man, deserving of all the accolades. As for me, I would rather have bits and pieces of you than nothing at all. This is the sacrifice that comes with being in love with everyone's hero."

He groaned. "No, Ella. You have *all* of my heart, not merely bits and pieces of it."

"Ah, all right. Then, to be more accurate, the sacrifice will be in having very little of your time. It is obvious England needs you as much as I do. The mere fact you were in a room with

Palmerston, Wooton, Wellington, and Grey for seven hours gives it away. I hope some good came out of your meeting."

"It did. Quite a lot of it."

"That's nice to hear. As for us, Caden, is it too late for us to marry today?" She shook her head. "Of course it is. But is there a chance we might marry tomorrow?"

Caden nodded. "I would say chances of it are excellent."

"You'll need witnesses," his grandfather said. "One of them shall be me."

Caden's eyes rounded in surprise. "How, Grandfather? Surely Dr. Farthingale will demand you remain in bed and rest."

"He can demand all he wants. I am not going to listen. I will require a pushchair. Blankets and a shawl, too. I may be frail, but I have not lost my mental faculties yet. Where's Talbott? Send him up to me."

His attendant now rose from her chair in the corner. "Your Grace, you know Dr. Farthingale told you to rest. Nothing strenuous for at least another week."

"This won't be strenuous. It will be a pleasure," the duke retorted. "My grandson is getting married tomorrow to the prettiest girl in London, and her father still needs to be convinced."

Ella blushed. "I don't know about my being the prettiest, but I do know my father will need more than a little persuasion to allow us to wed, especially after Caden failed to show up this morning. Thank you for helping us out, Your Grace."

The old man chuckled. "I knew my grandson would choose wisely."

Caden shook his head and simply grinned.

His grandfather had never been this amiable in his entire life. Perhaps Ella had worked her magic on the old man as she had on him. He dared not mention to her the odious Wycliffs or that his grandfather had been disparaging Ella throughout the entire hero tour. Nor did he need to remind the duke of Ella's chasing him around with a broom.

He took Ella's arm and escorted her out of his grandfather's bedchamber once Talbott bustled in. "Where do you wish to go on our honeymoon?"

She laughed softly as he led her into the study and shut the door behind them. "Assuming we marry tomorrow?"

"We *will* marry tomorrow. The world and everyone in it can go to blazes. Nothing is going to distract me from my purpose. By this time tomorrow, you will be Lady Mersey."

"That is quite an ardent declaration, Caden. I will understand if it proves impossible. Anyway, you are to give your speech to Parliament the day after tomorrow. Perhaps we ought to wait until after then."

He shook his head. "Marriage. Speech. Then honeymoon. The timing of the speech cannot be changed, but we can leave right afterward."

"No, we cannot." Her golden curls bobbed as she shook her head. "We both know you cannot leave. Stop trying to avoid the obvious."

"And what is that?" Nothing was obvious to him other than his desire to be with her.

"A hero must put England ahead of his honeymoon plans."

He frowned in response. "Not if it means losing you."

She gazed up at him with sparkling eyes. "You are never going to lose me. As for the honeymoon, I doubt there is a chance of our escaping London before the New Year. Whenever we do manage to break free, would you mind if I chose Moonstone Landing as our honeymoon spot?"

He grinned. "I should have guessed. Do moonstones shine in the winter?"

"Oh, yes. They always shine when there is true love, no matter the season."

"Even amid the cold and dark?" He picked her up and twirled her around. "I'll make sure to keep you warm."

"Just warm?"

"No, love. I'll have you glowing hotter than those moonstones." He could see by her smile that she thought he was jesting. "Care for a prelude?"

Chapter Twenty-One

"Do you, Lady Ella Stockwell," the vicar intoned, "take Lord Mersey to be your husband?"

"I do." Ella could not believe their wedding was actually taking place. Nor could she believe her father had agreed to it after yesterday's fiasco. Of all people, it had been the Duke of Seaton who finally convinced him it was the right thing to do.

Here they stood, before the altar in the magnificent St. Andrew's Church, exchanging vows. Ella decided she had to be dreaming when Caden responded with a clear "I do" when his turn came.

He then gave her hand a light squeeze.

Her parents, her Uncle Cormac, and Imogen were present. Also present were Caden's grandfather, who was warmly bundled in his pushchair and fussed over by both of his attendants, Mr. Stafford, and Lord Fielding—accompanied by his mother, the present Lady Fielding.

Ella had chosen to wear a white satin gown trimmed with pale green ribbon that matched the color of her eyes. Caden was in his dress uniform and had all his medals on impressive display across his equally impressive chest.

When the ceremony was over, everyone returned to the Seaton townhouse upon the duke's insistence for light refreshments and a toast to the newly married couple. But their party soon broke up because the duke was ordered back to his bed by Dr. Farthingale the moment he arrived to look in on his patient and saw the party taking place. "Upstairs with you, Your Grace. That is quite enough excitement for one day."

Ella did not mind this modest wedding celebration breaking up. They still had much to do today, since Caden still had his speech to finish, and she had yet to pack her belongings, as her father had refused to allow her to attend to it last night. He had not permitted a single trunk to be brought up to her bedchamber. "And have him not show up again?" he had said, showing complete lack of faith in Caden. "You will pack once you are well and truly married."

Ella did not argue, for her father was not to be reasoned with on this matter. They had a staff of maids to attend to most of it, so the chore would easily be accomplished today. What struck Ella hardest was the finality of leaving Imogen. Neither of them were prepared for this change, even though she was looking forward to starting her life with Caden.

The small reception had yet to break up when a messenger from Lord Palmerston's office arrived. "What now?" her father growled, noting the look on Caden's face.

"I've been summoned back to the Foreign Office. Ella..."

"Go," she said with more cheer than she felt. "I will be busy these next few hours bringing my things over here anyway. I do not need you waiting around for that."

"You are letting me off easy again," Caden remarked.

"I shall nag you like an alewife at a later time. Will that please you?" she teased. "You cannot refuse Palmerston, especially now that you have his ear. This is your moment, Caden. You must not waste it."

"All right. I love you, Ella." He groaned and then gave her a light kiss on the lips before striding out of the house and into Palmerston's waiting carriage. Stafford ran after him and jumped in, too.

Ella was now left alone to face her family, the Fieldings, and the Duke of Seaton, who had yet to obey the doctor's orders and retire to his bedchamber. Her father looked apoplectic. "Papa, we are married. You have no cause to be angry."

"He has abandoned you on your wedding day. Who does this?"

"England's hero," she replied. "He was summoned to the Foreign Office. It is not at all the same thing as a recalcitrant bridegroom running off. And he has a major speech to give tomorrow in Parliament. We will settle into married life once all the fuss dies down. Besides, it will allow His Grace and I to get to know each other better."

The Duke of Seaton nodded. "That's right, Stockwell. Stop complaining and rejoice in their love match. I've never had a granddaughter before. I think your girl and I will get on quite well."

"Like a house afire," her father muttered outside of the duke's hearing.

Ella stifled her laughter. "Papa, behave."

She smiled at the duke, believing they might actually get along. His near-death had jolted him and perhaps made him come to terms not only with what truly mattered in life, but *who* truly mattered in his life.

"She reads that romantic poetry," the duke said. "I've had Talbott order a dozen such books to stock in my library. Perhaps we'll form a poetry-reading circle. What do you say, Ella?"

"I would love it, Your Grace." Was this the same man she had chased around Caden's hospital room with a broomstick?

Her father regarded the duke askance. "Are you saying you enjoy that nonsensical drivel?"

"Ella has my grandson reading it, and I never thought such a thing possible. He spent an hour reciting Shelley's poems to me as I lay unconscious in my bed. It is not drivel. In fact, I shall invite you to our first poetry reading, Stockwell. You cannot get out of it. I shall demand your attendance." The old man winked at Ella, who could no longer contain her laughter.

"Yes, Papa. Do join us."

Her father threw his hands up in surrender and laughed along with her. "I shall be delighted…Lady Mersey."

The duke grunted in approval. "Well, now that's resolved, I had better take my nap before Dr. Farthingale boxes my ears. I shall see you later, my dear. We'll dine quietly together if Caden is not back by supper."

Lord Fielding had been avidly following the exchange. He and his mother now approached Ella to bid her farewell. "Call on us if you are in need of anything."

"Thank you. I will," she said, casting him a sincere smile.

After seeing the duke comfortably settled in his bedchamber, she returned downstairs to her family, who were waiting for her to return home with them in order to pack. "Papa, you are looking morose again."

He wiped a tear from his eye. "It feels so final. Ours is no longer your home. You are all grown up and Lady Mersey now."

Ella's mother took his hand. "Oh, John. She will always be our daughter. And she's hardly far away, not even a ten-minute carriage ride."

"That's right, Papa," Ella chimed in. "With Caden bound to be busy and his grandfather still requiring bed rest, I'm sure I'll be spending most of my time with Mama and Imogen."

"I hope you will visit us in Moonstone Landing soon, too," Cormac said. "Phoebe and I don't want that to change, although I suppose it will while Caden remains much needed in London."

Her father said nothing for the entire carriage ride.

They had hardly stepped inside their home before he took her into his arms and gave her an enormous hug. "My little girl," he murmured.

She gave him a heartfelt hug in return. "I'm sorry if I've disappointed you, Papa."

"You? Never, my child. I'm the one who ought to apologize to you. Cormac is right…although he rarely is," he added with a chuckle. "It's just that I love you girls so much and cannot bear the thought of not having you with us anymore. But this is life moving forward, and I am powerless to stop the advance of time. Let's get you packed and settled in your new home before your husband returns."

In truth, having time alone with her family eased the transition, because everything had been so rushed. Quick ceremony. Quick toast in celebration. Not even an hour with her husband before he was summoned away.

And what of tonight? Would he return for their wedding night?

Well, they had a lifetime together. Nothing needed to happen *tonight*.

By early evening, Ella was moved into the Seaton townhouse, her belongings placed in the room adjoining Caden's for now. This was also where she was to sleep until they worked out more permanent sleeping arrangements. It was a large, lovely room that reminded her of Cornwall summers because of its sunny colors and floral wallpaper and bedding. The bed itself was large and canopied, easily able to accommodate her and Caden—should he decide to join her in it.

There was no inner door between her room and Caden's, but Mrs. Nance suggested one could easily be put in for their convenience. "I'm certain His Grace would permit it."

Since Caden had not returned home by suppertime, Ella joined his grandfather for a light meal in his bedchamber. It was quite informal, for he had a tray set before him while he sat propped up in his bed with a dozen pillows behind him. She ate at a small table one of the footmen had moved beside his bed.

She enjoyed their supper tremendously because the old man could be quite charming when he wanted to be, and apparently, he had resolved to be nice to her. Perhaps it was merely because she loved his grandson.

"Your Grace, you must have been quite the rake in your younger days," Ella remarked, for he and Caden bore such a striking resemblance to each other.

"I was. All the ladies wanted me, mostly because of my wealth and title. I don't think any of them really cared for me," he said with a wistful note to his voice.

"I'm sure many did," Ella assured him, for he did not need his wealth or title to recommend him to the ladies of his time.

He shrugged. "Perhaps, but I could not tell who was real and who was lying. It was easier for me to follow my father's wishes and marry the young lady of his choice. It wasn't a love match."

"Did you ever regret this, Your Grace?"

"No, not until now—seeing you and Caden together, how certain you are in your feelings for each other and your determination to fight for each other. I'm sorry I did not have this for myself. She led her life and I led mine. I hardly saw her once she had given me a son. That was Caden's father. My son also married for love, but I would call it a gentler love. He never had the fire in his belly that Caden has. Did he ever tell you about them?"

"No, but I think he does not speak much about either of his parents because they died while he was young. He has very little memory of them."

"The girl was wealthy and her father was an earl, so I had no objections."

Ella pursed her lips in thought. "But you objected to Caden's marrying me. I am not lacking in funds, and my family is titled."

"It wasn't about you, Ella. In truth, I admired you from the first. But I objected to everything Caden was doing, mostly because he was challenging my authority. We have always been two rams butting heads. However, I think he chose wisely for himself. Don't tell him I said so, or I shall never hear the end of it."

Ella grinned. "My lips are sealed."

"You bring a fine dowry. You are the niece of a marquess. Your debut was a success and you were declared a diamond. You are clever, gentle, and, most of all, you make Caden so very happy. You should have seen his face the moment he first set eyes on you. We were standing together, squabbling as usual, and suddenly you walked into the room. It was as though he had seen a fairy princess. I think he forgot to breathe."

Ella's heart fluttered. "I had no idea."

"I also expect he is leaping out of his skin to get home to you. I hope Palmerston does not keep him too late. He also has his speech to give to Parliament tomorrow."

"He is ready," Ella said, feeling quite proud of him. "Are you going to oppose him?"

The duke sighed. "No. Sometimes it takes an old man time to come to his senses. The more I learn of Fulke and Abbott, the angrier I get. Of course, I must shoulder much of the blame for believing Abbott's lies and going along with his schemes that almost got my grandson killed."

His eyes began to tear as he continued. "I cannot talk of this, Ella. I was angry when Caden chose the Royal Marines over his duties as heir. That resentment carried through to this day. But no longer. I am very proud of that boy."

Ella kissed him on the cheek. "And he is proud of you, too."

"No, I don't know how he can look at me without his stomach churning."

"He knows you did your best to raise him and always meant well, whether he agreed with you or not." She rose to leave, for he had been at death's door only a day ago and she did not want him to overdo it. "Please rest now. All will be well. Goodnight, Your Grace."

He gave her hand a light squeeze. "Ella, will you call me Grandfather?"

She nodded. "Yes, if you wish. Goodnight, Grandfather. I will see you in the morning. Caden gives his speech to Parliament at eleven o'clock, and I'm sure they will want him there earlier."

"You must go with him, Ella."

"I thought I should ride over later with you."

"No, he needs you with him. I have plenty of toadies to fuss over me. Your place is with your husband, my dear. It will matter very much to Caden. He's been alone for so much of his life, but now he has you."

In a way, this saddened her. Both of these Seaton men had been deprived of loving care for most of their lives.

She returned to her bedchamber and readied herself for bed with the help of the lady's maid assigned to her by Mrs. Nance. "There, m'lady. Don't you look pretty? His lordship will not be able to resist you."

Ella blushed, for she knew what was to take place tonight. Of course, this assumed Caden ever returned. "Thank you, Polly. Have a good evening. I shall see you in the morning."

"Right, m'lady. Bright and early, because tomorrow is a special day for Lord Mersey. Although I'm sure tonight will be even more special for him." Polly giggled and bustled out.

Ella usually slept with her hair in a loose braid, but she had asked Polly to leave her hair unbound tonight so that it fell in a soft tumble down her back. She picked up her hairbrush and strode to the window to stare out over the garden. It was a moonless night, and the garden was too dark to make out any of the pretty landscape.

Not that it mattered. Her thoughts were on Caden. It suited her to simply stare into the blackness as she absently brushed out her curls and wished for his return.

It was not long before she turned toward the sound of a soft click at her door. "Caden, you're back."

He stood dimly illuminated by lamplight, looking tired but quite magnificent. Her heart soared as he approached. "Yes, love. I'm sorry it took longer than expected. Have you eaten?"

She nodded. "Earlier with your grandfather. And you? Shall I have Mrs. Nance bring up—"

"I had a veritable banquet with Lord Palmerston and several admirals and generals. They kept tossing questions at me, and all the while I thought of you. I was worried about your being alone with my grandfather. He is such a cantankerous old goat."

She laughed and shook her head. "He was a delight and docile as a lamb with me. We have decided to form a poetry-reading society."

Caden grinned. "What?"

"You will not recognize him, Caden. He is a changed man, and in a very good way. I suppose being on the verge of death has a way of clarifying what matters and what does not. I had a lovely time with your grandfather. Did you look in on him? He ought to be sleeping quite peacefully by now."

"I stopped in there first. He was still awake, and we spoke briefly. He said he enjoyed his evening with you, too."

She smiled. "I'm glad."

"I think I have walked into the wrong house," he teased. "First a doting grandfather, and now an angel for a bride. Lord, you're beautiful. I don't know why I am still talking when all I want to do is ravish you. Very gently, of course. This is your first time, and I am not going to rush anything."

"Says the man with so little time for himself."

"I'll have all night with you. And when I wake in the morning, I will be holding you in my arms. Ella, I'm so glad we are married."

"Me too." She melted against him as he took her into his embrace, her cheek pressed to the cool lawn of his shirt, although the look in his eyes was quite hot. "Come to bed, Caden. We can talk while you undress. What did Palmerston want of you?"

"My soul," he said with a mirthless laugh. "He offered me a position as second-in-command in the Foreign Office."

Ella gasped. "What did you tell him?"

"Nothing yet. You are my wife now. I said that I had to discuss it with you. But if it were up to me, I would refuse. There are good men who can handle the job. I suggested several candidates. But I was not on that list because it is time I attended to the Seaton holdings. Not to mention getting to know my new wife. I cannot keep putting you last, Ella. I will not. You are too precious to lose."

Did he not realize how deeply he was wrapped in her soul?

"You won't ever lose me."

He cast her a soft smile, his relief obvious. "Perhaps not, but I will leave you mightily disappointed if I keep running off and interrupting our precious time together. I will not shirk in my duty to king and country, nor in my duty to my grandfather. But above all, I mean to fulfill my duty to you."

His gaze raked over her body.

She was glad he found her enticing, although she knew this physical heat between them was only one aspect of their marriage that he meant to fulfill.

Still, she blushed.

He kissed her lightly on the lips. "Are you cold, love?" He ran his hands lightly up and down her arms when she shivered.

"Yes, a little." Her nightgown was more daring than any she had ever owned or worn before, but she and Imogen had read scandalous novels about wild dukes and their even wilder wedding nights. She knew Caden would appreciate her in this black silk confection. So she had purchased it without her parents' knowledge. Imogen had accompanied her because Ella was not very daring on her own. Her choice met with her sister's hearty approval.

She was not certain whether she was the bad influence on her sister or the other way around.

Caden obviously approved. His gaze was hot enough to burn straight through her.

His lips twitched upward at the corners as he smiled while drawing aside the bedcovers. "Why don't you climb in? I'll join you in a moment."

She set aside her brush and settled on the bed atop the covers to watch him as he began to remove his clothing. He had already taken off his jacket and medals before coming into her bedchamber, for those medals were precious to him and he was always careful to stow them properly. He had also removed his boots, so there was little left for him to do other than slip off his shirt and breeches.

She gulped as he removed his shirt first and set it aside.

Dear heaven.

The arch and strain of his body as he shrugged out of it was sheer balletic grace. There was not a blessedly soft thing about Caden. He was rippling muscles and rock-hard perfection, from his broad shoulders to his muscled arms and trim waist.

He began to undo his falls, then stopped. "I usually sleep naked, Ella."

Her eyes widened, for she never did.

However, she was not an utter goose. She knew what would be happening tonight and was eager for it. "I hope we will do a little more than sleep," she said, feeling herself blush once again.

He chuckled, for she could never be described as bold in the bedroom. "Yes, love. We will."

He studied her a moment longer, then undid his falls and slipped his breeches off.

"The thing about men," he said, settling beside her and drawing the covers over both of them, "is that we cannot hide our arousal."

She had tried to be subtle in her gaping, but she had never seen a naked man before. Oh, she had seen Caden partly undressed back in his hospital room in Moonstone Landing, but he'd made certain to cover up the most vital parts of himself.

But having seen him quite clearly now, she was not sure how they would fit because… Well, just because.

He nudged her onto her back and then shifted himself atop her, pressing down lightly but making certain to keep the bulk of his weight, which was all hot, solid muscle, onto his elbows. She was surprised he did not ask her to remove her nightgown, but as he slid his hand along her breast and then over her hips, she expected the garment would not stay on much longer.

In this, she was proven right.

She gasped as he undid the silk tie at her bosom and bared her to his view.

"Ella," he said in a whisper, his breath catching and his voice raw as he took his time with her, determined to be gentle. But their aching need for each other quickly took over. Her nightgown flew off, leaving her completely bared to his view.

She wanted to cover herself, but he stopped her gently. "No, love. Let me look at you."

His eyes were dark fire as he absorbed every detail of her body, and then emitted a soft growl to signal he was about to get down to the business of claiming her as his wife.

She was lost with his first kiss, the first touch of his hot skin to her cool flesh. The first touch of his lips to her breast and the soft flicks of his tongue as he teased and suckled the bud and then moved on to the other. She was liquid fire by the time his calloused fingers slid to the intimate spot between her legs and he began to stroke her there.

She had never thought of herself as wild, but this was how she wanted him. Savagely. Fiercely. Passionately. She clutched at him so awkwardly and desperately as new sensations overwhelmed her.

"Love, you are ready for me."

Was there ever any doubt?

She clutched the bedding and moaned breathily. Her body was in flames, and all she wanted to do was to have him inside her, because she was going to explode if they did not become one at this very moment. She ignored the pinch of pain when he entered her, for the rest of her was feeling nothing but exquisite pleasure. She shifted her hips upward to take more of him into her tight core. "Be patient, love," he whispered, his kisses soothing her and arousing her as he fitted himself into her.

Fire rushed through Ella as he began to thrust inside of her.

She could not say they moved as one, because her own movements were uncontrolled and sometimes she could not move at all, only feel those flames of desire burn through her. She had her eyes closed most of the time, but his were open and watching her with a scorching intensity, his need to conquer and possess her unmistakable as he maintained his steady rhythm.

She clutched his hair.

She grabbed his shoulders.

He laughed. "Ella, be patient."

"I cannot." She felt a molten heat build inside of her, ignited by the thrusts of his muscled body. Then suddenly, her body seemed to break apart, each piece of her turning to starlight, bright and bursting as she floated upward to the heavens and beyond. "Caden...oh, Caden!"

He kept up the onslaught, kissing her deeply on the mouth to absorb her cries that threatened to penetrate beyond the walls of their chamber. "Lord, you are glorious."

He kissed her again and again as he found his own release, dark and hungry, then growled like a jungle cat contented after devouring his prey.

"I love you, Ella." He entwined her hair in his fisted hands, buried his face in those long, golden strands as shudders ran through him and he emitted another animal growl before collapsing atop her. His big body momentarily pressed down on her with its full weight as the last of him spilled into her and his strength was drained.

But it was only a moment before he shifted off her and rolled onto his back with a contented laugh. He turned to her, smiling in smug conquest. "Lord, that was good. Ella, love—did I hurt you?"

Her little noises and purrs ought to have told him everything he needed to know, but she assured him anyway: "No, Caden. It was wonderful."

She nestled against him when he held his arms out to draw her up against him. "I thought so too," he murmured, kissing her on the forehead.

But after a moment, he rose.

She thought he was going to leave her now, but he only went to the washbasin and wet a cloth, which he then wrung out before returning to her side with it. "This was your first time," he said with affection. "There might be some blood on you. Not to mention some of *me* on you, too." He gave a ragged laugh. "I did a fairly poor job of maintaining my control."

"Were you supposed to keep control?" Her eyes widened. "Oh, dear. Was I not supposed to—"

"Heavens, you were the perfect amount of wanton. But you are innocent and I am experienced. I just thought… Well, no point in dissecting it. You were perfect, and I was lost to you. This is exactly how it ought to have been."

After taking care of her, he left her side a moment to set the cloth back beside the basin and then returned to take her in his arms. "Ella, I know you are worried I will leave you now."

She nodded against his chest.

"I have no intention of sleeping apart from you ever, unless you demand it. But I hope you won't."

"Oh, Caden. I would hate for us to sleep apart."

He kissed the top of her head. "We'll have to do a little rearranging of our two rooms. I'll ask my grandfather for permission to make those changes. First thing in the morning."

She looked up at him. "Don't fight him if he refuses."

"He isn't going to refuse. He likes you, probably more than he likes me," he said with a chuckle. "We Seaton men are going to be puppets in your hands."

"I doubt either of you can ever be manipulated. You are both too strong-willed."

"Not when it comes to you. I am completely in your thrall, my Moonstone siren."

She nestled against him once more. "A siren? That's rich. I'm glad you think so. I love you, Caden."

"Heaven help me, I am so in love with you, Ella. Those moonstones must be lighting up half of Cornwall tonight."

She glanced up at him again, smiling as he absently stroked her hair. "That's twice you've mentioned moonstones in under a minute. You believe in them too. Don't you?"

He nodded.

"I'm glad you do. After all you have been through, you deserve a bit of magic in your life."

"Ella," he said with aching tenderness, "you are the magic. It has always been you."

Chapter Twenty-Two

CADEN MADE LOVE to Ella once more in the night, inhaling the warm scent of her body that reminded him of meadow flowers in summer. She was so achingly lovely. One look at her in that black silk nightgown when he first walked into her bedchamber had sent a surge of desire through him powerful enough to drop him to his knees. Then to see all of her, the pink buds of her breasts and the gold of her hair, the green of her eyes framed by dark lashes, had his heart in a rampant beat.

She looked like a fairy princess.

She had cast her magical spell from the first moment he had set eyes on her. Those eyes would be watching him today from the spectators' gallery as he addressed Parliament. He knew what he was going to say, knew what sort of man he needed to be for Ella.

The *hero* he needed to be for Ella.

He stirred at first light, for he had to start getting ready for the day ahead. Ella was still asleep, curled up against him as soft as a kitten. He wanted to wish her good morning and kiss her, but he was not going to disturb her sleep for this.

He was disappointed, but still smiled as he recalled what they had done last night. Their coupling had been better than anything he had dreamed possible. None of it had quite gone as planned. A bit of fumbling. A lot of moaning and grunting. Ella so tight, she aroused him quickly. But he had been determined to have her experience her pleasure first before he turned into a wild, grunting ape and claimed his own release.

Even afterward, he needed more of her.

He had to have her. Touch her. Taste her.

Ella seemed pleased, for she was smiling in her sleep.

As the minutes passed, he knew he had to rise. But she was curled up against him and clinging to his arm. He tried to ease out of her grasp without waking her. She grumbled in her sleep and then turned so she was facing him.

Her eyes fluttered open. "Good morning, Caden."

Gad, they held starlight.

He kissed her smiling lips. "Good morning, love." All he wanted to do was remain in bed with her all day. But he knew Ella's maid and his grandfather's valet would be knocking at their door in a few minutes. "I am taking you straight back here after my speech, locking this door, and not letting us out of here for a full week."

She laughed. "I am sorry to spoil your fanciful dream, but I think we will be lucky to have a single undisturbed night together this week. Forget about the days, for I doubt I will have you to myself at all then."

He sighed. "I hate this, Ella."

"I know. You are a very private person, but the world will not leave you alone. I will always be here waiting for you whenever you feel the need to retreat."

"My gentle and safe harbor." He kissed her again before tossing the sheets aside and rising with a groan.

He had just tossed on his shirt and breeches, and handed Ella her robe—an equally sensuous black silk garment that hugged her curves and made him want to toss her onto the bed, bury himself deep inside her, and seek his satisfaction like a frenzied ape— when there came a light knock at the door.

He gave Ella one last kiss and then crossed the room to open the door.

"My lord," her maid said, sounding quite flustered as she bobbed a curtsy.

"Take good care of my wife, Polly."

"For certain, m'lord." She curtsied again.

He strode past her and walked into his own chamber, where his grandfather's ever-efficient valet, Cranford, was waiting for him. A tub had already been wheeled in and filled with steaming water. His uniform was already pressed, freshened, and set out on the bed. His boots were polished to a shine and neatly placed beside his bed.

Cranford was in the midst of taking out his shaving gear. "Good morning, my lord."

"Good morning, Cranford. Let's get to it, shall we? Time to make me look like a hero." Caden tossed off his shirt and breeches and settled in the tub's warm water, which still bordered on hot, but that was perfect for his aching muscles. Although he had fully recovered from his injuries, his leg was still tender, and he sometimes had to revert to using a cane. Also, his ribs had yet to heal all the way, and he occasionally felt twinges.

He'd felt a few after last night's exertions.

Worth it.

Within the hour, he was bathed, shaved, fed, and suitably clad. "Thank you, Cranford. Job well done."

The valet beamed. "You are most welcome, my lord."

As valet to his grandfather, Cranford would not be used to receiving compliments on his work. But this was not a battle Caden needed to take up with the duke just yet. He was not going to change the old man's ways after all these years.

He stopped by Ella's room, surprised to find her ready as well. She looked glorious in a moss-green gown and matching pelisse of softest merino. Her hair was done up in a stylish chignon. Perched atop was an elegant cap of black velvet that resembled a baker's cap. It looked spectacular on her. Her eyes were big and sparkling as she met him at the door. "Your grandfather suggested I go along with you to Parliament."

"Truly? You might be left to wait in the halls while I speak privately to the government ministers before the start of my speech."

She nodded. "I don't mind."

"Nor do I, then. I like having you near." He held out his arm to her. "Ready to tackle the world, my love?"

"That is your job, my hero." She reached up and bussed his cheek.

PARLIAMENT WAS ALREADY a hive of activity by the time the Seaton carriage drew up to it. Caden climbed down and assisted Ella, but they had made it no more than a step or two before they were met by Earl Grey's secretary and ushered straight to the prime minister's office. He had not officially taken power yet, but this was overlooked as Lord Palmerston also now joined them. Both powerful men greeted Ella, then Palmerston suggested that she be escorted to the private dining room to take tea while the men conversed.

"I have no secrets from my wife," Caden said. "There's no reason for Lady Mersey to leave, unless you wish to discuss confidential matters of national security."

Each of them arched an eyebrow but nodded their consent to have her stay.

"I did not realize you had married," Earl Grey said, resting his gaze a little too approvingly on Ella.

She did look beautiful, so Caden could not blame him for looking at her, although he would toss him a silent warning if he gazed too long. "Yes, yesterday."

"For the sake of his grandfather," Ella added. "As you know, he has not been well of late."

Palmerston groaned. "Why did you not tell me? I would have cut short our meeting or not troubled you at all. I must have taken you away from your wedding breakfast and your lovely bride."

"Your work is important," Ella said, "and the wedding will still go on as originally planned, although the ceremony itself will merely be a renewal of our vows already taken. The wedding breakfast will be the real celebration with all our friends and family. I do hope you will both be in Town to attend."

"Wouldn't miss it," each assured her, then they turned to Caden and discussed the points he was to make in his speech.

It was time for him to make his address.

Ella took her leave to join her family in the spectators' gallery while he made his way to the ceremonial floor in the House of Commons. He was surprised when he received a standing ovation from all those in attendance, although it was a frequent enough occurrence that he ought to have been used to it by now.

He smiled at Ella when he spotted her in the balcony with her parents and sister. She filled his heart with joy. On impulse, he blew her a kiss and noticed her cheeks immediately flush pink. She blew a kiss back.

The exchange, which was not as discreet as either of them had hoped, now had the crowd cheering loudly.

Yes, love always gave one hope and inspiration.

When the crowd quieted, he began his speech in a more solemn tone. "Who are we? Who do we promise to be to ourselves and others? What oaths have each of us taken to king and country? To our families? To the church? To our children? To all those who seek our help and protection? It is not merely the grand gestures and grand sacrifices that make a hero but the actions in our everyday existence. Stopping to help a child who has fallen and scraped a knee. Feeding a starving man. There is no kindness too small. This is how we inspire our children and others to be the best they can be, to stand up for what is right for no reason other than it is the right thing to do."

One could hear a pin drop in the audience, for all were listening with rapt attention, no doubt thinking he had all the answers.

But how could he when those answers resided in the heart of each man and woman—in what they were willing to sacrifice, in the kindnesses they were willing to show others, and the rights they were willing to fight for, not only for themselves but for others?

He then went on to speak of his regiment and how their lives were needlessly lost because of Fulke's greed and the absolute power he had been given. "Hate begets hate. Violence begets violence. He died in retaliation for all the deaths he had caused to friend and foe. He caused the deaths of countless others because he had the unrestrained authority to do so."

He saw his grandfather seated in the front row before him, but the aim of his speech was to inspire reforms, not sow discord. So he offered up the solutions he had discussed with Palmerston, Wellington, Wooton, and Grey.

He received another ovation when he concluded.

However, it came as little surprise when the newspaper reports that immediately followed spoke first of the kiss between him and Ella—an utterly harmless kiss, since he was on the dais and she was in the balcony. But this is what fascinated everyone. Only afterward did they report on his speech.

The gossip rags went wild.

This was the power of love, he supposed.

People loved to speculate. Had England's hero been secretly married to Lady Ella all these months? Was there a child on the way, and would it be an early arrival? Or were they not truly married yet and living in sin under the Duke of Seaton's very roof?

Caden paid little attention to the gossip, since Stafford knew their story and had their permission to print it with his exclusive interview. "You've gone and done it now, broken the heart of every lady under the age of ninety," he teased.

That did not stop those who were determined to capture Caden's attention anyway. Notes were still stuffed in his hands. Whispered trysts were still offered. Lord Wycliff and Melinda approached, still scowling and threatening to destroy his reputation.

Had they taken nothing from his speech about precisely their venomous behavior? It was easy to threaten and destroy, but what would be gained if they succeeded in damaging his reputation? In this instance, he doubted they would ever succeed, because the crowd adored him and Ella. Cheers resounded when Ella finally made her way to his side, beaming as she looked up at him in admiration. "You were brilliant, my lord."

He wanted to sweep her into his arms and kiss her soundly.

Hell, why not?

"I love you, Lady Mersey," he whispered, not sure whether she could hear him above the roar of the crowd.

She gasped and held on to his shoulders when she realized what he was about to do. "Caden! Put me down! Caden, it isn't seemly."

He did not care. He kissed her anyway, and did not hold back. No one was going to ban him from Parliament or censure him.

Besides, Ella did not sound all that distressed, even though her cheeks were adorably in flames. She appeared to be holding back her laughter and trying not to smile at him as he ended the kiss. "You are very naughty for a hero."

"Yes, I am." He kissed her again.

And had more kisses for her that night as they tumbled onto their bed, laughing as they shed their clothing and breathlessly undertook their romantic exertions. Wretched hound that he was, he could not get enough of her body. She was soft and sweet. Passion and heaven.

"Lord, that was good," Caden muttered with a satisfied growl once they finished together. They were still clinging to each other, their limbs and hearts gloriously entangled.

She grinned smugly. "Was I naughty enough for you?"

Their clothes were strewn across the floor.

Their bodies had yet to untangle.

They might have broken the bed in their zeal to couple...or

maybe it just squeaked a lot.

He kissed her, and then ran his fingers through the silken cascade of her hair. "You know, heroes have very high standards."

"Have I met them?"

"Yes, Lady Mersey. Your husband is a very fortunate man."

Her grin turned affectionately impish. "I shall tell him so when I next see him."

"I'm sure he will be delighted to hear it." Caden rolled her under him again. "I love you, Ella." He did not wish to be a hero in anyone's eyes—other than the fairy-pool orbs of his beautiful wife. "I love you, my sweet, lovely Ella. I surely do. Forever and always."

Chapter Twenty-Three

Moonstone Landing
July 1830

ELLA SAT ALONE at the top of the stairs leading down to the beach at Westgate Hall, staring into the sunset. Twilight was upon them, and the glimmers of a full moon could be seen on the horizon, its pale form almost unnoticed against the pinks and purples of the dazzling sky that reflected off the calm cove waters.

She held back a tear, for Caden was about to miss another turn of the full moon, and she was beginning to worry the moonstones would never shine for them. Oh, she loved him and he loved her—of this she was not in doubt. But he also loved the important role he was now playing in shaping England's future.

He had suggested they spend the summer in Moonstone Landing, because seeing those stones shimmer was important to him, and they had not had the chance to return to this lovely village as a married couple before now. They had not even managed a real honeymoon, merely snatching a day here or a day there to themselves in all these months.

Foolishly, she had gone on ahead to Moonstone Landing with Imogen because she expected him to follow in a matter of days. But half the summer was over and he was not here yet, nor had he written to her lately to advise her of his plans.

How would he ever see the moonstones if he remained in London?

"Where are you now, Caden?" she muttered, her words lost to the gentle wind.

She had only herself to blame for encouraging him to accept the role of second-in-command in the Foreign Office—this on top of slowly taking on more duties concerning the Seaton assets. While his grandfather had recovered somewhat, he was no longer the vigorous man he had once been. On the one hand, this was tragic. On the other hand, this had softened the old man sufficiently that he and Caden were developing a deep and loving relationship.

But in all the activity, and despite both men being loving and considerate toward her, she was somehow always last in line to command their attention. When was she going to start thinking of herself and demanding to be moved up in the ranks of importance?

No, that wasn't really fair. Attending a tea or a soiree with her was never more important than dealing with the security of England.

She remained seated on the top step as night fell and stars could be seen in the exceptionally clear sky. It was a beautiful sight, the big silver moon and myriad stars twinkling like diamonds across the dark expanse. Uncle Cormac and Aunt Phoebe would be worrying about her if she did not return soon. However, the sight of the moon hanging large over the tranquil waters fascinated her, and she could not draw her gaze away yet.

As the wind picked up slightly, she sighed. "Come on, Ella. You cannot sit out here all night."

Just as she was about turn away, something astonishing caught her eye. "What the…?"

A rainbow shimmer swept across the water like a tiny ripple, then disappeared. A moment later, another shimmering ripple swept across the cove waters. She looked around to see if there was a young couple close by, but could not see anything but shadows of rock on the beach below.

Perhaps a courting couple was standing somewhere on the cliffs above the beach.

To her disappointment, she saw no one.

Shaking her head, she rose and was about to start back toward the manor house when she noticed the outline of a man striding toward her. Perhaps Melrose, the family butler, had been sent to fetch her. Or her uncle had come to lecture her on standing alone in the dark outdoors.

But as the figure approached, she realized who it was. "Caden!" she cried, and ran toward him.

Who else would set those moonstones shimmering for her?

He swept her up in his arms. "I'm so sorry, love. I know I should have arrived weeks ago."

"You're here now, and this is all that matters."

"I was not going to miss another turn of the full moon," he said, wrapping her in his arms for a fierce hug before he let her go. "Sorry, I must still smell of horse sweat and leather."

Yes, he did.

She did not care. He was here, and that was all that mattered. "You made it."

"I would not miss our full moon for anything. Did you notice any moonstones yet?" He kissed her gently, for he hadn't shaved in several days and his jaw was all sharp bristles.

Ella laughed and kissed him on the lips, ignoring his scruff. "Yes, just a few quick glimmers. I thought the sea was shining for someone else. Have you slept at all these past few days?"

She planted more kisses on his face, still not caring that his recent growth of beard irritated her cheeks. He was with her, and it meant everything that he had pushed hard to reach her tonight, this night of the full moon.

"Thank you, Caden," she whispered brokenly, once more caught up in his treasured arms. Oh, how she had missed those strong arms of his.

"Love, I'm the one who should be grateful for *you*. You've

stood beside me, encouraging me to be everyone's hero, to belong to everyone. But I shall always and only ever belong to you, Ella. Nothing matters more to me. I love you so much."

He had no sooner gotten out the words than a veritable display of light erupted on the water, dazzling glimmers sparkling along the waves in every color imaginable. Ruby red, amber yellow, emerald green, sapphire blue, and the rarest diamond pink.

Caden sucked in a breath. "Are those the moonstones?"

"Yes, aren't they beautiful?" Ella turned in his arms so that her back was pressed against his chest. His arms remained around her, and they watched the illuminated waves dance to shore and break with a gentle whoosh.

"I love you too," she said, her heart soaring because she only ever wanted to be in his arms. Perhaps it was not the loftiest of dreams. He was still England's hero and would likely remain much sought after for the rest of his life. But she would share that life with him, perhaps making her mark as well. Her status as his wife allowed her to gain admittance in places she might otherwise be turned away from, and she meant to take full advantage if it meant saving lives or helping those who could not help themselves.

"Look at those brilliant lights," he said. "Is there any doubt how we feel about each other?"

She laughed. "No, but it's nice to have the confirmation, especially when we are apart so much."

"And especially since the gossip rags still accept stories from those who would wish us ill," he said ruefully. "I will always be faithful to you, Ella. *Always*. You were the miracle I needed to turn my life around. You are more wonderful to me than I deserve."

"You are pretty wonderful, too," she said with a sigh as he gently nuzzled her neck.

"I am the one who gained everything from our marriage. I loved you from the first moment I set eyes on you, Ella. Nothing and no one will ever change that. I hope you remember this as we journey through life and are constantly pulled apart. This new role for me is going to separate us from time to time. No matter the duration, I will never break my vows to you. I give you my oath upon those moonstones."

She nodded and emitted a trill of laughter. "I know, Caden. You pledged your heart to me when we married, and you are too honorable ever to break that pledge. I think it would hurt you as much as it would hurt me."

"It would destroy me," he said with a deeply felt ache. "It can never happen. But let's think good thoughts and not dwell on things that will never come to pass."

"You're right. Shall we return to the house? You must be hungry. When did you last eat? And you'll need a bath." She tugged on his hand, but he wouldn't budge.

"I have a better idea. Those moonstones are still sparkling like fireworks on the water. Come down to the beach with me, love."

"But it's dark and will be very difficult for us to see our way once those moonstones stop shining. Can it not wait until morning?"

"No," he said with a naughty grin. "And those lights are not going to stop shining for us because…"

She gasped. "You want us to make love down there? You do realize how impractical it is, don't you?"

He nodded. "I'll survive a little sand up my arse."

"Caden!"

"Come on, love." He kissed her long and hard again. "I think it's time we made a moonstone baby."

"Dear heaven, you are a naughty influence on me. All right, lead the way. I cannot even imagine what a moonstone baby will look like or turn out to be."

"Wonderful and special, like his mother." He took her hand and carefully led her down the stairs that were sufficiently illuminated by the display of light.

"*His* mother? You think we will have a boy?"

Caden shook his head and laughed. "I don't know why I said that. It just popped into my head, a little boy with green eyes like his mother."

"Well, we shall know in nine months, won't we? You had better not toss our clothes too far away from us. I will never forgive you if the tide carries them out," she said with a lilting laugh.

"Very well, no ferret-like frenzy, Miss Prude." He kissed her on the nose. "You know how wild you get me when you give me that prim look."

She smiled up at him. "I am only trying to be sensible."

"I know, love. Which is why it is so much fun to lead you astray. Lord, you are luscious." He proceeded to take off his clothes and then helped her remove hers.

The following day, everyone in the village commented on the dazzling display of moonstones the previous night.

"I told you Colonel Seaton loved her," the very wise and cheerful Elmer Angel said whenever anyone mentioned those moonstones.

Epilogue

London, England
April 1831

CADEN LET OUT a whoop and tore into his grandfather's bedchamber without bothering to knock. "It's a boy! Ella's fine and the baby is beautiful. He has Ella's eyes."

The duke laughed as he sat up in his bed and reached out to hug Caden. "Well done, but how can you know the color of his eyes, lad?"

"He had them open and was howling. Did you not hear him? He's going to be as insufferably arrogant as we are."

"Well, he's a Seaton, after all. Is Ella's family still here?"

"Yes, all of them. Imogen, Ella's parents, Burness, and his wife, Phoebe. Phoebe's sisters and their husbands. I'm sure Lord Fielding and his mother will stop by later this morning, too."

"What are we running, a marketplace?" the duke grumbled, but he did not appear put out. "Give me a moment to get dressed and I will come out to greet them. I'm so happy for you, my grandson."

Caden's expression softened. "It feels good, Grandfather. But are you sure you ought to get out of bed? Dr. Farthingale did tell you to take it easy."

"Pah! He did not mean for me to become a wilting flower.

This occasion calls for a celebration. Do you think Ella might allow me to see her and the baby?"

"Yes, of course. I'll come by in a few minutes to take you to our bedchamber."

Caden was eager to return to Ella's side, since he had been forbidden to remain while she was in labor. But now that the baby was born, he had no intention of leaving their side anytime soon.

Their door was open, and he was surprised to see only the midwife in attendance. "Where did everyone go?"

"Downstairs," Ella said, sounding ecstatic but exhausted.

"I'll give you two a moment alone," the woman said, and quietly left them now that the baby was clean and swaddled and resting comfortably in a cradle beside his mother.

Caden knelt by her side. "Ella, you are so beautiful."

She laughed. "I am a mess. But a happy mess."

"No, you are even more beautiful than the day I first laid eyes on you. I dared not believe my good fortune then, and I still cannot believe it. You've given me everything I ever hoped for—a loving wife, a beautiful child, a reconciliation with my former arse of a grandfather… Although I probably was as much to blame in constantly prodding him."

She caressed his cheek. "That the two of you continue to get along makes me very happy."

He nodded and kissed her lightly on the mouth. "Can I get you anything, love?"

"No, just hold my hand."

"Always, love. Have you told your family of the name we've chosen for our son?"

"Not yet. You can tell them. Your grandfather and my father ought to be very happy with what we've chosen. Good thing they both happened to be named John."

Caden chuckled. "I'm sure my grandfather will be delighted and convinced we chose John Caden Seaton because of him alone."

She gave his hand a light squeeze. "It's a fine name. My love, I'm so tired. Do you mind if I close my eyes?"

He shifted onto the bed to wrap her in his arms. "Sleep against me, sweetheart. The baby's fine in his cradle."

She nodded against his chest. "I like curling up against you, so solid and safe."

He kissed the top of her head.

Tears welled in his eyes.

He was never one for mawkish displays, but the happiness of this moment caught him by surprise and overwhelmed him. Taking Ella into his arms each night gave him a satisfaction he'd never dreamed possible. Even now, despite twelve hours of pushing their son out, she was sweet and warm as always, so perfect for his arms and resting in them.

There came a soft knock at the door.

Caden glanced over to the open door. "Come in, Grandfather. Ella fell asleep in my arms. Meet your great-grandson, John Caden Seaton."

"Is that to be his name? Well done, lad," the duke said as tears sprang to his eyes.

While his grandfather carefully and quietly cooed over their new arrival, Caden stared down at Ella's lovely face.

He hadn't needed the moonstones shining for them nine months ago for confirmation he would love this woman to the end of his days. But it was nice to see that magical display, and fitting too. It was a nice lore, and he could see why the villagers in Moonstone Landing held such faith in it. But for him, there was only one true magic in his life.

That was Ella.

The End

Also by Meara Platt

FARTHINGALE SERIES
My Fair Lily
The Duke I'm Going To Marry
Rules For Reforming A Rake
A Midsummer's Kiss
The Viscount's Rose
Earl of Hearts
The Viscount and the Vicar's Daughter
A Duke For Adela
Marigold and the Marquess
The Make-Believe Marriage
If You Wished For Me
Never Dare A Duke
Capturing The Heart Of A Cameron

MOONSTONE LANDING SERIES
Moonstone Landing (novella)
Moonstone Angel (novella)
The Moonstone Duke
The Moonstone Marquess
The Moonstone Major
The Moonstone Governess
The Moonstone Hero
The Moonstone Pirate

BOOK OF LOVE SERIES
The Look of Love
The Touch of Love
The Taste of Love

The Song of Love
The Scent of Love
The Kiss of Love
The Chance of Love
The Gift of Love
The Heart of Love
The Hope of Love (novella)
The Promise of Love
The Wonder of Love
The Journey of Love
The Treasure of Love
The Dance of Love
The Miracle of Love
The Remembrance of Love (novella)
The Dream of Love (novella)
All I Want For Christmas (novella)

DARK GARDENS SERIES
Garden of Shadows
Garden of Light
Garden of Dragons
Garden of Destiny
Garden of Angels

LYON'S DEN
The Lyon's Surprise
Kiss of the Lyon
Lyon in the Rough

THE BRAYDENS
A Match Made In Duty
Earl of Westcliff
Fortune's Dragon
Earl of Kinross
Earl of Alnwick

Tempting Taffy
Aislin
Gennalyn
Pearls of Fire
A Rescued Heart

DeWOLFE PACK ANGELS SERIES
Nobody's Angel
Kiss An Angel
Bhrodi's Angel

About the Author

Meara Platt is a USA Today bestselling author and an award winning, Amazon UK All-star. Her favorite place in all the world is England's Lake District, which may not come as a surprise, since many of her stories are set in that idyllic landscape, including her award-winning fantasy romance Dark Gardens series. If you'd like to learn more about the ancient Fae prophecy that is about to unfold in the Dark Gardens series, as well as Meara's lighthearted, bestselling Regency romances in the Farthingale series and Book of Love series, or her more emotional Moonstone Landing series and Braydens series, please visit Meara's website at www.mearaplatt.com.